M000020201

THE SEVENTY-FIVE FOLIOS AND OTHER UNPUBLISHED MANUSCRIPTS

By Marcel Proust
Edited by Nathalie Mauriac Dyer
Translated by Sam Taylor
Publication Date: April 25th, 2023
$35.00 | 368 pp.
ISBN: 978-0-674-27101-2

The Belknap Press of Harvard University Press

For more information, please contact:

Amanda Ice
Publicist
617.495.1693
amanda_ice@harvard.edu

Visit our website:
www.hup.harvard.edu

Advance Praise for *The Seventy-Five Folios and Other Unpublished Manuscripts*

"Can we read Proust's epic today and not care to know how it came about? In these pages, hidden from public view for a whole century, we can almost feel how Proust spent a lifetime planning and writing his book, picking his way towards what would become his great contribution to humanity."

— **André Aciman**

"The publication last year of the now famous seventy-five pages was a major literary and scholarly event, the 'lost' pages in question shedding valuable light on both the conception and the compositional history of Proust's novel. To have them now in translation is a real treat for English readers of Proust. Sam Taylor's rendering is also a treat in its own right, exact and fully responsive to nuance and to the rhythms of what Proust himself called 'the melody of the song beneath the words.'"

— **Christopher Prendergast, author of *Living and Dying with Marcel Proust***

"The recent discovery of the long-lost, seventy-five-page first draft that blossomed into *In Search of Lost Time* was one of the great miracles of modern publishing. Sam Taylor's magnificently deft and elegant English translation of that work is another. An indispensable read for Anglophone Proust lovers everywhere, *The Seventy-Five Folios* is a literary treasure in its own right."

— **Caroline Weber, author of *Proust's Duchess: How Three Celebrated Women Captured the Imagination of Fin-de-Siècle Paris***

The Seventy-Five Folios and
Other Unpublished Manuscripts

MARCEL PROUST

The Seventy-Five Folios and Other Unpublished Manuscripts

Edited by *Nathalie Mauriac Dyer*

Preface by *Jean-Yves Tadié*

Translated by *Sam Taylor*

The Belknap Press
of Harvard University Press

Cambridge, Massachusetts
London, England
2023

First published as *Les soixante-quinze feuillets et autres manuscrits inédits,*
Copyright © 2021 by Éditions Gallimard, Paris

Library of Congress Cataloging-in-Publication Data [to come]

Contents

Preface
The Sacred Moment

JEAN-YVES TADIÉ

And so here they are at last, the seventy-five folios that were for so long hidden, so long awaited, their legend growing over the years. In his book *The People,* the French historian Jules Michelet lamented the way that geniuses tend to cover the traces of their creations' genesis: "Rarely do they keep the series of drafts that led up to it." Historians seek to locate the unique moment of conception, the "sacred moment" when the great work burst forth for the first time. Here, we are close to that sacred moment. One of the great merits of these pages is that they were the first to be written in what would become *In Search of Lost Time,* even if they are the last to reach us. When the editors at La Pléiade and the researchers at the ITEM-CNRS[1] attempted to sift through the various strata of materials, marking the successive traces of Proust's masterpiece, they found they were missing the first step—like archaeologists searching for a small Merovingian or Roman church under the Gothic cathedral.

Bernard de Fallois, the original editor of *Jean Santeuil* and *Contre Sainte-Beuve,* had signaled its existence. He referred to the list of "Pages Written" that Proust had drawn up in the first of the notebooks he used in 1908 to sketch out the beginnings of the story, a list that does not match exactly with the contents of these folios. The list described only one stage. It was written in late 1907 or the first half of 1908. Proust had not attempted any fiction since 1899, when he abandoned *Jean Santeuil.* After that, he traversed a literary desert. Until 1905, all he produced were two translations

1. Institute of Modern Texts and Manuscripts at the National Center for Scientific Research.

of Ruskin and their preface. His mother died in September of that year, and he wrote nothing for some time afterward (although his friend René Peter claimed, in *Une saison avec Marcel Proust,* to have seen him writing constantly in Versailles, in the fall of 1906). His translation of *Sesame and Lilies* was published in 1906, as was an article on Ruskin's *The Stones of Venice.* Venice, "cemetery of happiness," which we will find in these folios.[2]

In 1907, he wrote an extraordinary article explaining his conception of the Oedipus complex ("Filial Sentiments of a Parricide"), another on the "death of a grandmother," and his "Impressions of the Road from an Automobile": in other words, he was blending theoretical ideas with autobiographical elements, along with a few reader's notes. All these themes would appear in his future masterpiece, but for the time being they were not enough to make their author's name. And then suddenly, in late 1907 or early 1908, the gates of fiction reopened. Paths branched outward but were abandoned before being followed to their ends. Ideas and themes came and went, like strange ghosts.

Because it would take Proust at least another two attempts before he wrote, not *In Search of Lost Time,* but "Combray," its two "ways," and a visit to the seaside, and it would be longer still before he described a trip to Venice. What was in those seventy-five folios? What qualities did they possess that made him write them? What flaws did they display that made him abandon them, like a computer program that self-destructs soon after first being used? Was it the fragmentary form, too reminiscent of the pages of *Pleasures and Days?* Had the plot, which could only be the story of a vocation, not yet been found? What story should he tell, essentially? What memories should he share? Which characters should the book be about? About a brother who disappears? About family life in a country house, located not in Illiers but in Auteuil? About the two "ways" of his mental territory? About provincial or Parisian nobles? About young girls at the sea-

---

2. There is a mysterious allusion to his mother in a letter from early June 1906 addressed to Lucien Daudet, in which Proust mentions "something I've started, which is all about her" (*Corr.,* VI, p. 100).

side? Where is the love? Where are Sodom and Gomorrah? And, above all, where is the notion of involuntary memory? These questions will be answered by Nathalie Mauriac Dyer in her commentary. Because the novel will only truly exist when Proust makes involuntary memory not only a crucial psychological event but the organizing principle of the whole story; in other words, the day when he imagined writing that all of Combray came from a cup of tea.

Proust himself described those scenes when one abandons a view, a face, an impression that could and should have been given more time and thought: the steeples of Martinville, the three trees at Hudimesnil, the milkmaid in Balbec. In his life, he abandoned loved ones like texts—Reynaldo Hahn to start with, Henri Rochat at the end—the eternal sketches, eternal drafts of a man worthy of being loved and never met. To read unpublished manuscripts is to read the story of an abandonment, an abandoned novel, like Balzac's *Deserted Woman*, like Baudelaire's *Passer-By*. Proust's head and heart were surprisingly restless; he is the Chérubin or the Don Juan of the written page.

He would become its Penelope. To read unpublished manuscripts is also to read the story of successive resurrections. Set aside, taken apart and put back together, night and day these pages would return. This return was a resumption and a moving beyond, an *Erlebnis*. It was what Proust had not done for *Jean Santeuil* and what would require time and a great number of aborted attempts for *Swann's Way*. Moreover, these folios had no title. Some novelists begin with a title and then write their book; Balzac, for example, drew up lists of titles for novels not yet written. The title is an ideal, something that drives and unites, before being a reason for glory. No title, and the book does not really exist, is merely a shadow, a puppet with the strings cut. You would not recognize, wrote Horace, Orpheus's scattered limbs. *Disjecti membra poetae.*[3]

The sense of *déjà-lu* is unfair: it is due to the fact that what was written first is being read last. Herein lies the paradox of the lover of unpublished

---

3. Horace, *Satires*, Book I, Satire IV, v. 61.

manuscripts: we seek out what the author himself rejected; we admire what was crossed out, removed, rewritten, because it's different. That difference makes it a new experience, a new Proust, despite its being older than the Proust we already know. We hope to find a secret there, the secret of the work itself, the figure in the carpet, the Aspern Papers. The miracle of manuscripts is that they allow us this return to childhood, impossible in real life. It is only in works of art, particularly in movies, that a child can appear in flashback, after the adult he has become. An inversion of the famous phrase by Bernard of Chartres that we are "dwarfs perched on the shoulders of giants." In this case, the giant is perched on the dwarf's shoulders—and that dwarf was he himself.

Here, the flood of childhood memories and grief is not yet under control; it flows endlessly, uninterruptedly. The reason for this is simple: the monologue we are reading is a form of confession, of autobiography, not a novel. This is what Proust began at the end of 1907. We know this because the author uses his family's real first names. The grandmother is called Adèle (Berncastell-Weil), the mother Jeanne (Weil-Proust), the narrator Marcel. Proust is always at his most moving when writing about his mother and his grandmother. The expression of his childhood sufferings, so different from those of adults, behind the cursory or denied goodnight kiss, behind or beneath, becomes almost unbearable, because many children would be happy to know that their parents were present, close by, in the garden or the dining room. The pages about the seaside testify to a frenzied desire to be known, as do those on the aristocracy. What could have happened to little Marcel, what injustice or blow of fate, that he should suffer so?

A young child weeps in Auteuil. Literature will gradually mask that raw wound, first in *Contre Sainte-Beuve*, then in the various stages of *Swann's Way*. Nathalie Mauriac Dyer's masterful study shows the progress of the creation, from these folios to their sequels, spreading like tree branches across successive notebooks. Slowly, over time, the wound was buried under the weight of pages. The involutions of the author's long sentences stifle the child's moan of pain. After this autobiographical beginning, Proust turns to the critical essay. After the essay, still unsatisfied, he starts his novel. After the last sentence of these seventy-five (or seventy-six) folios and the writing of pastiches will come the idea for *Contre Sainte-Beuve,* or rather the conversation with Maman about Sainte-Beuve. This method of resurrecting the mother is also a way of separating himself from her. Only when he has done this will Proust truly be able to begin his novel.

It is the use of the techniques of the novel that will give the Proustian monologue a form, boundaries, a method, a density, and also an emotional reticence that he still lacks, here, in early 1908. On the other hand, we have the impression that we have gained a better understanding of the work; everything that was hidden, we feel, is now explained. In the final text, we were left wanting more. Here, we know everything, and we feel a sort of indecency. But genius grows from sacrifices that talent never makes. A young child weeps in Combray, and from his tears emerges a masterpiece.

Note on the Manuscript

When they were discovered in Bernard de Fallois's home, the "seventy-five folios"—or, to be more precise, the seventy-six written pages—were inside a standard-sized burgundy cardboard folder, labeled in his handwriting "Dossier 3." That label covered up a previous title.

They were divided into five parts, each one placed inside a separate folder that Fallois had entitled "Combray Evenings," "The Villebon Way," "The Young Girls," "Noble Names," and "Venice," the titles written on inserts placed at the top of pages. With the exception of "The Villebon Way," they were accompanied by brief summaries of the contents of each section, also in Fallois's handwriting, on loose sheets. We have only partially kept these titles for the present edition (see below).

Many of the pages were damaged: outer edges torn (ff. 70, 83), a *reliquat* (a scrap of paper left over from a larger sheet and stuck to a folio) (f. 83), makeshift repairs (sticky tape on f. 53v), various stains; the lower part of f. 84 had been cut off, probably by Proust.

The manuscript of the "seventy-five folios" consists of 43 bifolios (or double folios), that is, 86 folios, or 172 pages, of vellum paper, unruled, no watermarks, in a 360×230 mm format. Those dimensions are approximate, because the folding of the folios is irregular.[1] Seventy-six pages contain Proust's handwriting, in ink, three of them on the verso (ff. 41v, 83v, 85v). With the exception of ten pages, the space has been completely filled, without leaving a margin. The author did not number any of the pages.

---

1. In places there are regularly spaced small perforations: it could have been a batch of paper originally intended for binding, according to the restoration team at the Bibliothèque nationale de France, whom we thank for their aid. Of course, we do not know in what circumstances Proust acquired this paper. The first pages of NAF 16636, identical to the "seventy-five folios," have some of the same characteristics in places (irregular folds, perforations).

There are a few drawings: small abstract doodles (f. 36), a woman's profile (f. 39), a church (f. 43).

Folios 8, 38, 42, 44–50, 52, 66, and 84 were left blank. Folios 44 and 49, 45 and 48, 46, and 47 were originally slotted together as a notebook inside folios 43 and 50.

The numbering of the folios follows the order in which the manuscript reached us, except in the case of folios 27–43, which were reclassified (see below). We adopted the following divisions and titles, which differ in part from those of B. de Fallois:

– ff. 1–26: [An Evening in the Countryside]. Thirteen bifolios, i.e., 26 folios, 25 pages with writing on the recto. Folio 8 is blank.

The last two pages (ff. 25–26) were published anonymously under the title "Separation" in the *Bulletin de la Société des Amis de Marcel Proust et des Amis de Combray* (no. 1 [1950]: 7–8). The last seven (ff. 20–26) were published by B. de Fallois in *Contre Sainte-Beuve* (*CSB*, chap. XV, "Return to Guermantes," pp. 291–297).

– ff. 27–52: [The Villebon Way and the Méséglise Way]. Thirteen bifolios, i.e., 26 folios, 17 pages with writing, all on the recto, except for folio 41, which also contains writing on the verso. Folios 38, 42, 44–50, 52 are blank.

We have used material and genetic evidence to reclassify this section, which came to us in the following order: folios 27–30, 39–41v, 43, 37–38, 35–36, 33–34, 31–32. With the exception of the first group, this order is the exact reverse of the order we obtained after reclassification. It is therefore likely that the bifolios had simply been put back in the wrong order after being consulted. Folio 51 is difficult to classify.

– ff. 53–65: [A Visit to the Seaside]. Seven bifolios, i.e., 14 folios, 13 pages with writing on the recto. Folio 66 is blank. We explain in the Notes at the end of this book why, unlike B. de Fallois, we have separated this "chapter" and the next one.

– ff. 67–74: [Young Girls]. Four bifolios, i.e., 8 folios, 8 pages with writing on the recto.

– ff. 75–82: [Noble Names]. Four bifolios, i.e., 8 folios, 8 pages with writing on the recto.

The first seven pages (ff. 75–81) were published by B. de Fallois in *Contre Sainte-Beuve* (*CSB*, chap. XIV, "Names of People," pp. 273–283).

– ff. 83–86: [Venice]. Two bifolios, i.e., 4 folios, 5 pages with writing, two of them on the verso (ff. 83v, 85v). A small fragment of the upper right-hand corner of another folio remained attached to the left-hand margin of folio 83, at the level of the second and third lines; two letters in Proust's hand can still be read there. Folio 84 is blank, its lower part missing.

The manuscript of the "seventy-five folios" is today kept in the Department of Manuscripts collections at the Bibliothèque nationale de France, under the classification number NAF 29020.

Note on the Present Edition

Principles for the Establishment of the Text

The writing of the "seventy-five folios"[1] was staggered between the first months and the fall of 1908; their creation might date back to the end of 1907. Given that we do not know how Marcel Proust organized these pages, we are presenting them in the order corresponding to the text of *In Search of Lost Time*, which is also the same order in which they were found.

The titles of the "chapters" are not by Proust. They are purely informative and were chosen to provide readers with familiar reference points.

In making the transcription, we have reduced the number of crossings-out to give a standard reading experience. Below, we set out the principles we followed in arranging the text.

A full diplomatic transcription (in French)—faithful on a page-by-page basis to the layout of the writing, with all of Proust's crossings-out and additions restored—can be downloaded from the gallimard.fr website and compared with the facsimile of the "seventy-five folios" when it becomes available on gallica.fr.

That transcription served as the basis for the standard transcription, as published in the French edition of this book and translated here. Both of them benefited from Bertrand Marchal's rereading.

The text of the seventy-five folios is followed by a series of documents ("Other Manuscripts by Marcel Proust") that illuminate both the genesis of the "seventy-five folios" and their place in that of *In Search of Lost Time*. These documents are from the Proust collection in the Bibliothèque nationale de France as well as from the Fallois archives.

---

1. We have kept the name "seventy-five folios" under which this manuscript was made known to the public in 1954 by Bernard de Fallois, despite the fact that Proust actually used seventy-six folios.

Proust's handwritten first drafts contain a large number of changes and additions. In the simplified version presented in this book, additions have been integrated into the text and deleted material left out, except with a note in the case of important passages, which can be consulted in the diplomatic transcription or in the critical notes.

Since Proust wrote very quickly, he would sometimes forget certain words or create inconsistencies between successive versions. Whenever it was necessary for the correct syntax and the intelligibility of the sentence, we have made the required changes (see the textual footnotes). In cases where the manuscript is damaged or incomplete, we have made a conjectural attempt at filling the gap; all such passages are placed inside square brackets.

The place where certain additions were to be inserted was not always clearly indicated by Proust; we have had to make those decisions.

Punctuation in the manuscript is used sparingly and sometimes inconsistently: we have completed it in order to make the text easier to read, except in the dialogue, where this lack of punctuation helps provide the oral style, and except where a change might alter the meaning. The spelling has been corrected where necessary, and the typographical presentation (abbreviations, titles of works) has been standardized. We have followed the author's paragraphing wherever possible.

This tidying up of the manuscript does not conceal its unfinished quality. Sometimes the story stops suddenly in medias res, even in the middle of a sentence; we have signaled such interruptions with a brief editorial commentary in square brackets. There are continuity errors between certain pages written at different times; we have left the repetitions. When there are several versions of the same passage, they are given in their most probable chronological order, with the oldest version first.

Notes

There are four types of notes:

— footnotes marked with letters, the textual notes indicate the lections in the manuscript (ms.) when we have had to make minor corrections to the text. We also indicate, wherever they differ, the corresponding lections in Bernard de Fallois's edition (*Contre Sainte-Beuve* [Paris: Gallimard, 1954], henceforth abbreviated to *CSB*);

— footnotes marked with numbers, the explanatory notes provide brief information that seems to us essential for ease of reading, for example variations in the identity of a character within the same passage;

— footnotes marked with T or TT are the translator's explanatory notes;

— endnotes, situated after the Commentary, attempt to illuminate the genesis of Proust's text and / or references, quotations, and allusions within it. In order not to disturb the smooth reading of the "seventy-five folios," these notes are not marked in the text itself; they are divided by folio and preceded by the extract, or the end of the extract, in question.

Abbreviations and Acronyms

col.   column

f.   folio (unless otherwise marked, a recto page)

ms.   manuscript

NAF   Nouvelles Acquisitions Françaises ("New French Acquisitions")—classification code for the Department of Manuscripts, Bibliothèque nationale de France

v   verso

[]   editorial intervention

*   conjectural reading

/   end of paragraph, or separation between two parts of an alteration, i.e., between the crossed-out part and its substitute

{f. #}   folio number

//   end of folio

See the Bibliography and Abbreviations for the editions used here. Where a book or an article is mentioned, it is followed by the author's name and the year of publication.

The transcription of the manuscripts was edited and simplified, except where indicated. The crossed-out passages are marked ~~like this~~, while additions appear between angle brackets, <like this>. A slanting line (/) separates the two parts of an alteration, i.e., the crossed-out part and its substitute.

The Seventy-Five Folios and
Other Unpublished Manuscripts

The Seventy-Five Folios

An Evening in the Countryside

{f. 1} We had brought the precious wicker armchairs back onto the verandah because a few drops of rain had begun to fall and my parents, after a brief struggle with the iron chairs, had returned to the sheltered area to sit down. But my grandmother, her graying hair tossed by the wind, continued her brisk, solitary walk along the paths because she believed we were in the countryside for the fresh air and it was a pity not to take advantage of it. Head raised, mouth inhaling the wind that blew and prompted her to say "at last one can breathe," she upped her pace and appeared not to feel the rain that was starting to soak her nor to hear my great-uncle loudly mocking her from the verandah: "It's nice, the rain, eh Adèle? It'll be good for your new dress." (This was a cowardly attempt to gain the support of my grandfather, who merely nodded.) "Funny, isn't it, how she's never like everyone else." He said this because he believed it. But he also said it because, since she was never like him, and since in a part of his mind that he didn't acknowledge he wasn't absolutely sure that he was always right, he was quite glad to place himself alongside "everyone else." The garden was not very big, so my grandmother never went long without passing close to us. As soon as I saw her emerging from the path I started to tremble because I sensed that they were going to call out to her, to say unpleasant things that broke my heart, and I was even afraid that my grandfather would force her to return to the house; in those moments I wanted to kill everyone to avenge her and sometimes, unable to bear it any longer, I would rush over and frantically cover her with kisses to console her and to prove that at least someone understood her, then I would run off to the bathroom, my sole refuge at that time, and sob my heart out. But my grandmother {f. 2} never responded to the mockery except with that beautiful, affectionate smile that seemed to join in with the others' taunting of her because she was never angry with anyone, she never had any feelings other than love and absolute devotion to others. The only hostile feeling she ever experienced, and she experienced it constantly, was indignation, but the only person on whose behalf she was never indignant was herself. It was as if, coming into the world, she had sacrificed her person and her life, so devoid was she of pride, vanity, and self-interest. She could have been wrongly imprisoned, or sentenced to death, without it exciting in her the indignation with which she trembled when my father, out of weakness, let me eat a coffee éclair or allowed me to stay in the living room an hour later than usual. Her walk had ended and so had the rain; she returned to sit with us, but naturally not on the verandah. Even though she had only gone for a short walk and the paths had not had time to become very wet, she had horribly soiled her plum skirt, because it should be noted that the legs of people blessed with an ardent imagination, an elevated mind, and without the counterweight of pride, do not cease for an instant as they walk, their heads buzzing with a thousand thoughts, to pick up all the mud from the paths and even, it seems, to spray it rapidly over their skirts, to rub it in such a way that it spreads across quite a wide span, and to splatter the parts of the dress or pants too far away to be directly hit by the alluvium. My grandmother looked out at the garden without saying anything and she was probably thinking about something else entirely, but my uncle, who {f. 3} knew that she strongly disapproved of the way that his new gardener had transformed everything, incriminated even her silences, which he interpreted as criticism. "You don't like the garden, eh, Adèle?" he shouted. "Naturally, since everything we like is bad." It was true that since the new gardener had pruned the branches from the trees in which she would become entangled every day and where she believed she could rediscover the freedom of nature, since he had, in the middle of a geometrically perfect lawn, planted houseleeks[1] in the shape of a cross, and since he had also persuaded my uncle to let him pick all the flowers from the little orange trees at the entrance on the pretext that he wanted to make orange flower water, my aunt[2] had suffered cruelly. I can say that she had never suffered so badly since the day when we had not been allowed to go out bare-legged. Sadly, the arrival of a new cook who made meals "dis-

1. Ornamental succulents.
2. *Sic.* The aunt becomes the grandmother again on folio 5.

guised" to look like other objects, then of a piano teacher for us who moved her body when she played and who refused to play with both hands at the same time because it inhibited the full expression of her feelings, soon provided her with other worries. Every year she would drive us to the seaside and there we would live life the way she wanted us to. She would have preferred,[3] if the prices were too high, to rent us simple attic rooms, just so long as they were on the beach. She didn't want a palace in town, wouldn't even take the time to visit one, because she didn't want to lose an hour of fresh air. She felt a profound pity for those people who visit the countryside in a car, who stay home, who go to the casino. We would leave for the beach in the morning and she would set up her folding chair at the very edge of the waves, moving it back and forth with the tide while we played on the sand. She barely allowed us time to go and eat lunch, leaving behind our folding chairs, which would regularly be stolen by the sea or by passers-by. On the way back she thought it too sad not to take advantage of the journey by stopping to see some famous site or monument whose great and simple beauty rivaled that of nature. So instead of catching the train to the place where we were staying, we would leave at five o'clock in the morning in a stagecoach, we would go twenty leagues out of our way, and we wouldn't manage to see the cathedral[4] nor catch our connecting {f. 4} train because the coach would break down and we wouldn't be able to warn our panic-stricken parents. I would generally go straight to bed when we arrived home after our two-week stay. During the vacation she would pen letters to our parents herself because it would have been a crime to make us write them and lose an hour of fresh air. But her letters were unreadable. "You can read your letters to me when you get back," my uncle would tell her every year when she went away. And since she was witty and educated and out of caution believed that she should never write anyone's names in those letters, she described everything with allusions, metaphors, and riddles, and no one could ever understand what she was talking about, and later if someone asked her for an explanation no matter how hard she tried she couldn't remember what she'd meant or

3. Ms.: preferred, ~~if it wa~~ the prices.
4. Ms.: to see any[thing] nor the cathedral.

who she'd been talking about. Not that it mattered because she always forgot to write the address on the envelope and her letters were always thrown away. After she died, I found some that had been piously kept by her daughter; a few of them had somehow reached their destination and by an equally rare good fortune were more or less legible and comprehensible. Despite that, they are all written in her usual style, making them quite difficult to interpret. Here is one, chosen at random:

> My daughter
> Yesterday drew Durandal the Hollandais volant with Sorry to bother you Madame. Ah! madwoman, madwoman. We were interrupted by the dreadful doc and my mother you are the queen of the ball. He declared that the children were anemic. That Machut. I looked at him from our forty centuries but you would have known better than me what to say, sadly I am in Étampes. I send you two or three little Hang yourself Sévignés that are worth their weight in gold. Have you received the hirondelles de Myroti.

Twenty years on, I was able to reconstruct almost everything. "Drew Durandal" is an allusion to Roland's sword in *The Song of Roland* and means to get angry, to stand up for someone. The *Hollandais volant* is the *Flying Dutchman,* the title of Wagner's opera, but also the "thieving Dutchman," the nickname we gave to a music-loving Dutch banker whom we strongly suspected of being a thief. My aunt often came to his defense. And obviously she had taken against: "Sorry to bother you Madame," a tedious person whom we met at the seaside and who whenever my aunt was chatting with us or reading an interesting book would come and sit down, regularly saying "Sorry to disturb you Madame" but without waiting for a protest of "Oh but not at all," which never came. She had no {f. 5} common sense and told my aunt ridiculous secrets about her marriage. It must be to some secret of this kind that my aunt is alluding with that quotation from Sganarelle in *L'Amour médecin:* "Ah! madwoman, madwoman!" They had been interrupted by the "dreadful doc," an incompetent physician to whom my uncle, while in the doctor's presence, unflinchingly applied the words of Labiche in *La Poudre aux yeux:* "Dreadful doctor who does not want to belong to the Académie!" because the only doctors he trusted were "specialist, hospital" surgeons and he was mercilessly sarcastic about the others. "My mother, you are the queen of the ball" was a line naively delivered by some young idiot, whose nickname it became, to his own— extremely ugly—mother, at a ball. His example was often cited to us to demonstrate that we should not pay compliments to our own family members, nor believe too easily in the compliments we heard about them. Whenever I complimented Maman, she would reply mockingly: "My mother, you are the queen of the ball." I already noted that "dreadful doc" was an allusion to Labiche's *La Poudre aux yeux.* Labiche must have been highly fashionable at the time because the following two phrases are also allusions to his plays. "That Machut" in *La Grammaire:* "That Machut, he looks a cow in the eye" . . . and can tell instantly what is wrong with it. And, also in *La Grammaire:* "How could I be in Étampes while my spelling is in Arpajon." Here, "my spelling" is my mother, more aware of the state of our health. "Our forty centuries" is of course an allusion to Napoleon's phrase: "From the tops of those pyramids, forty centuries look down on you." "Hang yourself Sévigné" meant badly written letters (because she enjoyed all those she received, not from a viewpoint of strict correctness, but from the elevation of feelings, the simplicity of the style, the elegance of the writing, etc.) thanks to an exclamation from a stupid gentleman whom we knew through the no less stupid letters of his daughter: "Ah! Go hang yourself Sévigné!" As for *"hirondelles de Myroti,"*[T] it undoubtedly means *"hirondelles demi-roties"*[TT] because my grandmother tended to write words wrongly when she was distracted. But what could those half-roasted swallows be? I have racked my brains, but sadly the last people who could have enlightened me on this subject are all dead.

I think I left my uncle saying to my grandmother: "You don't like the garden, Adèle, do you?" But after showing that he was not afraid of the discussion he preferred to avoid it by saying "let's go inside," and after pushing the little benches under the {f. 6} chairs so that we couldn't "trip over them," we went to the living room, since there was still a good hour

T. "Myrotis's swallows."
TT. "half-roasted swallows."

before dinner. Unfortunately, since that evening my uncle had invited a couple of his friends of whom he was very proud, the Viscount and Viscountess de Bretteville, to whom he was eager to show off his house, his nephews, his sister-in-law etc. (and he was no less desirous to show off M. and Mme de Bretteville to us), the gardener, who was adept at pleasing my uncle with little gestures of this kind, enough to make him turn a blind eye to the desolation of his garden whose most beautiful flowers he always sold, had arranged bouquets in all the vases. Now, the way in which the gardener arranged bouquets, which my grandmother naturally liked to be "natural," widely spaced and free, as if flung in there, had recently been the subject of a particularly tempestuous discussion between her and my uncle. She had declared that he didn't know how to make a bouquet. "I am not a gardener and yet if I was allowed to do it," just as she said I am not a piano teacher but I know one must not make those pretentious little diminuendo effects when playing Chopin's *Polonaise,* I am not a doctor but I know that shawls and candies can only harm children. The sight of the bouquets, while it pleased my uncle who thought immediately that it would give a good impression of the house's luxuriousness to the Brettevilles, also irritated him by reminding him of the recent discussion and making him fear that it would start up again. He wasn't wrong because as soon as she saw them my grandmother, despite swearing that she would never again express her opinion on such matters, could not contain herself and quickly pulled at a rose to make it look more casual and to let it dominate the bouquet, but the vase, which was probably not[5] plumb to the shelf where it stood, tipped over and water spread across the carpet. My grandmother apologized, but she laughed as she did so and said that if the vases and bouquets were destroyed it wouldn't be such a bad thing, which exasperated my uncle. Then the lamps were brought. Every night when I saw them, and when I heard the sound of the curtains being closed immediately afterward, I felt my heart contract. Because I sensed that in[6] a few hours there would come the dreadful moment when I would have to say goodnight to Maman, feel all life abandon me as I left her and went up to

5. Ms.: probably plumb.
6. Ms.: I sensed in.

my bedroom, and then suffer what nobody would ever know, in my room, from where I would hear the sounds downstairs, until the moment when I managed to fall asleep. If I managed it.

{f. 7} As soon as the lamps arrived I was unable to think of anything else, and I sat motionless in my chair, staring, not yet feeling the awful anxiety rise inside me, but sad and broken as I thought that little time separated me from it, and having no more happiness ahead of me. Only my grandmother did not want to go upstairs to dress because one did not dress in the countryside. When my uncle, coming downstairs, saw that she was still in her garden dress he made a furious movement thinking of Bretteville and whispered something that I didn't quite catch but I think it was "*la rosse.*"[T] He had already decided in any case that he would let his guest believe her mad. That evening my torture was even worse than usual because, since I wasn't supposed to eat dinner at the table, I had to say goodnight to Maman before she went to dinner, and go up to bed at half past eight as usual while she was still eating dinner. It was already painful to me every day, my thoughts entirely filled with the kiss I'd given Maman, having to quickly calm down after that sweetness and go to bed, believing that my lips were still pressed to her cheek and falling asleep before the anguish of my separation from her could overcome me. And alas I didn't manage it. For the half-hour that preceded the fatal minute, I was like a condemned man. Every now and then I would beg for a few minutes' grace, looking imploringly at my uncle, my grandfather, and everyone got involved, giving advice, saying half past eight was already late for a child, unaware of the hurt they were causing me. Then the last minutes arrived and I no longer knew what anyone was saying, I stared silently at Maman, her beautiful face so gentle, so cruel in not wanting (could I even conceive of such a life?) to remove this torment from her little boy's life, I sought out the exact place where I would kiss her, I tried to empty my thoughts of everything that wasn't the sensation of that place, so my eyes could perceive its color and its relationship with the essence of her face, so my mind could directly receive the notion of its flavor as soon as my lips touched it,

T. A mean, nasty person.

and finally so that this precious kiss, unique, because I was not allowed to kiss her several times, such a thing being considered ridiculous, so that I could keep the memory of that kiss whole, prolonging its presence in my mind, in such a way that when I was in my bedroom and starting to pant because I felt so lonely and separated from her, I would be able to open the memory intact and kept within reach by my[7] intelligence like {f. 9}[8] a Host in which I would find her flesh and her blood, or rather it was one of those modern scientific Hosts that the memory of her cheek resembled, because I broke it and raised it to my lips so that they could rediscover the softness of her cheek, and as in a[9] narcotic pill I found sleep. So I always tried to lure Maman into another room. Ah! if I could only persuade her to come up and say goodnight to me in my bedroom, after I'd gone to bed, then[10] I would keep her kiss like an indelible seal that would protect my heart from vain anxieties. Ah! there was the sound of her footsteps entering my room, almost dreaded because it announced, after her too-brief entry, the rustle of her dress as she moved away toward the door . . . once it was closed I wouldn't be able to kiss her anymore. Sometimes I would call her back: "Maman Maman" but I rarely dared do that because she would look saddened and irritated and then all the sweetness of the kiss would evaporate, leaving me only the awful anxiety. Sometimes after hesitating to call her back, hearing her footsteps at the top of the stairs and knowing she would soon be back down in the garden, I would leap out of bed and rush to catch her on the stairs. Almost violently I would beg her not to be angry. But that night I was going[11] to have to tell her goodnight half an hour before I went to bed. I'd tried everything, I'd begged her, summoned all my courage to ask Papa, written a little note to my grandmother, I'd thrown myself to my knees in front of Maman. It had done no good. And I was surprised by the sound of the bell, M. de Bretteville was at the door. The kiss whose sweetness I was going to have to protect for so long, without it vanishing, on the verandah, during my dinner, on the

7. Ms.: kept within reach my intelligence.
8. Folio 8 is blank.
9. Ms.: as a narcotic pill.
10. Ms.: while I would.
11. Ms.: that night to have.

stairs, all the way up to my bedroom, now I couldn't even give it to her, alone, concentrating all my thoughts upon it, like a neurotic concentrating all his attention on closing a door to be sure he has closed it and when he thinks about it a few minutes later applying to his fear the balm of his whole memory of that moment when he closed it. Maman kissed me quickly I held her back begging, she pushed me away worried that Papa {f. 10} would be annoyed, her blue summer dress from which were hung straw tassels escaped from my arms, and she said in a tone of reproach, gentler than her usual reproaches so she wouldn't make me even more anxious: "come on now my darling," just then my father turned around in a fury: "come on Jeanne this is ridiculous," and I escaped, but I sensed that my heart could not come with me and had stayed close to Maman who had not with her usual kiss given it permission to leave her and to accompany me. I tried to control my anguish while I stayed downstairs, forcing myself not to think about the moment (only ten minutes away) when I would have to go upstairs, I forced myself to read a few lines of a book, to look at the beautiful roses, to listen to piano music coming from the house next door, but nothing can penetrate the heart when one is too full of sorrow, the most beautiful things remain outside. This is what gives worried people that wide vacant stare where you can tell that nothing enters them, none of the words you say to them, none of the things they see, beautiful things or cheerful things. Their look is convex as their soul has become, extending its preoccupation toward the outside and letting nothing penetrate within. Even though I didn't want to anticipate my suffering, in my thoughts I had already arrived in the entrance hall, at the foot of the staircase that went up to my bedroom and each step of which could not have been crueler for me to climb had it led to the guillotine. And on the stroke of half past eight I did[12] indeed have to open the green wood-paneled door, smell that odor of varnish on the staircase and the boards that were hung above it and which amalgamated and impregnated every evening with my sad thoughts, expressing them in a way that was more painful still than a clear translation would have been, a full awareness of them. It obsessed me like those

12. Ms.: when I did.

dream demons which express through the rapid rush of an idea always {f. 11} the same painful sensation that we have at the time; a sensation so painful that upon waking we feel a sort of relief at knowing that this flower we desperately wanted to pick was actually our toothache, that this young girl we were trying to lift up was our struggle to breathe. At the moment when my sadness was obscured for me by the smell of varnish on the stairs, it oppressed me more cruelly perhaps than at any other moment. And so began that labyrinth of steps, each of which took me farther from Maman and led me closer to my prison, to the moment when it would be too late to pull myself together, to go back downstairs (already a very difficult task) to tell her goodbye again;[13] a labyrinth of sufferings so terrible that this staircase, even in daytime (when the day wasn't even halfway through, or I would still have hours to spend with Maman, or perhaps even when a pleasant smell from the kitchen filled it with the promise of delicious moments), if I had to go up to my room to fetch something and to climb the stairs without peril, that return to my bedroom from where I would re-emerge, that contemplation of my bed where I would absolutely not have to lie down, if that climbing of the stairs no more resembled the torturous evening climb than the representation of death in a play that we are watching from a comfortable box resembled death itself, I still couldn't climb those stairs without feeling vaguely troubled and even though I did not recognize, on those peaceful sun-yellowed steps that I raced freely up and down, the degrees of my passion on the ladder I could only ascend reluctantly, "against the heart," in the evenings, that theater of my nightly torture retained, and still awoke in me during the daytime, an impression of pain.

While lighting my candle in the entrance hall I already had the feeling that I wouldn't be able to climb the stairs, like someone fastening his packed suitcases for a journey even as he hesitates, already sensing that he won't go to the train station. How painful are those acts {f. 12} of preparation for an action that we are not yet certain we have the strength to accomplish and that seem to bring us closer to it and to make it more inevitable, the

13. Ms.: (already a very difficult task to tell her goodbye again).

gloves we button slowly while walking toward the door that we will not walk through, after a scene with a mistress. But once the candle was lit, I resolutely blew it out and tiptoed toward the living room where I wrote Maman a short letter begging her "for reasons that I couldn't tell her in writing" to come and talk to me when dinner was over. I told my old maid: "My word, I forgot to give Maman the information she insisted I give her for the gentleman who's dining here tonight. Hasn't she sent word to ask me for it? She probably hasn't thought of it yet. She's going to be very angry. Send Auguste with this note quickly or I'll be in trouble." My old maid, suspicious at first, went to take the note to Auguste who replied that it was impossible during dinner but that, when they left the table to drink coffee in the living room, he would give it to Maman. I waited delightedly; what I saw now was no longer my bedroom but Maman, even if she would be furious. Alas she sent word that it was *impossible* to come, that I should have been in bed long ago, that I should go upstairs quickly, that she was very unhappy with me. I went upstairs, I went into my room, I built my own prison by closing my shutters and my windows that overlooked the garden where they might go out to drink coffee later if the weather was fine, by pulling back my blanket, by opening up that bed which was the prison inside my prison, where I had just enough[14] room to wriggle my body. I lay in bed motionless, my heart pounding. Whereas in Paris between the furniture in my bedroom {f. 13} and my gaze there seemed to be a sort of sweet harmony that made everything I could see an extension of my gaze, almost as much mine as my gaze was, and that was[15] enclosed within me, in this new bedroom (we had arrived only a few days before) I felt surrounded by strangers, my soul didn't dare relax. The shape of the clock, the sound of its ticking, the positioning of the chairs, the smell of vetiver, the red color of the curtains, all this for me was like a new kind of food, indigestible, and which, absorbed by my eyes, my ears, my nostrils, which even if I closed them would absorb them all the same, made my whole being suffer a moral poisoning and left me feeling horribly sad. I tried to remain still and indifferent, I repeated to myself without even understanding the

14. Ms.: where just enough.
15. Ms.: and was.

meaning of the words some verses that I loved, I secured my gaze against
the hurtful shape of the clock and some enormous candelabras that stood
in the hearth with hostile aplomb, their appearance multiple, shaky, and
cumbersome, I forced myself to think that the smell of vetiver has no
painful significance and to think about the smell of the tea I made in my
Parisian bedroom in winter; all while regretting that this clock, one of
those unfamiliar, ugly people, indifferent to our unhappiness, imperturb-
ably cheerful and paying no attention to us, who in an instant removed for
us all the value of existence, did not let me for an instant forget its existence since it was speaking so loud and uninterruptedly in the bedroom
apparently unaware of my presence, I repeated to myself that in eight
days, as I knew from experience, all these demons of the bedroom would
be under control and I would no longer listen to the clock, which like an
old servant would speak only for me, and that I would think any atmosphere without that little dose of vetiver strange and unbreathable, and I
think I would have finally fallen asleep had I not got out of bed to fetch a
handkerchief and noticed lying there forgotten with a parcel for Maman
since that morning[16] her "mantilla," which she wore on her shoulders in
Paris the evenings when she had dinner in town. Now since she only ever
said: "Eugénie {f. 14} hand me my mantilla" when she was ready and
standing in the antechamber, in other words just over an hour after the
time for which she'd been invited, and an hour and a quarter after the time
Papa had spent waiting for her, furious, having rung the bell every quarter
of an hour to say: "Go and tell Madame that it is eight o'clock and we are
half an hour late," the sight of the mantilla immediately reminded me of
the anxiety I used to feel whenever I saw Maman getting ready, trembling
at my father's anger, pleading with him not to start a row, and suffering for
Maman because she was being rushed, feeling afraid she would catch
cold, wanting desperately to cry when I heard her say so gently[17] to Papa:
"I know I'm late." The thought of Maman (whom Papa always made the
happiest of women) feeling sad caused me such deep pain that I felt the irresistible need to kiss her to console her, to console myself, and knowing

16. Ms.: Maman that morning.
17. Ms.: heard her so gently.

that this would not be possible before the next morning, that I would first have to sleep, in other words give up on her, forget her, be dead to her, my heart began to beat intolerably, when suddenly I was filled with an immense joy because I'd decided to risk everything and to get up and wait for Maman who would pass by my room to go to her bathroom. Precisely at that moment I heard the bell on the front door ring, it was M. de Bretteville on his way out, and knowing that since my father had to leave the house early the next day my parents would soon come upstairs, I quietly opened my window and I heard the footsteps of my uncle and my grandfather who had accompanied their guest.

{f. 15} Soon I heard a lively discussion between my uncle and my grandmother. "No, say what you like," she said in a soft but firm voice, "he might be an excellent man, he might have many more horses than I do, but he is not distinguished." "Not distinguished!" shouted my uncle in a tone that made it clear that up to that very minute M. de Bretteville had for him embodied the supreme form of distinction, "not distinguished! But when I tell you," he repeated furiously, "that everything in Bretteville-l'Orgueilleuse belongs to him, that his estate includes two villages, a lake, a church, an army barracks. An army barracks!" "None of that has anything to do with distinction," replied my grandmother. "A man who says 'The streets aren't paved with gold' is not distinguished. Why, Auguste"—this was the manservant—"is a hundred times more distinguished than him!" My uncle did not feel at that moment how flattering it was to be served by a manservant more distinguished than M. de Bretteville and in a paroxysm of rage he yelled: "My word she's mad!" "Why, if he asked me for Juliette's hand in marriage," she added (Juliette was a young servant who came to the house during the day and whom my grandmother, remarking on her manners, her pretty voice, her letters, which were misspelled but always "elegantly written," the feelings she expressed or sometimes only hinted at, considered "extremely distinguished"), "I wouldn't let her marry such a common man." "My word she's rabid!" yelled my uncle, who did not have such an idealized notion of distinction or vulgarity. In truth, while he was a spendthrift and one might say a vain man, my uncle who denied himself half his income to provide for some poor cousins whom he never saw, and who refused to sell his property in return for a life annuity so that he could leave his entire fortune to[18] my grandmother with whom he argued so much, did in his own way possess a little of that moral distinction so prized by my grandmother. He {f. 16} possessed it but he didn't realize it. And he imagined that this moral distinction must be the prerogative of the Viscount de Bretteville, member of the Jockey Club and director of several finance companies, rather than some maidservant. Be that as it may, we never saw M. de Bretteville again. My uncle accused my grandmother of having caused a falling-out by greeting him so coldly. But I think in reality my uncle too had been enlightened regarding his character and he conceded with a reasonable amount of good humor that the Viscount had been a little ridiculous when, seeing eggs in the salad, he'd said "among polite society in Bayeux (the town next to Bretteville) eggs are never served in a salad." When there were eggs in the salad and someone ventured:[19] "Among polite society in Bayeux . . ." my uncle would not reply, but he wouldn't get angry and we sensed that deep down he was more inclined to take the side of his more intelligent relatives than the bigoted Bretteville. It wasn't until the next day that I learned about the disapproving attitude of polite society in Bayeux regarding sliced eggs in salads but I sensed that evening in the silence with which my parents listened to the argument between my grandmother and my uncle that if they weren't defending my uncle's guest out of politeness it was because they hadn't thought him entirely magnificent. For myself, I listened delightedly to the quarrel between my uncle and my grandmother; I was in that joyful mood that precedes a good fight, and despite myself I felt lightened by having put an end to the torment I was enduring, and I kept landing on my feet shouting "Zut, Zut, Zutiflor,"[T] and with a smile of infinite wellbeing as I jumped up and down those unconsciously spoken words seemed the highest expression of human bliss. With the last "Zutiflor" my happiness reached its zenith and I lifted my hand to my lips and tenderly kissed it.

18. Ms.: with.
19. Ms.: someone who ventured.
T. "*Zut*" is similar to a mild curse like "darn" or "blast." The nonsense term "*Zutiflor*" seems to have been a Proust family expression.

{f. 17} Once the last of the guests had been driven home and my parents had sat down again, I heard my mother ask: "Now that we're alone, tell me how was the fillet?" After a brief response from my father: "Yes I know the duckling was a mistake, but the lobster must have been excellent. And it seemed to me that they filled their plates. Did you notice whether Laure ate well? I don't think she had a second helping of the banana salad. And yet I thought it was very good. I should go and congratulate poor Angèle. Auguste did you notice if they took second helpings of everything? Did they seem to like it?" Auguste declared that the Viscount de Bretteville in particular had asked for more of everything and that he had seemed especially fond of the ortolans. My mother kindly reported this to my uncle: "Auguste says that M. de Bretteville appeared to like the ortolans." The coolness of the air, these familiar conversations, all of it calmed my excitement and brought me back to reality. However I was starting to fear the moment when I would have to talk to my mother. Soon I heard them getting up. Some more time passed. Then I heard my parents climbing the stairs; my mother went with my father into their bedroom. My maid had been waiting there to untie her bodice and let down her hair, then my mother came out again and went to her bathroom. I waited for her in the shadows like a thief. She was in a white canvas bathrobe, her beautiful black hair hanging loose, revealing all the sweetness and power of her nature, her hair that survived so long like vegetation unaware of the ruins it tenderly protects to the ruin of its own happiness and beauty, framing a face of adorable purity, radiating an intelligence and a cheerful sweetness that no pain could ever extinguish, but going out to meet life with a hopefulness, an innocent gaiety that quickly disappeared and that I saw again only on her funeral bed when all the pains that life had brought her were erased by the finger of the angel of death, when her face for the first time in years expressed no more pain or anxiety, returning to its first form like a portrait with too much impasto that the artist wipes away with a finger.

{f. 18} That first beloved face of my mother is not the one destined to remain for me definitively hers, the one that still appears to me now when I see her. The last time I saw my mother on those dark roads of sleep and dream where I sometimes encounter her she was wearing that crepe dress, which meant that she had, at the moment when I saw her in my dream, moved past the days that broke her life, leaving her only a few months to live. Her face was red with fatigue and poor circulation, her eyes tired from her constant worrying about me. She was dressed with a care that proved the effort she was making to remain connected to life, but she had been walking quickly and the hem of her dress was soiled, she was almost running toward the train station, I could tell that she was oppressed with anxieties, that she was suffering in her stout body, she clumsily lifted her skirts to avoid getting them dirty. And I choked with sobs seeing her rushing, tiring herself out like that, I wanted to give her those kisses that erase nothing, that would not help her arrive any earlier or more easily at the end of her hard road; she was walking faster and faster, which wrenched my heart more than anything, and there was a sort of irritation painted on her face, which was the form of suffering passing through and altering her health, upsetting her reason, an irritation that she hid so as not to cause me pain, but which made me more unhappy than anything because I sensed that it was in part directed against me and that she was in this way accusing me a little. I started running after her.

When Maman passed close to me I called to her quietly, "Maman," my mother turned around in surprise, then her face took on an expression of anger. "If you don't go to bed immediately, I will never talk to you again." But I knew now that she was so irritated, I would never be able to go back to bed while she looked like that: "I have something very important to tell you," and I started sobbing (every evening I said that, and she knew perfectly well that it was always a new excuse to see her again). "Go away, go away," but I didn't want to, so braving her anger I followed close behind, I threw myself to my knees, I kissed her dress; in the end defeated utterly exasperated she said to me {f. 19} "at least be quiet, you'll wake your father," and looking furious she entered my bedroom. It was a first victory but when she wanted to leave me after I had gone in there I started sobbing so hard that after a few more angry words, she stopped talking. She took my hand, consoled me; for the first time in my life in the eyes of my mother crying wasn't "not being good, being naughty, deserving to be punished," it was feeling sad, or even more than that, a malaise for which one was not responsible. And when, a moment later, my old maid trying to find my mother because she wanted to ask her if she needed anything else and coming into

my bedroom finding her next to my bed where she had forced me to lie
down and was holding my hands while I wept, and as if still under the impression that tears were a punishable act she asked with surprise seeing
me crying without Maman getting angry or walking away: "What's wrong
with him why is he crying?" Maman replied: "He doesn't know himself,
he's suffering," and she wiped the tears from my eyes with her beautiful
soft white hand that I so loved to kiss, where I saw the gleam of her gold
wedding band, which we had let her keep in her grave. Although I sensed
that this had not created a new order of happiness and that the same difficulties would recur every evening, the fact that my evening sorrows had
been in some way officially "recognized," that I had been relieved of responsibility for them, lifted a huge weight from my conscience. But I also
sensed that for the first time Maman had been defeated by life. Until then
faithful to what our doctor had doubtless told her, she hadn't wanted to
admit that I was sad for any reason other than a willful misbehavior which
I was at liberty to correct. She had persevered along this path, fought for
her desire to have a son worthy of her hopes, to whom she[20] would concede nothing that might be bad for him, whether that was tears at bedtime or
éclairs at teatime, or staying up an hour later when they had guests. She
saw only the main prize, true love, and sacrificed my momentary pleasure
for my happiness, which meant ridding me of my neuroses and making
me healthy enough to accomplish great things. Tonight, sitting next to me
despite the ungodly hour, despite my forbidden tears, letting them flow or
asking me to stop crying with a gentleness free of all reproach, she had
acknowledged as an illness what, in order to heal it, she had never wanted
to admit was an illness, and I sensed {f. 20} that this concession was a first
disappointment, a first abdication, that some of her strength had been
broken, confessing her helplessness, she who was so brave, so determined
to overcome the obstacles of life. It seemed to me that I had hurt her, diminished her in some way, that she had less value in that moment, that I
had succeeded in perverting her will and her reason, that this was my
victory. Without her having any idea why, my tears redoubled and, forgetting

20. Ms.: he.

herself for a moment, watching me cry, she said: "don't cry like that" in a broken voice; her eyes lost their luster and I thought she was going to cry, but she quickly pulled herself together and started to laugh. "You'll end up making me as silly as you, little idiot, little canary." And seeing me throw myself into her arms and weep even harder, she stood up and moved away, now fully in control of herself: "No, your father will be furious. What we're doing is as bad for you as it is for me." Above all I think she stayed because, however elevated her theories, she was first and foremost an admirably practical person who knew that the best solution is sometimes a compromise between the present evil and an even greater evil. She wasn't like those doctors who let you suffer indefinitely because they know that morphine is bad; she knew that suffering is sometimes worse. It was henceforth with tender sweetness that she would mock my fits of melancholy, and she would get angry only when I couldn't contain them, when I made a scene. She kissed me and said: "So my little canary, my little idiot," and caressed my head: "But it's sad that the mother bear should love her little cubs more when they are grumpy." A few days later, Mme de Z. having invited us to spend a few days at her house, it was decided that Maman would leave with my brother and that I would join them a little later with my father. They didn't tell me this so I wouldn't be too unhappy in advance. But I have never been able to understand how when someone tries to hide something from us the secret, however well-kept, acts involuntarily upon us, creating a sort of irritation in us, a feeling of persecution, a frenzied wondering. So it is {f. 21} that at an age when children can have no idea of the laws of generation they sense that they are having the wool pulled over their eyes, they have a foreboding of the truth. I don't know what obscure clues accumulated inside my brain. When on the morning of her departure Maman cheerfully came into my bedroom, concealing I believe the sorrow that she felt too by laughing and quoting Plutarch to me: "Amid great disasters Leonidas showed a yellow[21] face; I hope my little canary will be worthy of Leonidas." I said "you're leaving" in a tone of such despair that she was visibly moved, I thought perhaps I could make her stay

---

21. This word, "*jaunet*," is missing from *CSB*, with a note stating: Lacuna in the manuscript.

or take me with her; I think that was what she went to my father to say, but he presumably refused and she told me that she still had a little bit of time before she had to get ready, that she'd set aside this time to pay me a little visit. She had to leave as I said with my younger brother and since he was leaving the house my uncle had taken him to have his photograph taken in Évreux. His hair had been curled like the concierge's children when they had their photographs taken, and his plump face was surrounded by a helmet of puffed-out black hair with big white bows stuck to it like the butterflies of a Velazquez Infanta; I'd watched him with the smile of an older child for a beloved brother, a smile that mingled admiration, ironic superiority, and tenderness. Maman and I went to fetch him so I could say goodbye to him, but he was impossible to find. He had discovered that he couldn't take with him the goat he'd been given. which was, along with the beautiful toy cart that he always dragged around, his most treasured possession, and which he "lent" sometimes to my father, out of kindness. Since he would be going back to Paris after our stay at Mme Z.'s house, the goat was going to be given to some local farmers. My brother, hurt and despondent, had wanted to spend the last day with his goat, and perhaps also, I think, to hide so that he could get his revenge by making Maman miss her train. In any case, after searching everywhere for him, we walked alongside the small copse in the center of which was the cirque where the horses were tied so they could bring up water, a place where nobody ever went. Of course we had no idea that my brother might be there, but our ears were suddenly struck by a conversation punctuated with little moans; it was indeed {f. 22} my brother's voice and soon we spotted him, although he couldn't see us; sitting on the ground next to his goat and tenderly caressing its head with one hand, kissing it on its pure and slightly red nose, like some small, horned, blotchy-faced dandy, creating a composition that bore only the faintest resemblance to those paintings by English artists showing a child caressing an animal. While it was true that my brother, dressed in his best gown and his lace skirt, holding in one hand next to his beloved cart some satin bags in which his *goûter*[T] had been packed along

T. Traditional afternoon snack for children.

with his travel kit and some little glass mirrors, had the magnificence of
those English children close to the animal, on the other hand his face expressed, under all that luxury, which only heightened the contrast, the
fiercest despair: with his red eyes and his throat oppressed by frills, he
looked like a pompous, dejected princess in a tragedy. Now and again
he would lift his hand, the one holding his cart and the satin bags that he
didn't want to let go, because the other hand was busy hugging and
stroking the goat, to his hair and push it back from his face with the impatience of Phaedra: "What officious hand Has tied these knots, and gather'd
o'er my brow These clustering coils?"[T] "My poor little goat," he cried, attributing to the goat the sadness that he alone felt, "you are going to be
miserable without your little master, you will never ever see me again,"
and his tears made it hard to understand his words, "nobody will be good
to you nobody will stroke you like I do, you always let me do it though,
didn't you, my little child, my little darling," and as he choked on his tears he
suddenly had the idea of[22] crowning his despair by singing a song he'd
heard Maman sing and whose words in that situation made him sob even
harder: "Farewell the voices of strangers Are calling me far from you My
sweet sister of angels." But my brother, despite being only five and a half,
was by nature a violent boy and he quickly moved from tenderness over
his and the goat's unhappy fate to anger at his persecutors; after a second's hesitation he started violently[23] smashing his mirrors on the
ground, stamping on the satin bags, tearing out not his hair but the
little bows that had been put in his hair, ripping his beautiful Asiatic
gown and {f. 23} shouting loudly: "Who should I be handsome[24] for if I won't
ever see you again?" he cried while tears poured down his cheeks. Seeing
him tear the lace of his gown, my mother who had until then watched him
with tenderness could no longer remain unmoved. She advanced, my
brother heard a noise, he immediately fell silent, then saw her, unsure if
he'd been seen, and looking profoundly watchful and stepping back with a

T. Translation by Robert Bruce Boswell.
22. Ms.: had of.
23. *CSB:* swiftly.
24. *CSB:* Why should I be handsome (*pourquoi* instead of *pour qui*).

look of exaltation he hid violently behind the goat. But my mother went to him. He had to come but he made it a condition that the goat should accompany him to the station. Time was short, and my father at the bottom of the hill was surprised not to see us coming back; my mother had sent him word to meet us at the railway track that we crossed via a shortcut behind the garden because if not we might risk missing the train and my brother moved forward, guiding the goat with one hand as if taking it to be sacrificed while with the other hand he pulled the bags that we had picked up, the fragments of mirrors, the travel kit, and the toy cart, which dragged along the ground. Now and then he lifted up his hand holding the bags away from the cart, which he raised off the ground, up to his frilly tie and his gauzy veils: "Ah, how these cumbrous gauds, These veils oppress me!"[T] And occasionally, without daring to look at Maman, he caressed the goat and addressed it with words whose real intended recipient she could hardly mistake: "My poor little goat, you weren't the one trying to hurt me, to separate me from those I love. You are not a person, but you are also not nasty, you're not like these nasty people," he said, glancing sideways at Maman to judge the effect of his words and to see if he'd overstepped the mark, "you have never hurt me," and he started to sob. But when we reached the railway tracks he asked me to hold the goat for a moment and, in his rage against Maman, sat down on the tracks, looked up at us defiantly and refused to budge. There was no barrier at that part of the line. A train might pass at any minute. Terrified, Maman threw herself at him and tried to pull him away but—his backside hardened by his habit of sliding around the garden on it while singing on happier days—he stuck to the tracks {f. 24} and she wasn't able to tear him away. She was white with fear. Thankfully at that moment my father arrived with two servants who had come to see if we needed anything. He rushed over, picked up my brother, smacked him twice, and gave the order that the goat should be taken back. My frightened brother had no choice but to walk but, staring at my father with concentrated fury, yelled: "I'll never lend you my cart again!" Then, realizing that nothing he said could surpass the fury of

---

T. Translation by Robert Bruce Boswell.

these words, he fell silent. Maman took me aside and said: "You're a big boy so I want you to be reasonable: please don't look sad when it's time for us to go. Your father is already annoyed that I'm leaving—try not to make him find both of us unbearable." To prove myself worthy of the trust she showed in me, to fulfill the mission she'd given me, I did not complain. At times, however, I felt an irresistible rage against her, against my father, a desire to make them miss the train, to ruin the plan that had been hatched to separate me from her. But it broke against the fear of hurting her and I stood there smiling and broken inside, frozen with sadness. We had to [*passage ends here*]

{f. 25} We returned to eat lunch. In honor of "the travelers" we had a full meal with a first course, poultry course, salad, and dessert. My brother, still wild with suffering, did not say a word during the entire meal. Motionless in his high chair, he seemed fully submerged in sorrow. We were talking about one thing and another when a piercing cry rang out: "Marcel had more chocolate cream than me," my brother yelled. It had taken his righteous indignation against such blatant injustice to make him forget the pain of being separated from his goat. My mother later told me that he never again spoke about that friend of his, whom the restrictions of our Paris apartments had forced us to leave behind in the countryside, and we believe he never thought about it again either. We left for the station. Maman had asked me not to accompany her[25] but she had yielded to my pleas; since the previous evening she appeared to understand my sorrow, to take it seriously, and she asked me only to control it.[26] Once or twice on the way there, I was filled with a sort of fury, I felt persecuted by her and by my father who was preventing[27] me from going with her, and I wanted to take revenge by making her miss the train, preventing her from leaving, setting fire to the house; but these thoughts lasted less than a second; a single slightly harsh word could frighten my mother but I quickly rediscovered my passionate sweetness for her and if I didn't kiss her as much as I would

25. Ms.: accompany me to the station.
26. *CSB:* disregard it.
27. Ms.: were preventing.

have liked it was because I didn't want to hurt her. We arrived outside the church, then we passed the avenue;[28] this gradual progress toward what we fear, each footstep taking us closer, heart racing . . . then we turned yet again, "we'll be five minutes early" my father said, and at last I saw the train station. Maman squeezed my hand slightly and signaled for me to be strong. We went to the platform,[29] she got into the train car and we talked to her from below. They told us to move back because the train was about to leave. Smiling at me, Maman said: "Regulus showed surprising strength in difficult circumstances." Her smile was the one she wore when quoting something she thought pretentious, to anticipate others' mockery if she got it wrong. It was also to show me that what I thought was a source of sorrow was nothing of the kind. All the same, though, she sensed how unhappy I was and as she said goodbye to all of us she let my father walk away and called me back for a second and told me: "We understand each other, don't we, my wolf. My little one will get a note from Maman tomorrow if he's a good boy. *Sursum corda*," {f. 26} she added in that uncertain tone she used when quoting Latin so it would sound as if she were making a mistake. The train left, I stayed there, but it seemed to me that something of me went away too.

28. *CSB:* then we walked more quickly.
29. *CSB:* the platforms.

The Villebon Way
and the Meséglise Way

{f. 27} I was surprised to be told by my mechanic that if you turned right from Chartres on the road to Nogent-le-Rotrou then turned left two or three times you would arrive at the Château de Villebon. For me, that was like being told that if you took one path and then another path you would arrive in the land of dreams. In the ancient world the well that you descended to reach the realm of future life had a precise geographical location, surrounded by real places. For a long time I wasn't even sure what Villebon was. After lunch, after we'd lingered comfortably over a cup of coffee, after one last glass of plum brandy three-quarters of an hour after finishing lunch, someone would say: "The weather's good, there won't be a storm. Why don't we take the road to Villebon?" The road to Villebon was a foreign land, completely different from the road to Bonneval, for example, which we took on days when we'd spent the afternoon at the park. So around five o'clock, to give ourselves an appetite for dinner, we shut our books or stopped our games and we went out for a short walk on the road to Bonneval, which was at the top of the slope after the asparagus plant and the white wooden wickerwork door, a road where it was always already quite cool (perhaps because we went there in late afternoon), where the setting sun turned all the fields crimson and in the distance you could hear the bells ringing to bless the fruits of the earth. I would have loved to know more about Bonneval, which lay beyond the compass of my acquaintance; from farther off I could glimpse only little oak woods forever out of reach, where I sensed that another life began. But Villebon was even more foreign and mysterious. To go on the road to Villebon you had to leave from the house, and not only that but from the back of the house; instead of leaving from the entrance hall onto the street as you did to go to church, or the market, or the park, or the station, you left from the back; in other words, from the entrance hall you went into the little {f. 28} garden and you went out through a door that I took only rarely and that was mostly used by the gardener, the milkmaid, the butcher; and immediately after that you arrived at the river, which was apparently the same one that passed through the park and that you followed before arriving there. But down there it was a sleepy trickle of water that you crossed on a wooden bridge and into which a little boy, amid water lilies and buttercups on the riverbank, was forever plunging a bottle that filled in the sunlight with tadpoles and minnows. Here it was almost a little town river spanned by a big stone bridge. Since I'd never followed it[1] from the little wooden bridge to the big stone bridge, and since the two parts of it that I saw belonged to two different lands, to completely disparate days, to another side of the house that seemed to me another side of the world, I made no connection between them. On this side I knew nobody. And sometimes we would go down there to take a look at a small garden on the edge of town belonging to my uncle, who let us cut across it, bringing us directly to "the Villebon road." That garden was the most wonderful thing I had ever seen. Rather than being worn out as in other gardens by the variety of flowers I had not yet learned to love or that were starting to leave me indifferent,[2] here there were only a few species that I loved in a delightful abundance. The minor miracle of a sweet red strawberry hanging from a stalk with round, veined leaves that looked like none other was repeated thousands of times. The equally charming miracle of a large asparagus held in the earth by its end and raising from the ground its light plume of mauve and azure was repeated with no less grace. A few lizards of a beautiful green color were always in the sun by the well where you could see a thousand little minnows, as in the river. Lastly there were cherry trees laden with a profusion of cherries. Between the myriad sunshades of transparent crimson that they graciously fostered, and the garden of creamy reds that was the strawberry garden, the pale blue garden too, with the unshining but oh-so-soft silk of its forget-me-nots and the less silky, more celestial blue of its periwinkles, and the dark blue, violet-blue, velvet blue of its cineraria, and the

1. "It" refers to "the river," a few lines up.
2. Ms.: would be starting to leave me indifferent.

barely bluish blue of its asparaguses, there passed countless butterflies
with pale blue wings. And not one of those flowers that {f. 29} bored me in
the park and that I would learn to love only later. No begonias, which I
would never love, no[3] large fuchsias of that ugly red like the cheeks of the
gardener's daughter, which were constantly dropping their flowers into
their ugly green boxes where I was sent to learn my lessons, no enormous
pink peonies which seemed to me so heavy, so common, which smelled so
bad in the big flower bed where it was always so hot that you never stopped
sneezing and which always had a caterpillar inside them despite the attentions of the gardener. None of the boring geraniums that we walked past
every time we had to give some strangers a tour of the park and whose
flowers were so ordinary, so poor, so short, with a hairy leaf and a common
scent, flowers that the gardener was obsessed with, that seemed made for
him alone, and that for me did not yet have a connection to any poetic idea
that would revive them in my mind, make them as desirable as the strawberry plants, the periwinkles, the forget-me-nots, the asparaguses, the
roses. And those flowers, which I dreamed of and which I marveled at
seeing in real life before me, it was a delight to find so many in front of me
and to have such a complete vision of them uninterrupted by things I
didn't like. The other gardens were like Mérimée's *Colomba* or Musset's
Merle blanc, which I liked far less than Saintine's *Picciola* because no
sooner did he talk about something beautiful that I liked, about a moon
[*passage ends here*]

Leaving the garden, we came upon a big street where we passed in front
of the notary's garden, a garden of another kind altogether with big flowering trees in strange colors that struck me as very ugly, a pond, a foun-
tain. We could see it only through the bars of a high fence. There was a
lawn with houseleeks in the shape of the cross of the Legion of Honor; the
rest of the facade consisted of high walls covered in clematis and . . . a
pink hawthorn. The shrub I have always loved most, which I loved so
much that at times, when it leans down, smilingly displaying its confusion
of pink flowers, it is almost impossible for me not to believe that I am

---

3. Ms.: which I would love, no.

someone special for the hawthorn just as it has always been someone special for me; even when I was a little boy, people would joke about my passion for that beloved flower. When I fell very ill there, the first joy of my convalescence was the visit of a cousin I loved, whom I had never thought would come to the house, and the long pink hawthorn branch that she brought me. It was a wonderful adornment for an altar and something that, in pathways filled with the divine, fragrant grace of the hawthorn that I loved, added {f. 30} color, the same color as the pink cookies from Tours that we took out of their box after lunch on days of special privilege, or as cream cheese mixed up with smashed strawberries. Seeing my beloved hawthorn, the enchantment of church and of springtime, painted pink, was for me the intoxication felt by a music lover when he hears a Beethoven symphony played by an orchestra that he has previously known only by reading the score, or by an art lover who is mad for a painting by Vermeer that he has only ever seen in a photograph, now witnessing it with all its colors. Even today when I think that there are paths lined with pink hawthorns they have, for me, a particular substance like that of a dream, and it seems to me that if my sad infirmity did not prevent me walking there I would penetrate them in my twelfth year and that so many things that strike me as possessing the insignificant color of experience would once again become, for me, beautiful, mysterious, akin to that divine reality that we touched everywhere then and that, having never found it in life, we try so desperately later, when we are artists, to discover and elucidate in our brain. In the sunken paths that we took afterward there were other hawthorns, and merely its leaf, like later the leaf of an apple tree, appeared to me as something absolutely different from a leaf, like the name of a woman we love, but the promise of a particular happiness. Already I would have liked to remain alone in front of it, to try to understand what it was that I liked so much about it, but my parents were calling me. And anyway the bush couldn't tell me anything more. It could only give me its image. It was up to me later, intuiting from the pleasure it gave me that this corresponded with something real in my thoughts, to try[4] to lift up the image remaining

---

4. Ms.: to later try.

intact in its place and to seek what was hidden beneath, not in the tree, but in my brain. And in passing I cut a few of those dog roses that one day are more pleasing than roses, four pieces of fragile pink fabric pointing with a pistil, and all of it blown by the wind before being taken home.

[New version]

{f. 31} For a long time I knew Villebon only by these words "the Villebon road, the Villebon way." "I was sure," my great-aunt would say when we got home late for dinner (in other words only half an hour early, leaving us just "time to get ready" before the bell was rung), "I was sure, I said to myself if they're not back by this time they must have taken the Villebon way. You must be so hungry! I hope you're going to have enough to eat . . ." "Taking," impulsively, in this way, "the Villebon way" (in other words walking along the Villebon road on our way back) was very rare. When we went to walk the Villebon way, we knew it when we set out. And we didn't leave the house by the same door as for the other walk. There were two walks, "the Méséglise way" and "the Villebon way."[5] The "Méséglise way" began above the park for us. For poor people, and local people during holidays, there was a sunken path of hawthorns that ran up alongside the park and ended at the same place as the gate at the top of the park, in other words in the fields. The "Méséglise way" was open-air, immense, and it would rain sometimes because, since it was the shorter walk, we reserved it for uncertain weather; and the sun was always close to setting there because we would only leave after the hot hours in the park were over. We went to the park first, so we left by the door that opened from the entrance hall onto rue de l'Oiseau bleu, greeting the gunsmith, "Monsieur Orange" (the grocer), crossing the thin trickle of river on a little wooden bridge where we would stop to contemplate the tadpoles that gathered there for an instant, or were scattered; sometimes little boys would put bottles into the river to catch them, and sometimes a man in a straw hat who knew my uncle would be fishing from the bridge. And barely past the bridge, more than a hundred meters before reaching the park, we were

---

5. Ms.: ~~and the Villebon way~~. We have restored the line.

greeted by the fragrance of the big lilac bush that was held prisoner behind the little white gate where it shook its limbs with distinction and a thousand shivers and manners from its supple waist, sending its scents out to meet us. Such was the entrance to the "Méséglise way." We probably never went all the way to Méséglise, but Méséglise was not very far {f. 32} from the place where we stopped. We could sense that the country was beginning to change, that there were thickets of trees, that the road was beginning to slope down again. And on Sundays near the park we would see people that nobody knew, "strangers" who came from beyond Méséglise. Méséglise remained as mysterious as the horizon. (Maybe put here: it was in the fields that led to Méséglise that I first saw the sun set, noticed the shadows around their feet, saw the pale crescent moon, heard the angelus bells on the way home, experienced the sweetness of getting back before everyone else. It was in those fields of Méséglise that twelve years later I felt the thrill of going out after everyone else when the moon was already in the sky, seeing sheep blue in the moonlight, etc.)[6] But Villebon was as distant, as abstract as the North or Spain. To go the Villebon way, after my father had checked with the gardener who promised that it wouldn't rain, we would leave after lunch. And we didn't leave by rue de l'Oiseau, the wooden bridge, etc. where the path was marked as with milestones by the gunsmith, "Monsieur Orange," the fisherman in the straw hat who greeted my uncle, the scent of lilac.

[*Resumption and development of the previous two pages*]

{f. 33} For a long time I knew Villebon only by these words: "the Villebon road, going the Villebon way," as opposed to the "other" walk, the Méséglise road, the Méséglise way. "I was sure," my great-aunt would say when we were late home for dinner (in other words only half an hour early and having just "time to get ready" before the bell was rung), "I was sure, I said to Félicie" (the maid she had sent to wait for us on the doorstep) "if they're not back by this time they must have taken the Villebon way. I hope you're going to have enough to eat after a hike like that, it's only a tiny little

6. This editorial note, which we have put in parentheses, was written at the top of the folio.

leg of lamb." But "taking," impulsively, the Villebon way, in other words joining the Villebon road to lengthen the Méséglise walk, was something exceptional and for me it always remained incomprehensible, since the Villebon way and the Méséglise way were parts of the universe as opposed as the East and the West, that there could be any means of communicating between them along a side road. Usually when we were going to walk the Villebon way, we knew before leaving. And we didn't leave on the same side as to go "toward Méséglise." To go toward Méséglise we left as we would to go to the park that we had outside the town, in other words we left the house by the front door from the entrance hall, which gave onto rue de l'Oiseau bleu; and on the way to the park we would encounter on the path, at roughly equal distances, like so many milestones dividing it, first the gunsmith who was closing his shop,[7] then, as soon as we had turned onto rue du Saint-Esprit, "Monsieur Orange"[8] the grocer who passed us,[9] bareheaded, carrying sugar-loaves, then, on the edge of town, the little wooden bridge over which we crossed the river as thin as a thread where a man in a straw hat I didn't know was fishing and who greeted my uncle, {f. 34} and[10] lastly, walking alongside the river on the elevated path, the scent of the big lilac bush that we couldn't yet see, imprisoned behind the white bars of the little wooden gate, which would cry so softly on the stones later when we pushed it, in its flower bed where it would exaggeratedly and endlessly shiver at the slightest breath of wind, showing off the great distinction of its manners, the lightness of its beautiful mauve plumes, its waist that was still so supple; it sent its perfume to meet us on the little towpath, and we encountered it more or less midway between the unknown fisherman in the straw hat and the gate of the park, at the spot where little boys would always place bottles in the river, the bottles looking cooler because they sparkled between the water that filled them and the water that surrounded them as on a set table, and where would be caught many of those minnows

7. Ms.: who was closing his shop to us (previous versions: who greeted us from his shop, whom we greeted outside his shop).

8. Ms.: by "Monsieur Orange."

9. Ms.: who passed us at the corner of.

10. Until "suddenly scattering," we give here the second version of the manuscript. Proust did not cross out the previous version.

and tadpoles that here and there in the river we would enjoy watching abruptly gathering as if the supersaturated water had until then contained them in solution, then suddenly scattering. Since the Meséglise way was short, we first stayed in the park to play for an hour or two and then, when the heat faded, around four o'clock, we left through the gate at the top. The country of Meséglise was lit by slanting sunlight then. Its climate was quite rainy, its soil often soaked, because we reserved the walk on that path for days of uncertain weather when we were unwilling to risk the Villebon way. The country of Meséglise [*the rest, crossed out, is resumed at the start of f. 35*]

{f. 35} The country of Meséglise consisted of fields of wheat, rye, and buckwheat stretching all the way to the horizon. Only at the very end, on the right, was a small thicket of trees that seemed to signify that the land started to change character there, and beyond that apparently lay Meséglise itself. But we never went that far.

The only information I might have gleaned about Meséglise would have come from strangers in peaked caps or knit caps or even in hats whom sometimes on Sundays we would see walking in town, looking through the gate at the park, and whom we said came "from the Meséglise way," probably from beyond the little thicket of trees. But I was not allowed to speak to people I didn't know. Moreover I never understood anything I was told, even by my parents. And, absorbed by I know not what, I didn't even listen. And for me Meséglise was as mysterious as the horizon. But Villebon was as abstract as a cardinal point. Everything about going the Villebon way was different from the Meséglise walk. And first of all we left from the small door to the garden through which only the butcher, the milkman, and the grocer entered, and immediately we found ourselves in a part of the town where we never went, whose inhabitants were unknown to us. We crossed the river on a broad stone bridge, sometimes cluttered with carts. And how could I imagine that this broad, deep river was {f. 36} the same one as the thin trickle of water completely covered in places with water lilies, green plants, and buttercups, spanned so easily by a wooden plank at the entrance to the park? We passed in front of the notary's garden where the Japanese trees with red flowers, always scattered outside the door by the wind, seemed ugly to me, and where purple velvet clematis

covered the wall from the month of May on as if born from the warm air.
We passed the Calvary and then there was only a single row of houses, an
arm of the farmers' village reaching out toward the countryside, in a sleeve
of pink silk and scented muslin made by the dog rose and hawthorn
hedges. Then a tree-lined path that seemed to know where it was leading
[*a line connects this page to the next one*] {f. 37} We took a sort of avenue of
tall trees that gave the impression it knew where it was leading. Often
since then, seeing similar trees in Normandy, in Burgundy, I would suddenly feel a sort of sweetness pour through me and my present state of
consciousness would gently slip aside, revealing a very old one beneath.
"I've seen those trees before, where." It was so vague that I thought it had
only been in a dream. And then I remembered, it was the avenue we took
as we were leaving town to go on the Villebon road. I so often wanted to
see it again, that avenue, that it constantly grew, in my dreams, even more
mysterious than it had been in my memory, in my desire, full of women
mysteriously in the shade, with only their faces illuminated, and above all
with that startlingly specific feeling of a place that resembles no other, such
as we imagine every place we have not yet visited, and which we never find
when we do go there. This obsessive desire to exhaust the singularity of a
country and to express it became in the end a sort of intellectual malaise
that returned to me in dreams, like a physical malaise. I sensed the extreme singularity of that avenue, I sensed its inexpressible nature, I was
about to express it, and I woke up. Then the trees multiplied, it was a
forest, but the path turned, the trees lit up, and we arrived on a very high
road, with deep blue valleys sweeping down on either side, quickly closed
by hillsides before sweeping off elsewhere, out of sight. Then the road
turned again and it was a vast plain, empty under a vacant blue sky where
a few white clouds had been left [*passage ends here*]

[*Resumption of the previous page*]

{f. 39}[11] Before reaching what was actually the Villebon road we took a
sort of wide avenue of trees that seemed to know where it was leading. Even
today when all the places of the earth have one after another refused the

---

11. Folio 38 is blank.

mysterious essence that I dreamed for each of them and taught me one after another the uselessness of those journeys for which their name awoke in me an insane desire, it seems to me that this avenue must genuinely contain something similar to what I dreamed. Sometimes I see it in dreams, women half-hidden in the shade busy at invisible tasks. I sense, and this time no longer with my imagination, I sense directly the mysterious essence of a country, it is my imagination that sees, it is my dream that I am going to live, but then I wake up. Other times I feel this wonderful sensation while awake, but at the very moment when I am about to grasp the mysterious singularity of that tree-lined path, I fall asleep, or if I force myself to stay awake I can no longer see it. Because there really are things that must not be shown to us. And seeing that my whole life has been exhausted trying to see these things, I think that this is perhaps the hidden secret of Life. The trees multiply, we walk for a moment through the forest of Barbonne, then they light up and we join the real Villebon road, overlooking on one side deep blue valleys that open and close by turns between high hillsides, sweeping toward a horizon, hidden from us by the hillsides, to which they seem to belong. We were, so to speak, surrounded by the shapes of another land that only passed through there, and of which we could see only the beginning, or the end, above us, in a blue light. The other side of the road was on the same level as a vast plain, completely empty because we normally arrived there at the hour when the peasants stopped working; above empty fields, the vacant sky was all blue, with fat white clouds left on the sides like farm tools in the furrows. Everything seemed eternally motionless, as in an artist's painting. But the white clouds, like natural sundials, showed by the angle at which they received the light that the sun was very low and would soon set. Soon the road {f. 40} left this plain and we were facing an immense valley, very high hillsides on which a forest shredded the sky like crosses, and on another more distant hillside a church steeple, the only human trace in the entire landscape, engraved its little pale triangle in the blue sky. "What a magnificent view," said the deputy mayor who had accompanied us one day. I was stunned by this.

Sources of the Loir[12]

---

12. Editorial note, indicating that the corresponding piece should be inserted here.

It is probably due to the walks on the Méséglise way that I cannot see, while walking along the embankment of a field, perched on a green stalk amid wheat, the two red wings of a poppy, without feeling a profound joy that the beauty of a flower would not in itself be enough to give me. I say of other flowers that I find them beautiful, but for poppies and several other varieties, if I spot them from a car, I will ask the driver to stop so I can get out to take a closer look, the way I used to slip away from my parents to pick them. And without them a field for me is not a field. A field full of poppies makes me think that poetry is a reality and that joy and blessings can descend upon the earth. It must also be due to the walks on the Méséglise way that I love cornflowers, and almost as much the purple fleece of clover, and a thousand times more the white blossom of the apple tree, which I could pick out from a thousand others, because of the emotion it inspires in me, just as you could not mix up a woman you loved with any other. But it is to the "Villebon way" that I owe my even deeper tenderness for the hawthorn, so powerful and persistent throughout my life that I can hardly believe the hawthorn itself is unaware of my predilection. Crying out with joy at an age when I couldn't even pronounce its name, because I'd glimpsed the fragrant muslin of its flowers held out on its little branches with their openwork leaves, had I already seen it on the church altar, and was it this that began to give it for me a sacred quality that it has never lost? But my tenderness for it has nothing of that simple admiration for a beautiful flower that might turn to boredom like any purely aesthetic satisfaction. For me, its flowering brings to mind the indescribable charms of delicious life, between games in the park, the wonders of reading in the house, the months of Mary at the church. And when I glimpse it in a hedge, I stop before the miracle of its flowers as before a dream turned real that would contain the joy of living its sweetness, all the philosophy of understanding it, and all the art of recreating it. It is also to the Villebon way that I owe the love I feel, a thousand times less but still a little, for the {f. 41} miracle of strawberries under their large curled leaves, agate cherries in the cherry trees, periwinkles, and pale blue silk forget-me-nots. It was on the Méséglise way that I learned to love the bracing air in the middle of a field, the softness of stamping on plowed soil, the black shadows at the feet of apple trees, the sadness of the sounds of autumn as in a house without furniture. But it

was on the Villebon way that I noticed for the first time the mysterious pink-
ness that rises above woods after sunset, making the branches appear
black, reflecting red in water, and that would make you sad and dreamy if
it didn't make you so desperate to get home, to sit at the table before nightfall in front of a good fire, with the lamp lit, and the prospect of a pleasant
dinner close to you. Many years later[13] on the Villebon road I knew a pleasure different from that of walking all day long and going home at night,
namely that of staying home to work all day, and with the Duchess of Villebon, who was in the habit of eating dinner at the hour when I used to go
to bed years before when I was a little boy, going out for a walk at night. So
it was as we were leaving that we encountered the last people on their way
home, crossing through the village as we saw above the rooftops the already golden moon in the still pink sky. Then the moon reigned supreme
and we walked on the paths overlooking those valleys where we saw lines
of sheep with bluish fleeces and reddish noses, noble as Greek gods,
walking home confusedly, and we stood aside to let them pass, enjoying
the surprise caused by our unusual walk, and soon found ourselves alone
in the fields, the silence, the moonlight. When you are alone with another
being in the empty universe, it seems that only you exist for her. Sometimes as we descended the valleys fantastically lit by the moon for our
whimsical walk, I had the feeling that I truly existed for her in the universe, that I was not merely a fleeting, fading image. But I remembered
friends I had heard her speak about so tenderly, her voice held up by their
existence, that I didn't think she could live without them, who had become
merely "poor so-and-so" whose name was never mentioned, could not be
mentioned. And after a long walk we went back and we saw in the village the
houses showing us[14]   and we rejoiced when the looming silhouette of
the château presented us with the two big lighted windows, presaging for
us at the hour when everyone else was asleep, the delicious dinner, conversations with friends, music very late at night.

{f. 41v} To return to the time when I knew only the "Villebon way" and
the "Meséglise way," when I was in love, during the walks in those flat,

13. Ms.: ~~Later~~.
14. Blank in the ms.

infinite fields of Méséglise, where a breath of wind could sweep across leagues without meeting any obstacle, where no rose bush could emit its scent, no angelus could ring out, no breeze could stir within ten leagues of there without reaching us, I would say to myself: "she breathed this air, breeze go to her, tell her of my tears, unite our thoughts, song of bells." But when we went the Villebon way, I saw deep below me a small house that looked remote from everything, hemmed in with no view, bound to a fold of the river hidden under water lilies and aquatic plants, sad, unknown, rooted to the damp earth. And I thought of the sadness of coming to live there forever, without her, to forget her, to silence one's evening revolts, to accept oblivion, isolation, to return to the soil, to immobility, lost in those lonely lands. An elegant woman with a sad face was standing on the balcony, and I thought that she must have come to that place to forget a lover. But when you have to marry the land like that, what better way to know the soul of its lost places, their inhabitants, than by becoming their inhabitant, by having this place to yourself, this forsaken house, this sleepy fold in the river buried under water plants, by being the person whose soul we seek to penetrate. But I sensed that I would have quickly destroyed the soul of these lands by perpetually dissolving my own, would have penetrated them with my thoughts, already well known to me, rather than receiving, except in the first days, the impression of theirs, a malaise without thought. Cars passed, trains whistled, telegraph wires sang, I felt united with the one I loved. Perhaps that train is bringing me a letter. Perhaps it is her tender thoughts running toward me that those wires are singing to me. I could have her letter tonight, I am going to have it, it begins with these words. And I knew now that I wouldn't have it, because there is no reason why precisely what we imagined should immediately come true. And if that had happened, it would have seemed to me that it wasn't real, that reality was merely a sort of imagination emanating from me, that it wouldn't have brought me something independent from myself that could give me joy. It's not for me that those wires are singing, I told myself, it isn't a letter for me that they're sending, and yet, I added {f. 43}[15] in tears,

15. Folio 42 is blank.

"if you wanted, if you had wanted, it would be your letter, and I would have it when I got home, you bad girl"; I took pleasure in running far from my parents, feeling alone, sitting in a place where they couldn't see me, crying, singing and listening to my voice "Reproaches are no use" or "Farewell the voices of strangers are calling you[16] far from me," praying to Christ of the Calvary when we passed him on the way home, and as it was often late since my parents did not calculate the precise time needed to return from Villebon, watching the stars light up, telling myself that she was probably looking at them just then too, telling myself that she loved me if I spotted five at once, starting over if I'd only seen four, and if I still saw only four telling myself that it made five, four stars and one phrase: "I love you."

{f. 51}[17] Once we went farther than usual on the Villebon road, we went to the Sources of the Loir.

I never saw Villebon. Sometimes Madame de C. would tell Maman, one day you must come to Villebon.

16. Ms.: calling me.
17. Folios 44–50 are blank, as is folio 52.

A Visit to the Seaside

{f. 53} The question of whether or not one should make new relationships during a trip, a question posed, I imagine, many times by all our readers during the months that have just passed, is in reality resolved by the best portion of humanity in a way that seems to me deplorable in that it is destructive of sincerity and of life. My grandmother, I may say, ignored quite sincerely the people staying in the hotel. If she spotted some friends of hers in the dining room, the constant thought of never wanting us to miss out on ten minutes of sea and sun, or more often alas of cold and rain, would have prevented her from "recognizing" someone she would have had to speak to, from "going through the motions" of politeness. On the beach we never left the sea, going up and down its slope in time with the tide, while my grandmother (whose skirts were always soaked) followed the waterline with her folding chair, and we only ever left the beach for long enough to go eat lunch. Even then we didn't let it out of sight because my grandmother, after the hotel manager had categorically refused to serve us outside, insisted on reserving a table next to the patio door, which she always asked to be opened despite the recriminations of the other guests. Sometimes if the maître d' had refused her request, she would try to open it herself. And as soon as it was open, everything would go flying, menus fluttering through the lobby, tablecloths blown outside. My grandmother would laugh at length about this, but the other people took it far less well. Amid a general outcry, the maître d' would be obliged to close the patio door again, not without addressing a few observations to our table, to the despair of my brother and myself and to the complete indifference of my grandmother, who thought these other people "common" and, looking at the sunlight on the sea, said: "Such a pity not to make the most of this good weather, to be shut up here just like in Paris. Children, eat quickly so we can get back to the sea." {f. 54} While my grandmother didn't suffer from not being known by the other hotel guests, and even being somewhat despised by them, perhaps it wasn't the same for a few other people. But people are so used to saying about something that vexes them that it is perfectly pleasant, because they regard it as more flattering, that they long ago got into the habit of telling themselves this and believing it. Consequently our soul lives surrounded by a series of pleasures that are in fact only unconfessed dissatisfactions or at best a vague boredom labeled as pleasure, and out of human respect distances itself from and forgoes the natural pleasures, which in truth when they are experienced are not particularly lively but at least offer the advantage of not giving us the impression that we always live amid distorted impressions. So with the old lady eating dinner at a table close to ours, I am sure that when she arrived at a hotel she would have wanted all the people chatting in the lobby—the financier, the well-known doctor, the provincial viscountess—to read from her face that she knew the Duchess of T. and had a letter from her in her pocket and many other things that would have given them an esteem for her that her black-and-white mourning dress signally failed to give them. But she had gotten into the habit of telling herself that she was indifferent to the opinions of others and that she had no desire to know any of the people she met while traveling. And so as not to have to explain who she was and not to suffer from the contempt of others, she had placed between herself and others—between herself and life—a number of people whose task it was to act like a series of living barriers {f. 55} between herself and life. In each new city, in each new hotel, she arrived preceded by a housekeeper who reserved rooms, and accompanied by a chambermaid and a chauffeur. And when her automobile arrived outside the hotel and she went up to what was already her room, with her housekeeper waiting for her at the door, her chambermaid, she enjoyed a sort of extraterritoriality, the feeling that she wasn't really setting foot on foreign soil at all but continuing to live in the same microcosm that moved around with her, its borders guarded by her housekeeper, her chambermaid, her butler, and her chauffeur, and she entered a room where all the objects from her home in Paris had already been prepared. And when she walked quickly through the lobby to reach her room, not looking at anyone around her and replying as tersely as possible to the hotel manager to whom she did not have to be introduced since her housekeeper had already made him aware of everything she desired, then the hotel manager probably thought that this was a very proud lady who did not want relations with anyone; and when she went down to eat lunch and she reached her table and glanced at the people around her with a look that seemed to signify her indifference and superiority but that probably signified this only in her own eyes since the others appeared to laugh a little when they looked at her, I wonder if all of that was nothing more than a lie in which she lived, intended to hide reality, but which had ended up hiding her instead. I wonder if she hadn't in fact been intimidated at the idea of arriving in a new hotel, {f. 56} worried about the opinions of the handsome gentlemen who were smoking or chatting there in the lobby, or going out for a walk, I wonder if she wasn't in fact eager to meet them, to be liked by them, perhaps for one of them to be her lover, if she wasn't merely anxious about entering an unknown room. But her pride and her sensitivity suffered from those first minutes when she had to be looked at suspiciously, or so she thought, by the hotel manager—like some not-very-chic client, perhaps—and the fear that she would not be able to quickly, or perhaps ever, let those other people know who she was, that she might be scorned by the very people whose approval she craved; her sensitivity and her health suffered perhaps from that first encounter with a foreign land, with a new room, amid pieces of furniture that didn't know her. Even if within a few moments she could have provided references to the hotel manager, maybe later gotten to know and made herself known to the handsome gentleman with the gardenia, to the young man in riding boots flirting with another lady, maybe if she could have gotten used to her room, become friends with those unknown portraits, with those two Chinese vases that greeted her so coldly, that initial period when she had to accept a new reality was too much for her. Maybe in two months she would be an acquaintance of the young man in riding boots and it would be he who wished to visit her in Paris. Maybe in a few days when she thought about leaving, the ladies holding a rose above the door would give her a look {f. 57} to make her heart melt at the thought of being separated from them, and in the Chinese vases she would recognize a pair of old friends who had silently begun to love her and from whom she would not willingly be separated. As for the hotel manager, after half an hour he would almost certainly have understood that this was a particularly choice client. But even with him there was that first minute, that first word addressed to her that was the acceptance of being thought of *for one minute* as a possibly contemptible stranger. And she had rid herself of that minute by sending her housekeeper in her stead. She'd had the Chinese vases removed in advance and had the room made to look as close as possible to her own bedroom in Paris. She had rid herself of that entire period when the gentleman in riding boots whom she wanted to like her might despise her by denying that she wanted him to like her, just as she had denied that she was afraid of that first encounter with the hotel manager or with her room. And to heal her soul she had fed it the same lie that she told to others and under whose intoxicating, medicinal influence she would eventually fall: "It's so tedious to have a conversation with the hotel manager that I send my housekeeper. The rooms are so ugly that I bring my little {f. 58} belongings to brighten them up. I like traveling as long as I don't know anyone and I don't have to meet anyone. It's so tedious making new acquaintances." And so, with a delicate, shivering sensitivity similar to a shivering snail followed by its entire *house,* she went through life followed by her chauffeur, her butler, her housekeeper, her chambermaid, her belongings, hardening the shell that came between life and her over-delicate sensitivity. But now that delicate sensitivity was no longer directly touched by life, since there was between it and reality always that shell which rid her of the need for contact. She had rid her life of the work we are obliged to do to adapt to new places, to new people, to perpetually rebuild on unknown sand the house of cards of one's "situation," but in doing so she had rid her life of new places, new people, life. And isn't the same true for the rich, elegant man I saw at a table farther off with his mistress and two friends? His mistress was charming, intelligent, and witty, and had embraced all his tastes in art, reading, decoration, conversation and his friendship for four or five charming beings who liked one another, and she and he and they only ever traveled in one another's company and on the condition that they could eat dinner together as they did in Paris, go on outings together, attend the theater together. {f. 59} They came down to eat dinner only very late when there was no one else in the hotel dining room so they could relax together, and if there was anyone else they didn't throw contemptuous glances at them as the old lady did because they felt admired and envied and they had no need to assert their superiority because they believed it was obvious in their elegance and their charm. But that elegant mistress drew a veil between that rich man and life, a soft and perfumed veil but one that separated him from it nonetheless. The different outfit that she wore each evening to come down to dinner was the outermost boundary of the universe for him, just as the housekeeper had been for the old lady, and when they decided to go out every night so as not to be surrounded by the other guests in the hotel dining room, very late, just as everyone else was finishing dinner, to an elegant restaurant where they had a private room, the automobile that waited for them and into which they disappeared made them turn their backs on life. Even that wonderful country that their automobile might have allowed them to visit, those paths where the sea could be glimpsed between apple trees and hawthorn bushes, they reduced it to nothing more for them, since they only went out in the black night when others were going to bed, than the black and always identical image of the journey they must take from their hotel bathroom to the private room of a restaurant, or to a high-society dining room, from the place where they combed their hair one last time, and fastened a flower to their buttonhole, or applied some lipstick and hesitated between two hats, to the moment when they hand their overcoat to the footman and where, perhaps after a glance in the mirror and a quiver of skin in a white shirt, they go inside and hold out their hand to shake. That unremarkable rue des Capucines, {f. 60} unrecognized even from the back of the car where they finish putting on their gloves and where, noticing that it is half past eight, they wish death on the passers-by who are making them late, yes that is what became for them the wonderful paths of Normandy. To bring your belongings with you to a foreign land is to not want to commune with its unknown rooms, to enter into a new life, but to take your mistress with you is to not want to commune with unknown women, to enter into a new life. My uncle was not that way and whenever, having failed to meet any of the elegant women in a land, to be introduced to any of its young maidens, to put his arm around the waist of any of its serving girls, he wrote in desperation to his mistress to come and stay with him, it seemed an act of renouncement, a lie, because by pretending to lead a full life there he was simply substituting the part of life that he couldn't explore with something that did not belong to it. He was not someone who remained enclosed in his old relationships, who stayed aloof in his "situation." His situation was, for him, no longer something that existed but something that was over and that had taken the form of a useful tool to help him make a new one. The situation he had in the Saint-Germain quarter of Paris, now that he knew all the women there, was nothing more than a sort of inert mass, without any value in itself, but very useful as a trowel to help him build one in the village or the spa town {f. 61} where he arrived and where he found a woman he liked. The situation in Saint-Germain, all of whose women he already knew, no longer meant anything to him. But the possible situation in Quimper-Corentin where the daughter of the judge was attractive and seemed to pay no attention to him, that was everything. In a word, his situation was not a home where he was stupid enough, like some people, to lazily remain. It was a kit house that could be taken down and brought with him whenever he traveled and which he endeavored, in accordance with the possibilities and customs of each land, to reconstruct wherever he found himself so that he made a good impression. Perhaps he might have succeeded with the pretty women of each land without making this effort to show himself an elegant man. But his vanity was used only in the service of love and in itself it meant nothing to him; on the other hand, he was not one of those people like my grandmother who do not understand what vanity is, who even if they could be imagined inside the body of a young man in love would make no attempt to dazzle the one they loved. And if I consider my uncle now, with the perspective to understand and reconstruct his life, as being much closer to life than the old lady preceded by her housekeeper and followed by her chauffeur, or the elegant man living always with his mistress in the same select society, nevertheless I believe that this need to shine in front of whomever he loved or was courting, to approach women *from above,* from a situation that they would envy, with an air of condescension, I think that there too there was to a certain degree {f. 62} as with the old lady a sensitivity and timidity unwilling to be put to the test, a renouncement not of life or its new joys, as with the old lady, but of total contact with life. But as for his relationships, I repeat that they were just useless gold chains until the day when he found a dish to his taste—like a man who has a gold chain and needs jewels—and he sold it to the first money changer for silver that could be more easily spent. All the courtesies he had paid in his life to a duchess, the entire "situation" that he had forged with her, he summed up with an imperious request for a letter of recommendation allowing him access to a farmer, because the man had a pretty daughter. So, as the movements of our blood, for example, are revealed to others, even to those who we claim do not understand them, by sphygmographic lines, always identical, so did we recognize him in those letters that we often received from him, asking with feigned indifference, on invented pretexts, with a tact in which {f. 63} the persistent originality, well-known to all, of his character, rendered his competency more damning than his blunders, for a letter of introduction, an invitation, or simply an opportunity to get back in touch with friends he hadn't seen in a long time and in whose orbit he thought he might be able to meet the woman he liked best at that moment. I remember with a certain sadness the way my parents would always flatly reject his requests. They were suspicious of every letter he sent them, and refused to arrange a meeting with this or that woman whom they would put in contact so easily with so many other people who had no real desire to meet her, people whom they loved less than my uncle and who were "less" than him. As soon as my father recognized his handwriting, he would say: "It's Florian about to ask us for something. On your guard!" And they made the excuse that the woman in question was not going out much at the moment, that even they weren't able to see her. And each time (when I'd guessed my uncle's request from snatches of conversation) that I saw this woman come to visit us, and often be bored alone in the house, since my parents had found no one else to invite, I thought how happy my uncle would have been to be there, in what blissful mystery our dining room would have been bathed, had he known that it was that evening the world where she was shining, that the lamp which lit up our dining room was the one she saw, its light illuminating her slightly pale cheeks, her short blonde hair. There was on my uncle's part {f. 64} undeniably a certain boldness in the way he expected, at a time when he was ceaselessly offered new forms of life, the whole world to serve as his matchmaker. You must not imagine, however, that he pictured all the people he knew and all the people that those people knew and through whom he had access, this vast crowd of scholars, princes, generals, duchesses, financiers lined up on either side of the room he wished to enter, each of them holding a light, my uncle dismissing them after paying in kindnesses of one sort or another for the price of the candle, the indemnity for the inconvenience, and as they say the hour of waiting. That would be even less true since sometimes my uncle from the first glance did not want to sleep with them, and even if he had desired that from the beginning—which was not always the case—he often gave up the idea en route for reasons that we will see, and so, his intentions, if not his desires, for fornication having been abandoned sometime between the moment he first glimpsed the object of his attentions until the moment he knew her well enough to be able to put them into execution, on the rare occasions when the intention had accompanied him until the end, the harshness of circumstances that was usually the virtue of the maiden would force him to give it up. What drove him was desire but it was also a sort of sincerity; it was taking desire for what it is, a path we hope will lead us to a real knowledge of particular things, of individuals. It was not "passing on" to his usual mistress {f. 65} the desire inspired in him by the milkmaid with white sleeves who had looked at him on the street corner when, busy walking an old lady home, he hadn't dared, whatever desire he'd felt, or hadn't been able to, on some pretext suddenly invented, ditch her then and there, or the *trottin*[1] that he had—without having seen her, let's be honest—searched for (because it is possible to provoke experiences: scientists call this experimentation) and searched for in vain while he was on foot and, having seen that no more women would appear, he had hailed a taxi, and then the girl had passed right in front of him without him having the time or the nerve to stop the car, it was [*passage ends here*]

---

1. Outdated term meaning a young worker who was sent to do errands, often for shop-keepers; a courier.

Young Girls

{f. 67}[1] One day, like two seabirds walking on the sand and about to fly off, I spotted on the beach two *fillettes*,[T] no longer little girls but not yet young women, whose unknown appearance, whose unfamiliar outfits, made me take them for foreign visitors whom I would never see again. They were walking, laughing haughtily, apparently unaware of the other humans on the beach, and speaking in loud voices. Soon two or three others of the same species had joined them and they had formed a chattering conventicle, constantly swelling, for whom the rest of the universe seemed not to exist. If they had been new arrivals I would have seen them again that evening, or the next day before and after lunch on that little beach where everyone saw one another ten times a day. But a few days later, gathered around a beautiful *break*[TT] that had stopped at the corner of one of the streets that led to the beach, I spotted them, perhaps not exactly the same girls, but I felt as if I recognized several of them. The ones already in the *break* were saying goodbye to the others who soon went over to the horses waiting for them a little farther on, reined in by grooms. This time I clearly distinguished one of the foreign girls who had a quick, determined look, long red hair that floated in the wind behind her, and a hat in the form of a seagull with wings outstretched, which seemed to be just as much a part of her person as her pure nose or her pale eyes that stared as she rode past, but the way the eyes of a seagull might stare into ours, without the slightest awareness of us, or like someone of another race. She wore a little guipure

---

1. Folio 66 is blank.

T. The most obvious translation for "*fillette*" would be "young girl," since "*jeune fille*" in French generally corresponds to "young woman" in English. This is confused, however, by the fact that *Jeunes Filles en Fleurs* has always been translated as "Young Girls in Flower." So I am leaving "*fillette*" untranslated, with the understanding that the word describes a prepubescent girl who is no longer a "little girl."

TT. A *break* was an open-top horse-drawn carriage with four wheels.

collar, which became charming, like {f. 68} something that had no other purpose than to cover her neck and that carried out its duty quite badly, because she kept twisting and pulling it, which added to its charm, from being constantly touched by her hands and from being close to her neck.

Maman's attitude was probably the most beautiful. But she is so rare, and indifference to what surrounds them is for most [*passage ends here*]

[*Resumption and new development of the two previous folios*]

{f. 69} One day on the beach walking solemnly on the sand like two sea-birds about to fly off, I spotted two young girls, two young women almost, whose new appearance, whose unfamiliar outfits, whose haughty and deliberate gait made me take them for two foreigners whom I would never see again; they didn't look at anyone else and didn't see me. I didn't see them again in the days that followed, which confirmed my intuition that they had been only passing through on the little beach where everyone knew everyone else, lived the same life, saw one another four times a day playing innocent beach games. But a few days later, gathered around a beautiful *break* that stopped in front of the beach, I saw five or six of the same type, the ones in the *break* saying goodbye to the others, who soon went over to the horses that were being reined in nearby and on which they rode off. I thought I recognized one of the two I'd seen walking on the sand but I wasn't sure, but this time I could clearly distinguish one of them by her red hair, her pale and haughty eyes, which rested on me, her nostrils quivering in the wind, and a hat in the form of the outstretched wings of a seagull that seemed to be flying in the same wind that blew the {f. 70} curls of red hair. They rode away. Occasionally I would see them again. I recognized two that I wanted to keep seeing. When I spotted [their] strange assembly sometimes those two weren't there and I [was] sad. But not knowing where they came from nor at what time they would be there, I could only wait for them to appear and I would desperately hope to see them without actually seeing them, or if they suddenly appeared when I hadn't been expecting them I was too flustered to take any great pleasure from the sight. They were the daughters or nieces of the main château owners in the neighborhood, nobles or rich people who mixed with the nobility and who came to spend a few weeks in C. every year. A few of them, whose châteaux were very close by, frequented the beach in that season without staying at the resort itself, since their château was only a few kilometers away. Although in their milieu there were probably exceptions to this elegance, this group all happened to possess a grace, an elegance, an agility, and a disdainful pride too that made them seem like a race apart from the young girls of my own world. They were also dressed in what struck me as an extraordinary way, a style I couldn't define, which was probably just a result of the fact that, spending their time playing sports that my girlfriends knew nothing about—horse riding, golf, tennis—they generally wore riding skirts, golf outfits, tennis shirts. Presumably they played all these sports far from the beach and came only at fairly spaced-out intervals, the timing of which I had not yet discovered; for example, I suppose that after golf on the day there was no dance at the Château de T., etc., they would come just for a moment, as in a conquered country, without granting the natives who usually lived there anything more than a haughty and frankly impolite look that signified "you are not from our world," and sometimes unashamedly exchanging a smile between them that signified: "What style!" Our old friend Monsieur T. would constantly object to their poor education. Maman, on the contrary, paid them no attention and was surprised, as almost all intelligent people are, that anyone could be so concerned about people whom we did not know, and whether or not they were polite. She {f. 71} thought they were chic but *mauvais genre,* but essentially she was utterly indifferent to what they might have thought of her. I will freely admit that I did not share Maman's philosophy in the slightest and that I would have passionately loved, not even to know them, but for them to have the highest possible idea of me. If they could have known that my uncle was the best friend of His Highness the Duke of Clermont and that, at that very moment, if Maman had wanted and hadn't preferred the sea air for our health, we could have been in Clermont where His Highness had invited us. Ah! if only that could have been written on my face, if only he could have told them himself, if only the duke could have come to spend two days here and introduce me to them! In reality, if the Duke of Clermont had come here they would have thought him merely a badly dressed, bourgeois old man with a politeness that they would have seen as proof of his common birth and they would have looked down on him. Because they didn't know him, coming as they did from a world that imagined itself illustrious but was nothing of the kind. And I don't see how the Duke of Clermont, even by descending to his most humble acquaintances, could have introduced me to them. Their fathers were wealthy industrialists, or small provincial noblemen, or recently ennobled industrialists. Monsieur T. knew the fathers of several of them from the neighborhood, and for him they were illustrious men, and even if they had come from essentially the same starting point as him, they were leading more illustrious lives. Twice I saw him chatting in a friendly way with gentlemen whom I had seen with the young girls and who could only be their parents. When I discovered this I was in a fever; this way I could, if not get to know them, at least be seen by them in the company of someone who knew them (I didn't know at the time that he criticized them for their rudeness). Suddenly I felt for Monsieur T. the warmest friendship, I hugged him a thousand times, and with Maman's permission, although she had no idea of the reason, I bought him a beautiful pipe that his stinginess had prevented him from buying for himself. And the day I spotted them on the beach, I ran to T.'s house. Just before going there I went back home and combed my hair, borrowed a pink tie from my older brother, put some of Maman's rice powder on a small pimple I thought I had on my cheek, and took Maman's parasol because it had a jade handle and seemed to me a sign of opulence. "Monsieur T. please come for a walk on the beach with me." "But why, my friend?" "I don't know, because I love you so much it would make me happy." "Hmm, all right, if you like, but wait until I've finished this letter." He laughed at my parasol, wanted me to leave it at his house, and I fiercely took it back from him, saying that Maman had forced me to carry it to protect me from the sun. I lied pitilessly in defense of my desire. "Oh, you can finish the letter later!" I thought they must have left already, I was in a rush, in a fever, {f. 72} and just then through his window I spotted the six young girls (all of them were there that day; it would have been perfect) picking up their belongings, whistling for their dogs, getting ready to leave. I begged him, he didn't understand my insistence, we went down to the beach but it was deserted, I had tears in my eyes, I felt cruelly the useless beauty of the pink tie, the combed hair, the powdered pimple, and the parasol. I didn't want to stay on the beach any longer. I accompanied him to the post office, where he had a letter to mail, then on the way back from the post office we found ourselves suddenly face to face with the six young girls who had stopped *break* and horses to make a purchase. I held Monsieur T. warmly by the arm so they would see that I was with him and began to talk animatedly to him so they'd notice us. To make sure they would see us, I suggested to Monsieur T. that we go into the store to buy something; however, I unbuttoned my overcoat so they would see my pink tie, I tipped my hat backward to reveal the curled lock, I glanced furtively in the mirror to check that the pimple hadn't reappeared from under its coating of powder, and I held the parasol by its very end to exhibit in all its splendor the jade handle, which I twirled in the air. Literally hanging on Monsieur T.'s arm, oppressing him with the marks of my intimacy, I chatted to him with surprising animation. Then suddenly at a moment when I could tell they were all looking at us and when, I have to admit, the parasol did not seem to be producing exactly the effect I had hoped for, on some absurd pretext, to prove that I was very close to someone their parents knew, I threw my arms around Monsieur T.'s neck and kissed him. A ripple of laughter seemed to spread through the youthful crowd, I turned around and looked at them with an expression of surprise and superiority as if I had just spotted them and was suddenly aware of these people. At that moment, Monsieur T. greeted the father of one of the girls, who had come to find them. But while the father responded very politely with a tip of his hat, his daughters, whom Monsieur T. had greeted at the same time, instead of replying just looked at him impolitely then turned, smiling, toward their friends. In reality their father considered Monsieur T. as a nice man who was not from what he had for several years called his world. And the girls, who {f. 73} believed that they had always belonged to the "world" that their father had entered, and who considered this world—the world of the former notary T., of the successful biscuit salesman, of the manufac-turer of artificial mountains, of the Viscount of Vaucelles etc.—to be the most elegant world in the universe, or at least the second most elegant just after the world, as divine as a gleaming infinity stretching all the way to the horizon, of the Marchioness of C. whom they had seen while visiting the Viscountess of Vaucelles and out shopping, and who had once said to them:

"Hello young ladies," considered Monsieur T., with his wide-brimmed straw hat and his habit of riding the tram and his lack of pale ties and horses and knickerbockers, as a man of the people to whose greetings they were not obliged to respond. "What badly raised children," T. cried. "They don't know that without me their father wouldn't have his château, nor would he have made his marriage." He always defended the father, whom he considered a good boy. But all the same the father, perhaps less ridiculous than his wife and daughters, was content to wear those knickerbockers that T. found comical and to walk on the beach with the Viscount of Vaucelles. Except even then he greeted Monsieur T. very politely. I vaguely sensed that the effect produced by my efforts was disappointing, but with a sort of wisdom that never abandons me and which, in a different and higher form, also existed in my father and my mother, I knew I couldn't complain. I had the advantage of knowing a friend of their father, I wanted them to see me with him, and they had seen me. They knew, driven into their attention and their memory by perhaps the very features of ridiculousness, what I had wanted them to know. I had nothing to complain about. If it had no real effect on them, that was something else altogether. They knew what they had to know and there seemed to me a sort of justice in that. The advantage that I had, they knew about. That was justice. If they had thought it paltry or even derisory, it was simply because what I had thought an advantage was nothing of the kind for them. So I had nothing to regret. I had given my hair the best combing I could give it and they had seen it, they had seen the jade parasol, which might even have given them an exaggerated idea of our opulence, since Maman carried it to please her own mother who {f. 74} had given it to her, but she thought it far too beautiful for her, far too luxurious for our situation. So I had nothing to complain about. The powder still covered my pimple, the pink tie was still tight around my collar, in a mirror I thought myself handsome, so overall the experiment had taken place in the most favorable conditions. I returned disappointed and yet content, less lost in the immensity of the unknown than I had been before, telling myself that at least they would recognize me now, that I had an identity in their eyes, the small boy with the parasol, even if the friendship with the businessman had not consecrated me in their eyes. We were

returning via one of those streets shaded by plane trees, with the store-
fronts[2] of the pâtissier, the shellfish seller, the target shooting range, the carousel, the gymnasium smiling up at the sun beneath the foliage, and
where one is surprised to see, between trees, coming from the sea, headed
toward the countryside, a tram passing, when we found ourselves face to
face with the Viscount of C. who was staying in C. for a few weeks and was
going home with his daughters, two of the famous gang, perhaps the prettiest two of all, one of whom was the famous redhead. The viscount stopped
for a moment to speak to us. My heart was beating so hard that I couldn't
feel this pleasure that I had not had time to imagine and that was already
beside me. The Viscount of C.[3] asked to walk with us, Monsieur T. introduced him to me. He introduced me to his daughter. To my extreme surprise, because the young girls of my world did not have her airs and graces,
she held out her hand and with a friendly smile said: "I see you sometimes
in C., I'm pleased to meet you." And yet I was sure that she'd laughed and
been impolite earlier. We parted and the next day, when I had to stand to
the side of a road because of a passing car, I had not had time to recognize the entire gang piled inside the car before the redhead, smiling as if
we were two old friends, gave me a little wave of hello to which I didn't
have time to respond.

2. Ms.: storefront.
3. Ms.: The Viscount of.

Noble Names

{f. 75} It is still today one of the great charms of noble families that they seem to be located in a particular patch of land, that their name, which is still a place-name, or that the name of their château (and it is still sometimes the same) instantly gives your imagination the impression of the residence and the desire for travel. Every noble name contains within the colored space of its syllables a château at the end of a difficult path with a warm welcome on a cheerful winter evening, and all around the poetry of its pond and its church, which in turn sometimes repeats the name, with its coat of arms, on its gravestones, at the foot of its painted statues of ancestors, in the rosy glow of its heraldic stained-glass windows. You might tell me that this family, which has resided for two centuries in a château near Bayeux that gives me the impression of being pounded during winter afternoons by the last flakes of foam, a prisoner in the fog, internally dressed in tapestries and lace, that its name is in reality from Provence. That does not prevent it from evoking Normandy for me, like many trees from the Indies or from Cape Town are so well acclimatized to our provinces that nothing seems less exotic and more French than their foliage and their flowers. If the name of this Italian family has stood proudly for three centuries above a deep valley in Normandy, if from afar when the terrain dips we glimpse the facade of red schist and grayish stone of the château on the same level as the crimson steeples of Saint-Pierre-sur-Dives, it is as Norman as the apple trees that[1]   and that came from Cape Town only in[2]   . If this Provençal family has for two centuries had its mansion in Falaise on the main square, if the guests {f. 76} who have come to play cards in the evening and who leave after ten o'clock risk waking the bourgeois inhabitants of Falaise and if we hear their footsteps echoing endlessly in

1. Blank in the ms.
2. Blank in the ms.

the night all the way to the castle keep, as in a novel by Barbey d'Aurevilly, if the roof of their mansion can be glimpsed between two church spires where it is embedded like a pebble on a Norman beach between two per-forated seashells, between the pinkish, veined turrets of two hermit crabs, if the guests who arrived earlier before dinner can, as they descend to the main reception room filled with precious Chinese ornaments acquired during the great age of trade between Norman sailors and the Far East, walk with members of different noble families who reside between Cou-tances and Caen or between Thury-Harcourt and Falaise, in the sloping garden lined with city fortifications down to the fast-flowing river where, while waiting for dinner, they can fish on the property, as in a Balzac short story, what does it matter if this family came here from Provence or that its name is Provençal? It has become as Norman as those beautiful pink hydrangeas that you can glimpse from Honfleur to Valognes and from Pont-l'Évêque to Saint-Vaast, like an imported embellishment that now charac-terizes the countryside it adorns, and which gives a Norman manor house the delightful, ancient, fresh color of an earthenware Chinese pot brought back from Peking by Jacques Cartier. Others have a[3] château lost in the woods and the road to reach it is long. In the Middle Ages there were no other sounds around it than the blare of a trumpet, the barking of dogs. Today when a traveler comes to visit them in the evening it is the sound of the car's horn that has replaced both and that, like the other horn, matches the damp atmosphere through which it echoes under the foliage, then is satu-rated by the scent of roses in the principal flowerbed, and poignant, al-most human, like the dogs' barks, its repeated[4] calls inform the lady of the house, who comes to the window, that she will not be alone tonight to eat dinner then to play cards with the count. No doubt when I am told the name of a beautiful Gothic château near Ploërmel I think of the long gal-leries of the cloister, where we walk[5] {f. 77} among the broom, and the roses on the graves of the abbots who lived there beneath those galleries, with

---

3. Ms.: Others a.
4. Word omitted in *CSB*.
5. Ms.: of the cloister, and of the *abbés* [abbots] where we walk. *CSB:* of the cloister, and of the *allées* [paths] where we walk.

the view of this valley in the eighth century, when Charlemagne did not yet exist, when no one had yet built the towers of the Chartres cathedral nor the abbey on the hill in Vézelay, above the deep Cousin river, teeming with fish, no doubt if in one of those moments when the language of poetry is still too precise, too full of familiar words and consequently familiar images, not to disturb this mysterious current that the *Name,* that thing which predates knowledge, sets flowing, unlike anything that we know, as sometimes in our dreams, no doubt after having rung the doorbell and having seen a few servants appear, one of them whose melancholy flight, whose long curved nose, whose rare and hoarse yelling make us think him the incarnation of one of the swans from the pond after it was drained, the other in whose mud-brown face the terrified eyes remind us of a dexterous mole under duress, we will find in the grand entrance hall the same coatracks, the same coats as everywhere else, and in the same living room the same *Revue de Paris* and *Comoedia.* And even if everything there still smelled of the eighteenth century, the guests, although intelligent, or rather because they were intelligent, would say intelligent things about our own times. (Perhaps it would be better if they were not intelligent, and their conversation was concerned only with things of local interest, like those descriptions that are meaningful only if they contain precise images and not abstractions.) The same is true for the foreign nobility. The name of this or that mediatized[6] German lord is shot through with a breath of fantastical poetry in the midst of a stale odor and the bourgeois repetition of first syllables makes one[7] think of colored candies eaten in a small grocery store in an old German square, while in the chameleonic sonority of the last syllable Aldegrever's[8] old stained-glass window darkens in the old Gothic church across the street. And such another is the name of a stream born in the Black Forest at the foot of ancient Wartburg that crosses all the valleys haunted by gnomes and is overlooked by all the castles where the old lords reigned, then where Luther dreamed, and all of this is in the possession of the lord and inhabits his name. But I dined with him yesterday, and his face

6. Word omitted in *CSB.*
7. *CSB:* might make one.
8. Ms., *CSB:* Aldgrever.

is of today, his clothes are of today, his words and thoughts are of today. And so elevated and open is his mind that if you speak of the nobility or of Wartburg he says: "Oh, there are no more princes these days!"

{f. 78} Doubtless there never were any. But in the only sense, imaginative, where there can be any, all that remains today is a long past filled with dream names (Clermont-Tonnerre, La Tour[9] et Princes des Dunes,[10] from Clermont-Tonnerre). The castle, whose name is in Shakespeare and in Walter Scott, of this[11] "duchess" is from eighteenth-century Scotland. On her lands is the admirable abbey that Turner painted so many times, and it is her ancestors whose graves are lined up in the destroyed cathedral where cattle grazed among the ruins of arches and the flowering brambles, and which impresses us all the more when we think that it is a cathedral because we are obliged to impose upon it the immanent idea of things that would be otherwise without that and to call this meadow the flagstones of the nave, and this copse the entrance to the choir. This cathedral was built for her ancestors and still belongs to her now, and it is on her land, this divine torrent, all coolness and mystery under two beech trees[12] with the infinity of a[13] plain and the sun descending through a large patch of blue sky, surrounded by two clouds[14] that mark like a sundial the slant of the light that touches them in the happy hour of a late afternoon, and the whole town ranged in tiers in the distance, and the joyous fisherman we know from Turner and that we would roam[15] the entire earth to find, to know that beauty, the charms of nature, the joys of life, the singular beauty of the place and the time[16] exist, without thinking that Turner—and after him Stevenson—simply portrayed as unique and desirable in its own right the place that they happened to choose, just as their brains could have rendered desirable and unique the beauty of any other place. But the duchess

9. Ms.: Latour.
10. *CSB:* P . . . of the dukes of C. T.
11. We have restored this word, since the ms. here is illegible.
12. *CSB:* roofs.
13. *CSB:* of the.
14. *CSB:* orchards.
15. *CSB:* would roam.
16. *CSB:* the time and the place.

invited me to dinner with Marcel Prévost and Melba will come to sing, and I will not cross the strait.

But had she invited me among the lords of the Middle Ages, my disappointment would have been the same, because there can be no identity between the unknown poetry contained in a *name,* in other words an urn of the unknowable, and the things that experience shows us and that correspond with words, with known things. We could, out of the inevitable disappointment arising from the encounter with things whose names we know, for example a man bearing a grandly territorial and historical name, or better from any journey, conclude that this imaginative charm that does not correspond with reality is a poetry of convention. But beyond the fact that I don't believe this and that I plan one day to establish the exact opposite, from the simple point of view of realism, this psychological realism, this exact description of our dreams would merit {f. 79} the other realism, since it is concerned with a reality that is far more enduring than the other, that tends to be perpetually reshaped by us, that if it deserts the country that we visited still extends its aura over all the others, and covers again those that we knew as soon as they have been slightly forgotten and have become for us once again *names,* since they haunt us even in dreams and in that way give the countries, the churches of our childhood, the castles of our dreams the appearance of *the same nature as names,* the appearance fashioned from imagination and desire that we no longer find in a waking state, or only at the moment when, glimpsing it, we fall asleep; because it causes us infinitely more pleasure than the other, which bores and disappoints us, and is a principle of action and always sets in motion the traveler, this lover forever disappointed and forever setting off again with high hopes; because only the pages that succeed in giving us this impression give us the impression of genius.

Not only do nobles have names that make us dream but, at least for a large number of families, the names of the parents, grandparents, and so on are also among those beautiful names, so that nothing without poetry intercepts this constant grafting of names that are colored and yet transparent (because no base matter adheres to them), enabling us to trace them back through time from bud to colored crystal bud, as in a stained-glass Tree of Jesse. In our minds those people take on the purely imaginative purity of their names. To the left a pink carnation, then the tree rises again, to the right a dog rose, then the tree rises again, to the left a lily, the stem continues, to the right a blue nigella, his father had married a Montmorency, rose France, his father's mother was a Montmorency-Luxembourg, clove pink, double rose, whose father had married a Choiseul, blue nigella, then a Charost, pink carnation. At times a very local, ancient name, like a rare flower no longer seen except in the paintings of Van Huysum, seems to us darker because we have looked at it less often. But soon we have the amusement of seeing that on two sides {f. 80} of the stained-glass window where this Tree of Jesse blooms other windows begin, recounting the lives of people who were at first only nigella and lily. But as these stories are ancient and also painted on glass, the whole is wonderfully harmonized. Prince of Württemberg, his mother was born Marie de France, whose own mother was born in the Kingdom of the Two Sicilies.[17] But then her mother would be the daughter of Louis Philippe and Maria Amalia who married the Duke of Württemberg, and so we see to the right in our memory of the little window, the princess in a garden dress at the wedding of her brother the Duke of Orléans to show her irritation at seeing her ambassadors rejected after they had gone to ask for the hand of the Prince of Syracuse on her behalf. Then here is a handsome young man, the Duke of Württemberg, come to ask for her hand and she is so happy to leave with him that, smiling, she kisses her weeping parents on the doorstep, to the disapproval of the servants standing motionless in the background; soon she falls ill, returns, gives birth to a child (that very Duke of Württemberg, yellow calendula, who took us the length of his Tree of Jesse up to his mother, white rose, from where we leaped to the window to the left), without having seen her husband's only castle, the Schloss Fantaisie, whose name alone had prompted her to marry him. And immediately after that, without awaiting the quatrefoils at the bottom of the window showing us the poor princess dying in Italy, her brother Nemours hurrying toward her, while the Queen of France organizes a fleet to carry her to her daughter, we look at that Schloss Fantaisie where she would never spend

17. *CSB* puts this phrase in quotation marks.

her disordered life, and in the following window we see, because places
have their own history as do races, in that same fanciful castle, another
prince (and another fantasist) who would also die young and after similarly strange loves, Ludwig II of Bavaria; and in fact below the first
window we had already read, without[18] being aware of it, these words of the
Queen of France: "a castle near Bareut."[19] And we think again of other sad,
fanciful, almost royal lives that ended at Fantaisie, "a castle near Bareut."[20]
But we must return to the Tree of Jesse, prince of Württemberg, yellow
calendula, son of Louise de France, blue nigella. So he still lives, that son
she barely knew? And "when she asked her brother how she was, he said:
not too bad, but the doctors are concerned. She replied: Nemours, I understand you, and after that she was tender toward everyone but no longer
asked to see her child, for fear her tears would betray her." So that child
still lives, he lives, the royal prince, in Württemberg? Perhaps he looks
like her, perhaps he inherited from her {f. 81} some of her tastes for
painting, dreaming, fantasy, which she thought would be so at home in her
Schloss Fantaisie. How his face in the little window is given new meaning
by our knowledge that he is the son of Louise de France! Because those
beautiful noble names are either without history, dark[21] as a forest, or they
are historic, and always the light from the eyes, well-known to us, of the
mother, illuminates the whole face of the son. The face of a son who lives,
a monstrance where a beautiful dead mother placed all her faith, is like a
profanation of that sacred memory. Because it is that face to which those
imploring eyes addressed one last goodbye that should not be forgotten for
a second. Because it was with that sublime line of his mother's nose that
his own nose was made, because it was with his mother's smile that he seduced girls into debauchery, because it was with the movement of an eye-
brow that his mother made to gaze upon him most tenderly, that he lied,
because that calm expression his mother wore when speaking of everything
to which she was indifferent, in other words of anything that was not

18. *CSB:* without even.
19. *CSB:* Barent.
20. Phrase omitted in *CSB.*
21. *CSB:* and dark.

himself, he wore now when saying of her, indifferently, "my poor Mother." Beside these windows are secondary windows where we can find a name obscure at the time, the name of a captain of guards who saves the prince, the owner of the ship that goes to sea to rescue the Princess, a noble but obscure name that has since become well-known, born in a crack of circumstances like a flower between paving stones, and that bears forever within it the afterglow of the devotion that illustrated[22] it and that even now hypnotizes it. I find them even more touching, these noble names, I would like to penetrate even more deeply into the souls of sons illuminated only by the light of that memory, which see all things in the absurd and deformed vision given by that tragic glow. I remember having laughed at that gray-haired man forbidding his children to talk to a Jew, praying before meals, so correct, so miserly, so ridiculous, that enemy of the people. And his name now lights him up for me when I see it again, the name of his father who rescued the Duchess of Berri on a boat, a soul in which that glimmer of blazing life that we see reddening the water in the moment when the duchess, leaning on him, sets sail, has remained the only light. A shipwrecked soul, a soul of flaming torches, of unreasoning fidelity, a stainedglass soul. Perhaps beneath those names I will find something so different from me that in truth it will be almost the same matter as a Name. But how nature plays with all of us! Here I have made the acquaintance of a young man of infinite intelligence, more like a great man of tomorrow than of today, having not only attained and understood but surpassed and refreshed socialism, Nietzscheism, etc. And I learn that he is the son of the man I saw in the hotel dining room, so simple in its English decorations that it could have been the bedroom in *The Dream of Saint Ursula*, or the room in the window where the Queen receives ambassadors who beg her to flee before she leaves for sea, its tragic reflection lighting up for me her figure as I imagine her innermost thoughts lit up for her the world.[23]

{f. 82} The name of the Belleuses is so clear that I see it more through a display window than through stained glass. A display window with beau-

---

22. *CSB:* illustrates.
23. This last word is almost illegible at the very bottom of the folio.

tiful shelves displaying the royal family's precious memories: that is how I imagined the mansion where the Belleuses lived; since they received, I know, only other glass people, people who are only names, and nobody, nobody else, I sensed that nothing would be in their home as it was in others', not a door, not even a wall, a window, with shelves, and precious people, in animated Saxon porcelain, a dream whose extraordinary nature it must be said did not degenerate in any way their[24] daughters, truly in pink Saxon porcelain, with blue eyes, proud and hard as if painted, and adorable red hair. Knowing that they were free of vulgarity, welcoming only other immaterial names, I had expelled from their home the idea of any walls, anything that was like other places, and it had remained . . . glass. Moreover their house meant above all their privacy, the place where no one entered, like the church taken more in the mystical sense than in the sense of the dwelling itself. The universal church.

24. Ms.: its.

Venice

{f. 83} While I was reading these pages on Venice, the sun entered my bedroom, bathing half of it in light. And soon I left the bed, I walked over the sunlight spread across the floor of my room, descended the marble stairs where badly closed doors let in drafts of cool sea air on those hot days, and arrived in front of the blue Grand Canal, on which my gaze leaned, rested, delighted and enchanted, like a cheek still soft from sleep rests, leans, enchanted, on a soft pillow, I arrived at the door three steps from the hotel, of which the first two were in turn hidden by running water, because while elsewhere people live by the sea, here they live in the sea. The palaces are magnificent and the gondolas crowd the water like cars in the main square of a city on a holiday. Jump into the gondola and let's say: "Doge's Palace, San Marco," where your friends are already waiting for you with the books. Because ever since your childhood, on beautiful sunny days you have known the charm of saying: "I'll join you there," when the hour is [late],[1] the rendezvous certain, and the way there walked alone to find your [friends] who left before you filled to the brim with the joyousness of a sunny day, [whether] you have to follow the river where you hear fish leap from the water and tadpoles converge around a breadcrumb, where buttercups and daisies crowd the surrounding fields, and where the little bridge creaks as you cross over it and walk in the scent of hawthorns that, when you raise the flower to your nose, no longer smell of anything, or whether gliding in a gondola[2] . . . Here you will not pass in front of the pâtissier, you will not cross the street to find shade. But the gondolier, taking you where you asked him to go, will point at them and tell you: "Palazzo Foscari." Over there, rising from the blue water, approached, passed, then left

---

1. The edge of the ms. is torn across five lines. We have restored the missing words.
2. We have restored "gliding in a gondola," crossed out in the ms. The sentence is unfinished.

behind by the gondola are those who have inflamed your dreams as Anna Karenina and Julien Sorel did. But you couldn't get to know them. These, the heroes of Ruskin novels, existed somewhere, here where you have come, in this street without stores, without convertibles, without paving stones, and you have to pass by them in the evening when you go out to dinner or before dinner when you go sightseeing. {f. 83v} Naturally all these words— "the glorious private architecture of Venice," "the glorious Foscari Palace"—had a charm that you do not rediscover here when the gondolier points and tells you: "Palazzo Foscari." But one day "Foscari" spoken by the gondolier, passed by the gondola before you go to visit the Grand Hotel, will be no less poetic than the other[3] Foscari, the one from before, which you were disappointed not to find, "the masterpiece of that glorious private architecture school of Venice"; because these are the moments of our life that sensory perception, the tyranny of the present, the intervention of intelligence, the network of activity, the succession of selfish desires, prevents us from living but that become glorious again on the day, come at last, of the resurrection.

{f. 85}[4] I descended the marble stairs in my overcoat, holding the tartan blanket to cover my shoulders and the books by Ruskin, and we left as for a sea voyage, rowing out to the expanse of the great canal, in the blue, beneath the sun, inhaling the breeze, to reach some temple risen from the waters where the gondola was moored. Other days they went to wait for us in San Marco and I left through little streets that felt like the interior corridors of the hotel courtyard, so close were the houses on either side, so little did they look like two sides of a street. The streets in Venice are canals. And this is perhaps the most surprising thing about Venice: elsewhere, canals, however numerous they may be, are canals that cross the city. In Venice they are not canals, they are streets of water with all the social personality that the word street implies. So the various actions of life are transposed in the way this singularity implies. Going out means navigating. Not even walking alongside the water, as on the wharf of a river, on

3. Ms.: poetic the other.
4. Folio 84 is blank.

a lakeshore or by the sea, but setting foot, straight from your door, into the gondola. Where the doorway ends, the street—in other words, the water—begins, and the doorway is perpetually splashed, washed, covered, abandoned when the tide ebbs, and covered again by the rising water. The gondola is not used only for promenades and visiting, but for all traffic, for life in its poorest, most active, most hurried aspects; despite its appearance of luxury, it is used by everyone, for everything. The doctor visits his patients by gondola, the housewife does her shopping, the employee carries out his duties. And with a slowness, a silence, a grace that seem reserved for the idleness of the rich or the spare time of dreamers, the gondola transports luggage to the train, meat from the butcher's to the hotel, the newly arrested criminal to prison. So there are Black Maria gondolas. And there are hearse gondolas too, since funerals must take place at the island cemetery; and the friends and family who follow the gondola, weeping, follow it in gondolas. In this sense it is more the idea of the city that is unique in Venice than the appearance of the city. Venice's founders did not bring to the world only an incomparable work of art. They created a new social form quite different from the previous idea {f. 85v} of the city as an urban conglomeration and above all as a new form of social operation. The idea of taking away from the sea and its canals the immemorial meaning of what it imposed on them and still imposes on us now, as an intermediary element whose crossing, whether for the purposes of fishing, travel, discovery, or war, remains temporary, and assigning it the social meaning until then indissolubly attached to streets, making it a place where one goes from one house to another, goes shopping, goes to see friends, goes to Mass, goes to the Council, goes to prison, goes to the cemetery, is a genuinely brilliant invention in that it required the strength to cut oneself off from what is and to create what did not yet exist. Are not we ourselves, to shake up the commonplace idea of Venice's originality (this city divided by canals) and to attempt to see its true originality, are we not obliged to try to give our minds a little of that strength which the Venetians instill in us in some ways, even if it costs us infinitely less effort and is worthy of infinitely less merit than theirs? So, all the meaning and personality of the street being [altered] (transposed in so many ways by the needs of the element so opposed to earth in which they are inscribed), the streets of Venice are in some way decerebrated of what makes a street a street, and resemble streets only in the way that the dead resemble the living. From the windows of the hotel, you cannot believe that you are not looking down at a tiny backyard, that this amalgam of houses that all seem to depend on yours, to form a single whole, could be a street. In a street, what belongs to everyone and separates like strangers those who live in different houses and are separated by the street, which is impersonal, which belongs to everyone, seems not to exist here and these windows all have[5] the look of horrible outbuildings of the hotel.

With my blanket in my arms and my Ruskins in my hand, I arrive in San Marco, which seems to me as different from a church as Venice is from a city. The personality of the church, delimited and comprehensible in height, is extensive in width, raised very little above the ground, and the God that we know to be our {f. 86} God but who appears almost like a foolish Oriental pasha is so little raised above us that we must send ebbing back the waves of marble that encroach on either side of Him and follow the personality of the building, tracing its entire width, no longer looking up but right and left, somehow separating the nonexistent height between its long lines of right and left, and feeling our idea of a church decapitated and extended indefinitely, steeple turned to facades, transposed, embodied in this new monument, festival, low, and stretched out. And in the church at the very back we see Our Lord looking effeminate, Oriental, and bizarre, his gesture transformed into the pretension of some fat, suspect Syriot,[6] and we understand how much the signs of the same moral dispositions change and how difficult it would be for us to recognize in beings of another race the equivalents of those things we call distinction, kindness, courage, simplicity, delicacy, tact, nobility, and which have in those of our blood their own signs, sometimes imitated, sometimes misleading, but aesthetically certain.

5. Ms.: all these windows all have.
6. Literally, an inhabitant of the Greek island of Syros. Presumably intended to mean: inhabitant of Syria.

Other Manuscripts
by Marcel Proust

The following manuscripts were chosen based on their genetic significance: because they form part of the antecedents of the "seventy-five folios" or because they show the use that Proust made of them afterward.
They are presented in the most probable chronological order of writing.
We are not reprinting the relevant passages from Carnet 1,[T] cited and
commented upon in the Chronology.

In each case, we indicate the origin of our transcription (*Sketch* of *In
Search of Lost Time* in the "Bibliothèque de la Pléiade," if necessary revised and supplemented; article or critical edition; original transcription).
We have prioritized the readability of the texts: consequently, the transcrip-
tions do not include Proust's crossings-out, except for those we considered
the most significant, and sometimes certain passages where relevant. The
specialist may refer to the facsimiles available on Gallica.[1]

Concerning the previously unpublished manuscripts from the Fallois archives, our original transcription was checked against the facsimiles by
Bertrand Marchal.

For the notebooks of rough drafts and the typed version of "Place-Names:
The Place," we have followed the dating of Anthony Pugh in *The Birth of
"À la recherche du temps perdu"* (1987) and *The Growth of "À la recherche
du temps perdu": A Chronological Examination of Proust's Manuscripts
from 1909 to 1914* (2004):

T. There are two words for "notebook" in French—*cahier*, translated throughout as
"notebook," and *carnet*, which is a smaller-format version of a *cahier*. Since there is no
equivalent single word for this in English, *Carnet 1* will be left untranslated.

1. See the home page of the Institute of Texts and Modern Manuscripts at the CNRS
(National Center for Scientific Research): http://www.item.ens.fr/fonds-proust-numerique.

– Notebook 3, January–February 1909;

– Notebook 2, January–February 1909;

– Notebook 1, February 1909 (for the folios in question);

– Notebook 4, May 1909 (for the folios in question);

– Notebook 12, August–October 1909 (for folio 42 sq.), October–November 1909 (for folio 111 sq.);

– Notebook 64, October–November 1909 (for the folios in question);

– Notebook 69, January–March 1910;

– Notebook 65, January–March 1910;

– Manuscript pages of the typed version of "Place-Names: The Place," March–June 1912, or just after.

I

"The Belle-Île Manuscript"

This five-page unpublished manuscript from the Fallois archives contains what is, at the time of writing, the oldest known version of the "evening kiss."[1] Proust altered this version from the first to the third person when he took it up again for the corresponding scene in *Jean Santeuil* (*JS*, pp. 202–211).

This text was written in graphite pencil on folios of graph paper in a 207 × 264mm format with the heading "Hôtel du Commerce/Jules Petitjean/Le Palais/Belle-Île-en-Mer (Morbihan)." Proust had arrived at Belle-Île with Reynaldo Hahn on September 5, 1895, for a brief stopover before going to Beg-Meil, which gives us a *terminus a quo* for the writing of this fragment.

There were few crossings-out, and we retained only the most significant in the transcription. We have kept Fallois's title.

My childhood twitched miserably at the bottom of a well of sadness. Later, activities, ideas, memories were placed on top of one another like an easy ladder that I could use to escape from creature to creature or from thought to thought until the great day in my hopes or in centuries, ~~every time I had the strength to grasp it. But until I was 7 or 8 nothing could divert me from my despair, which was as deep as it was dark~~. Even today if I don't have the strength to grasp it as soon as I feel myself falling to the bottom of my sadness, I am plunged into a despair as deep as it is dark and which makes me feel a terrible pity for my gloomy childhood. Nothing then could divert

---

1. Although we must bear in mind this passage from "The Confession of a Young Girl" (1894), a short story printed in *Les Plaisirs et les jours* (1896), where the transposition is obvious: "The two evenings that she [my mother] spent at Oublis, she came to tell me goodnight in my bed, an old habit that she had lost, because I took too much pleasure and too much pain from it, because I wouldn't fall asleep since I kept calling her back to tell me goodnight again, not daring to do it anymore at the end, but feeling the passionate need to do so even more strongly, forever inventing new excuses, my hot pillow needing to be turned over, my frozen feet that she alone could warm up with her hands. . . . So many sweet moments received an extra sweetness when I felt that my mother was truly herself and that her usual coldness must be hurting her too. The day she left, a day of despair when I clung to her dress all the way to the train car, begging her to take me to Paris with her [. . .]" (*PJ*, p. 86).

me from my sorrow, not even the idea of its cause, which was unknown to me and for which I have substituted today its secondary and apparent cause, my nerves, because I am hardly any more aware of its primary cause now than I was in the days of my childhood. In truth it must be what lies deepest inside me and I could not break free from it without giving up on myself. I never went within myself after long or short absences outside without first seeing it on the threshold with its face of long ago. Since they wanted to cure me of my nerves, they never gave in to its prayers and its lamentations. They constantly reproached me for it and I grew up with the idea that it was shameful. From that period when I felt nothing but sorrows—because the joy that shared my character with the sadness did not have such old claims upon me, and although it was certainly mine, it wasn't born until later—here are three that I remember.//

[. . .] Another day I was so sad to be without Maman on the Champs-Élysées with my maid that, despite the fear and the shame I felt in the sight of other people, I started weeping on the bench, sitting still and letting myself freeze, with a strong desire to die. In the evenings these sadnesses were infinitely worse. Even today, if I am not distracted by a visit, a walk, or a book, the moment preceding the arrival of the lamp and the first moments of its brightness are filled for me with indefinable suffering. But the truly tragic hour, the horror of which is no less oppressive for its vagueness, is the moment when I go to bed. Habit alone among the old powers of the world is stronger than suffering, and habit alone can lessen it. And even today when some ordinary circumstance breaks it, my immense anxiety, as old as myself, is reborn if I go to bed much later or much earlier, or if an unusual light or noise or especially a new bedroom prevents me from unconsciously accomplishing the act of going to bed or falling asleep. Every time I go to bed for the first time in a hotel room, even if I ask all the great writers to keep me company, all the heroes with whom I am friends and who//put my life and its troubles into perspective by teaching me to let it be blown away like a grain of wheat on the wind of centuries, even if I forcefully attach myself to the next day and to all the days that will follow to help me effortlessly overcome this difficult minute through the power of thought, the small inconsolable soul of the child who could not fall asleep returns to my side and moans, and I am powerless to stop it flying like a bat through the dark, unknown

room, crashing into corners and circling endlessly like a worry. The third
sorrow I talked about still darkens one of those evenings of my childhood,
the one when Maman did not come to tell me goodnight before I fell asleep
in my bed and merely kissed me in the garden surrounded by all the others.
Yet that kiss in my bed was for me the last rites, the small offering that the
Ancients [atta]ched to the dead man whom they lay in his tomb so he could
make the gloomy voyage without fear. After tasting Maman's cheeks for a
long time she would kiss me, and the imprint of her lips pressed to my forehead would remain there like a sweet sedative that through my childish
bangs sent my little soul softly to sleep. This was the gift I feverishly awaited
while I undressed; I forced myself not to think about it until she arrived. It
was the beloved gesture that swept away anxiety and insomnia. And I was
going to miss it, and I would miss it every night. It took me a long time to get
used to it. When I had made an honest attempt to fall asleep, I wai[ted] a
little longer to be able to touch her late at night. Then I ran in my white
nightshirt, my eyes filled with tears, to her bedroom, begging her to come
up and warm my feet.// And she stayed sitting there for a while until I [fell]
asleep, adding to all her other sweetness that of not telling me off, of calling
a truce on severity, of letting me glimpse behind the broken rule possibilities of something more whimsical, a delicious and unmerited charity. One
evening when I had wept dreadfully in my bed, rung the bell after Maman's
first visit, called her back again after the second, and since no one came
anymore after that I had rung the bell endlessly, and yelled so much that I
feared they would be angry with me for a month, after all of that Maman sat
next to me and the chambermaid came in and asked what was wrong with
me and Maman said in a sad voice: But you see Victoire, Monsieur Marcel
is suffering, he himself doesn't know why, it's his nerves. Happiness flooded
me. The weight of responsibility for my sadnesses was lifted and the weight
of my sadness lightened. And so [deep] down Maman didn't [blame me, and
I wasn't][2] guilty. For a long time while I wept I kissed her calm, [sw]eet,[3]
cool face.

2. Passage almost erased.
3. This word is almost erased, and its meaning is conjectural.

II

"There were other innovations during lunch . . ."

In this unpublished fragment of *Jean Santeuil* from the Fallois archives,[1] Proust attributed to "Mme Santeuil the mother" the character traits that would be those of the anonymous "great-aunt" in "On Reading" (*La Renaissance latine*, 1905),[2] then those of the "aunt" who would fleetingly replace the grandmother Adèle in the "seventy-five folios" (f. 4). The culinary "discussions" already take place there, in an addition, with "my uncle," the sudden appearance of the first person seeming almost, here, a Freudian slip; "my uncle" would become "my grandfather" in "On Reading."

We present a simplified transcription of this text with few crossings-out.

[. . .] There were other innovations during lunch, dishes of all sorts. For those that were successful, Madame Santeuil showed a justifiable approval, which she pronounced in a distinguished tone of voice that grew easily irritated if anyone claimed to be unaware of its superiority. Because she had pretensions//about it, as we have for everything we have learned. For a novel, for a poem, she would give her opinion modestly, leaving the matter to others of greater competence even though when it came to such things she had excellent taste. But for her it had always been the floating domain of whimsy. Whereas she had been taught by her mother the way to cook certain dishes, to play Beethoven's sonatas, and to receive visitors in a friendly manner. And in fact perfection for those three things was very similar: it consisted of a sort of simplicity of means, a sobriety, and a charm. She rejected with horror the idea of putting spices even in dishes that seemed to require them, or of playing with affectation and abusing the pedals, or of acting in a way that was not perfectly natural and talking

1. The part transcribed here appears on pages 6–9 of a series of three bifolios (195×300 mm).

2. Text used in 1906 as the preface to his translation of *Sesame and Lilies*, then in 1919 with the title "Reading Days" in *Pastiches et mélanges* (for the present passage, see *PM*, pp. 162–164).

about oneself with exaggeration when receiving visitors. From the first mouthful, the first notes, the first words, she had the pretension of knowing if she was dealing with a good pianist, a good cook, or if the woman//who had come to ask her for information about her maid or who had written her a New Year's wish on a card was a tactful, well-raised person. So she commented endlessly on these details until she had little by little trained M. Santeuil, for whom the constantly added principles had become to an extent his own principles, or rather who left such matters to his wife.

"She might have many more fingers than me but she lacks taste, playing that simple andante with such emphasis."

"She might be a brilliant woman with many qualities but it shows a lack of tact to talk about oneself in such circumstances."

"She might be a very skillful cook but she doesn't know how to make steak and potatoes" [. . .]//[. . .] Madame Santeuil in truth barely ate and was certainly no gourmand. She tasted the dish to give her opinion. And the gentle but intransigent belief that she had in the excellence of her own opinion, with that sureness that principles provide, that unshakable gentleness given by faith which smiles sweetly and perseveres in the face of attacks from coarse men who know nothing, like Mme Santeuil's uncle who thought a very spicy duck delicious, that belief was not a gastronomic pretension. [. . .]

[*Addition written at the top of the third page:*]

Often to avoid discussions with my uncle who took infinite pride in the thought of all the dishes being successful and knew too little to ever tell if they were not[,][3] after tasting she would not give her opinion, which immediately let everyone know that it was unfavorable. We read in her gentle eyes an unshakable disapproval, which had the gift of sending my uncle into a paroxysm of fury. But we sensed that she would have borne martyrdom rather than admit my uncle's belief that the dessert was not too sweet.

---

3. This relative clause added lower down between the lines replaces a first version, which Proust omitted to cross out: "[. . .] who put in this [*illegible*] great pride and little discernment." Cf. *PM*, p. 163.

III

"I certainly hadn't loved my mother
for a long time . . ."

This unpublished text from the Fallois archives could have been written in the fall of 1907: it is on a bifolio of graph paper in a 198 × 305 mm format, identical to that which Proust used before mid-November for rough drafts[1] of his article "Impressions of the Road from an Automobile" (*Le Figaro*, November 19, 1907). Proust wrote on pages 1 and 3, and continued on the versos 2 and 4, pivoting the folio a quarter turn as he was in the habit of doing with his correspondence.

The previous versions of the "evening kiss"—the one from "The Belle-Île Manuscript" (no. I) and the one from *Jean Santeuil*—had been written while Mme Proust was still alive; this one is subsequent to her death, which is immediately mentioned. This version predates that of the "seventy-five folios," from which Proust would remove certain details relating to his family.

The transcription only includes the most important crossings-out in the manuscript. The additions, also few in number, were all integrated.

I certainly hadn't loved my mother for a long time as much as I loved her when I was a child. Were it not for that, how could I have survived her? Every summer evening in Auteuil, when after dinner they would sit out in the garden, I had to go upstairs to bed. My heart sank at the thought of leaving Maman, and often by five o'clock in the afternoon I could think of nothing other than that terrible moment and when I sensed that dinner was nearly over, that they would soon tell the manservant: Auguste, serve coffee in the garden, I sensed that I would have only a quarter of an hour, I stared constantly at Maman, my eyes too anxious to weep as yet, I replied to what was said to me only as a man condemned to death can talk about little incidents that interest others. They went through to the garden, my old uncle[2] remaining on the verandah out of prudence, sometimes even in the living room where he would have liked everyone out of courtesy to

1. Fallois archives.
2. Regarding this uncle, the owner of a large villa in Auteuil, see the Commentary.

stay with him; my grandmother on the other hand, as a person enthused by nature and health, even when everyone else was in the living room because it was cold or raining, would drag her wicker armchair to the front of the garden near the lawns, where we would see her letting drops of water fall onto her plum dress, and her headbands undone and her hair floating in the wind as if to let the rain fall more easily onto her forehead. "You're too hot Adèle! It's a beautiful day Adèle!" would yell my uncle, who considered her a crank. And from time to time she would from afar (because he owned the house; we lived in his home) give him a few gentle, scornful criticisms of the way his garden was kept by the gardener, the too-straight borders, the stiff flowers, the unnatural flowerbeds. This exasperated my uncle who was extremely vain. But she loved nature, and that gardens should resemble it was one of her theories, as was not playing the piano "dryly," or cooking meals "disguised" to look like other objects, or talking about oneself to someone who is very sad, for example writing: I couldn't attend your son's funeral because I had a toothache and needed to book//an appointment with my dentist. One also had to travel in an intelligent manner. And when we left the seaside to return to Paris, she would organize the journey to see two or three curiosities on the way back, so that we would leave by car at five in the morning to catch the noon train, having seen two towers and a famous villa. Naturally at noon we were still a long way from the station, we hadn't seen any towers or a villa, and after some scenes with the parking valet whom we'd had to pay in the end anyway, and having sent reassuring telegrams to Paris, we would finally get home a day late, not having seen anything. This excursion was reserved for the very last day because while we were at the seaside, as long as the swimming season lasted, we had to *make the most of it,* in other words leave the house (which was of course on the beach, in the wind) at dawn, venture onto the sand or the pebbles with some spades, a book, and a folding chair, right on the water line, and go up and down the beach with the sea. To my grandmother, staying only ten meters from the waves seemed "a pity." We went back to the house to eat lunch (where we always had something simple, and whenever possible a local dish), returning immediately afterward. We didn't wear stockings so that the air could penetrate more easily, and she was so fanatical about the idea that our bathing costumes should be reduced to their simplest expression, allowing our entire body to be in contact with the bracing sea air, that several times she almost got us in trouble with the police for breaking the rules on modesty. I need not say what she thought of casinos and gaming rooms. For the rest, the great elevation of her mind gave her a genuine disgust for all foolish nonsense and all artificial pleasures. She was relatively open-minded and when Maman was a young girl my grandmother used to let her read pieces considered inappropriate as long as they were well-written and had a "feeling of beauty." But the thought that Maman might have read about "society life" or have cared about frivolities would have killed her. She said *cullière* instead of *cuiller*,[3] believing that it was more harmonious, and told Maman: My daughter, I will never get used to saying *cuiller*, it's too horrible.//Since the death of her mother, my dear little Maman would have liked, I can tell, that we should find it completely natural to say *cullière*. Because it was sweet for her to speak like her mother. But she didn't want to say it in an affected way to quote her, she said the word with respect, gentleness, care, and infinite sadness, as she had during a funeral when dropping a shovelful of dirt into the ditch, thinking no doubt about those she had already buried, and those who would join them one day.[4] She couldn't say anything about her mother without the humility of her respect, the depth of her grief, the pas-

3. In 1922, Proust attributed in extremis this trait to a character, Mme Poussin, for whom that appearance would be the only one in *In Search of Lost Time*, in a passage regarding the attachment of the hero's mother to her own mother: "Living quite withdrawn from Combray in an immense garden, nothing was ever soft enough for her and she would soften words and even names in the French language. She thought it too hard to call the piece of silverware used to pour syrups a '*cuiller*' and instead said '*cueiller*'" (*SG*, III, p. 168 and note 1 of A. Compagnon). In one of the two later notebooks where Proust prepared this addition, "the old lady of Combray and her daughter" draw from the grandmother the same criticisms that the gardener previously drew for his treatment of orange tree flowers: "They had known my grandmother who reproached them for having outside the salons [in] the entrance hall about thirty beautiful orange trees in pots, which they stripped of their beautiful white flowers to make that liqueur named '*fleur d'oranger*'" (Notebook 60, f. 123; cf. above f. 3). See also Notebook 62, f. 34v.

4. Cf. Notebook 3: "[Maman] had kept something of the gesture of infinite respect, infinite shyness, infinite gentleness with which at the cemetery she had let drop, as if horrified, in light and broken dust the shovelful of dirt onto her Mother's coffin" (f. 17; *CS, Sketch I*, I, p. 639). Adèle Berncastell was buried at Père-Lachaise, in the Weil family vault.

sionate tenderness of her memory, making her hesitate before she spoke. My grandmother was very generous despite being the daughter of a woman so miserly that in her old age she had to be persuaded that through political means it had been decided by the President of the Republic that due to her kinship with M. Crémieux (she was his sister-in-law)[5] she wouldn't have to pay for her seat on the omnibus. And they secretly paid for her seat because it would have made her blood boil to pay six cents.[6] I think this mother of my grandmother was every bit as mean as my grandmother was saintlike in her gentleness and generosity. Maybe she wasn't positively mean but she had a sort of wandering imagination that amused itself turning people's lives into novels. She would leave you in the best mood in the world. Then she would start thinking about you, imagining to distract herself that you had played some kind of dirty trick on her; she would become agitated and excited while thinking about this alone, and in the end she would send you the most offensive letter imaginable and never see you again. I never knew her, except when she was very old and I was very young,[7] and from what I heard said about her by Maman, whose memories of her were not particularly tender, not that this prevented her from going to pray at her graveside on the days when she knew her mother used to pray there[8]—but despite that it seems to me that I have inherited from her that tendency to suddenly fall out with people *at a distance.*

5. Proust's maternal great-grandmother, Rachel "Rose" Silny (1794–1876), wife of Nathan Berncastell, was the sister-in-law of the lawyer and politician Adolphe Crémieux (1796–1880), who had married her younger sister Amélie (1800–1880). The death certificate for "Louise-Amélie Silny, Marx," Crémieux's wife, was signed by Nathé Weil and his son Georges Weil (Digital Archives of Paris, V4E 4696, no. 116). Crémieux survived his wife by only a few days.

6. This anecdote was not lost: years later, in 1920 or early 1921, Proust included it in the words of Mme Verdurin at La Raspelière, in an addition to Notebook 62 that would join *Sodom and Gomorrah* (*SG*, III, pp. 301–302; see the Commentary in this volume). The grandmother's mother was then replaced by the grandfather's father.

7. When his great-grandmother died aged eighty-two, Marcel Proust was five years old.

8. Rose Berncastell was buried at the Montparnasse cemetery. Her remains were then transferred to the ossuary at the Cemetery of the East (i.e., Père-Lachaise) on February 10, 1986 (Digital Archives of Paris).

When I said that my grandmother was saintlike in her gentleness, I didn't mean that she led a saintlike life, although this is somewhat true. Maman, who loved her father // and her mother too passionately and too equally to ~~prefe~~ ever rule against one of them, would not have admitted this, but in reality I believe that my grandfather, who was the best of men but also the most despotic and the most ~~refractory~~ fastidious, often left her worn out and hurt.

I sensed that the last seconds of respite were about to end, I stared constantly at Maman, seeking out the place on her beautiful face where I preferred to kiss her (because if I kissed her several times Papa would say to me: come on now no ridiculous scenes and Maman would turn away) I chose it in advance so I would know it perfectly, would be able to take from the moment of the kiss itself all the pleasure of the act, consciously, so that I could remember exactly, when I went to bed, in tears, in my lonely bedroom, the softness of her cheek and the beautiful look in her eyes. That kiss in the middle of everyone, embarrassed by my father, could not be savored. Often I would find an excuse to call Maman to the stairs or to the parlor. And she herself, to avoid that scene which always irritated my father, often preferred to kiss me beforehand, and alone. But then I felt that nobody knew about it, and consequently I had the right to come back and kiss her again when it was time to go upstairs. In an awful indecision, out of fear that I would anger her, I hesitated, then unable to stand it any longer I went back to the garden, carried out the ceremony of saying goodnight to everyone and ended with Maman. But then Maman was cross at seeing me start over, and the goodnight kiss that I tried to plant on her cheeks, which she turned away beneath her frowning brow, gave me no relief, and I left her feeling so anxious that when I arrived in the antechamber and began to climb the fatal staircase that led to my bedroom and on the first steps of which my heart sank as I felt myself becoming more distant from Maman [*passage ends here*]

IV

"There is a Breton legend that says . . ."

This unpublished text is on the same graph paper[1] as that used by Proust for the previous document (no. III). In the Fallois archives, it was grouped with it and the Other Manuscripts nos. V and VI. It is possible that it was part of the project of the "seventy-five folios."

This is the oldest known version, at the time of writing, of what would become the episode of the madeleine. Only the first page of the bifolio was filled. It is difficult to say whether Proust ended the passage there at the bottom of the page or whether the sequel was lost.

There is a longer, rewritten version at the start of the manuscript that Fallois used for the "preface" to *Contre Sainte-Beuve* (Other Manuscripts, no. VII).

We have restored the first paragraph, which was crossed out. For the rest, we have kept the most significant deletions.

[*Paragraph crossed out with an X*] There is a Breton legend that says that the soul[s of] men at their death pass into their dog, [a] ~~peal of bells~~, into the stone of their house's doorstep, into their bracelet etc. and remains there indefinitely if they do not see someone they knew in their former destiny.[2] But if they are encountered by someone who knew them they immediately retake their previous form. It seems to me that of all beliefs on the beyond, this is one of those in which I would have the least difficulty placing my faith.

Often when I read one of those legends of which there are so many in Brittany about how the souls of the dead pass into familiar objects and remain there ~~bound~~ <captive> until the day when they meet someone they knew and who releases them, I would feel that it was a belief in which it wouldn't take much effort for me to place my faith. This is due to the fact that each time the great things of my life have died ~~for me~~, or at least I have believed them dead, they had in reality passed into tiny things and

---

1. Format: 198×305 mm. The bifolio, stained, is less well preserved than manuscript no. III; patches of decoloration show that it has been more exposed to the light.
2. The writing of this sentence is confused and unfinished.

would have remained ~~there~~ dead if I hadn't encountered those little things. I strove with my intelligence to evoke them but I couldn't. Alas, I thought, that whole part of my past is dead. How could I have known that those summers, the garden where I spent them, the sorrows that I felt there, the sky that stretched above, and all the lives of my loved ones, that all of this had passed into a ~~spoonful~~ <little cup> of ~~hot~~ boiling tea where ~~a~~ some stale bread was dipped. If I had never encountered the cup of boiling tea—and that might very well have ~~been~~ happened because I have never been in the habit of drinking it—it is probable that that year, that garden, those sorrows would never have been resurrected for me. But a few days ago, when the weather was ~~cold~~ icy, I came home frozen and I [*passage ends here*]

V

"Innocence and virtue in a woman
also have their poetry . . ."

This piece was grouped with nos. III, IV, and VI in the Fallois archives. It is written on two bifolios of the same graph paper.[1]

The contents of its first two pages correspond to the third item on the list of "Pages Written" found in Carnet 1 (f. 7v): "Vice ~~interpre~~ seal and opening of the face. Disappointment as a possession, kissing the face ~~under~~." Even if Proust didn't rework it in the "seventy-five folios," it belongs, like everything on that list, to their immediate antecedents (see below in Chronology). Its presence strengthens the probability that this is also true for the other manuscripts in this batch of texts found in Fallois's home.

This text also includes the first draft of a famous passage from the novel that, heralded in Carnet 1, was first reworked in Notebook 2.[2]

This is a complete transcription.

Innocence and virtue <in a woman> also have their poetry. But vice has its own and it extends our personality in the universe by making of the innumerable faces ~~and~~ encountered so many possibilities for happiness. When I learn retrospectively that a pretty face is not shy it is as if I could penetrate it, become the thought behind its eyes, hear <myself> addressing ~~through~~ through this mouth words that others should not hear. For my personality this is a new way out. The ~~knowledge~~ collection of society gossip that extends indefinitely the number of loose women is for us a little like the story that allows us to assimilate unknown or intractable* eras and to find hospitality within the thoughts of Louis Philippe or Marie Leckzinska [sic]. We probably won't possess these women. But ~~what wa that is not what for us~~ what for us excites the imaginative joys of gourmandise or

---

1. Format: 198×305 mm.

2. Carnet 1, f. 20: "Sadness of thinking travels = 2nd theme 1st the woman selling café au lait"; Notebook 2, ff. 28–26v (cf. *JF*, II, pp. 16–19). For a conjunction with another theme of the "seventy-five folios," see in this volume, f. 60.

physical strength is not fine dining or strenuous exercise, it is reading in Dumas ~~in~~ or in Walter Scott about wonderful dinners or how Lord Dufferin after quickly finishing his urgent business went rowing on the Bosphorus. What we need to know is that gourmandise, agility, the possibility of physical possession exist. Those affirmations suffice to extend our ideal faculties of desire and possession and we feel happy as soon as we sense that the universe is full of happiness. ~~What we put back every day to the next day~~ What is troublesome to us is ~~not~~ to sense parts of the nature of humanity where we are not. The possibility that a woman desires us, that we might be an aim for her, immediately extends for us the field of our existence. It is another barrier that falls // another closed field that we enter. The face that appeared closed to us until now half-opens. ~~Between~~ Earlier it was the face of a passer-by, now it is a work of art whose hidden underside, whose deep meaning we can sense. Sometimes it is only at life's end that we know that such-and-such a woman considered virtuous and cold had in reality kept lovers, that we could have been one of them. Retroactively an entire part of the past is acquired by us and like a sculptor's ~~marble~~ receives on its blank face a deep meaning, a delightful expression of beauty. But sometimes that face we have loved without being able to put any intention under its eyes whose <sometimes glimpsed> sadness we would have liked to be ~~caused~~ <experimentally provoked> by our coldness, years afterward when ~~red~~ fat has thickened the cheeks, when eczema has damaged the skin, when happiness and stupidity have forever dissipated the melancholy in those eyes, when the mad flowering of hair like capricious weeds in springtime on the edges of fields has withered, that same face is offered for our kisses, held in our hand. While we hold it we say: Don't speak, wait a moment, and during that time we tell ourselves: It's the same, and approaching our lips to those cheeks we loved so much we have the feeling that by touching them, we touch our once unattainable dream. Regardless, a disappointment is still a dream come true. The young girl who appeared to us out of reach, whom we never knew if we would be able to captivate, to possess, she was beyond our powers. Today she is a dream ~~fulf~~ deflowered and therefore fulfilled[,] she has entered into the domain of what we know[,] of what our experience can attest, of what our fingers have held. I can certainly say that an entire part of my life has been spent this

way, seeking in particular cases to make my dreams come true, organizing
~~jour~~ a journey to the town whose name//inspired me, going to see the
Gothic church whose description had enchanted me, in knowing the name,
the relatives, the friends, in seeking to meet the young girl I had glimpsed.
Sometimes things became mixed up, and I took endless trips to find [her]
<in> a train station [where] we met at four in the morning, at daybreak when
the rivers were shining, with her cotton sleeves, carrying into misted-up
train cars a steaming café au lait. It is her image that made me decide to
take the trip[,] that made me overcome my anxiety at separations, the sadness of arrival. Always in my hesitations that lasted months, and until the
torments of the last minute, what I glimpsed was the morning, in the remote little station between <wooded> mountains <like a green crystal> beyond which it has never seen anything, close to the torrent that falls from
a height of two hundred* feet under the shaky, tatty* bridge, the young girl
with cheeks more crimson than the morning [that] rises behind the woods,
bringing me my café au lait and whose eyes had appeared to follow me three
years before. And since what happens is never what we thought, this vision, which was for me the entire journey, never appeared there, never occupied the slightest space. It happened so inexorably that now every time
such a thing enters my mind during a journey, I can eliminate it knowing
that it will not be like that, that we will not see the sunrise, and that it will
be a man this time who brings the café au lait. But I also know that
someday encountering a friend by chance, returning unexpectedly to this
station, I will learn that the beautiful girl let herself be closely followed
into a train car, and every day ~~will arise~~ a new and chilling testimony will
arise to endlessly expand the history of loves I never lived.

VI

"Every time I find myself in a circumstance . . ."

This fragment from the Fallois archives belonged to the same group of manuscripts as the previous three; it is written on the first two pages of a bifolio of the same graph paper.[1]

Although it is written in the first person, it has thematic similarities with the end of the unfinished portrait of the uncle in the "seventy-five folios" (ff. 64–65). It is difficult to say if it is a previous version that was condensed or a later development intended for a different project.

The transcription does not include most of the crossings-out in the manuscript, although we have kept the introduction.

<Of course> There is love, and there is loving friendship, which I am not going to talk about today. But beyond those there is this.

A pretty woman who passes

Every time I find myself in a circumstance where it seems to me impossible to follow a woman, I am almost immediately passed by one who is pretty and whom I watch walk away, powerless and bound to some wretched necessity, with the anxiety that an unknown and possible happiness is being left to disappear forever. Never have I walked an old lady home without meeting under [*sic*] the door a seventeen-year-old milkmaid who walked away willowy and laughing, noticing my look and seemingly slowing down or even imperceptibly turning her head. But even if I managed to come up with a sudden reason not to go up to the old lady's room or even not to walk her to the elevator, by the time I have said goodbye to her and answered all her interminable last-minute questions, even if I run as fast as my legs will carry me, I find the milkmaid must have taken a different direction to the one I followed because she is nowhere to be seen. [. . .] If while out shopping I stroll for a while, eyes peeled, no pretty woman will pass. But if at that moment I have to stop to speak to one of my former

1. Format: 198×305 mm.

professors, or a member of the clergy, or some elderly relative, within two minutes I will see three pass by on the opposite sidewalk. If having walked pointlessly for two hours I decide to hail a taxi, then no sooner am I//inside it than the most delicious little servant girl will pass carrying a parcel. I hesitate, given pause by scruples of politeness toward the driver, then quickly ridding myself of these I knock on the window with all my strength, he doesn't hear me, I knock even harder, he stops, doesn't understand what I am saying, and finally, no longer knowing which way she has gone, I ~~send him in pursuit~~ tell him to drive as fast as possible up a street that she probably hasn't taken. In two minutes we are so far from any of the places where she might conceivably be at that moment that there is no longer any possibility of finding her and I know I should give up. But the mere possibility of an improbable encounter, unmingled with anxiety, is in itself a source of pleasure. [. . .]

VII

"Every day I attach less value to intelligence."

The relationship of this text to the "seventy-five folios" is in the first instance material: these six pages are written on three bifolios identical to the forty-three bifolios of this manuscript;[1] the written form, and the occupation of the space of the page, are similar. In the second instance it is intellectual: the beginning resumes and develops the Other Manuscripts no. IV, which as we have seen may have been an antecedent of the "seventy-five folios"; and we find here the echo of their dreamlike "tree-lined path" (ff. 36, 39).

Because of its conclusion announcing the essay against Sainte-Beuve's method, Fallois decided to make this text Proust's "preface" to *Contre Sainte-Beuve* (1954), in accordance too with the note in Carnet 1: "Begin with mistrust of Intelligence" (f. 17v).

Our transcription restores the most significant modifications of the manuscript and respects the paragraphing. It differs from both Fallois's (*CSB*, pp. 53–59) and Clarac's (*CSB* Clarac, 1971, pp. 211–216).

[NAF 16636,[2] f. 1] Every day I attach less value to intelligence. Every day I understand more and more that it is only outside of intelligence that the writer can recapture something of our past impressions, in other words attain something of himself and the sole substance of art. What intelligence gives us under the name of the past is not the past itself. In reality, as happens to the souls of the departed in certain popular legends, every hour of our life, as soon as it is dead, is incarnated and hidden inside some material object. It remains captive there, captive forever, unless we encounter the object. Through the object we recognize it, call it, and it is released. The object where it was hidden—or the sensation, since all objects are for us sensations—we might very well never encounter. And so it is that there

---

1. Fallois had suggested this (*CSB*, p. 14). In the Proust collection following the present manuscript there is a draft of the beginning, also written on the same paper (NAF 16636, f. 11).

2. This manuscript was originally labeled in the critical literature with its first provisional notation at the Bibliothèque nationale de France: "Proust 45." The habit has sometimes remained.

are hours of our lives that will never be resurrected. Sometimes the object is so small, so lost in the world, there is so little chance that it will be found on our path. There was a house in the country where I spent several ~~years~~ <summers> of my life. Sometimes I would think about those ~~years~~ <summers>, but what I thought about wasn't *them*. There was a good chance that they would remain forever dead to me. Their resurrection was due, as are all resurrections, to simple chance. The other evening, coming home frozen from the snow, and being unable to warm up, I was about to go up to my bedroom to read beneath the lamp, when my old cook suggested making me a cup of tea, which I never drink. And chance had it that she brought me a few slices of toast. I dipped the toast in the cup of tea and, in the moment when I put the toast in my mouth, and I felt the sensation of its softened matter infused ~~with the smell of~~ <with a taste of tea> against my palate, I felt a confusion of scents, of ~~roses~~ geraniums, orange trees, and a sensation of extraordinary light, and happiness; I sat motionless fearing ~~by~~ a single movement might stop what was happening inside me, which I didn't {f. 2} understand, and still clinging to that taste of soaked bread which seemed to produce so many wonders, when suddenly the shaken walls of my memory gave way and it was those ~~yea~~ summers that I spent in the country house I mentioned that burst into my consciousness with their mornings dragging along with them the whole parade, the incessant flood of joyful hours. And I remembered: all those days when I got dressed I went down to the bedroom where my grandfather had just woken and was sipping his tea. He dipped a *biscotte*[T] in it and gave it to me to eat. And when those summers were over, the sensation of the *biscotte* softened in tea was one of the refuges where those dead hours—dead for my intelligence—went to nestle and where I would probably never have found them again had not, that winter evening, returning home frozen by the snow, my cook suggested the beverage to which the resurrection was linked by a magical pact unknown to me. But as soon as I tasted the *biscotte*, it was a whole garden, until then vague and lifeless to me with its forgotten paths, which was painted flowerbed by flowerbed, with all its flowers in the little

---

T. A kind of sweetened, twice-baked bread popular in France.

cup of tea, like those little Japanese flowers that open only in water. Likewise, certain days in Venice that my intelligence hadn't been able to restore to me were dead when, last year, walking through a courtyard, I
stopped suddenly ~~on a flagstone of t~~ in the middle of some shining, uneven
flagstones. The friends I was with feared I had slipped, but I signaled to
them to continue walking and that I would catch them up[,] a more important object had my attention, I didn't know what yet, but I sensed quivering deep inside me a past I didn't recognize, it was when I'd placed my
foot on that flagstone that I'd felt it first stir. I felt a happiness filling me
<that I was going to be enriched> [by] a little of that pure substance of
ourselves that is a past impression, of pure life preserved in its pure state
(and that we can only know is preserved at the moment when we live it
[because] it doesn't present itself to our memory, but amid sensations that
suppress it) and [which] asked only to be released, only to increase my trea-
sures of poetry and life. But I didn't sense within myself the power of re-
leasing it. I was afraid that this past would escape me. Ah! my intelligence
was useless to me in such a moment, I took a few steps back to {f. 3} stand
once again on that shining, uneven flagstone in the hope that it would return me to the same state. Suddenly a flood of light rushed through me. It
was the same sensation I'd felt beneath my foot on the smooth and slightly
uneven paving of St. Mark's baptistery. The shadow that lay that day on
the canal where a gondola awaited me, all the happiness, all the treasure
of those hours poured forth after that familiar sensation, and I lived through
the day itself again. Not only can our intelligence do nothing for us ~~in~~ <for>
these resurrections, but those hours of the past nestle only in objects where
our intelligence hasn't sought to embody them. The objects in which you
have sought to consciously establish connections with the hour you are
living through, in those objects it cannot find refuge. <And furthermore if
something else can resurrect them, when they are resurrected they will
be stripped of poetry.> I remember traveling one day, looking through the
window of a train and desperately trying to extract impressions of the
landscape flashing past. I wrote as I saw the small country cemetery pass,
I noted the luminous stripes of sunlight on the trees, the flowers by the
path like those in *The Lily of the Valley*. Often since <I have tried by>
thinking again of those trees striped with light, of that village cemetery, to

evoke that day, I mean the day *itself,* and not its cold ghost. Never had I managed it and I was in despair of ever succeeding when the other day while eating lunch I dropped my spoon in my plate. And it produced exactly the same sound as that of the signalmen's hammers hitting the wheels of the train that day whenever it stopped. In the same minute the hot dazzled hour when that noise rang out was brought back to life for me and all of that day in its poetry, with the sole exceptions of the village cemetery, the trees striped with light and the Balzac-esque flowers by the path, [which had been] acquired by willed observation and lost to poetic resurrection. Alas sometimes we encounter the object but the lost sensation makes us shudder, but the time is too distant, but we cannot name the sensation, call it, it {f. 4} is not resurrected. Walking through a pantry the other day, a piece of green cloth blocking part of a broken window made me stop dead, listen within myself. A glimmer of summer came to me. Why[,] I tried to remember. I saw wasps in a beam of sunlight, a smell of cherries on the table, I couldn't remember, for an instant I was like one of those sleepers who wake in the night and do not know where they are, try to position their body to become aware of the place where they find themselves, not knowing in what ~~bedroom is~~ bed, in what house, in what corner of the earth [nor][3] in what year of their life they find themselves. I hesitated for an instant, ~~groping~~ searching [ ][4] around the pane with the green cloth for the places, the time where [my] barely woken memory had to situate itself. I hesitated between all the confused impressions, known or forgotten, [of] my life; this lasted only an instant, soon I saw nothing more, [my] memory had fallen asleep forever. So many times friends have [seen] me stop like that during a walk by a path o[ ][5] that opened up before us or by a group of trees, asking them to leave me alone for a moment. It was in vain, even if sometimes to regather my strength afresh for my pursuit of the past I have closed my eyes, thought of nothing, then abruptly opened them, hoping to see again those trees like the 1st time[,] I still didn't know where I had seen them. I recognized their shape[,] their disposition, the line they

3. Lacuna in the manuscript.
4. Id.
5. Id.

drew seemed traced from some mysterious beloved drawing that trembled in my heart. But I couldn't say more[;] they themselves from their naive and passionate attitude seemed to express their regret at not being able to speak to me, to tell me the secret that they sensed I couldn't untangle. Ghosts of a dear past, so dear that my heart {f. 5} was beating fit to burst, they reached out with helpless arms like those shades Aeneas saw in hell. Was it in hell in the walks around the town where I was so happy as a small child, was [it] only in that imaginary land where later I dreamed of Maman so ill, by* a lake, in a forest where it was bright all night long, a land only dreamed but almost as real as the land of my childhood, which was already nothing more than a dream, I didn't know. And I was obliged to join my friends who were waiting for me at the corner of the road, <with the anguish of turning my back forever on a past I wouldn't see again, of rejecting the dead who reached out with helpless, tender arms and seemed to say, resurrect us.> <and before catching up and chatting again with my companions> I turned back for a moment <to throw one last ever less perceptive glance> at the curved and vanishing line of silently expressive trees that still snaked before my eyes and said nothing more to my heart.

Next to this past, intimate essence of ourselves, the truths of intelligence seem hardly real. And so, particularly once our forces begin to diminish, it is toward what can help us rediscover it that we head, even if that means being misunderstood by those intelligent people who do not know that the artist lives alone, that the absolute value of the things he sees is not important for him, that the scale of values can be found only within himself. It could be that a pathetic musical on the stage of a provincial theater, a ball that people of taste consider ridiculous, either evoke memories in him or connect him with an order of daydreams and preoccupations, far more than an admirable production at the Paris Opera might, or an elegant party in St. Germain. The names of stations in a railway timetable for the North, where he likes to imagine himself getting off the train one evening in fall, when the trees have already lost their leaves and there's a strong scent in the crisp air, a book that people of taste would find dull, filled with names he hasn't heard since he was a child, can for him have a far greater value than beautiful works of philosophy and make the people of taste say that for a talented man he has awful taste. Perhaps it will surprise some that, attaching so little importance to intelligence, I have written the following few pages about some of those {f. 6} ~~truths~~ remarks that our intelligence ~~reveals~~ suggests to us, in contradiction with the banalities that we hear read aloud or that we read ourselves. At a time when my hours are perhaps counted (although isn't that the case for everyone?) it is perhaps frivolous to perform only *intellectual* work. But the truths of intelligence, while less precious than those secrets of feeling about which I was talking earlier, do have their interest. A writer is not only a poet. Even the greatest of our century, in our imperfect world <where masterpieces of art are merely flotsam from the shipwrecks of great intelligences>, connected the pearls of feeling to a thread of intelligence where they appear only here and there. And if we believe that on this important point we hear the best of their age making mistakes, there comes a moment when we must shake off our lethargy and summon the urge to say so. Sainte-Beuve's method is at first sight perhaps not such [an] important subject. But perhaps during the course of these pages you will be led to see that it touches upon some very important intellectual problems, perhaps the greatest of all for an artist, [namely] that inferiority of intelligence which I mentioned at the beginning. And that inferiority of intelligence must, however, be established by our intelligence. Because if intelligence does not merit the supreme crown, it is intelligence alone that can bestow it. And if in the hierarchy of virtues it warrants only second place, it is intelligence alone that is capable of proclaiming that instinct must occupy first place.

VIII

Notebook 3

In Notebook 3 Proust explores the sensations that assail a "barely woken sleeper," when his "soul, on the threshold of space and time, hesitates between places, conditions and years" (f. 15).[1] The sensations given by the body itself, sparking an internal memory, a sketched recollection of bedrooms, are succeeded by atmospheric impressions from outside (the color of a stripe of daylight, sounds from the street, etc.), and then those sparked by the world seen through the window (dazzle of sunlight, passers-by, etc.), all of which stimulate the memory and inspire desires.

It is easy to spot in Notebook 3 traces of the "seventy-five folios," as in the portrait of Maman as she enters the bedroom with the article from *Le Figaro* (*CS, Sketch I*, I, p. 639), and especially in the spectacle of the young girls glimpsed through the window. These clearly recall the haughty, nouveau riche *"fillettes"* by the seaside who, in the "seventy-five folios," were admired and unattainable (f. 67 sq.).

This is a highly worked draft left unfinished, which we give in the 1954 version, revised (*CSB*, chap. III, *"Journées,"* pp. 81–82).

{f. 30v} Sometimes I would go to the window, I would lift up a corner of the curtain; in a golden puddle, followed by their schoolteacher, on their way to catechism or to classes, I would see those young girls pass, their supple gait purged of all involuntary movement, forged in precious flesh, who seem to be part of an impenetrable society that doesn't see the vulgar masses through which they pass, unless it is to laugh at them with a shamelessness and insolence that seems to them the affirmation of their superiority.[2] Young girls [who seem with a look to put between themselves and you that distance that their beauty renders painful; young girls not of the

1. He develops an intuition from the "preface" given above: "[. . .] for an instant I was like one of those sleepers who wake in the night and do not know there they are, try to position their body to become aware of the place where they find themselves, not knowing in what bed, in what house, in what corner of the earth [nor] in what year of their life they find themselves."

2. Other version of folio 32: "[Young girls] appearing not to see the vulgar masses through which they pass unless it is to laugh out loud at a ~~ridiculous~~ poor outfit or a clumsy deportment with a shamelessness that seems to them a mark of their superiority [. . .]."

aristocracy][3] {f. 31} because the cruel distances of money, luxury, elegance are nowhere erased as completely as in the aristocracy. Aristocrats can seek wealth for pleasure but they place no value in it and sincerely, unceremoniously regard it as being equal to our clumsiness and our poverty. Young girls not from the world of intelligence, because with them there might be other divine ways of finding an equal footing. Young girls not even from the world of pure finance, because it reveres what it wishes to buy, is still close to work and the consideration of merit. No, young girls raised in that world which can put between them and you the greatest and cruelest distance, a clique from the world of money that[,] thanks to the wife's pretty figure or the husband's frivolity[,] begins to mix with the aristocracy at hunts,{f. 32} seeking tomorrow to form an alliance with them, while today it still holds bourgeois prejudices against them; but already [the members of that clique] are pained that their commoners' names do not let anyone guess that they visit a duchess, and that their father's profession of foreign exchange broker or notary might suggest he leads the same life as most of his colleagues, whose daughters they have no desire to see. A milieu that is difficult to penetrate because already the father's colleagues are excluded, while nobles would have to lower themselves too far for you to allow them entry; [. . .] {f. 33} [. . .] refined by several generations of luxury and sports, how many times in the very moment when I was enchanted by their beauty did they make me feel with a look all the[4] distance that there is between themselves and me, the only truly unbridgeable distance of luxury and elegance, which to me made them more unattainable and more desirable, all the more unattainable for me since the nobles I know did not know them and couldn't introduce me to them, and being introduced to them by people of their own world [*passage ends here*]

---

3. We have put in square brackets a passage that B. de Fallois wrote in ink on Notebook 3, folios 30v–31, presumably based on the upper part, torn off and today missing, of folio 31.

4. From this word until "desirable," the text is crossed out: we have restored it.

IX

Notebook 2

This passage from Notebook 2 was transcribed only recently:[1] irrelevant to the issues explored in *Contre Sainte-Beuve*, developing a scene that was apparently anecdotal and largely inconsequential, it did not hold the attention of the researchers. But it is a rewritten version of a scene in the "seventy-five folios" (f. 1).

"My uncle," initially here the protagonist with the grandmother, metamorphoses in the course of a single sentence into a female character (f. 8), becoming an "aunt" (f. 7v), then a "great-aunt" (f. 8v); the grandmother is here named "Cécile." We can wonder about the function of part of this passage (f. 7v) in the economy of the *Contre Sainte-Beuve* "story," such as it takes shape in Notebooks 3 and 2, unless, written on the verso pages and perhaps a later addition than the rest of the Notebook, it was already part of the *Contre Sainte-Beuve* "novel." It could be a "preparation" for the delicious sensations triggered by the flavor of the bread dipped in tea, in the first form of the reminiscence (see the Commentary).

Our transcription has been edited; it differs slightly from Bertrand Marchal's,[2] notably in the order of the fragments.

{f. 8} ~~My great-uncle sha~~ Sharing none of my grandmother's taste—for his taste was detestable—and determined to follow only his own taste[,] my great-uncle never received my grandmother's approval, [*passage ends here*]

My great-uncle ~~suffered~~ haughtily scoffed at the criticisms of the gardener that my grandmother spoke aloud or silently implied, but they pained him all the more since he had decided to keep this gardener, whom he greatly admired. Since he did not share my grandmother's taste—his taste was detestable—when something gave him contentment, he was sure it wouldn't receive my grandmother's approval and she did without it. But deep down she needed it and she was unhappy. She suspected [that] {f. 7v} my grandmother's judgment appeared to us superior to hers and to destroy those suspicions she would try to ambush us into approving her acts and

1. Marchal 2021.
2. Id.

criticizing my grandmother's whenever my grandmother did something that nobody could approve, when for example the [*passage ends here*]

{f. 7v} "Come back in then Cécile! Why always stay in the garden if you think it so badly laid out?" All the new gardener's actions gave my aunt great pride and my grandmother great pain. My grandmother gazed with pain at the bare orange trees whose flowers he had all torn off to make a [*one word ill.*] syrup that he sold to ~~pharmacists~~. But since from that amount he kept one bottle that he gave to my aunt, she was thrilled to be able to announce when she had it "served" to visitors: It's homemade. Whenever she came home from a walk she would stop next to the storeroom in front of the gardener's laboratory while the servants took her belongings from the car, fearing only that he would tire himself out like a cook she had once had who had spent his nights making sugar cakes, who had won first prize in various regional contests, and who had then died of exhaustion after two years. And she would also stop for a few minutes, while her belongings were taken from the car and carried up to the house[,] before the varieties [of] geraniums invented by the new gardener, which around the large smooth lawn in the sunlight, on summer afternoons, when all the shutters [of] the house were tightly shut to keep out the heat, gave in passing simply the most joyful and brilliant image.[3] The prefect had asked for her gardener to pay them a visit. My aunt was flattered that people were coming from the capital, from the prefecture itself, to see her geraniums, but she feared that in showing them she would be helping a rival to grow equally beautiful flowers, [so] she hesitated but her very hesitation, at the hour when the gardens are empty, [when] the houses have their shutters closed against the heat, giving an impression all the more brilliant and joyful since one sensed that this sunlit splendor did not make anyone hot and that during that time the happy houseowners must be taking naps in their darkened bedrooms, was full of charms [*sic*]. She knew that my grandmother expressed, usually with her silence, the poorest opinion regarding the new

3. See *Jean Santeuil* for the first appearance—in that case referring to the "notary's gardener"—of the gardener, the orange trees he strips bare, and the "magnificent geraniums" he breeds (*JS*, pp. 327, 328).

gardener. And she haughtily scoffed at my grandmother's opinion while deep down it pained her. Not having {f. 8v} the same taste as my grand-mother—my great-aunt had detestable taste—she knew whenever she loved something [that] it would not meet with my grandmother's approval and[4] she did without it. But she needed it and so her contentment was not complete. She sought to persuade herself that my grandmother's opposition was unfounded, but she did not succeed. If she had thought that the doubt she had regarding the quality of her own tastes was not shared by us, it would have been a great help to her, but she suspected that on the contrary we considered my grandmother's judgment finer than hers, and to destroy those suspicions she sought to ambush us into total disapproval of what my grandmother did. She chose a moment when, taking refuge on the ve-randah, or in the living room, the patio doors open to the garden, we watched the rain fall, and seeing my grandmother who continued to walk around the garden in the downpour, she called out: Come on Cécile, come inside. But no, she can't do anything the way we do it. She's the same way with the rain as she is with everything else. *All it takes is for you or me to think something good and she has to criticize it.* Alas the only response was our silence, and my great [*passage ends here*]

4. We have not included after "and," "she sought only her own contentment. ~~But~~," which, for sense, should have been completely crossed out. This sentence and the fol-lowing one are rewritten in the second paragraph of folio 8.

X

"But come inside then, ~~Octavie~~ \<Bathilde\>"

The fragment from Notebook 2 we have just read is reworked and developed by Proust in a long addition to one of the typed versions of "Combray" (NAF 16730, ff. 21v–23v). The intention was to insert it between the grandmother's walk in the garden and the scene with the cognac (ibid., f. 22; *CS*, I, p. 11). The grandmother is still called Cécile, whereas she is already Bathilde in the typed version (NAF 16730, f. 22).

Perhaps this addition, partly crossed out, dates from the period when Proust possessed only one typed copy of "Combray" ("First Typed Version," NAF 16730), the other being in the offices of *Le Figaro*, theoretically awaiting publication ("Second Typed Version," NAF 16733), namely between December 1909 and early summer 1910.[1] Written on a small bifolio,[2] the present piece from the Fallois archives condenses this addition to the "First Typed Version." If Proust planned to insert it in the other copy, the one intended for the publication of the book, he didn't go through with it: perhaps he considered this illustration of the antagonism between the grandmother and the great-aunt to be superfluous, less striking than the cognac scene, and the pairing of geraniums and orange trees would no longer find their place in the episode of the madeleine (see the Commentary).

This text shows few alterations. We have included the most significant.

"But come inside then, ~~Octavie~~ \<Bathilde\>, ~~shouted my great-aunt from the verandah or the parlor whose glass door remained open~~ can't you see that it's raining? Why do you always stay in the garden since you think it so ugly?" she added ironically because she couldn't forgive my grandmother for criticizing the new gardener. While he cut down her trees, while he stripped her orange trees of all their flowers to make a syrup most of which he sold, reserving one bottle for my aunt who went to fetch it whenever she had a visitor, this did at least give her the pleasure of saying: "It's homemade; my gardener makes this." In the evening when she came home, while the servants gathered around the car to take the parcels off the top, she

1. Wada 2012, p. 45. A third copy is conserved in the *Reliquat* NAF 16752.
2. Blank paper, watermarked "Imperial Diadem," 134×181 mm. Proust wrote on pages 1 and 3.

made a stop outside the gardener's laboratory[,] fearing only that he would tire himself out, then before the geraniums whose rim of red and pink looked so good around the large green lawn that even in the hot hours when//nobody wanted to hang around on rue Sainte Hildegarde,[3] you would see passers-by who couldn't help stopping to marvel in front of the fence, gazing enviously at the house with its closed shutters at the back of the shadeless garden. On the other hand my great-aunt knew that ~~the garden did not have~~ my grandmother's approval was lacking. She scorned it but ~~she had~~ sought it. Unable to obtain it she tried to disparage it. "I don't know why I bother telling you to come inside. As soon as we like something you think it's bad" she said looking at us from the corner of her eye, vainly hoping to draw from us a mass condemnation of my grandmother's opinions.

3. This street in Combray is first mentioned in Notebook 8 (ff. 10 and 47v; CS, I, p. 48).

XI

Notebook 1

Having found the formula for it in Notebook 5, Proust develops in Notebook 1 the outline for a dual retrospection: the protagonist recalls the nights during which, in his waking moments, he remembered the various bedrooms he has inhabited. The body's memory suggests places and sometimes triggers the story.

At the end of the masturbation scene (f. 67), the mention of lilac brings about the rewriting of the entire passage, which, in the "seventy-five folios," was connected with it in the walks of the "Méséglise way" (f. 34). It is only at the proof stage of *In Search of Lost Time* that the lilac is removed from this part of the story, replaced by a "wild currant bush," then by the wild blackcurrant of the definitive text.[1]

For the memory of the nocturnal walks as an adult—which follows soon after that of "a wicker armchair in the garden at Auteuil"—Proust borrows from a passage he had written in the "seventy-five folios" for the "Villebon way" (f. 41). In *Search*, this account, prefigured in the novel's opening, is placed during the trip to Tansonville at the home of Gilberte de Saint-Loup, but Proust wasn't able to give that development its final form.[2]

We present the revised text of the *Sketch*.

{f. 66v} Finally an opal jet arose, in successive surges [. . .]. At that moment I felt a sort of tenderness surrounding me, it was the scent of lilac that in my excitement I had ceased to notice and which reached me, as on all those days when I used to go and play in the park outside the town, long before I had even spotted from a distance the white gate near which they swayed in the wind* on their flexible waists like attractive, affected old ladies, and shook their feathered heads, the scent of lilac coming out to welcome us on the little path that runs above the river, where the bottles are put into the current by kids to catch fish, giving a dual idea of coolness because they contain not {f. 65v} only water as on a table where they give the impression of a crystal, but are contained by it and receive from it a sort of liquidity, in that place where around little breadcrumbs that we

1. NAF 16755, p. "13," f. 9; NAF 16758, p. "15," f. 7a; *CS*, I, p. 12.
2. *CS*, I, p. 7; *AD*, IV, pp. 266–269. See in this volume f. 33.

tossed in there gathered in a living nebula the tadpoles held in solution in the water and invisible the instant before, just before crossing the little wooden bridge at the angle of which in springtime and summer a fisherman in a straw hat would stand between the blue plum trees; he would wave to my uncle who must have known him and who signaled to us not to make any noise and yet I never knew who he was [. . .] I only ever saw the fisherman fishing, at the time of year when the path was dense with plum tree leaves, in his alpaca jacket and his straw hat, at the hour when even the bells and the clouds were strolling idly through the empty sky [. . .].

{f. 60v} But already my body evoked another attitude. It is no longer lying but sitting in a wicker armchair in the garden at Auteuil, no it's too hot, in the salon of the gaming club in Evian where they must have turned off the lights without noticing that I had fallen asleep there. But the walls close in, my chair turns around and leans against the window. I'm in the bedroom of the château of xxx, which belonged at one time to my grandparents and where before dinner I would go upstairs to rest for a second, and I would fall asleep, they must be at dinner, perhaps they have finished eating. But they won't be angry with me. Because years have passed since I lived at my grandparents' house. Now we do not dine until nine in the evening, after the walk for which we leave at the hour when long ago I used to come home. It was a pleasure when we saw the setting sun make a red stripe behind the château to hurry home to find the lamp lit and dinner served. It is also a pleasure, of a very different kind, at that same moment of {f. 59v} preparing to go out, walking through the village [. . .], encountering the blue triangular moving mass of sheep returning home in moonlight, and beginning in the silence under the moon one of those walks that we used to take in sunlight, taking care to be home before nightfall.

[*New version*]

I am in my bedroom at the château of x, I went upstairs as usual before dinner for a rest, I fell asleep, dinner is perhaps already over. They wouldn't be angry with me. Years had passed since the time when I lived at my grandparents' house. In Réveillon we didn't eat dinner until nine o'clock, after returning from the walk for which we left just after the moment when in the old days I used to get home from the longest walks. The pleasure of returning to the château when the château stands out against the red sky, when the water in the {f. 60} ponds is red too, and reading for an hour by lamplight before eating dinner at seven o'clock, was followed by a more mysterious pleasure: we set out after nightfall [. . .]. Soon we arrived in the countryside; half of the fields were drab and still light {f. 59}; on half of the fields the setting sun had gone out; on the other the moon was already shining; [. . .] we now encountered only the irregular bluish moving triangle of sheep returning home, I arrived in the fields; on half of them the setting sun had gone out; on the other the moon was already shining, soon the moonlight filled them completely. I advanced like a boat sailing alone on the waters; already followed by my wake of shadow, I had crossed then left behind me an enchanted expanse. Sometimes the lady of the château accompanied me, we quickly passed those fields whose far end I never reached on my longest walks as a child, my afternoon walks, we {f. 58v} passed that church, that château that I had only ever known by name and which it seemed to me should only be found on a map of Dreams; the country changed, we had to go up and down slopes, climb hillsides, and sometimes, as we descended into the mystery of a deep valley painted with moonlight we would stop for an instant my companion and I before descending into that opal chalice and the lady indifferent spoke one of those words in which I saw myself suddenly placed unwittingly and seemingly forever in her life, where I hadn't believed I could enter, and from where the next day when I left the château she had already expelled me.

XII

Notebook 4

It has been said that Notebook 4 was where *In Search of Lost Time* was born,[1] since it was perhaps there that Proust performed the crucial graft of the retrospective narrative outline from *Contre Sainte-Beuve* onto some of the abandoned novel pages of 1908.[2] And it is true that Proust does recycle substantial parts of [An Evening in the Countryside], [The Villebon Way and the Méséglise Way], and [A Visit to the Seaside] in Notebook 4. But this recycling is far from being a simple copy.

First of all, he continues his tireless work on the walks of those two "ways": this is the most heavily reworked part of the "seventy-five folios." The Villebon way—which in folio 35 becomes the "Garmantes way"—inherits most of the traits that in the "seventy-five folios" were attributed to the Méséglise way (the little bridge over the river, the fisherman, the bottles for catching tadpoles), enriched by new descriptive elements (including the aquatic plants and water lilies)[3] and emblematic characters (Mlle Swann and the Countess of Garmantes).[4] In Notebook 12, where the development of the "ways" is continued, everything related to the river passes back to the Méséglise way—as in the "seventy-five folios"—before being reassigned, for good this time, to the Guermantes way.[5] As for the park, the family estate still close to the Pré-Catelan in Illiers in the "seventy-five folios," while it initially remains on the Méséglise way in Notebook 4 (f. 26), a few pages later it has been moved in its entirety to the Villebon way, with its "little white gate," its metaphors characterizing the scent of lilacs (f. 30), and even the "hedge of hawthorns" (f. 32) that it discreetly possessed in the "seventy-five folios" (f. 31): from this point on, it

1. "One can confidently assert that it was in that exercise book that Proust's novel was born" (Pugh 2004, p. 3).
2. The theory that some of the "seventy-five folios" were the antecedents of Notebook 4 was advanced well before their rediscovery: see Bardèche 1971, I, pp. 210–211; Quémar 1975, p. 212, and 1976, pp. 21–22; Pugh 1987, pp. 28, 65–66, 83; *Cahier 26* [2010], p. XXIV note 2; Leriche 2013, pp. 23, 24.
3. Both *nymphéas* and *nénuphars*, the latter of which were barely hinted at in the "seventy-five folios" (ff. 28, 36, 41v).
4. There is even a fleeting mention of "Mme de ~~Forcheville~~ <Guerchy>," a precursor of Mme de Saint-Loup (f. 42).
5. Notebook 12, f. 18 sq., and f. 27. See Quémar 1975, p. 179 sq. and note 5, p. 196 and note 3.

is "M. Swann's park" (Notebook 4, f. 30). It will ultimately end up on the Méséglise way in Notebook 12 (f. 21), along with the famous hawthorn.[6]

Next, the first two "chapters" of the "seventy-five folios," which were merely juxtaposed, are joined in Notebook 4: the ceremony of the evening kiss introduces and provides the setting for the walks along the two "ways" (ff. 25, 44), under the aegis of a single location, Combray, making its first appearance here.[7] Positioned first in the "seventy-five folios," the important scene of the grandmother in the garden now seeks its place: Proust initially positions it at the moment of the nocturnal visitor's arrival (f. 53), then inserts a more finished version in the part about the walks along the Méséglise way, the days when because of rain the family had to stay at the house (f. 24v). All of this would prove ephemeral: from the first consistent version of "Combray" (Notebooks 8 then 12), the episodes of the grandmother in the garden and the evening kiss would be, as in the "seventy-five folios," clearly separated from the walks along the "ways," with the episode of the *biscotte* acting as the border.[8]

Lastly and perhaps most importantly a new character, Swann, ousts the bland M. de Bretteville from his role as nocturnal intruder and the uncle from [A Visit to the Seaside] from his role as womanizer. His lengthy portrait, an opportunity to immediately flag both his Jewishness and the grandfather's anti-Semitism, leads to a vacation at the hotel where the grandmother and her grandson frequented him. But even more rapidly than in the "seventy-five folios," Proust breaks off before describing the Don Juan's adventures. We find once again the portrait of the grandmother as an eccentric, although the little society of the four friends is held in reserve and replaced by other "strange characters" met at the seaside (f. 65). Mme de Villeparisis must wait until Notebook 12 to be formally identified as the dowager of the "seventy-five folios." But this is the starting point for the cycle of the Guermantes in Balbec (the encounter with Mme de Villeparisis in Notebook 4 succeeding that with her nephew Montargis, the future Saint-Loup, in Notebook 31, then with Guercy/Charlus in Notebook 7),[9] and for the Swann novel, the rough outline of which Proust traces in the following Notebooks (Notebooks 31 then 36), from his marriage to a courtesan to the Guermantes' obliteration of his name after his death, the sign of assimilation's crushing defeat.

6. The hawthorn is already discreetly present on the Méséglise way in the "seventy-five folios" (f. 31), but it is principally featured on the Villebon way (ff. 29–30, 36, 40), and on the Garmantes way in Notebook 4 (ff. 32, 41).

7. The mention of Combray in Notebook 1 (f. 68v) is a substitution, in a different ink, which seems to have been added later than the principal lines. Pugh 1987, p. 122 note 29; in this volume, f. 1.

8. Although there remains a reminder of the bedtime drama after the return from the walks along the Guermantes way, *CS*, I, pp. 180–181.

9. Although a "marchioness of Gurcy" is mentioned as early as Notebook 4, f. 57. *CS*, *Sketch* IX, I, pp. 670–671.

To better show the imprint of the "seventy-five folios" in Notebook 4 and their first "montage," we have chosen to present an almost continuous extract from this notebook (ff. 23–65), omitting only the insertion "To add to the Balzac of M. de Garmantes" (ff. 49v–52) and the developments that clearly diverge from the 1908 pages—like the main part, completely new, of the portrait of Swann in Combray (ff. 47–60)—since these passages are easily accessible anyway.[10]

Overall, we follow the *Sketches* of the Pléiade edition, the text of which is sometimes revised; two pages had never been transcribed, and we keep the most significant crossings-out from them.[11]

{f. 23} Often I could not fall back asleep and my thoughts conjured my life in one of those rooms of old where in that moment I believed I had gone to bed. One of those whose memory for me remained something painful was the bedroom I had in Combray when I was a little boy. Every evening, the moment of going upstairs, leaving behind Maman and the garden with all the family, was torture. Thankfully she came upstairs to kiss me a few minutes later, when she thought I must be in bed. But that lasted so little time, she went down again so quickly, that the moment I heard her footsteps and the sound of her dress—a garden dress, of blue muslin with straw tassels— entering the hallway that led to my room was almost painful, because it brought me closer to the moment when she would close the door again and descend, leaving me alone with the anxiety of being separated from her until the next morning. All the time she stayed downstairs without coming to me seemed like hours of grace that distanced me from the moment when she would go away again. Sometimes when, after kissing me, she reached the door and was about to leave, I wanted to call her back to kiss me again. But {f. 24} I knew that I would see her face grow angry, and all the peace she had brought me for the night, by giving me her lips, for a soft communion, her face happy and tender as a Host [*unfinished*]

10. See *CSB* 1971, pp. 295–296; *CS*, *Sketches VIII* and *IX*, pp. 667–668 and 669–672.

11. For folios 23–26, 25v–26v, 27, 24v, 27–47: *CS*, *Sketch VIII*, I, pp. 665–667 and *Sketch LIII*, I, pp. 805–814; for folios 60–62: *CS*, I, p. 672 var. *a* (p. 1437) and original transcription; for folios 62–65: *JF*, *Sketch XXXVI*, II, pp. 910–912. For f. 62 see also Yoshida 1978, I, pp. 5–6.

When after kissing me, she opened the door again to leave me, I would
have liked to call her back, to tell her, "Kiss me once more," but I knew
that then I would see her face grow angry (coming upstairs to kiss me was
already a concession to my sadness of which my father disapproved) and
seeing her face angry erased all the peace that her kiss a second before
had brought me when leaning her happy and tender face over my bed she
gave me her lips like a Host and I would taste her real presence to keep it
near me until the next morning; a soft Host for a communion of peace, which
would assure me for the whole night long a calmer, sweeter sleep than the
sleep {f. 25} we find in those other Hosts, miraculous though they are too,
which the pharmacy prepares for us and which he who no longer has his
mother's cheeks is very happy to find when the need to kiss her returns too
cruelly. But if that bedroom where my mother brought me peace left me
with such a painful memory, it is because on certain evenings—evenings
when we went walking along the Villebon way or when M. Swann came to
dinner—Maman did not come up to my room. For walks in Combray, there
was the Méséglise way and the Villebon way; in fact, all I ever knew of
Méséglise was the famous "way," and some unknown people who went for
walks on Sundays and whom it was said came from Méséglise. {f. 26} Going
the Méséglise way was nothing, it was an hour-long walk. We left as if to
go to the park, through the street door, generally we would spend the afternoon in the park, and around four o'clock if we felt like it and if the weather
was good, we would leave the park through the gate at the top, and we would
go into the fields on the Méséglise road until the bells ringing to bless the
fruits of the earth reached us to let us know that it was time to go home, as
did the fruits of the earth itself, making flights of gold shimmer horizon-
tally above the lilacs at the corner of the path between the rays of the setting sun. We retraced our footsteps and a half-hour later we were home.
But the "Villebon way" {f. 25v} was far more formidable. When we weren't
home by dinner time, my great-aunt who was waiting at the door would say
to Françoise: "You see they've gone the Villebon way. They're going to be
hungry. You see your leg of lamb won't be big enough." And when we came
home and she said: "I was sure you'd gone the Villebon way." Maman said:
"But aunt, didn't you see us leave through the little garden door?" Because
the Villebon way was so opposed to the Méséglise way that we didn't leave

the house by the same door. We went out the back, through a door to the garden that was for tradesmen, we didn't go on the street, we didn't pass the grocer,[12] the church. It was {f. 26v} another country. Why, when I heard my cousins who had gone for a walk along the Méséglise way say upon their return that to "lengthen" it they had gone by Villebon that seemed as inconceivable to me as someone talking about joining the East and the We[13] [*passage ends here*]

{f. 27} The Méséglise way was only a plain in the setting sun, where the weather was always good, because if ever it "looked like rain" we would return directly from the park to the house.[14]

{f. 24v} If on the contrary it looked like rain, we didn't go on the Méséglise road and as soon as we felt the first drops we went home. We read in the living room. We had brought in the wicker armchairs so they wouldn't get wet and in the empty rain-whipped garden all we could see was my grandmother who, thinking it "a pity to leave the children cooped up when we're in the countryside," pushing back her gray disheveled hair to let her forehead be soaked by the wholesomeness of wind and rain, sighed: "At last one can start to breathe," and walked along the drenched paths, which were too symmetrically aligned for her tastes by a gardener bereft of a feeling for nature, her footsteps unsteady and impassioned, more attuned in truth to the contrary movements excited in her soul by the intoxication of the storm, the stupidity of our education, and the symmetry of the garden than to the desire—unknown to her—to avoid getting mud stains on her plum skirt, which was in fact disappearing entirely under mud up to her blouse in a time whose shortness always remained a problem for us.

{f. 27} The Villebon way had a completely different character. One of its charms was that you could always see the Loir, whose course quickly moved

12. In the first version of this page, the grocer is described as follows: ". . . bareheaded in front of his door, a head that was itself of sugar-loaf with a pencil at the corner" (f. 27). Cf. this volume, f. 33.

13. The development in folios 25v–26v rewrites the bottom of folio 26 and the top of folio 27, which Proust did not cross out.

14. In the "seventy-five folios," the Méséglise way was, on the contrary, associated with uncertain weather: "The 'Méséglise way' was open-air, immense, and it would rain sometimes because, since it was the shorter walk, we reserved it for uncertain weather" (f. 31; cf. f. 34). That would also be the case in the definitive text: *CS*, I, p. 148.

away from the path only to return to it a little farther on. The first time
coming out of town, we crossed it on an old wooden bridge (not much more
than a plank with a rope running above one side like a railing) {f. 28}
at the end of which there was a plum tree covered with blue leaves and
under the plum tree a fisherman in a straw hat and an alpaca jacket who
seemed to have grown there too in the springtime. He must have known
my grandfather because he took off his straw hat when he saw him and my
grandfather signaled us not to make any noise. But just as the gallant little
stucco gardener in the notary's garden was only a gardener and had never
let go of his wheelbarrow, I think that fisherman was only a fisherman and
had never left his line. Because while I knew that the cantor was M. Ron-
deau the grocer when he'd finished singing and that the verger became once
again the blacksmith's boy once he'd taken off his cassock and handed out
the blessed bread, I never knew who that fisherman was and I only ever
saw him at the end of the little wooden bridge under his plum tree. So we
silently embarked {f. 29} upon the little path with the plum tree that overlooked the Loir from quite high up. It was in those vacant hours of the first
afternoon when even the sky is empty, except for a scrap of cloud or a sound
of bells still hanging there, when children already want to open the basket of
snacks and when their nanny tells them it's not time yet. In the Loir too
occasionally a carp would come to the surface to yawn with hunger or annoyance, in a sort of big annoyed sigh, and of desire for the beyond. We
always stopped to look in the river at those bottles that the kids put in to
catch little fish; the crystal contains water, as on a table, but gives an even
greater impression [of] coolness, because it is itself contained by the water;
you can no longer tell if it's the river that's a crystal bottle or if it's the bottle
that's icy liquid. Between the two there's that sort of alliteration that there
was in Guermantes in certain cider cups, whose cloudy glass, pink and as
if moistened with droplets of crystal seemed like a drink in itself, kindled
the desire to drink even while interposing between the cider and our lips
an obstacle too compact that our teeth wish to {f. 30} bite just as they wish
to bite the flesh of too plump women, where it seems that without the bite
one will not be able to kiss fully. Halfway down the little path and while
we threw breadcrumbs into the river around which gathered tadpoles in
vast systems of an identical crystallization, as if the water had held them

until then in solution and that our breadcrumb by some unknown chemical similarity between itself and the tadpole had supersaturated it, there came to meet us, and we welcomed it, the scent of the lilac bush that grew there at the corner of the little path, at the spot where it left the Loir, on the grass at the entrance to M. Swann's park, passing over the little white gate, their heads covered with violet feathers like women of a certain age attending a garden party, showing off their supple waists, and expressing to all with the aid of a thousand little movements their delicate essence. In that way the lilacs swayed like female relatives M. Swann had asked to be friendly and their pleasant scent came to meet us before we had {f. 31} even noticed the white gate. But they were wrong, we didn't go in, we hadn't gone in [since] M. Swann had married, since he'd chosen for a wife someone who wasn't exactly a courtesan but at any rate someone whom Maman, it appeared, could not see. He still came to the house sometimes to visit my grandfather, but alone, and he never brought his wife or his daughter, but Maman when my father wasn't there always spoke to him a great deal about his daughter and he was very grateful to her. I understood that he loved that little girl, she was so pretty. One day when we had gone the "Villebon way" she was standing at the gate of the park in a little pink coat, I couldn't help looking at her [. . .] [*meeting with Mlle Swann*] {f. 32} We took the Villebon path that runs alongside the park fence a little farther. And she on the other side of the hedge of hawthorns took the same path [. . .] [*description of the walk along the Loir: aquatic plants, "unfortunate" water lily leaf*] {f. 35} [*vision of the Countess of Garmantes*] One day we went as far as the Sources of the Loir. I saw only a sort of square little washhouse with a few bubbles bursting at its surface. And I leaned down in surprise over that washhouse where that immaterial and immense thing was: the Sources of the Loir, as a Roman might have leaned over the [ ], where the gates of Hell are located. Such was the "Garmantes" way and what I loved in those places was, as is always true when one loves, not their beauty, but themselves. [. . .] {f. 36} Because a woman can live elsewhere, but a beloved or simply desired place cannot. For things, place is the strongest mark of their individuality. [. . .] But for places, location is what matters: it is their very person. This is why for places we love without knowing them, if the voyage is disappointing—as when it comes to romantic love, meetings with the

person we love are always disappointing—it is nevertheless the very essence of our desire. The departure, the approach, the arrival, everything
that leads us toward the only place in the universe where Quimperlé exists, where Bayeux exists, where Venice exists, it is this that makes us feel
that these places are individual and worthy of being loved. [. . .] Because it
is the necessity of the voyage that guarantees the individuality of the
country. To know them, themselves and not something like them, one must
go to the only place where we hear that name anew, shouted out by railway
employees. [. . .] But I who as a child never knew more of Garmantes
than the "Garmantes way," for whom Garmantes was only the almost ideal
extremity of that famous way, something mysterious like a cardinal point,
the day when, lost after a long day in an automobile in a place I didn't
know, my chauffeur told me that if we took the first road to the right we
would arrive [in] {f. 38} Garmantes, it was absolutely as if he were telling
me that if I took the first path to the left and then the second to the right I
would fall right into my youth or my first love. [. . .] On the Meséglise way,
when I knew that Mme Swann had gone with her daughter to Chartres I
felt the sweetness of being on that same rolling plain where she herself
was, leagues away. Occasionally a breath of wind would pass, bending the
wheat, and I thought that it was the same breath of wind that had passed
over her[,] that nothing had stopped it and that at the moment when it
came to my lips I told myself: she told it, take him my kiss. But on the
Garmantes way when we had long ago left behind her estate on the main
road it was the quivering telegraph wires that would bring a telegram from
her. I would find it when I got home, I arranged each sentence then frightened at the idea etc. At some meander of the Loir sometimes isolated from
everything by the woods that surrounded it was a little house. I thought of
the sadness of going to end one's days in a place unknown to she whom I
loved, where I would myself be unknown, accepting the thought: I have
voluntarily distanced myself from everything that would have allowed me
to see her again, from those who could speak to me about her, perhaps
speak to her about me. I will no longer know anything but these water
lilies and this hedge, I will no longer be known to anything but this little
door that rings for a long time when you open it. Nobody will see me beyond this path, I will not see any farther than that moored boat. And at the

window there appears a woman with a sad face, of a delicacy that is not
from these parts, who must have come here to end, to renounce her life. I
would like to do the same thing, but by the second evening I would be
crazy, I would leave. And yet if one wishes to know the land, in that great
anxiety that we have to be what is not us, to marry the land, to taste the
secret life of those who inhabit it, wouldn't it be by becoming an inhabitant, by being the castellan of that castle lost in the woods, by becoming
a citizen of this hamlet, by paying taxes to the collector of Garmantes? But
no! It's impossible, we never inhabit a new home. Like the snail we carry
our home around with us, our atmosphere, our past, our habits.[15] In a few
days the little house on the Loir will be full of me, it is this country that
will {f. 40} become my residence, it is not I who will become its inhabitant, it will not leave its mark upon me, it will be I who leave my mark
upon it. Despite myself I would spread out on the ground this carpet that I
carry out around with me like a street performer and I would not know
the smell of the earth. The first stars were already out when we came
home late from the Garmantes way and I thought that she could see them
at the same time, in Chartres, or even in Paris to where she must have returned. If I saw three at once, she was thinking of me! But I only saw two.
But two and my desire made three. She was thinking of me. It was on the
Méséglise way that I first fell in love with cornflowers and poppies, apple
tree blossoms, and that there was for me between those flowers and the
flowers sold by florists the same difference as between the Méséglise way
and a pretty foreign landscape. [. . .] {f. 41} [. . .] It was on the Méséglise
way that I first noticed the beautiful round shadow made by apple trees in
sunlight, and that the white moon, not yet wearing make-up, would sometimes pass through the sky in the middle of the day, like an actress in her
street clothes during a rehearsal where she has no part to play. But it was
on the Garmantes way that I began to love the hawthorn, then with an even
greater joy, with an extra color, the pink thorn, like loving a piece played
on the piano then hearing it with a full orchestra [. . .] {f. 42} [. . .]. It was on
the Méséglise way that I first noticed the setting sun, that I knew the

15. The same image is used in the "seventy-five folios" with regard to the old lady on
vacation at the hotel in C. (f. 58).

sweetness when the sky was red between the trees, associating that redness with the idea of the kitchen stove, and of going home early, when the
day ended, before the usual time so that I could read before dinner. But a
curious thing: the Méséglise[16] way one day taught me a completely opposed
pleasure. Years later I was with Mme de ~~Forcheville~~ <Guerchy> of whom
I will write more later and we had to leave Combray at the hour when I
used to come home [*passage ends here*]

Then we came back, ["]retaking" the Garmantes way. Because I learned
then that the Méséglise way and the Garmantes way were not as irreconcilable as I used to think and that we could leave the Méséglise way and
take a shortcut via Garmantes. But in the years that I am talking about,
joining the Garmantes way and the Méséglise way appeared to me {f. 43}
as impossible as bringing the East close to the West and placing them next
to each other. I didn't know then that there wasn't so much difference between the Garmantes way and the Méséglise way. [. . .] But what distinguished Garmantes above all for me was that the days when we {f. 44}
went walking along that "way," since we came home late we would be sent
to bed almost immediately after finishing our soup and on those evenings
Maman would not come upstairs to tell me goodnight in my bed. All day
long during the walk I thought about the Countess of Garmantes or about
water lilies, as if I didn't have that apprehension for the evening. But on
the way home when night started to fall, my anxiety took hold of me. And
so it was on the Garmantes way that I learned to distinguish within myself
those distinct, almost opposed states that succeed one another in my life,
even within each day, when the sadness returns at a certain hour with the
regularity of a fever, and during which what was desired, feared, accomplished in the different states appears almost incomprehensible.[17] Returning from Garmantes, I knew that I had barely a half-hour before the
moment when I would have to say goodnight to Maman. Sometimes not
even a half-hour, because there was always someone, my grandfather, my

16. This is the only time in this passage that Proust places an accent over the first e. The
spelling "Méséglise" is also used in the "seventy-five folios," with one exception (f. 34).

17. In the "seventy-five folios," on the other hand, the staircase, that theater of "nightly
torture," awoke "an impression of pain" during the day as well. On this important modi-
fication, see f. 11.

uncle, to let slip with {f. 45} careless cruelty: "Nine o'clock already! The children should be in bed, they must be tired." And then that kiss with Maman which I had to try and carry intact up to my room, so that it did not evaporate in the corridor, the entrance hall, the staircase, I had to give [it] to her quickly, almost surreptitiously, in front of everyone, without even having the time to devote to what I was doing that neurotic attention paid by those who do not want to think about anything else while they are closing the door so that when they start to doubt whether it is really closed they can oppose their doubt with the clear and certain memory of the moment when they closed it. But Maman, so as not to annoy my father who thought that letting children get used to kissing their parents only perpetuated their neuroses, would withdraw her face almost immediately. And for a few instants I stared at the place on her cheek where I would kiss Maman, I did all the groundwork for my kiss that I could manage alone in advance, I chose the spot, I prepared my thoughts, I "worked from memory" like artists who know that their model cannot pose forever. But from that point of view the evenings when M. Swann came to dinner were even crueler than those when we had walked the Garmantes way because even if I was allowed to eat dinner at the table, as I sometimes was, I had to disappear as soon as dinner was over without saying goodnight, which meant I had to kiss Maman a long time in advance, before M. Swann's arrival. Thankfully M. Swann no longer came often since his marriage. Based partly on what I knew of him myself, but mostly on what I found out later from what people told me, he was one of those men to whom I feel most close and whom I could have liked more than most. M. Swann was Jewish. He was my grandfather's best friend despite being much younger than my grandfather and despite the fact that my grandfather did not like Jews. It was one of those little weaknesses in him, those absurd prejudices that exist in the most upright, the most rigidly moral natures. For example the aristocratic prejudice in a Saint-Simon, the prejudice against dentists among certain doctors, against actors in certain bourgeois circles. My grandfather claimed that each time we brought a new friend home from school to introduce him, he was always an Israelite. He welcomed them politely but during the meal he would always hum the chorus of *The Jewess* "O God of our Fathers among us descend, Hide our Mysteries from

Evil Men" or the chorus from *Samson and Delilah* "Israel break your chain Arise display your might!" without the words of course but we recognized the tune and that would make us laugh and shake. He guessed ~~their~~/the Jewish ~~race~~ <origin>—whose full nobility he would later know—of our new friends before he had seen them, even when there was nothing Israelite about their names. "Dumont . . . Dumont, I don't trust that" and he would launch into the chorus "Archers on your guard, Be vigilant and silent" and after one or two adroitly asked questions he would shout "<Archers> On your guard, on your guard" or if the patient was there he would be content to whisper while looking at us to show that he had no doubts left "Israel, break your chain." <and "O God of our Fathers among us descend"> [. . .][18] {f. 60} [. . .] I have perhaps already talked too much of M. Swann and yet I have given only one aspect of his person, undoubtedly the least interesting. Other traits of his nature, which I perhaps reconstructed later based more on my family's accounts of him than on my own observations, are so sympathetic to me, so close in a way to certain traits in my own nature that I would like to devote a few words to them. I had noticed at home[19] that we often received letters from M. Swann asking[20] (and his marriage, the bad marriage that I will describe {f. 61} later barely interrupted this mania for correspondence) saying that for reasons too long to explain we would be doing him a great favor if we arranged a meeting for him with this or that person of no apparent interest. But you could be sure that the person of no interest always had a daughter or a niece or a wife or a chambermaid who, on the contrary, was

18. For the rest of the portrait of Swann, see *CS, Sketches VIII* and *IX*, I, pp. 667–668 and 669–672.

19. Another version appears in folio 61v, but the paper is damaged: "As for Swann's situation, it would in itself be without interest, had I not understood later when I questioned my uncle and my cousins about how he used them, at least before his marriage, in a way that was obviously shocking, but [which] is strangely and closely related to several of my own ideas [on] pleasure and on life; so much so that in trying to de[scribe] his, it was mine too that I en[joyed]* setting out for myself during those long nights./I had heard my grandfather say 'it's like Swann's letters, it won't wash.' This is to what [he was] alluding. Back when Swann wasn't married, [the family] would never go very long without receiving a [letter from] him saying that 'for reasons that he would [*passage ends here*].'"

20. This word should have been crossed out.

of particular interest. Because what lay behind his request was always some fleeting love affair. Swann couldn't meet a pretty woman without falling in love with her and right away he would have to find out where she lived, who she was, and then get to know her. Hence, whenever he thought that she might have some close or remote relationship with my family, the little notes whose contents we could guess in advance, the permanent and unchanging original character of their author giving to his little ruses [s]omething [a]lways [id]entical [th]at made them [*the rest is illegible due to the state of the paper*] Alas poor Swann, my family always refused him, whether out of morality, or out of fear of complications and difficulties, or because unconsciously they wished to support the unwritten law that the simplest pleasures—like finding oneself at dinner with a completely insignificant young woman—belonged to everybody except those for whom these pleasures would really be a pleasure. As soon as he saw the name on the envelope my grandfather would say it's Swann again ~~wanting~~ [*the rest is illegible due to the state of the paper*] {f. 62} always a pretext to refuse him. <I heard it said by my cousins that> Sometimes it pained ~~me~~ them to see that each week a young woman whom Swann had asked to meet was invited to the house, that they would rack their brains thinking who they could invite with her, excluding the only person whom the invitation would have made happy. If Swann had known that she was eating dinner there, what mysterious charm our dining room would have been suffused with for him. Thinking that our dining room that evening was a part of the delicious unknown that is the universe of the woman he loves, the table where she sits, the lamp that lights her, the friends with whom she is close. But if Swann had no fear of trying to rope us in, always in vain as it turned out, when chance made him believe that my family's connections might prove useful to him, he knew that this was nothing to the favors he asked of his famous "situation." I must admit that in this desire to go bravely to the ends of what reality offers us, I feel he is so close to me that I will never tire of talking about him. I remember one year when we were at the seaside with my grandmother (it was[21] always to my grandmother that we were en-

---

21. The rest of the page after this word was crossed out by Proust until "and visiting it." We have included this passage nonetheless: see this volume, ff. 3–4 and 53.

trusted[22] during those months, and we always returned home with sore
throats because she believed that [sea] air and water never did any harm,
having been kicked out of the hotel because she always opened the windows of the dining room during lunch on stormy days at the risk of causing
the verandah to collapse, a little panicked by *Indiana* and *Lélia,* because
masterpieces could never do any harm, and having driven our parents mad
with worry the day of our return by arriving several hours late because it
would have been too sad to pass near a famous town that was on the ~~way~~
~~route~~ without getting off the train and visiting it[)] and we were in the same
hotel as Swann {f. 63} or rather we had been there to start with because
my grandmother, thinking it "a pity" to have the windows closed at the seaside, demanded that the patio door of the dining room be left wide open
despite the complaints of other people whom she did not want to hear, and
one stormy day when they had closed the windows despite her, she tried to
open them again herself while the waiter's back was turned, the glass
smashed and they showed us the door. From the day of our arrival my grandmother had spotted Swann and also an old marchioness of Villeparisis
with whom she had been at Sacré-Coeur, whom she didn't see often but
who still felt a great deal of friendship toward her and to whom my grandmother had turned, and never in vain, when she'd had favors to ask. But
my grandmother had pretended not to see them (to my great sorrow because
I sensed that this would "place" us in the hotel) because any time given to
people would have been so much time taken away from the famous "sea
air," which we had to breathe from morning until evening. As for the other
people in the hotel, I don't think my grandmother could have told you after
a month what they were like. The {f. 64} thought that one might take an
interest in someone one didn't know was something she could not understand and that she considered the very depths of vulgarity. Now since from
that point of view my mind was far less elevated than my grandmother's (I
don't know what I would have given to be seen saying hello to Mme de Villeparisis or even occasionally to Swann) there were at least two gorgeous
young girls who couldn't see me without elbowing each other and laughing,

22. Cf. Notebook 12, ff. 42v–43.

perhaps, in the most favorable hypothesis, because of my grandmother who would open the windows every day during lunch and smilingly brave the insults of various "families" with the smile of Saint Blandina among the lions, lost in ecstatic contemplation of the paradise of health and vigor to which the famous "air" would allow us entry. [. . .] Mme de Villeparisis, having noticed that my grandmother was avoiding her, politely lowered her eyes whenever she saw her so as not to embarrass her. And I couldn't dream of making my grandmother understand my desire. She would have been baffled by it even more than she despised it. {f. 65} And if it was impossible to make her understand about the two pretty young girls, how much harder would it have been even trying to explain to her the kind of charm held during the time one spends at a seaside town by certain strange personalities who enjoy a sort of prestige there, this courtesan married to a deposed pretender to the throne of a South American country [. . .], that frighteningly pale young man [. . .], all these personalities to whom the originality lent them by the absence of any point of comparison [. . .] gives a sort of supremacy that enables them to gaze upon the crowds with a sort of disdainful and ironic regard, which, less elevated in my sentiments than my grandmother, I lowered my eyes from the shame of being included in it. O [ ]

There are two words missing at the bottom of the page due to a tear in the paper; Proust could not continue this passage on the verso because it had already been filled with the end of the part from Notebook 4 written upside down. The rest (immediately interrupted) of this development features at the start of Notebook 31, folio 1.[23] It returns to the portraits of [A Visit to the Seaside]:

All this reality that my grandmother's natural elevation prevented her from even perceiving and in the grips of which my undoubted vulgarity left me disarmed, I realized then how many people for other reasons elude it.

---

23. This sequence had been noted before the rediscovery of the "seventy-five folios": see Leriche 1988, p. 80; Pugh 2004, p. 13.

XIII

Notebook 12

Notebook 12 includes a new version of the walks along the two "ways" (ff. 17–42).[1] They are clearly distinct, this time, from the bedtime drama, and the definitive separation of their traits is gradually established: the Guermantes way is the river landscape, and the Méséglise[2] way the landscape of the plain.

This is immediately followed (ff. 42v–73) by the account of the seaside vacation with the grandmother at a resort now named Querqueville, including the two passages given below, which draw on the "seventy-five folios." Mme de Villeparisis, who appeared in this place in Notebook 4, starts to slip into the role of the dowager from [A Visit to the Seaside], though as yet without the effect of surprise and "recognition" that we find in the definitive text. The main part of her portrait is kept in reserve until the additions to the typed version of "Place-Names: The Place" (see no. XVII).

After several complements to "Combray" and "Querqueville," Proust writes a new version of the appearance of the gang of young girls (ff. 111–124). But it differs so substantially from the one found in [Young Girls], notably in the description of the *"fillettes"*—now brunettes and blondes, including a "Spanish brunette" who replaces the redheaded favorite from the "seventy-five folios."—that it is likely we are missing some transitional drafts. During this trip the hero is accompanied by his grandmother, and no longer by his mother as in the "seventy-five folios."

Notebook 12 also includes the rewritten version of the episode's "punchline" as it existed in the "seventy-five folios," when the protagonist, walking along the road, sees the young girl in a car who, to his great surprise, gives him a friendly wave. In both cases, the scene (which would disappear)[3] acts as narrative punctuation.

Our edited transcription keeps only the most significant crossings-out.

{f. 42v}[4] Other times I did not fall back asleep and my thoughts continued to visit the bedrooms I had inhabited[5] from Combray to Querqueville where

1. See *CS, Sketch LIV*, I, pp. 814–830.
2. This spelling appears on folio 37.
3. See f. 74.
4. See also Yoshida 1978, I, pp. 7–8.
5. Compare with the start of the long passage in Notebook 4, Other Manuscripts, no. XII: "Often I could not fall back asleep and my thoughts conjured my life in one of those rooms of old where in that moment I believed I had gone to bed" (f. 23).

we went for several years on seaside vacations. It was my grandmother who took ~~us~~ me there; ~~we would get sore throats by we~~ I <generally> got sore throats there, because to be in direct communication with the sea she made me spend the whole day with my feet in the water, and as soon as we were inside she opened all the windows. The journey home was an occasion of deathly fears for my parents who awaited us uselessly at the train station, because my grandmother thought it too sad to pass near a curious town or some historical ruins without stopping there. We got off [the train] in the middle of the journey, we couldn't find our luggage, we miscalculated our connections, we no longer had a train. In Querqueville we were held in low regard in the hotels because my grandmother dem- {f. 43} anded that the windows of the dining room be left wide open in all types of weather, which led to continual complaints from the other people whose belongings went flying, when the windows didn't break.

{f. 49} I was ill when we left, we stopped en route to visit Caen, we did not arrive until very late at night, [and] when opening the door of the pyramidal bedroom that my grandmother had reserved off plan* for me because it had more air, my spirit broke as the smell of vetiver attacked my nose, and I collapsed into an armchair in front of my closed suitcase and the unmade bed in a state of such exhaustion and sadness that I thought I would never go to bed. [. . .] {f. 50} [. . .] The next day the first person that my grandmother saw in the hotel lobby was the Marchioness of Villeparisis, that old lady with whom she had been at Sacré-Coeur and who, followed by her chambermaid<s> carrying her coats, preceded by her footman who went up next to the driver on the coach emblazoned with her coat of arms into which she climbed, seemed within the hotel to move around inside her own little world, descending the staircase, without having to submit to direct contact with the hotel, in a sort of extraterritoriality like that of ambassadors in foreign countries in the embassy is [*sic*] an enclave of their homeland. She wanted to say hello to my grandmother. But already my grandmother had turned away {f. 51} in accordance with her principle that "one does not know anyone at the seaside," without which one would lose to conversations and good manners the time that one should be devoting entirely to the "good sea air." I was sorry about this because I sensed that relations with Mme de Villeparisis would have "placed" us in the hotel and would perhaps have diminished, in the minds of the two pretty young girls who elbowed each other laughing when we passed and considered Mme de Villeparisis on the other hand with great respect, the deplorable reputation that my grandmother ~~gave~~ us by demanding that the windows be opened during lunch despite the high winds. Doors slammed. Newspapers went flying. People complained. The hotel manager came, ordered them closed, and barely had he left the room than my grandmother surreptitiously opened them again amid a volley of insults that, as she looked out to sea, inhaled the breeze, tasted salt on her lips, already lost in a vision of the joys of vigor and willpower that the good sea air was bound to give me, she heard with the same holy indifference, the same indestructible serenity as Saint Blandina ecstatic in the arena amid the roars of the lions and the rabble's yells of rage. [. . .] {f. 52} Soon I had a deeper reason to regret that my grandmother refused to "recognize" Madame de Villeparisis. [. . .] [*his desire to be introduced to Mlle de Quimperlé*][6] {f. 57} Insofar as it might serve me with Mlle de Quimperlé, I couldn't dream of making my grandmother understand my desire to be "well regarded" in Querqueville. But I have to say that as far as other people {f. 58} were concerned, I had no more chance of making her understand. The idea that one might be interested in people one didn't know, and care about the opinion they might have of us, would have appeared infinitely vulgar to her but above all inexplicable. If I had told her about various people in the hotel whose disdainful looks and ironic smiles made me unhappy and in whose minds the sight of our intimacy with Mme de Villeparisis would have neutralized the negative effects produced by the inconsiderately opened windows, I do not say that she would have despised me, because I don't think that was possible for her, but she would have been saddened to find in me a sentiment so different from anything that she or Maman could ever have felt, so different from anything she hoped

6. For a transcription of folios 52–57, see *JF, Sketch XXXV.2*, II, pp. 907–910.

for me, and above all she would not have understood me. After a month I do not think she had looked at a single other person inhabiting the hotel and if she had been asked the names of any of these "strangers" she would not have been capable of giving a single one.

{f. 111}[7] One day when I had a light fever it had seemed prudent that I not spend too much time by the sea, and I was walking along the esplanade in front of the casino when I saw four unknown *fillettes* as different from the rest of the people on the beach as four seagulls who had suddenly appeared out of the blue, who were walking without seeing the humans around them and who would soon fly away. In their clothing and their entire person they were absolutely different. Jodhpurs, short skirts, riding boots, waists made supple by all that exercise which made only the desired movements, faces by chance all delicious and all different but to which so much insolence, self-confidence, disdain, insensitivity, and arrogance provided that absence of nervousness, distraction, and human respect that is so favorable to beauty. [. . .] {f. 112} [. . .] They never sought to avoid anyone because in their contempt for all that was not themselves, they walked as if Querqueville had been made for them alone [. . .]. I walked past them twice, but it was impossible to be noticed by them, they had in their eyes a gaze directed {f. 113} outward that let nothing penetrate, a gaze so hard that instead of welcoming the objects it encountered, it went through them and beyond without seeing them. [. . .] Never had the impression of a special, impenetrable world, leading a life all its own, where it would be impossible and delightful to enter, struck me so powerfully as when I saw those four gorgeous young girls who evidently all led lives filled with horse riding, long walks, games, and hunts, which I would have liked so much, who {f. 114} were not weighed down by any sadness or shyness or clumsiness or shame or respect, and to whom it would certainly have been impossible, even under the most fearsome duress, to make them address a word or even give a look of welcome or merely neutrality to anyone outside their circle,

7. *JF, Sketch XLV.2,* II, p. 935–936, revised.

with the exception of a few peers who were not there at that moment, or anyone they didn't know but whom they recognized as a peer by dint of their beauty, elegance, independence in movement, or their riding clothes, their grace, their rudeness and insensitivity.

{f. 122}[8] A few days after that[9] I returned with my grandmother[10] from the beach, covered in dirt and hoping nobody would see me. Thankfully the people we encountered where friends of the judge, in an even worse state than ourselves, and we were returning in convoy when we heard an engine roar and we stood aside, and the judge's daughter said: "Ah, here's the countess's car." She was watching the car with a curiosity {f. 123} that embarrassed me, adding to the appearance of our mediocrity an air of envy for their greatness, when I spotted with a pang sitting next to old Madame de Chemisey who was very busy being terribly gracious to her, the beautiful Spanish girl, more beautiful than ever; the extraordinary impression with which she announced herself to me, the fact of feeling that *she* was there, that the air, the middle of the road, the day, were suddenly imbued with extraordinary value, were bringing to life my constant thoughts, were putting her, my dream, in material things, in real time, all this caused within me a delight so deep that I forgot the humiliation of being seen in that state; besides, she had hardly seen me, she hadn't even noticed me at the artist's house, she couldn't recognize me; at the same moment I saw her nod and pouring from her eyes and her mouth the blue and flowered rainfall of a smile[11] that showered upon me the thousand perfumed droplets of her light. I wondered to whom this smile could be addressed and I was about to pretend not to have noticed anything when the car slowed at the bend, and as she was passing me she raised her gloved

8. *JF, Sketch LXV,* II, pp. 993–994, revised.

9. In other words the same day as the tea party at the artist's house, where the hero was introduced to the "Spanish brunette." *JF, Sketch LXIII,* II, pp. 989–992.

10. In the "seventy-five folios," the presence of Maman in the corresponding scene was crossed out.

11. This image would be transferred to the Duchess of Guermantes at the Opera (*CG,* II, p. 358).

hand and waved it in a sign of friendship: "How've you been since the other day at XXX's house, see you {f. 124} soon"; and taking my hat off, stunned, embarrassed, intoxicated, thrilled, I noticed that Madame de Chemisey, seeing her friend's amiability toward me, was greeting me too, nodding her mitered head over her episcopal bosom [. . .].

XIV

Notebook 64

Notebook 64 dates from 1909 and can still be connected to the *Contre Sainte-Beuve* project by its critical section on Leconte de Lisle at the start of the verso pages. The next, longer section is devoted to the young girls at the seaside. Before being invited to the artist's house, where he will finally be introduced to the "Spanish brunette" (f. 118v), the hero attempts, through the intermediary of the artist, to make the young girls' acquaintance. In the two unpublished versions of the attempted introduction—on the beach and in the street—there are still a few traces of the "seventy-five folios," in particular the way the intercessor goes about his business, oblivious of the hero's torment, but also the lavishing of gifts and the pointless dressing up, treated mockingly here as well. The luxurious parasol with the jade handle (f. 71 sq.) has now become an amusing *"en-tout-cas"* (i.e., a parasol that can also serve as an umbrella).

Our transcription does not include Proust's crossings-out.

{f. 127v} I had always admired the artist but, sensing that he might be the key to all this happiness, I began to adore him to the point that I never left him, spent all my savings on gifts for him, came up with the [most] absurd excuses to drag him to the beach at times when I thought the girls might be there, after first putting on the most elegant clothes, spending an hour at the hairdresser's, and making myself grotesque by trying to add some ridiculous accessory to my attire such as my grandmother's jade *en-tout-cas,* which I thought would impress them. When he was outside with me and he wanted to go back in, I would think: the girls might arrive in five minutes, so I would tell him I still have something to ask you: I would love you to see the glimmer of light that will appear later on the sea, and while I was saying this my eyes would devour the horizon and I would hold the useless *en-tout-cas* in my gloved hand, its beauty lost.

{f. 123v} At the times when I thought they might come to the beach, I would tell the artist, whom I hardly ever left now, and on whom I spent all my savings, to buy him flowers, shells, and books that he liked, wanting only one thing in the world: to make him grateful, so that he would bring me into contact with those young girls. <{f. 126}[1] All that I would have given to them, I gave instead to the man who could introduce me to them, who knew them> [. . .] I went to see him before the hour when they sometimes came to the beach, after spending a long time at the hairdresser's, trying desperately to smarten my appearance in ways that those who love us don't really care about, and which have no power to make us loved; once he burst out laughing when he saw that I'd enhanced the three hairs on my upper lip with make-up, and [that I was carrying], as a sign of elegance that I thought must impress them, my grandmother's tortoiseshell *en-tout-cas*, the only thing of beauty {f. 122v} I had been able to find, on the pretext that the sun gave me a headache. And indeed it was very hot. Unfortunately he was lost in his work, and as the sun grew lower in the sky and I said to myself they must have arrived, they're going to leave and I won't get to meet them, he continued with disheartening slowness to paint one of the beautiful roses that I'd given him in the hopes of getting to know them. "You really are desperate to go out." And he continued to carefully examine the flower and his canvas, probably without any idea of the reason why I wanted to go out. [. . .] Finally at my insistence he put down his paintbrush, [. . .] and we left his studio. How I loved him. "Wouldn't you like to go to the banks of the Epte?" "Oh, no, monsieur! Let's go to the sea." "It's just that we'll see so many awful people. All right, let's go." The blue sea regularly uncovered the beach. [. . .] I forced him to sit down, and I {f. 121v} tried to keep him from noticing the passing time, asking him a thousand questions while my eyes scanned the horizon. [. . .] At last he had to leave. Regretfully I led him back, still holding the now ridiculous *en-tout-cas*. We took one of those avenues lined with trees and here and there with such singular houses. For, despite the presence of a tram line, a gymnasium, a dentist's office, the houses looked like they belonged to the countryside, and that odd mix made me think of those avenues that lead to certain small towns in Holland. [. . .] {f. 120v} [. . .] How sad all this seemed to me. Suddenly one of those green avenues opened in front of us and I saw,

---

1. Addition on the facing page, today separated by an interleaved bifolio (ff. 125v–124).

like the promised cluster of grapes, five young girls advancing, we were headed straight toward them, I pretended not to have seen them and began talking animatedly, cheerfully to the artist, so it looked like I wasn't interested in the girls and was on very good terms with the artist. Happiness was inevitable now, we were moving toward it as toward a necessary accident, and as we came close to them I stepped off the sidewalk and continued walking as if I hadn't noticed that the artist was stopping or as if I were being discreet, and a few feet away from them I came to a stop. I played casually with the handle of the *en-tout-cas*. From the corner of my eye, without appearing to look, I saw that they were talking to him. [. . .] He didn't call to me, and soon after he joined me. "Why did you walk off like that?" he asked me. "They wouldn't have eaten you."

XV

Notebook 69

In Notebook 4 (no. XII), Proust only partially transferred to Swann the portrait of the womanizing uncle written in the "seventy-five folios": he limited this transfer to the passage about the letters vainly sent to the hero's family, a brief complement to the very first portrait of the character, in Combray. The decisive change takes place in Notebook 69, which contains the first coherent draft of "Swann in Love." Proust opens the passage (as he would in the definitive text) with the portrait he'd begun based on the portrait of the uncle, and adds to it with elements drawn more broadly from the "seventy-five folios" (ff. 60–65).

This piece is also remarkable for two features. The first is the explanation of Swann's romantic psychology—approaching women "from above"—in terms of his Jewishness (i.e., in this case, because he feared humiliation). The uncle, on the other hand, had never been described as Jewish, despite the fact that his portrait was almost certainly based on Louis Weil.[1] The second remarkable feature is an editorial note written in the margin beside this explanation, referring to the portraits of the dowager, the grandmother, and the little society of four friends, with the intention of inserting them into the beginning of "Swann in Love." Before the rediscovery of the "seventy-five folios," there had been no way of understanding that this was a direct, unambiguous reference to those writings. Proust would not follow through on this plan, and the explanation of Swann's behavior in terms of his Jewishness would disappear when these pages were tidied up in Notebook 15.[2]

We reprint here the text of the Pléiade *Sketch*, revised and with the addition of certain crossed-out passages.

{f. 1} This was not the first time that Swann, for romantic reasons, lowered himself from his grand social situation and migrated to inferior circles. He did it every time he fell in love, something he had often done, albeit not very seriously and always with someone new. Indeed Swann was not ~~someone who inhabited his "situation" as if it were a home with high walls that hid him from the outside world~~ [. . .] {f. 2} ~~In this home, St. Germain, he knew all the women and had nothing left to learn about them. So in a~~

1. On this question, see also the Commentary.
2. Pages kept in the *Reliquat* NAF 16703, ff. 93–95.

~~sense this situation no longer had any value to him as a situation that ex-~~
~~isted in St. Germain. It became interesting once again only when~~ one of
those people who shut themselves inside their situation, inside their
aloofness, inside their relationships, and never come out. And soon he
sensed that, as an acquired situation, his situation in St. Germain where
there wasn't a woman he didn't know or who had something new to teach
him, his situation was no longer of any interest for him. It represented only
a sort of potential value, like a bill of exchange, enabling him to create a
new situation in Quimper-Corentin, or in some Quimper-Corentin in
Paris, if he liked the judge's daughter. How many times did he sell the
precious jewel that was a duchess's accumulated desire to be agreeable to
him for way below its market value to procure the dish that he fancied at
that time, asking this duchess, with an indiscreet telegram sent on an
absurd pretext, for a letter that would introduce him into the home of one
of her farmers whose daughter had caught his eye. His situation was
something that could be taken down and transported; better still, it was
like those huts of which the pieces, once they have been taken apart, can
be transformed into tools that enable you to build a suitable home wherever you go.

All Swann's friends were used to receiving occasional letters in which
Swann, with {f. 3} a diplomatic skill that, persisting through a succession
of affairs and various pretexts, was more revealing of his character and his
true objective than a faux pas would have been, requested a letter of recommendation or invitation. My cousin told me that at home, before the time
when Swann had his liaison, we often used to receive his letters, and that
as soon as he recognized the handwriting on the envelope, my ~~grandfather~~
<great-uncle> would say: "Uh-oh, it's Swann who's going to ask us for some-
thing. On your guard!" And always, whether out of suspicion or simply out
of that strange feeling that drives us to only ever give something to people
who don't ask for it, they would flatly reject his requests when it would have
been so easy to grant them. I was sad sometimes my cousin told me,
hearing my parents wonder aloud whom they could invite with a young girl
who came to dinner occasionally, and not finding anyone, deciding to let
her be bored on her own rather than inviting the only person whom that
dinner would have made so happy, for whom our dining room would

suddenly have been illuminated with a delicious mystery, Swann who had asked us to help him meet that young girl, who asked us practically every week, and must have been surprised to hear us say each {f. 4} time that we hadn't seen her recently, when he knew we were so close to her. [. . .] {f. 5} [. . .] No doubt Swann had a nerve, wanting to force the entire world—this whole host of duchesses, generals, members of the Académie, and even members of the bourgeoisie whom he knew—to act as go-betweens. But that {f. 6} was down to two aspects of his nature, the first of which always struck me as truly remarkable. If I understand it correctly, I would define it as a sort of sincerity in the desire that ~~drove him to make made him consider women as distinctive individuals and prevented him from cheating on~~ <with> ~~another the excessive pleasure of that another had inspired in him~~ made him wish to get to know a particular being, to know this or that woman whom he happened to meet. When traveling he did everything he could to make the acquaintance of the local women he liked and to send for his mistress only as a last resort, regarding such an act as a sort of abdication, a confession of his powerlessness to penetrate the new reality that was offered to him. Instead of shutting himself up in his old relationships, and asking his mistress for a pleasure equivalent to what he would have received from the woman he'd met at the hotel or the port, it was the singularity of their face, the meaning of their look, that he wished to taste. ~~But since he was not one of those haughty souls like Of course if one could~~ I cannot of course compare him to people like my parents who showed so little interest in anyone they didn't know that they could barely tell them apart and would not have been capable of recognizing them, but even supposing that my grandmother's soul was one day implanted in the body of a young man in search of good {f. 7} fortune, that soul was too free of all vanity to understand Swann might want the woman from Quimper that he met to *know* that he was friends with the Duchess of S. etc.[3] Perhaps

3. Here, Proust inserts this addition, but it was written after the editorial note in the margin of the following phrase: "<In truth it generally did him no good. Often, perhaps, he would have gotten better results with women of other backgrounds had he not turned up accredited in that way, thanks to a brilliant intuition he had of more distant connections with some great lady. Either because he didn't want to appear {f. 6v} to care about that, or because such an excess of preparation and the rather unnatural-seeming desire of

his Jewish origin ~~had something to do~~ was part of the cause, which, <making him> (as ~~the~~ <certain> Romans found a greater charm in penetrating certain Oriental captives) particularly attracted to pious young ~~Cath~~ Christians in whom his infidel soul greedily drank the new taste of holy water and French soil—like the ~~Gothic~~ <Lombard> style merging with the Byzantine—also gave him, through the memory of those humiliations that it is rare for a Jew not to have experienced during his childhood, a sort of fear of being despised, misjudged. <Perhaps put here the dowager, my grandmother, the Monsieur and his mistress. Anyway show that all this is useless for Swann and that it's just so he isn't despised.> ~~Obliged to Of course~~ He did not do what most people do, he didn't shut himself up in a flattering situation, he went back down into the arena each time, creating, at a new cost, for new beings, a new situation, and starting his life over each time. But out of a final attachment to vanity he wanted it to be from above, wanted to show that he had no need for the relations he sought, so that, a sensitive man, he could be rejected, but not despised.

When Mme X started to like him, then, {f. 8} and when he started to enjoy her company he found it only natural to visit the Verdurins.

---

such an illustrious man to mix with people below him aroused suspicions, he was less successful than he would have been had he simply made their acquaintance, remaining incognito as he did for such a long time with us. But despite not being vain, he was sensitive. We knew him, we couldn't suspect his behavior, and that was enough for him, he had no need for us to recognize his relations. When traveling he would have been afraid to appear scheming.>"

XVI

Notebook 65

Notebook 65, which mainly concerns the visits to Querqueville with the grand-mother but also with Maman, is an important notebook on death and grief, the first notebook to include the resurrection and dreams of the grandmother. It contains a series of four dreams, following the experience of the hero's awakened memory in a hotel room ("sleep that is more truthful and unsparing remade this blend of my enduring tenderness and her nothingness," f. 39). The first three dreams develop those of his parents that Proust had noted down in 1908 at the start of Carnet 1 (ff. 2, 3v, 4, respectively in ff. 41v, 39–40, 40–42 of Notebook 65). The fourth, not mentioned in Carnet 1, retranscribes and develops (by attributing it to the grand-mother) (ff. 42–44) the dream of Maman as it appears in the "seventy-five folios" (f. 18). The presence of "Maman" in the present passage (f. 44), despite the ambiguity, seems almost a Freudian slip: in the next version, she will have disappeared from the corresponding phrase (Notebook 50).[1] This dream did not make it into the published text.[2]

We complete here the partial transcription provided by Jo Yoshida.[3]

{f. 42} Then by train./The noise of the train, I dozed off, ~~and. Then my grandmother~~ my eyelids sealed my eyes and my gaze turned inward saw only inside me, that interior world (the organs etc. see other page).[4] Then my grandmother appeared to me. ~~She ha~~ I hadn't seen her since she died, ~~and she was~~ on ~~the way~~ <the little path that leads to the station>, in traveling clothes, ~~her ha she~~ she was walking quickly, almost running, ~~because~~ the whistles of the departing trains were audible, she was hurrying, she'd

1. *SG, Sketch XIII*, III, pp. 1033–1034.
2. See f. 18.
3. Yoshida 1992, p. 52.
4. Reference to ff. 38v–39v. The "great solemn figures" that we encounter in our dreams "are seen inside us, from a more internal, more corporeal, more organic aware-ness, seen in the transparency of our organs [. . .]" (f. 38v); "in the catacombs of the or-gans" "suddenly turned translucent," "we see them, with a perception in which all the organs participate, internal, organic, subcutaneous" (f. 39v).

dirtied her dress,[5] almost lost an ankle boot and her hat was all askew and she had a splash of mud up to her veil, she was red-faced, and she looked so ill that the rings around her eyes went down almost to her mouth. Her eyes were unspeakably sad but with a fierce sadness as if furious and bitter. Perhaps she had she was angry with me as she was sometimes <, for such a brief time, she was>, and more to teach me teach me a lesson than out of any real anger; perhaps she was was she had pere before dying, understood suddenly my at that moment when with life leaving us we cling more tightly to it, when even the most selfless {f. 43} think for an instant of their body, which feeling it give way beneath them they want to hold together, perhaps at the moment of dying she had suddenly seen the swindle perpetrated on her by her life of devotion, of sacrifice to others, perhaps she had my immense selfishness abruptly ceasing to be hidden from her by the sophisms of her loving heart had suddenly appeared to her, and the rigors she had borne for me which perhaps* I would not have borne for her[,] which had marked* a life, and was it that, that reproach without forgiveness that she <any remaining love>, that by <without> any possible forgiveness, that verdict rendered she delivered to me with resentment with fairness—in that look which truly pierced me because it wa her very eye was in me—to the one <the child> who had hurt her most, because he was the one she had loved most, to the one who had caused her death, because he had been her life. I felt that I didn the depth of her reproach, the the bitterness of her grief, while she struggled breathlessly not wanting to look at me, staining herself with mud, tiring her belly and her legs toward the station. An immense of desire [sic] to catch up with her, kiss her, beg her forgiveness lifted me up, but at the moment when I came close to her she turned her face away, fierce and red with breathlessness and fatigue, implacable, irreconcilable, and suddenly I couldn't move anymore, the already an employee {f. 44} was signaling to her that the train was about to leave, she was going faster, I sensed her fatigue, sensed she was in pain, that her heart might

5. The term "soiled" (*crotté*), present in the "seventy-five folios" (f. 18: "the hem of her dress was soiled") and absent here, would be reintroduced in the next version: "She had dirtied <soiled> her dress, almost lost an ankle boot" (Notebook 50, f. 19; *SG, Sketch XIII*, III, p. 1033).

stop beating. All the anxieties I might have felt in my life at being separated from Maman[,] at feeling the approach of evening, at leaving on a trip,
evoked by the memory of the dream, without my intelligence being able to
tell them apart, swelled this memory. My whole life was a cry*[,] to be able
to join her, to have her close to me like I used to. ~~I~~ I couldn't move a
muscle now, ~~she~~ the train was leaving she climbed ~~onboard~~ the steps of
a car, half-stumbled, an employee roughly <perhaps hurting her—ah! if
only I could be sure that she hadn't been hurt—> shoved her like a piece
of luggage into the car and closed the door on her, the train moved away
and I sensed that she ~~was leaving for~~ <~~was moving away~~ was going away
with no intention of coming back ~~toward~~> from lands I didn't know ~~and~~
~~from where she~~ where I would not be able to go and find her ~~and from~~
~~where~~ I sensed [that] she ~~was going~~ had gone <~~without any~~ thought of
coming back idea of ~~intention of returning~~> forever!

XVII

Handwritten pages of the typewritten version of "Place-Names: The Place"

In the spring of 1912, Proust, who was tidying up his draft of the first visit to Cricquebec/Balbec, asked his secretary Albert Nahmias to set aside several blank pages in the version he was typing up (Notebook 70, f. 53). He used them for a long handwritten "addition." The portraits of the dowager (who had become Mme de Villeparisis) and the little society of four friends who had been sketched in the "seventy-five folios" were reworked, intertwined, and expanded; the bourgeois clientele of the hotel (the notary, the barrister, the chief magistrate, and their wives) inherited the social pusillanimity skewered at the start of the 1908 pages (f. 54).

It was this text that would be printed in Grasset's galley proofs for the first volume (1913) and then the second volume[1] (1914), before the war interrupted publication of *In Search of Lost Time*; Proust would further expand this piece for *In the Shadow of Young Girls in Flower* (*JF*, II, pp. 38–42). But the final allusion to Swann's character would have disappeared (ibid., p. 42).

We present here a lightly revised version of the transcription produced by Richard Bales in his edition of the 1912 typed version.[2]

[NAF 16735, f. 212] The little colony perhaps had less opportunity to feel this way,[3] toward an actress, known less for her professional achievements, because she had played few roles at the Odéon, than for her grace, her wit, her elegance, her taste, her precious collections of German porcelain, and who was staying at the Grand Hotel in Cricquebec with her lover, a very rich young man for whose benefit more than anything she had bettered herself, and with two men close to the aristocracy, the four of them forming for the pleasure they took in chatting together, playing cards together, eating

1. See NAF 16754 (1913), galley proofs 80 (ff. 142v–143) and 81 (ff. 144v–145), and NAF 16761 (1914), galley proofs 49 (ff. 41v–42) and 50 (ff. 43v–44).
2. Marcel Proust, *"Bricquebec": Prototype d'"À l'ombre des jeunes filles en fleurs,"* edited and introduced by Richard Bales (Oxford: Clarendon Press, 1989), pp. 71–87.
3. On the previous page, Proust had described the contempt shown by the Grand Hotel's regular customers toward the false "king of a small island in Oceania" or the rich young man with tuberculosis.

together (because all four were gourmands) a little society that refused to be separated by the summer's travels and which transported itself, intact and complete, here and there over time. But the chief magistrate's wife and the notary's wife were denied the joy they would have felt at suffering the close proximity of this demimondaine. Because the little society, which always had special menus, for the creation of which one or two of its members would always have long meetings with the chef, never ate lunch until very late, when everyone else was about to leave their table. They took their meals apart, entering through a little door and never bothering anyone; the woman always admirably elegant, in dresses that were never the same but were not particularly conspicuous, with a singular taste for scarves that her lover appreciated. None of them were ever seen during the days, which they spent playing cards together. In the evening when they left the table, the three men were sometimes spotted in tuxedos waiting for the woman who was late and who soon, after calling the elevator from her floor, would emerge from its doors as from a toy box, all dressed up with a new scarf, glancing at herself for an instant in the mirror, adding a little rouge to her cheeks, and then, the whole society diving inside a closed carriage drawn by two horses that was waiting outside for them, they would go out for dinner, driving a half-hour from there to a little restaurant renowned for its fine food, where since there were few other diners the chef could devote more time to each dish and they themselves could have a longer discussion with him over whether or not to add this or that ingredient. In this way they passed almost unnoticed by the inhabitants of the hotel. The same could not be said of an elderly, rich, aristocratic lady who, although she was staying on another floor, the valet on our floor had told us about, impressed as he and his colleagues were by the fact that she had brought with her her own chambermaid, driver, horses, cars, and had been preceded into the hotel by a butler tasked with choosing the rooms and making them, with various trinkets and precious old ornaments that he had brought with him, as similar as possible to the rooms that his mistress inhabited in Paris. The barrister and his friends were full of sarcastic remarks regarding this respect shown by the hotel staff for a grande dame who never went anywhere without her full entourage of servants. Every time the notary's wife and the magistrate's wife saw her in the dining room at mealtimes, they examined her insolently through their lorgnettes with the same fastidious, mistrustful look that they might have given some pompously named but unappetizing dish of the kind that is often served in luxury hotels, which after the unfavorable results of methodical {f. 213} observation is rejected with a vague gesture, a knowing air, and a grimace of disgust. In doing so, the notary's wife and the magistrate's wife probably wished to show, as everybody does, that while there may have been certain things that they lacked—some of the old lady's prerogatives, and a relationship with her—it was not because they couldn't have them but because they didn't want them. But the sad thing was that, in seeking only to convince others of this, they had ended up convincing themselves. And it was the suppression of all desire, all curiosity for forms of life that one does not know, the hope of being liked by new people, the effort made to be liked, replaced in these ladies by simulated disdain, by feigned cheerfulness, that had the drawback of making them mask their displeasure as contentment and constantly lie to themselves: two reasons why they were unhappy. But everybody in that hotel probably acted in the same way as they did, even if under different forms, and sacrificed if not to their own pride as those ladies did, at least to certain principles of education, or to certain intellectual habits, the delicious agitation to be found in getting mixed up in a stranger's life, in pursuing the object of one's desires, in seducing, in growing attached, by reinventing oneself, to the mysterious sympathy of new beings. No doubt the microcosm in which the aristocratic old lady was isolated was not poisoned by such virulent bitterness as the one where the magistrate's clan gloated, sneering its rage.[4] But it was scented with a fine, old-fashioned perfume of politeness that was no less false. I liked to think that perhaps deep within her she had sensitivity and imagination and that the charm of an unknown person might have had a more profound effect upon her, that the pleasure without mystery to be found in frequenting only people of one's own world and in reminding oneself that this world is the best there is; who knows whether it was not in thinking that had she arrived incognito at the hotel {f. 214}, going more or less unnoticed or being considered a figure of

4. *Sic.*

fun with her black wool dress and her unfashionable hat, if seeing her in the lobby a boisterous young man whom she thought rather handsome—like the one this year who lost all his money gambling—would even have snickered from his rocking chair "What a pauper!" or if some worthy man with salt-and-pepper hair, like the chief magistrate, and a wholesome face and spiritual eyes, the type she liked best, would, smiling, have pointed out to his wife this bizarre sight, upon which she would have turned (not bad-temperedly) the lens of her lorgnette like a precision instrument, who knows if it was not out of fear of that first minute which everyone knows to be brief but which is no less dreaded anyway—like the first toe dipped in the water—that this lady sent a servant ahead of her to make the hotel aware of her imminent arrival, of her personality and her habits, and that emerging from her car she advanced rapidly between her chambermaid and her footman, cutting short the greetings of the hotel manager with a curtness in which he saw arrogance but in which there was perhaps only shyness. Quickly she gained her room where, her personal curtains having taken the place of those that were hanging at the windows, the screens and photographs and trinkets she'd brought with her having built, between herself and the outside world to which she would have had to adapt, the dividing wall of her habits, it was her home in which she stayed that traveled, rather than she herself. Subsequently, having placed between herself and the hotel's staff, the suppliers, her own staff who in her place received the painful or charming contact with this new humanity and maintained around their mistress her accustomed atmosphere, having put her prejudices between herself and the other tourists, strangers, and bathers, unworried about upsetting people whom her friends would not have received, it was in her own world that she continued to live, through correspondence sent and received, through memory, through the private awareness that she had of her situation, the quality of her manners, the proficiency of her politeness. And every day when she went downstairs to take a tour in her horse-drawn carriage, her chambermaid carrying her belongings behind her, her footman walking out in front of her {f. 215} seemed like those guards flying the flag of the country they represent who, at the gates of an embassy, guaranteed for her on foreign soil the privilege of her extraterritoriality. She did not come down from her room and we did not see her in the dining room that first day [. . .]. But after a while we did see there a squire and his daughter [. . .]. {f. 216} [. . .] And of course in the desire for isolation that drove the rich young man, his mistress, and his two friends to always travel together, to always take their meals after everyone else had eaten, there was no bitterness or malice toward others and consequently no unpleasant feelings or bitter aftertaste for they themselves. But only the demands of a taste that they had for certain witty forms of conversation, for certain elegant refinements, which made it unbearable for them to share a life with people who had not been initiated into those tastes. Even at a dinner table or a gaming table where such knowledge had no use, each of them needed to be sure that inside the guest or the partner who sat facing him there lay dormant a certain knowledge that would enable them to recognize the junk in which so many Parisian hotels deck themselves out to look authentically "medieval" or "Renaissance," the subtlety of mind that prevents them enjoying an idiotic pun, an experience of polite society that allows them to instantly detect any pretentious or common manners, in short a criterium common to all of them for distinguishing between the good and the bad in all things. It was probably in those moments only at some rare and amusing interjection made amid the silence of the meal or the card game, or in the charming new dress that the young actress had put on for lunch or to play poker with those three men, always the same, that was manifested the special life in which the little society of friends wished to remain immersed wherever they went. But by enveloping them in habits that they knew by heart already, that life also protected them against the mystery of the unknown life of people and of things. During the long afternoons that they spent playing cards, the sea hung before them like a pleasantly colored painting hung in the boudoir of some rich bachelor, and it was only in a pause between two hands that one of the players, having nothing better to do, glanced up toward it in search of an indication of the weather or the time, and reminded the others that it was time for tea. They felt the same way about the countryside as they did about the sea and about people. And in the evenings when they went out to eat, the road lined with apple trees that leads out of Cricquebec was for them merely a distance to be traveled—in the black night barely distinguishable from the distance that separated their Parisian dwellings from

the Café Anglais or Le Joseph—before arriving at an elegant, rustic restaurant where they ate their fine dinner, and where while the friends of the
rich young man envied him having such a well-dressed mistress, the mistress's scarves stretched out before the little society like a perfumed,
supple veil that separated it from the world.

{f. 217} Unfortunately for my tranquility I was nothing like those people,
and I worried about many of them; I wouldn't have wanted to be despised
by them; back then, I had not yet had the comfort of discovering the character traits of Swann who, if he'd summoned his mistress from Paris to take
out on her the desire inspired in him by an unknown woman, would have
thought he didn't believe in that desire, a particular reality for which
one could not substitute an[other].

Critical Apparatus

NATHALIE MAURIAC DYER

Commentary

Their disappearance, the fruitless investigations carried out by several generations of researchers since the early 1960s . . . all of this has imprinted the "seventy-five folios" with a particular aura of mystery. The manuscripts that the Proust aficionado Bernard de Fallois (1926–2018) kept about his person for more than half a century were not the least remarkable of the writer's oeuvre. The "seventy-five folios" are the foundation of *In Search of Lost Time*. Proust had carefully kept them, as he did most of his manuscripts. He wrote them between the first months and the fall of 1908[1] and continued to refer to them until at least 1912. They accompanied him throughout all his changes of residence, from boulevard Haussmann to the sad rue Hamelin.

With their entry into the Bibliothèque nationale de France, it is as if the immense ship of the "Proust collection," all at sea for decades, has finally reached land. Proust did not know it yet, but this was the beginning of *In Search of Lost Time.* In these pages, surprising the novel's characters at an unknown moment of their "revolution," we recognize, at once strange and familiar, the grandmother in the garden, the evening kiss, the bedtime drama, the walks to Méséglise and Guermantes, the farewell to the hawthorns, the lessons of the two "ways," the portrait of Swann, the bedroom in Balbec, the clientele of the Grand Hotel, the three trees in Hudimesnil, the little "gang" of young girls, the poetry of names, the death of the grandmother, the posthumous dreams, Venice, and other episodes besides . . . A *Search* before the letter,[2] in short, even if Charlus and Albertine, Sodom and Gomorrah do not yet figure. (Sodom, however, is not really absent, just cloaked in allusions.)[3]

---

1. But they were perhaps prepared in late 1907. See the Chronology.
2. I borrow the expression from Bertrand Marchal.
3. See below, p. 218 *sq.*

If the existence of the "seventy-five folios" was already known, it is thanks entirely to Bernard de Fallois, who devoted a page to them in his 1954 preface to *Contre Sainte-Beuve*. That page merits rereading.[4] It states the essential truth, namely that Proust, after *Jean Santeuil* but before *Contre Sainte-Beuve*, had started writing a novel again, "in a personal form this time" (i.e., in the first person). This is not an insignificant point, and the "seventy-five folios" would perhaps have merited, even then, publication in their own right. But Fallois preferred to turn to the draft notebooks, which were also hitherto unseen back then in the early 1950s, and he invented what he himself admitted was only "the dream of a book, an idea for a book":[5] *Contre Sainte-Beuve*. Logically, there was no place in that volume for the "seventy-five folios," which—as Fallois himself said— belonged to another, earlier writing project. But, probably because he could not completely resist their charms, he included about fifteen pages from the "seventy-five folios" in *Contre Sainte-Beuve*.[6] He did so surreptitiously, but by quoting in his preface the note from the 1908 Carnet in which Proust briefly described the contents, he allowed attentive readers to guess what he had done.

In 1962, the numerous manuscripts that Robert Proust had inherited from his brother and bequeathed to his daughter Suzy Mante-Proust entered

---

4. The "group [of manuscripts] consists of seventy-five folios, in a very large format, and includes six episodes that would all be reworked in *Search:* these are the description of Venice, the visit to Balbec, the encounter with the young girls, bedtime in Combray, the poetry of names, and the two 'ways.' This ensemble is clearly indicated by a note in the agenda [here Fallois provides the contents of the note from f. 7v of Carnet 1: see the Chronology]. With the exception of *Jean Santeuil*, it is the oldest draft of *Search*. Guermantes here is called Villebon. Swann does not exist: his role is shared between the narrator's uncle, and for the evenings in Combray a certain M. de Bretteville. The young girls in flower are sketched out by two *fillettes*. And Balbec does not yet have a name. There is no mention of Sainte-Beuve in these episodes and we would not have brought them up here did they not contain three important pieces of information: firstly, they give us proof that Proust had begun a new draft of his novel, in a personal form this time, before starting *Sainte-Beuve*. Next, because these episodes constitute a store of details on which he would draw constantly to expand his work. Lastly, because on folios of the same format, in identical handwriting, we find a piece about twenty pages long, which is the essay on Sainte-Beuve" (*CSB*, p. 14).

5. Ibid., p. 26.

6. Today ff. 20–26 and 75–81. *CSB*, pp. 291–297 and 273–283.

the Bibliothèque nationale de France.[7] But not all of them. In particular, curators and researchers noted, not without surprise, that the "seventy-five folios" described by Fallois in his preface and partially reprinted in *Contre Sainte-Beuve* were not included. The mystery, soon to become the myth, of the "seventy-five folios" of 1908 was born.

There is always a form of artifice in the posthumous publication of manuscripts, in other words of documents that their author chose not to publish in that form. It is probably greater in the case of *Contre Sainte-Beuve*, which exists only as a result of choices made by its successive editors regarding the fragments and their assembly, giving rise to the artifact. The "seventy-five folios," even if we do not know in what order their author arranged the pages (or even if he arranged them at all), have the advantage of appearing to be a homogeneous, clearly circumscribed whole. Proust certainly considered them an ensemble in their own right.[8] They belong to the novel, even if they are not yet "a" novel. The "solidarity of the parts"[9] that characterizes *In Search of Lost Time,* in which a highly organized system of preparations and echoes, rhymes and reminders, saturates the text, was the result of about fifteen years of patient composition. Proust first worked on a series of independent sections, which he then juxtaposed: in the "seventy-five folios" (and, from the following year, in the draft notebooks), they are still enclosed as if in different rooms, with no communicating doors between them. The slow work of weaving and assembling would come later.

Even so, we can guess that the first "chapter," [An Evening in the Countryside], is already the product of the careful stitching of pieces that were previously separate,[10] and already Proust is trying to weave a few connections: the portrait of the health-obsessed grandmother could pave the way for the visit to the seaside; in that chapter, too, the character of the uncle,

---

7. For the history of the collection, see Fau 2013.

8. This can be deduced from the note "Pages Written" in Carnet 1, f. 7v, quoted by Fallois (*CSB*, p. 14), even if this note only designated, for the most part, the antecedent texts (see the Chronology). In the absence of a title, we name them here the "seventy-five folios."

9. Letter to Paul Souday, November 10, 1919. *Corr.,* XVIII, p. 464.

10. See the Chronology, and f. 1.

already well drawn in [An Evening in the Countryside], reveals another unexpected aspect of his personality; in Venice, the gondola rides "recall"
the walking of the "ways" . . . Sometimes the author even intervenes, prom-
ising us future developments.[11] But the narrative horizon imagined by
Proust escapes us.[12] As does what he wanted to do with these pages on the
Parisian literary scene, although publication in *Le Figaro,* as was still de
rigueur for many novels, may have crossed his mind. Such an approach
could be suggested by various appeals, direct or indirect, to the "reader";[13]
it could also have been inspired by his then-recent journalistic triumphs:
three brilliant articles in 1907.[14] Temporarily setting aside his novel project
at the start of 1908, he turned again toward *Le Figaro* for his literary
pastiches—it was another way of attracting attention to himself as a writer
and of clearing the way for his own book.

But the seventy-five or seventy-six folios that he assembled did not sat-
isfy Proust, who in the fall of 1908 set them aside and began reading the
works of Sainte-Beuve. The conventionally crafted essay that he began
against the critic's method[15] metamorphosed into another personal account: "Maman would come close to my bed and I would tell her about an
article I wanted to write on Sainte-Beuve."[16] He abandoned the loose sheets
on which he had begun his essay—some in the same format as the "seventy-
five folios"—and began to write in school notebooks, immediately drawing,

11. F. 64.
12. Perhaps, for example, he was planning to develop the scene sketches noted early
in 1908 in Carnet 1: "In the 2nd part of the novel the young girl will be ruined, I will
keep her without seeking to possess her due to inability to be happy."; "in the second part
young girl ruined, kept without enjoying her [. . .] due to inability to be loved" (Carnet 1,
ff. 3 and 3v; *Cn*, pp. 34–35).
13. See particularly the beginning of folio 53, which suggests an "end-of-the-holidays"
chronicle in a newspaper whose readers had gone on vacation.
14. "Filial Sentiments of a Parricide," "Reading Days," and "Impressions of the Road
from an Automobile," which appeared in *Le Figaro* on, respectively, February 1, March 20,
and November 19, 1907. Also in *Le Figaro*, there appeared "*Les Éblouissements*," a review
of Anna de Noailles's poetry collection (June 15, 1907), and two obituaries, "A Grandmother" (July 23, 1907) and "Gustave de Borda" (December 26, 1907).
15. I refer to the seminal works of Claudine Quémar (1976) and of Anthony Pugh
(1987). See also the clarification by Leriche 2012.
16. [Late November or first half of December 1908], letter to Georges de Lauris.
Lettres, pp. 465–466. See also the letter to Anna de Noailles, ibid., p. 466.

here and there, on details and inspiration from the novel of the previous months for his new project. [17] The writing of the morning preceding Maman's arrival, and of the night preceding that morning, brought about the appearance of a character who, during his nocturnal half-awakenings (at the time when he still went to bed early), fooled by the position of his body, remembered bedrooms where he had lived before: without seeking it, Proust had found the "opening" that had been missing from his recent attempt at a novel. In the spring of 1909, it was within this retrospective framework that he "recycled" not only fragments but whole pages of the "seventy-five folios": the evening kiss, the walks along the "ways," and the start of the visit to the seaside.[18] From a single source—the memory of the bedrooms—he began to weave together those abandoned narrative threads.

The crucial creation, also in Notebook 4, is that of "M. Swann."[19] As, five years later (in 1913), the musician Vinteuil would be born from the fusion of the naturalist Vington and the composer Berget, Swann was a composite: he brought together two characters from the "seventy-five folios"—M. de Bretteville, the evening visitor and third wheel, and the narrator's womanizing uncle.[20] In Notebook 4, his character is immediately fleshed out, far beyond the character of the maternal uncle, explicitly introducing to the nascent novel the question of Jewishness. In 1908, in the "seventy-five folios," Proust had not yet reached that point.

How can we describe the encounter produced in Notebook 4? Should we call it a reciprocal "contamination" of the two projects, a "transplant," or the "explosion" of *Contre Sainte-Beuve* under pressure from the "seventy-five

17. See in Notebook 3 the motif of the insolent young girls (Other Manuscripts, no. VIII), in Notebook 2 the remarks on love affairs during travels (f. 60), in Notebook 5 the Guermantes family portrait (f. 82), in Notebook 1 the lilacs on the walks (Other Manuscripts, no. XI). Fallois had said, without going into further detail, that Proust had "draw[n] constantly" from the "seventy-five folios" to "expand his work" (*CSB*, p. 14).

18. Notebook 4. See Other Manuscripts, no. XII.

19. See Leriche 2013, pp. 23–25.

20. Fallois had indicated this, but in a way that was difficult to understand, given the inaccessibility of the "seventy-five folios": "Swann does not exist: his role is shared between the narrator's uncle, and for the evenings in Combray a certain M. de Bretteville" (*CSB*, p. 14). Proust acknowledged the role of Charles Haas in the character's genesis, but never that of his uncle Louis Weil. See *Corr.*, XII, p. 387; XVI, p. 321; XIX, p. 660.

folios"? We could also see in it the happy confluence of two rivers, one of which would reveal itself to be far more powerful. In this writer who had described himself as having "no imagination,"[21] fiction ultimately triumphed over the autobiographical and autofictional elements.

In 1909, then, the "seventy-five folios" were given new life: they would accompany Proust until 1912, from *Contre Sainte-Beuve, souvenir d'une matinée* to the birth of "Intermittences of the Heart." The trace of their presence is visible even now in the definitive text of *In Search of Lost Time*.[22] We didn't know this before, because "the luxuriant grass of fertile works, on which generations will cheerfully come, without a thought for those who sleep beneath, to eat their 'luncheon on the grass,'"[23] had grown over them.

Adèle, Jeanne, and Marcel

One of the great surprises of the "seventy-five folios" is the sheer amount of manifestly autobiographical material. This can be summed up in three names: Adèle, Jeanne, and Marcel.

"Adèle" appears three times in the first "chapter," and it was there in the antecedent text too;[24] "Jeanne" and "Marcel" each appear just once.[25] Adèle was the name of Marcel Proust's maternal grandmother, née Berncastell[26] (1824–1890), wife of Nathé Weil (1814–1896); Jeanne was his mother's name—Jeanne Clémence Weil (1849–1905), Mme Adrien Proust, daughter of Adèle. Never before had we seen Proust—not in his correspon-

---

21. "All is fictional, laboriously since I have no imagination [. . .]" (Carnet 1, f. 16v; *Cn*, p. 59).

22. See the Table of Concordance below.

23. *TR*, IV, p. 615.

24. Other Manuscripts, no. III. There are other autobiographical clues in this draft.

25. Ff. 10, 25.

26. Most biographies spell her surname "Berncastel." But it is "Berncastell" on her birth and marriage certificates (Digital Archives of Paris), on her death certificate, and on the monument in Père-Lachaise (for which, see Compagnon 2020, p. 14). She signed the marriage certificate for her daughter and Adrien Proust with the name "A. Berncastell" (see a reproduction in Wise 2017, p. 80). See also Proust noting "Berncastell" in Carnet 1, ff. 34v, 36v (*Cn*, pp. 90, 95).

dence, nor in his literary manuscripts—refer to his mother and his grandmother by their first names.

They would be removed. "Jeanne," the rarest of all, written only once,
would vanish immediately: from the notebooks for *Contre Sainte-Beuve* and
Search onward, she would never be anything other than "Maman" (Proust
always capitalized the initial M). "Adèle," the grandmother, would become
Cécile, then Octavie, and lastly Bathilde[27] (and for Françoise and more
customarily, from her husband's first name, "Mme Amédée").[28] As for
the name "Marcel," it remained in a few 1909 notebooks, then disappeared, only to reappear belatedly in the drafts of *The Captive*, where it
was tenderly spoken several times by Albertine-Agostinelli.[29] Upon rereading, Proust blurred it rather than removing it completely.[30]

Marcel Proust's maternal grandmother, Adèle Berncastell, a woman "wholly
transmitted to her children" according to her daughter Jeanne Proust,
quoting Mme de Sévigné to Marcel,[31] appears in the photographs that have
reached us to have a very gentle face, and yet she does not seem to have
sought or aroused unanimous approval among her family. This is what her
grandson wrote to her when he was twelve: "I wish you a happy holiday
[. . .] and no more teasing from maman, and no more impatience from grandfather and no more culinary discussions with my uncle or medical (hygiene) discussions with papa."[32] We must only add one word to a sentence
from "Combray" to describe the situation accurately: "she had brought to
my [*grand*]father's family a mind so different that everybody teased and

27. See Other Manuscripts, nos. IX and X.
28. *CS*, I, p. 101.
29. See f. 25.
30. See Mauriac Dyer 2006, pp. 72–75.
31. "Sometimes, reading Madame de Sévigné, I come across thoughts and expressions
that please me. She says [. . .]: 'I know another mother who hardly considers herself at all,
who is wholly *transmitted* to her children.' Isn't that true of your grandmother? Except
she, she wouldn't say it" (Letter from [April 23, 1890], *Corr.*, I, p. 138).
32. Letter from Marcel Proust to Mme Nathé Weil, [soon after August 3, 1883], *Corr.*,
XXI, p. 542; verified against a facsimile of the original, thanks to the kind agreement of
Caroline Szylowicz (Kolb-Proust Archive), whom I thank.

tormented her."[33] In the "seventy-five folios," Proust uses the same word, "discussions" (a "lively" discussion, a "tempestuous" discussion, a "recent" discussion),[34] to characterize what seems to have been a very tense relationship between Adèle and her brother-in-law Louis Weil.[35] Of course, according to the narrator, Adèle has an "elevated" moral character: with an "absolute devotion to others,"[36] she would be completely devoid of "pride, vanity."[37] And yet the traits that are attributed to her immediately afterward depict her rather as an eccentric unconcerned with the real needs of those around her: disastrous vacation plans, incomprehensibly quirky letters, a tyrannical obsession with health, repeated rudeness . . . Even if she is subject to the uncle's interminable sarcastic remarks, Adèle the grandmother of the "seventy-five folios" is certainly no victim: in their incessant squabbles,[38] she stands up to her brother-in-law and succeeds in exasperating him just as, when labeled the "great-aunt," she exasperated the "grandfather" in "On Reading."[39]

This woman with her "elevated mind"[40] can also be irritating to say the least, and her first appearance in the "seventy-five folios" is a degrading one: the image of her walking in a "horribly soiled" skirt.[41] The description is long, almost indulgent.[42] It contradicts the cowardly escape "to the bathroom" to which this painful vision, aggravated by the uncle's sarcastic remarks, is supposed to drive the young narrator. A trace of this would remain in *Sodom and Gomorrah,* when the hero, after his grandmother's death, remembers the woman "who once couldn't take two steps without

33. Cf. *CS*, I, p. 11. The phrase is "corrected" in this way, with *grandfather* instead of *father,* by D. Mayer (1984, p. 25) and E. Bloch-Dano (2004, p. 97). It appeared in Notebook 9, f. 32, in the cognac scene: "she had brought to my father's family a 'mentality' so different that everybody mocked and teased her."
34. Ff. 6 and 15. See also f. 5.
35. On Louis Weil, see below, p. 188 sq.
36. F. 2.
37. Ibid.
38. Ff. 2–3, 4, 5–6, 7, 15–16.
39. In culinary "discussions" (*PM*, pp. 163–164; see also Other Manuscripts, no. II).
40. F. 2.
41. Ibid.
42. Ibid.

soiling herself."[43] The term had disappeared from the walk in the garden by the time of the first draft notebook,[44] but the "mud stains" that replaced it are not free either of vulgar connotations, at least for a reader in the early twentieth century.[45] In the "seventy-five folios," the grandmother's "soaked" skirts suggest an image of defilement.[46]

In this rather complex and possibly composite portrait, which part is the "real" Adèle Berncastell? It is impossible to know, but it is notable that in the early pages Proust tries, as if to reduce the resemblance, to attribute some of her behavior (the extravagant excursions, the abstruse letters) to an "aunt."[47] In the next stage of the genesis, the grandmother remains "mad" in the eyes of the father, and "a bit nutty" as far as Françoise[48] is concerned, but some of her flaws would be reduced to a couple of lines (the extravagant excursions)[49] while others would disappear (the refusal to change her clothes) or would be redistributed to other characters (the taste for allusion to "my grandmother's sisters,"[50] the knocked-over vase to Bloch[51]). And in the fall of 1909 Proust would add the cruel episode of the cognac[52] as an opportunity to "motivate" the hero's flight to the toilet with

43. "[. . .] I left to walk alone toward that main road that Mme de Villeparisis's car used to take when we went walking with my grandmother; puddles of water, not dried by the shining sun, turned the ground into a real swamp, *and I thought of my grandmother who once couldn't take two steps without soiling herself.* But when I reached the road I stared in amazement. There where with my grandmother I had never seen, in August, more than the leaves and the trunks of the apple trees, now, as far as the eye could see, they were in full, luxurious bloom, dressed in ballgowns *with their feet in the mud, taking no precautions not to ruin the most glorious pink satin* ever seen as it shone in the sun [. . .]" (*SG*, III, p. 177; italics are ours).

44. Notebook 4, f. 24v (Other Manuscripts, no. XII); Notebook 8, ff. 14–15 (*CS, Sketch XII*, I, pp. 679–680); Notebook 9, f. 31; *CS*, I, p. 11.

45. *"Boue"* (mud or sludge) is a mix of earth and various excreta. See Alain Corbin, *Le miasme et la jonquille* (Paris: Flammarion, 1982 [1986]), p. 28; Antoine Compagnon, *Les Chiffonniers de Paris* (Paris: Gallimard, 2017), p. 61 sq.

46. F. 53.

47. Ff. 3–5.

48. See ff. 7, 15.

49. See f. 4.

50. See f. 4.

51. See f. 6.

52. Notebook 9, ff. 30v–31v, pages thereafter copied by Proust's secretary in ff. 32–35; *CS*, I, pp. 11–12. On this scene, see also p. 191.

its scent of irises, and to make the grandmother of the novel a victim in a way that she hadn't been before, that she had hardly been in the "seventy-five folios." The character traits that would be retained (her somewhat ridiculous health obsession) or would be added (her questionable taste for "higher degrees of art," which rather distorts judgment)[53] would be compensated with positive elements: the grandmother becoming the sweet and tender woman who, in Balbec, rescues her grandson from his anxiety. Her death scene would make her a tragic, moving, and—above all—a pure character. But all of this she would owe to Jeanne Proust.

The portrait of "Maman," Jeanne Clémence Weil (1849–1905), Marcel Proust's beloved mother—"what I loved most on earth"[54]—is marked in the "seventy-five folios" by pathos and suffering. We knew how crucial the scene of the evening kiss was: one of the earliest scenes in Proust's novel, he wrote it again and again. The Fallois archives present us with three extra versions.

The earliest is the direct source of the scene in *Jean Santeuil*, and—surprisingly—is already written in the first person.[55] Next comes an important antecedent text to the version of the "seventy-five folios," which ends abruptly,[56] and to which we will return. The "seventy-five folios" version, the longest and most complete, is clearly the matrix of the definitive version, which Proust patiently continued to refine until 1913 in several draft notebooks, then in typed versions and proofs. But the version in the "seventy-five folios" differs substantially from all those known versions, both in terms of what is there and what isn't.

In terms of what isn't there: here, the father merely intervenes when the mother behaves tenderly toward her son—"just then my father turned around in a fury: 'come on Jeanne this is ridiculous'"—and, as in *Jean Santeuil*, it is the mother's decision (and the mother's fault?) to finally give

53. *CS*, I, p. 40.
54. Letter to François, Viscount of Paris, June 12, 1908, *Corr.*, VIII, p. 136.
55. Other Manuscripts, no. I. This version dates from the fall of 1895 at the earliest.
56. Other Manuscripts, no. III. It is possible that this version was preceded by that "something [. . .] on Maman" that Proust admitted in a 1906 letter to Lucien Daudet having "started," and which "is all about her" ([early June 1906], *Corr.*, VI, p. 100).

in to the little boy and go into his bedroom. It was during the rewriting of the "seventy-five folios" that the father, overtaken by a sudden and surprising magnanimity, encouraged the mother to spend the night in the child's room ("come on we're his parents not his torturers").[57] The "seventy-five folios" version also does not include Maman reading to her son from one of George Sand's pastoral novels, the climax of their night of intimacy, which also appeared in 1909[58] and would be rewritten and refined until the galley proofs of *Swann's Way*.

But the "seventy-five folios" version of the evening kiss scene is even more surprising in terms of what Proust added to it, and what he would later remove: its hostile decor, for a start. The reader will recognize a first sketch of the inhospitable hotel room that adds to the hero's anguish on the evening of his first arrival in Balbec.[59] Perhaps out of a concern for plausibility (the bedroom in a family home, even if you have just arrived there "a few days before,"[60] could hardly appear so strange), the following year Proust transformed this country-house bedroom into a banal, familiar place and transferred the hostile decor to the seaside hotel room.[61] We first discover it through the memory of the woken sleeper at the beginning of "Combray," after the various bedrooms of the past have finished parading through the insomniac's mind, and the contrast between the bedrooms in Combray with their "grainy, pollinated, edible and pious" atmosphere and those of the Grand Hotel in Balbec will become paradigmatic.[62]

It is true that, in the antecedent text of *Jean Santeuil*, the torture of bedtime is related to the experience of spending the night in a strange bedroom.[63] Was it the one in Cabourg that supplied Proust with the striking physical details that enabled him, in the "seventy-five folios," to embody what had until then been an abstract malaise: that heady smell of vetiver,

57. Notebook 6, f. 47; *CS, Sketch X*, I, p. 675. In the rest of this scene, the father acquires the stature of a biblical patriarch: see Notebook 8, f. 40; *CS, Sketch XII*, I, p. 692.

58. Notebook 6, ff. 43–51; *CS, Sketch X*, I, pp. 673–677.

59. *JF*, II, pp. 27–28.

60. F. 13.

61. See f. 13; Notebook 8, ff. 6, 7–8, and 6v; *CS, Sketch IV*, I, pp. 655–657.

62. *CS*, I, p. 8 and p. 376.

63. Other Manuscripts, no. I; *JS*, pp. 209–210.

that loudly ticking clock, those red curtains (which would turn purple), even the candelabras? A note written in Carnet 1 after his arrival in Cabourg in 1908 could suggest it: "Smell of a room, the body isn't used to it, and suffers, the soul notices."[64] In any case, it is to Cabourg that we can trace the "square mirror" that would be added to the decor of the room in Querqueville/Balbec after the "seventy-five folios," when that room was moved to the seaside. That square mirror evokes the one in the Hotel Splendide in Evian where Proust took one last tragic vacation with his mother in September 1905, during which she suffered from the bout of uremia that would take her life. The memory of this is noted in Carnet 1 just after his arrival in Cabourg, on July 18, 1908, with the exclamation point—something Proust used only very sparingly—a sure indication of his emotion: "Maman rediscovered during journey, arrival in Cabourg, same room as in Evian, the square mirror!"[65] This mirror would return again, associated a little farther on in Carnet 1 with the pyramidal shape of the bedroom in Dieppe that, according to an early draft, the hero shared with his mother:[66] "Bedroom with pyramid-shaped ceiling, hard mirror."[67] Even if the hostile bedroom is no longer the one where the bedtime drama played out, it remains connected to Maman, both through those secretly poignant details of decoration and because it was another maternal figure who, in Balbec, saved the young boy from asphyxiation.[68] It is easy to understand why "Intermittences of the Heart" was set in Querqueville (Balbec) from its very first version.

Of course, there had never been any doubt that the grandmother of the novel, whose death scene forms the most poignant chapter of *In Search of*

---

64. F. 8v. *Cn*, p. 45.

65. F. 5v. *Cn*, p. 39.

66. See Notebook 1, f. 60v: "I am in this bedroom, convalescing, and Maman sleeps close to me." There is a record of Proust staying in Dieppe as a child in September 1880 and September 1881, the second time most likely in the company of his grandmother Adèle (*Corr.*, I, p. 95; XXI, p. 541).

67. Carnet 1, f. 10. *Cn*, p. 48.

68. "Deprived of a world, of a bedroom, my body menaced by the enemies that surrounded me, shaking to my bones with fever, I was alone, I wanted to die. Just then my grandmother entered and, as my pent-up heart expanded, vast spaces opened instantly around me" (*JF*, II, p. 28).

Lost Time, was a mask for Mme Proust. Even so, it is striking, and touching, to see the death of "Maman" herself mentioned in the "seventy-five folios," further darkening the scene of the bedtime drama. This occurs in the space of two events that follow in quick succession with almost no transition, and which would have two contrasting genetic fates. First there is the description of a "face of adorable purity" that Proust, in a single phrase, leads to the ruin. of her reappearance on her "funeral bed"[69]— here we see the very first sketch of the grandmother of *Search,* "lying like a young girl" on that same "funeral bed."[70] Next comes a posthumous nightmare in which Maman, her body now heavy and ugly, "the hem of her dress [. . .] soiled" like the grandmother in the garden, is suffering, her son powerless to help her, and she cannot conceal her irritation toward him.[71] This anxiety dream would have a meandering genetic trajectory,[72] and Proust would end up cutting it while correcting the typed version of *Sodom and Gomorrah,* a few months before he died.[73] It is possible that guilt got the better of him, that the son recoiled before the idea of showing—in a work that was her mausoleum, even concealed by the identity of the grandmother—Maman humiliated with "a splash of mud up to her veil," Maman "irreconcilable," Maman shoved into the train "like a piece of luggage": a terrifying, hallucinatory, almost prophetic vision.

In the 1907 article "Filial Sentiments of a Parricide," Proust depicted himself, and all sons, as their mothers' murderers.[74] The drafts of that

69. F. 17.

70. *CG,* II, pp. 640–641; see f. 17.

71. F. 18. The bedtime scene enters the logic of the dream: this is how the little boy hidden in the shadows calls his mother and is able to touch her.

72. Rendered even more tragic when it was first rewritten, in 1910, as part of "Intermittences of the Heart" in Querqueville (Notebook 65; Other Manuscripts, no. XVI), it was then set on the return train journey from Italy with Maman, after the erotic adventure with Baroness Putbus's chambermaid (Notebook 50), before returning to Balbec, in *Sodom and Gomorrah.* See f. 18.

73. See *SG,* III, p. 368 var. *a* [pp. 1553–1554]. Proust replaced it with a long, recently written, scientific essay on deep sleep. Ibid., p. 370 and note 1 by A. Compagnon; see also Compagnon 1992, p. 60.

74. "'What have you done to me? What have you done to me?' If we think about it, there is perhaps no truly loving mother who couldn't, on her last day, or often long before that, address this reproach to her son. As we get older, we kill everything we love with the

article were written on mourning letter paper,[75] the very same he had used to write grief-stricken notes to his friends just after his mother's death. In the "seventy-five folios," it is the son's simple involuntary resemblance to his mother when he feels desire, when he reaches orgasm, that is profane (Proust struggles to even write the word correctly, and spells it "pronafation"): "The face of a son who lives, a monstrance where a beautiful dead mother placed all her faith, is like a profanation of that sacred memory. [. . .] Because it was with that sublime line of his mother's nose that his own nose was made, because it was with his mother's smile that he seduced girls into debauchery [. . .]."[76] It is the face of a Jewish mother that is profaned, for how can we not recognize, in "that sublime line of his mother's nose," "the sublime lines of her Jewish face," the lines written about Maman-Esther in a Notebook for *Contre Sainte-Beuve* a year later?[77] Profanation, connected to Jewishness, is also connected to homosexuality, because it was about Charlus that Proust would write: "Sons, who do not always resemble their fathers, even without being inverts, even while chasing women, [. . .] perpetrate with their faces the profanation of their mothers."[78]

---

worries we give them, with the anxious tenderness that we inspire in them, constantly alarming them. If we could see in a beloved body the slow work of destruction carried out by the painful tenderness that animates it [. . .]" (*Le Figaro*, February 1, 1907; *PM*, pp. 158–159).

75. See Ritte 2017 and *Bulletin d'informations proustiennes*, no. 32 (2001–2002): 155. Other drafts of "Filial Sentiments . . ." were found in the Fallois archives; they were also written on mourning letter paper.

76. F. 81.

77. Notebook 2, f. 6; *CSB*, p. 128.

78. *SG*, III, p. 300, and note 1 by A. Compagnon (see also ID. 1989, chap. 6, "The Quiver of a Heart That Is Hurt," pp. 160–165). Proust went on: "But let us leave here what would deserve a chapter of its own: profaned mothers" (ibid.). He never published this "chapter of its own," although in reality he had already addressed the subject in the scene at Montjouvain where Mlle Vinteuil can only reach orgasm after first spitting on the portrait of her father. Even if Proust inverted the roles, it is clear that a profaned mother looms behind the profaned father in this scene: "what she profaned, what she used for her pleasures but what remained between them and herself and prevented her tasting them directly, was her resemblance to her father, *his mother's blue eyes* that he had passed on to her like a family jewel [. . .]" (*CS*, I, p. 162). Italics are ours.

Guilt does not prevent (can, in fact, provoke) ambivalence. The painful wait for Maman's kiss, its brevity, give rise to incomprehension and resentment toward that "beautiful face so gentle, so cruel in not wanting to remove this torment from her little boy's life."[79] Difficulty breathing is directly associated with separation anxiety: ". . . starting to pant because I felt so lonely and separated from her."[80] In the episode of "Robert and the goat" that follows the bedtime drama scene without any solution for continuity, the announced separation between Maman and Marcel sends him into a delirium of persecution and violent impulses.[81] And it is just after the description of Maman's "adorable" face that her face appears "red with fatigue" in the dream where she shares the grandmother's humiliation of being soiled and mistreated. What is unique in the "seventy-five folios," and which obviously couldn't be maintained in later versions, is the juxtaposition of those two images of Maman.

The Three Metamorphoses of Uncle Louis

There can be little doubt regarding the identities of Adèle, Jeanne, and Marcel, and the same is true for the identity of the "old uncle" who, in the antecedent text, owns the house "in Auteuil" where the whole family lives: this is Lazard[82] Baruch, a.k.a. Louis, Weil (1816–1896), son of Baruch Weil and his second wife Marguerite Sara Nathan, Proust's maternal great-uncle and the younger brother of Proust's grandfather, Nathé Weil (1814–1896).[83] In the "seventy-five folios" he became "my great-uncle"[84]

79. F. 7.
80. Ibid.
81. Ff. 24, 25.
82. Lazard and not "Lazare," as it is sometimes spelled. See the death certificate, written on May 11, 1896 (Digital Archives of Paris, V4E 8723, certificate no. 860), as well as the register of burials at Père-Lachaise, May 12 (id., CPL_RA18951899_01, p. 556).
83. "Louis Weil" signed the birth certificate of "Valentin, Louis, Georges, Eugène, Marcel Proust," and it was probably in his honor that Proust was given the second of these names—it would have been more usual, after naming him after his paternal grandfather (Valentin) to give second place to his other grandfather, Nathé, but, as was the case with Lazard, that name could have complicated the planned Catholic baptism. Georges was the name of his maternal uncle, Eugène that of his godfather, Eugène Mutiaux.
84. F. 1.

(in accordance with his place in the line of descendance), then systemati-
cally "my uncle" (which, based on correspondence, seems to have been
what he was called by the family).[85] It was in Louis Weil's home, 96, rue La
Fontaine, that Marcel Proust was born in 1871, followed two years later by
his brother Robert.

But Auteuil is named only in the sketch of the evening kiss scene: "Every
summer evening in Auteuil, when after dinner they would sit out in the
garden, I had to go upstairs to bed. My heart sank at the thought of leaving
Maman [. . .]."[86] In the "seventy-five folios" version, the "precious wicker
armchairs" that are brought inside to protect them from the rain, already
present in the sketch, are the only clue to this being Uncle Louis's house.
Proust would mention that "Auteuil of his childhood" only once more—in
1919, in the preface to Jacques-Émile Blanche's *Propos de peintre*—and
without ever again referencing the memory of the maternal kiss.[87] Combray, which did not yet exist in 1908, would bring together the memories
of Auteuil (the maternal way) and those of Illiers (the paternal way), but
"Combray I" would secretly remain the Auteuil way.

Louis Weil was a successful button manufacturer, at the Trelon-Weldon-
Weil factory (from 1845), which became the Trelon-Weldon-Weil-Hartog
and Marchand factory in 1865.[88] His death notice indicates that the
"former manufacturer" was a Knight of the Legion of Honor, an honorary
member of the Committee of Customs Values, and a former member of the
CNE bank.[89] Unfortunately his dossier at the archives of the Legion of Honor
is almost empty,[90] probably because Louis Weil's nomination dates from
August 8, 1870, in other words at the very end of the Second Empire.
Curiously, Dr. Adrien Proust was named a Knight in exactly the same year

85. See *Corr.*, I, pp. 102, 110, 137, 141, passim.

86. Other Manuscripts, no. III.

87. *EA*, p. 570. See also pp. 572–573: "That house where we lived with my uncle, in
Auteuil in the middle of a large garden that was cut in two by the opening of the street
(from Avenue Mozart), was as bereft of taste as is possible."

88. Source: "Trelon Weldon Weil," Wikipedia; Bloch-Dano 2004, p. 89.

89. *Corr.*, II, p. 62 note 2.

90. Base Léonore, online. The dossier contains traces of a posthumous investigation
by the Police Prefecture of Paris on June 26, 1912, at 68, boulevard Haussmann, which
the administration mistakenly believed to be his house, rather than number 102.

group (his dossier had time to grow as he was promoted to the grades of Officer and then Commander), with the two nominations, which came from the same ministry, occurring a few weeks before the union of the Weil and Proust families.[91]

Louis Weil was a generous man who regularly hosted his family in his large house with garden at 96, rue La Fontaine. Little Marcel Proust probably lived there during the years 1872 and 1873, when Dr. Adrien Proust was head of department at the Sainte-Périne hospice,[92] only ten minutes' walk from the uncle's house (by way of rue de Perchamps).[93] They stayed there frequently until Louis Weil's death in 1896. A childless widower, he bequeathed most of his fortune to his nephew Georges Weil and his niece Jeanne Proust, including his house in Auteuil (which they quickly sold) and the building at 102, boulevard Haussmann in Paris.[94] After his mother's death, Marcel Proust finally moved there in December 1906, and it was there that he wrote the "seventy-five folios" and most of *In Search of Lost Time:* "[. . .] I have sublet an apartment in our house on boulevard Haussmann where I often went to eat dinner with Maman, where together we watched my old uncle die in the bedroom that I will occupy."[95] That same year he would refer to this "old uncle"—an old uncle whose place he had taken—as "a less rich Nucingen," a way of suggesting both a fondness for prostitutes and perhaps a certain credulity.[96]

We learn from the "seventy-five folios" that the role of uncle Weil was more important than previously thought in the genesis of *Search.* He shows three

91. Base Léonore, online. The two promotions were made "on the report of the Ministry of Agriculture and Commerce," which makes sense for Louis Weil, "button manufacturer," but also for Adrien Proust, "medical doctor in Paris," who was at the time returning from an important healthcare information mission in the East, expedited by that ministry (see Panzac 2003, pp. 33, 58).

92. Panzac 2003, pp. 104–105.

93. Even if, officially, Adrien Proust's family was then domiciled in Paris, on rue Roy. They moved to boulevard Malesherbes when Dr. Proust was transferred to the Saint-Antoine hospital.

94. Duchêne 2004, p. 673.

95. *Corr.*, VI, pp. 230–231.

96. Ibid., p. 326. See Balzac, *A Harlot High and Low.*

faces, only one of which—the last—was known before: the uncle in Auteuil, exasperated by his sister-in-law Adèle; the womanizing uncle on vacation; and, lastly, Uncle Adolphe in "Combray."

The host of the house in Auteuil is part of a comedy double-act with his
sister-in-law Adèle. His attempts at acerbic comments hardly seem to af-
fect her at all. But that particular uncle soon disappeared.[97] When Proust
rewrote these pages in *Contre Sainte-Beuve* as it was in the process of becoming *Search*, he would remove this comic couple and replace them with
two others: the grandmother and the father, arguing over the children's education[98] (and in *Search* the father makes several other cutting remarks to
his mother-in-law);[99] and, in a discussion about the gardener (which was
soon cut), the couple formed by the grandmother and the aunt, or great-
aunt.[100] However, the antagonism between the uncle and the grandmother
reappeared when "Combray" was being revised. At this point Proust introduced a scene mirroring the vanished scene from the "seventy-five folios" where the great-uncle taunts his sister-in-law for her soiled dress: this
is the scene where he torments her by encouraging her husband to drink
cognac, and this scene too ends with the hero running away.[101] When he
corrected the typed version of this passage, Proust again substituted the
great-aunt for the great-uncle[102]—at the moment when he grafted the cognac scene onto the garden walk scene, the story was no longer taking place

97. Although he did make an appearance in *Jean Santeuil:* see Other Manuscripts,
no. II.

98. Notebook 8, f. 14; cf. *CS*, I, p. 11. The disagreement between the father and the
grandmother is introduced during the walk in the rain, when the father is telling his son
to go inside.

99. See *JF*, I, p. 431 and II, p. 7.

100. Other Manuscripts, nos. IX and X.

101. Notebook 9, ff. 30v–31v, pages then copied by Proust's secretary in ff. 32–34.

102. NAF 16733, ff. 23–24; *CS*, I, pp. 11–12. There remains a trace, perhaps involuntary, of the former presence of the uncle in the cognac scene when, in *The Guermantes
Way*, a young actress is preyed on by a cabal: "I tried hard to make myself think no more
about that incident than I had about my grandmother's suffering when my great-uncle, to
tease her, made my grandfather drink cognac" (*CG*, II, p. 471). In the early notebooks,
the uncle generally had a cruel role: we find him, in competition with the parish priest
and a "private tutor," pulling the hero's hair in his dreams (Notebook 5, ff. 114v, 112v;
CS, Sketch II.i, I, p. 649); giving a "sales patter" for the magic lantern in a passage
crossed out during the revision of "Combray" (Notebook 9, f. 25); and briefly taking the

at the uncle's house "in the country," but at the great-aunt's house,[103] even if the grandfather and the grandparents would compete for the honor at the start of "Combray."[104]

However, this eviction of the uncle—split in two and reincarnated as the great-aunt and the father—was accompanied by another change that proved hugely significant for the novel: the "other" uncle—not the uncle with his country house, but the womanizing uncle depicted on vacation—"became," through a merger with M. de Bretteville, Charles Swann.[105]

This can be seen in the first notebook where Swann appears: Notebook 4 from the spring of 1909. Now armed, thanks to a detour via *Contre Sainte-Beuve*, with the "opening" he had lacked before—the woken sleeper's memory of past bedrooms, enabling the author to set off on a number of narrative paths—Proust "tries out" most of the "seventy-five folios," inserting the walks along the "ways" in the middle of the evening kiss scene, and replacing the insipid M. de Bretteville with "M. Swann," of whom we are given the first—lengthy—portrait. It is at the end of this portrait that the character of the uncle is transferred to Swann: the narrator mentions those "letters" that Swann would send to his family, even after he was married, asking for an introduction to this or that woman, behind which lay "always some fleeting love affair."[106] The father's unkind ritual remark about the uncle in the "seventy-five folios"[107] was now echoed by the grandfather's words about Swann: the anti-Semitic barb, "On your guard!"[108]

---

place of the anti-Semitic grandfather (Notebook 8, ff. 18–20 [*CS, Sketch XII*, I, p. 681682], Notebook 9, ff. 39–42).

103. See Notebook 9, ff. 7 and 24; *CS*, I, p. 9.

104. Ibid., p. 6. The faltering genetic trajectory is interesting: first we read "at my grandparents' house" (Notebook 8, f. 6; *CS, Sketch IV*, I, p. 655), then in the fair copy "at my great-uncle's house," corrected as "my great-aunt's house" (Notebook 9, f. 7), and lastly, in the galley proofs, "at my grandfather's house" (*Bodmer*, galley proof 1, col. 5).

105. Fallois had suggested this in his preface but, without the corresponding pages from the "seventy-five folios," his remark made little impact (*CSB*, p. 14; see above, p. 178 note 4).

106. Notebook 4, f. 61; Other Manuscripts, no. XII.

107. F. 63.

108. In Notebook 4, it was unfortunately written on the torn bottom part of folio 61. But it is found in all the following stages after Notebook 69, f. 3 (Other Manuscripts, no. XV).

The narrator embarks upon the "services that [Swann] asked of his famous 'situation,'" but the expected resumption of the corresponding part of the "seventy-five folios," though anticipated by a connecting sentence ("I remember one year when we were at the seaside with my grandmother"),[109] does not occur. In all likelihood Proust realized that there was an implausibility in the narrative: the invention of Mlle Swann a few pages above in the same notebook presupposed that Swann was already married; it was hardly credible that the father of a girl more or less the same age as the hero would be pursuing love affairs while on vacation. But the influence of the womanizing uncle from the "seventy-five folios" on Swann's genesis would be powerful: it certainly explains why Proust originally imagined Swann's affairs in Querqueville, even if, for the sake of the story's consistency, those affairs took place during the character's youth.[110] When this plotline dried up,[111] Proust "recycled" the portrait of the womanizing uncle, this time in full, for the opening of "Swann in Love," in the shadow of the Verdurins' little Parisian clan.

Now for the second important turning point in the story of the uncle from the "seventy-five folios." It happened at the beginning of 1910, in the first fair copy notebook of the episode.[112] From this point, Swann would be given two portraits: Proust placed each at the start of the first two parts of the book that would bear his name.[113] Like the uncle in the "seventy-five folios" approaching women "from above," out of a "need to shine in front of

109. Notebook 4, f. 62; Other Manuscripts, no. XII.

110. Swann's brief affairs with young women at the seaside, probably actresses, risked being thwarted by the arrival of "his father" (Notebook 25, ff. 46v–45v; *JF, Sketch XLV,* II, p. 928).

111. But the relationship of the characters and the penchants of the uncle and nephew, then of Swann and the hero, are doubled in the drafts with a sort of porosity of roles: the uncle's love affairs are very like those of "I" (Other Manuscripts, no. VI), and Swann's seaside affairs draw on *Jean Santeuil* and would be recycled for the hero who was jealous of Maria and then Albertine (Saraydar 1983 and Wada 2012, pp. 115–116). Examples of the sudden transition from "he" to "I" (*Cahier 26,* 2010, f. 28) or of their coexistence (Notebook 25, ff. 47v–42v and ff. 44–43; *JF, Sketch XLV,* II, p. 927 sq.) remain disconcerting.

112. Notebook 69; Other Manuscripts, no. XV.

113. *CS,* "Combray," I, p. 15 sq. and "Swann in Love," ibid., p. 188 sq.

whomever he loved or was courting," Swann does the same thing "out of a final attachment to vanity [. . .] so that, a sensitive man, he could be rejected, but not despised."[114] In the version from Notebook 69, this behavior is explained:

Perhaps his Jewish origin was part of the cause, which [. . .] also gave him, through the memory of those humiliations that it is rare for a Jew not to have experienced during his childhood, a sort of fear of being despised, misjudged. <Perhaps put here the dowager, my grandmother, the Monsieur and his mistress. Anyway show that all this is useless for Swann and that it's just so he isn't despised.>[115]

The editorial note written in the margin ("Perhaps put here the dowager [. . .]") can now be deciphered, of course, as a reference to the "seventy-five folios," proof that Proust has the uncle in mind as the model for Swann. But in these pages, no explanation of Jewishness is given, even though Louis Weil was Jewish: not because that explanation couldn't cross the author's mind, but because, with the family connection between the character and the real person being evident, it could not or should not have been stated.

Now, while the explanation links Swann to Jewishness in a way that never happened with the uncle, it also presupposes an intimate knowledge of the situation it describes: the person speaking must at least have witnessed the humiliations that "it is rare for a Jew not to have experienced during his childhood," or he must have experienced them, being Jewish himself. This is one reason that could in itself explain the disappearance of this phrase in the next version. It began, before the expression of sympathy for the Jews' fate, with anti-Semitic words that could have come from the mouth of a Charlus, as if the author were giving voice to another character:

Perhaps his Jewish origin was part of the cause, which, making him (as certain Romans found a greater charm in penetrating certain Oriental captives) particularly attracted to pious young Christians in whom his

114. Notebook 69, f. 7; Other Manuscripts, no. XV.
115. Ibid.

infidel soul greedily drank the new taste of holy water and French
soil—like the Lombard style merging with the Byzantine[116]— . . .

Two opposing philosophies collide in this strange phrase, because the
lustful assault of the "infidel" is immediately compared to the "Lombard
style merging with the Byzantine," that is, according to Ruskin, to the very
thing that was (in addition to the Arab influence) at the root of one of the
wonders of Western architecture: Venice.[117] We can surmise that it is not
only architectural syncretism that Proust is defending here after appearing
to borrow the voice of anti-Semites—just as, when he mentions in the
"seventy-five folios" the acclimatization in Normandy of families from
the South and of exotic species, he isn't talking only about botany and
the French aristocracy,[118] but of assimilation. All the same, caught between two contradictory philosophies, the phrase could not be kept as it
was, and it disappeared completely from the next version.[119]

To memorialize a womanizing uncle without mentioning his Jewishness (or
to talk about Jewishness without it being linked to his own family), Proust
decided to make this uncle wear the mask of a fictional character[120]—
Swann, the alter ego of the novel's hero. But Swann did not entirely use up
the memory of the uncle, who would also become Uncle Adolphe, visited
by the "lady in pink,"[121] the courtesan who captivates the young hero when

116. Ibid.
117. See *The Works of John Ruskin*, Library Edition (London: George Allen, 1903), vol.
IX, p. 38: "The work of the Lombard was to give hardihood and system to the enervated
body and enfeebled mind of Christendom." Cf. also p. 38: "The reader will now begin to
understand something of the importance of the study of the edifices of a city which includes,
within the circuit of some seven or eight miles, the field of conquest between the three pre-
eminent architectures of the world" (i.e., Roman/Byzantine, Lombard, and Arab).
118. Ff. 75 and 76.
119. The insufficient elegance of his name and the universal fear of being despised by
an "inferior" now explain Swann's behavior (start of Notebook 15, pages kept in the *Reliquat* NAF 16703, ff. 93–95; cf. *CS*, I, pp. 188–189).
120. Proust might have thought earlier about detaching him from the uncle, to go by
this note from Carnet 1 in early 1908: "Character writing from time to time to ask if he
can be introduced etc." (f. 3; *Cn*, p. 34).
121. *CS*, I, p. 74 sq.

he turns up unannounced. "Like certain novelists, he had split his personality between two characters"[122] . . . This method was an effective way of cutting off further questions. Who could imagine that Charles Swann was not only Charles Haas—whom Proust could mention without difficulty[123]—but also Louis Weil? Of course, there was never any doubt that the famous Laure Hayman, who sent a wreath to Louis Weil's funeral,[124] was a model for Odette de Crécy, but from there to thinking that Uncle Louis could be . . . Uncle Adolphe shielded him. He alone absorbed the memory of Louis Weil, known for his supposed escapades with actresses and demimondaines, and whose collection of signed photographs had been partly conserved by his nephew.[125] After the great-aunt and Swann, this was the third and final metamorphosis[126] of the uncle from the "seventy-five folios."

The Memory of a Jewish Family

So the draft found in the Fallois archives mentions the house in Auteuil belonging to an "old uncle" who could hardly be anyone other than Louis Weil, even if his name is never mentioned.[127] And it also includes the first name of his sister-in-law, Adèle Berncastell Weil, Proust's maternal grandmother, whom he calls out to in the "seventy-five folios" as she is walking in the rain: "You're too hot Adèle! It's a beautiful day Adèle!" But Proust also mentions Adèle's mother in that sketch—his great-grandmother—about whom he tells a comical, cruel anecdote to illustrate her miserliness.

122. Ibid., p. 373.

123. See above, p 178 note 4.

124. See the letter from Proust to Laure Hayman [just after May 12, 1896], *Corr.*, II, p. 64.

125. It was sold at Sotheby's on May 31, 2016: "Books and manuscripts, collection of Patricia Mante-Proust," lot no. 119 (*Bulletin d'informations proustiennes*, no. 47[2017]: 138–139).

126. The episode of the visit to Uncle Adolphe was one of the additions to the "Second Typed Version" of "Combray" (NAF 16733, ff. 104–116); it was prepared in Notebooks 13 (ff. 18–25) and then 11 (ff. 32–37), notebooks dated by Akio Wada between the beginning of 1910 and the spring of 1911 (Wada 1998, pp. 58–59).

127. Other Manuscripts, no. III.

In the course of this anecdote he slips in a real family name, the only one associated with his maternal family that, to our knowledge, Proust ever wrote in a draft of his novel: the great-grandmother is told that "M. Crémieux" has arranged for her to have a free seat on the omnibus, freeing her of the obligation to pay six cents. The words in parentheses following this revelation tip the sketch into the realms of autobiography: "she was his sister-in-law." Starting with this couple, then, a whole section of Marcel Proust's maternal family tree falls into place. The miserly great-grandmother was Rachel "Rose" Silny (1794–1876), wife of Nathan Berncastell; her younger sister, Louise Amélie Silny (1800–1880),[128] had married the lawyer and politician Adolphe Crémieux (1796–1880). If Proust mentions this great-grandmother he barely knew, given that he was only five when she died, it is because, he says, he "inherited from her [a] tendency to suddenly fall out with people *at a distance*." Even if this is an unfortunate character trait— "Once we have passed a certain age, the soul of the child we were and the soul of the dead from whom we came shower us with their gifts and their curses"[129]—it adds to the supposed supremacy of the maternal lineage. Maman imitates her dead mother out of love; Marcel involuntarily takes after his great-grandmother. They are both from the same "side."

But why refer to the maternal family through the intermediary of Adolphe Crémieux, a great-great-uncle by marriage? Proust never mentions in any other piece of writing the name of that lawyer and politician committed to the rights of Jews, not even in his correspondence (except regarding the translation of Ruskin's *The Stones of Venice* by Crémieux's daughter Mathilde). Was it snobbery at being related to a "famous man"? What role did Crémieux play in the family story? He signed the marriage certificate of Adrien Proust and Jeanne Weil on September 3, 1870, just after the Battle of Sedan: was he, then, in some sense the godfather of this union between the rich heiress and the young medical doctor?[130] A few weeks before the alliance of the Weil and Proust families, Uncle Louis and Adrien Proust

128. The name on her death certificate reads: "Louise-Amélie-Silny, Marx."
129. *P*, III, p. 587.
130. On the theory, still unsupported but highly plausible, of a "meeting between Nathé Weil and Dr. Proust in Masonic circles," under the aegis of Crémieux, member of the Supreme Council of the Grand Lodge of France, see Compagnon 2020, p. 23; A.

were, as we have already stated, promoted to the grade of Officer of the Legion of Honor in the same year group (August 8, 1870) and on the proposal of the same ministry:[131] was this really just coincidence? Was it inevitable that it should be Nathé Weil, Crémieux's nephew by marriage, who, accompanied by his son Georges, should declare the death of Amélie Crémieux on February 1, 1880? A great deal of mystery surrounds a family history that Proust seemed to want to evoke in 1908, at least fleetingly.

Fleetingly because the "seventy-five folios," even if they seem to us from that point of view a little more forthcoming than *Search*, already mark a withdrawal into more obscure territory. In these pages, the somewhat baleful great-grandmother disappears, and so does the name of Crémieux; it is true that she will reappear, years later, reincarnated in *Sodom and Gomorrah* as the father of the hero's grandfather, the one reluctant "to pay three cents to ride the omnibus," his "rare miserliness" contrasted with the "slightly too lavish generosity" of the great-uncle.[132] The name of Auteuil was also removed, as we have seen, leaving no recognizable traces in the final text of *Search*, for readers of this sketch like ourselves, except those "precious wicker armchairs."[133] One of Proust's cousins on the Crémieux side, Valentine Thomson, would later remember seeing Mme Proust sitting in one of those armchairs;[134] in the text, they are brought inside to protect them from the rain, but their place in Proust's novel would provide those precious armchairs with the ultimate shelter, protecting them from the passing of time as they discreetly bore the memories of an entire family life.

Compagnon also established that Godchaux Weil, Nathé's half brother, was a freemason (ibid., pp. 31–32).

131. See above, p. 189.

132. As for Crémieux, he was replaced by a supporter of Napoleon III, the Duke of Persigny. My thanks to Francine Goujon for reminding me of this passage (*SG*, III, pp. 301–302). It was a late addition, prepared in Notebook 62, whose pages following folio 11 were cut and pasted as a *paperole* to the typed version (NAF 16738, f. 170; Goujon 1997, t. 2, p. 184). (We have kept the French word *paperole*, which is commonly used to designate the strips of paper Proust pasted onto his manuscripts for additions. The word appears in *Le Temps retrouvé* [IV, p. 611].) The passage closely follows the remark about "what would deserve a chapter of its own: profaned mothers," which also appears in the form of an addition to the typed version (NAF 16740, f. 48; *SG*, III, p. 300).

133. This volume, f. 1; *CS*, I, p. 11.

134. "My Cousin Marcel Proust," *Harper's Monthly Magazine*, May 1932, p. 713.

As the grandmother Adèle would say when she was briefly transformed into an "aunt" in the "seventy-five folios," one "should never write anyone's names in [. . .] letters."[135] Apparently Proust believed that one should never write anyone's real names in novels either: after the "seventy-five folios," both "Adèle" and "Jeanne" would vanish from the text. But deletion probably doesn't equal silence. The grandmother's favored epistolary style, describing "everything with allusions, metaphors, and riddles," gives rise to a comic, almost caricatured moment in the "seventy-five folios" to which Proust would not return. But he himself would deliberately, discreetly practice that same art of disguise and encryption in his novel where, through a minor detail, the relative, friend, lover, or enemy might "recognize" a meaning that would escape most readers.[136] This cloaked use of allusions is already present in the "seventy-five folios," when the little brother resembles "a pompous, dejected princess in a tragedy," a description that immediately suggests Racine's Phèdre, and more obscurely the same playwright's version of Esther, the Jewish queen of Persia . . . Some things must be said only obliquely, understood only slowly.

Was this discreet form of expression a way of remaining faithful to the ancestral demand for prudence: "O God of our Fathers, / Among us descend, Hide our Mysteries / From Evil Men"?[137] Proust was no more likely to write about a Jewish family from the French bourgeoisie than he was to give his hero his own sexual preferences. He was not going to write a *roman à thèse* when the enemy, in the shape of venomously reactionary newspapers like *La Libre Parole* and *L'Action française,* were spreading derogatory stereotypes of "the Jew" and still, as late as 1908, fanning the embers of the Dreyfus affair.[138] He chose to depict individuals, characters: a mother, a grandmother, a great-grandmother, an uncle, a grandfather, a brother, with

135. F. 4.

136. See on this subject Francine Goujon, *Allusions littéraires et écriture cryptée dans l'œuvre de Proust* (Paris: Honoré Champion, 2020).

137. Here, Proust slightly misquotes *The Jewess* (1835) by Scribe and Halévy, act II, scene I; quoted in *SG*, III, p. 329; cf. *CS*, I, p. 90.

138. *L'Action française* ran a daily column on the Dreyfus affair starting on March 21, 1908, despite the fact that the case had officially been closed after the rehabilitation of Captain Dreyfus on July 12, 1906.

their virtues and their flaws, combining tenderness, mockery, empathy, sometimes cruelty. If he didn't name them, it was to protect them. And if he couldn't use their names—family names, first names—except in the secrecy of his manuscripts, then he wouldn't use his own name either.

Should there be some regret that Proust never intended to tell the story of life in an assimilated Jewish family in France at the end of the nineteenth century? Perhaps, but all families, Jewish or otherwise, are first and foremost a little society in their own right. Religious observance, for example, was not followed equally in the Weil and Berncastell households. Nathé, Jeanne's father, insisted on being incinerated after his death even though Judaism condemns this practice: it was a formal declaration of freedom of thought,[139] even anticlericalism—and probably anticlericalism of a more virulent kind than Proust admitted in a 1908 letter to Daniel Halévy in which he mentioned that grandfather.[140] He also, as an aside, made the narrator's grandmother a "free-thinker."[141] On the other end of the scale, Amélie Crémieux, Jeanne Weil's great-aunt, converted to Catholicism and had her two children baptized without telling her husband, a passionate champion of the rights of Jews and president of the Universal Israelite Alliance, who had to resign from the Central Consistory.[142] Lazard Weil chose a first name, Louis, that revealed his fantasy of assimilation into the historical France of the ancien régime, which matches the portrait of the somewhat vain man described in the "seventy-five folios," but does not match the line about Nucingen that Proust uses about him in the letter already cited, which suggests a failed assimilation.[143] Of all the family members, it was perhaps Lazard who was most indifferent to Judaism but who most faithfully practiced the Jewish virtue of charity, constantly inviting his relatives to stay at his house and giving generous dowries, and he was the only who would remain at all Jewish in the novel, disguised by

139. See Compagnon 2020, pp. 20–23.
140. See ibid., p. 15, and below.
141. *CS*, I, p. 64 var. *a*.
142. In 1845. See Daniel Amson, *Adolphe Crémieux: L'oublié de la gloire* (Paris: Éditions du Seuil, 1988), p. 154 sq.; Bloch-Dano 2004, pp. 43–44.
143. In 1908, in his pastiche of Balzac, Proust imitates what the author of *A Harlot High and Low* called "the dreadful patois of the Polish Jew" Nucingen (*PM*, pp. 9–10).

the name Charles Swann (while also borrowing, as Uncle Adolphe, the first name of the illustrious Crémieux). As for Jeanne Weil, she married outside the faith and allowed her children to be baptized, but she never converted; after her death, Marcel and Robert Proust summoned a rabbi to say the last prayers.[144] And Nathé, for all that he was a free-thinker, took his grandson to rue du Repos, in the Jewish section of Père-Lachaise, to place a stone on his parents' grave.[145] Despite being an atheist, he remained faithful to the old traditions, while Proust, an agnostic, wrote during the war to Emmanuel Berl: "They've all forgotten that I'm Jewish. But I haven't."[146] But in truth we know nothing of what might or might not—in Auteuil or at 40a, rue du Faubourg-Poissonnière, where Nathé Weil and his family lived—have been kept of the old habits of a "traditional" Jewish family, despite the jokes, in *Search*, about strangers who do not understand why things are done differently on Saturdays, or the allusion to a "half-German, half-Jewish dialect"[147] spoken in the Bloch family.

Nathé Weil remained faithful to his origins to the point of rejecting a certain form of assimilation, or at least of being annoyed by it. In 1908, while he was working on the "seventy-five folios," Proust used a condolence letter to Daniel Halévy after the death of his father Ludovic Halévy,[148] to write, in a curious digression, a description of his own grandfather, in which the empathic qualities of "the best of men,"[149] "tender and good"[150] like his daughter Jeanne, are emphasized, while passing over in silence the "despotic and [. . .] fastidious"[151] character of this man who, in the sketch, causes his spouse suffering and, in the "seventy-five folios," prompts the

144. *Journal des débats*, September 30, 1905: "The funeral of Mme Adrien Proust, widow of the member of the Academy of Medicine, took place at the home of the deceased, 45, rue de Courcelles, where a rabbi came to say the last prayers."

145. See Compagnon 2020, p. 13 sq.

146. Emmanuel Berl, *Interrogatoire*, by Patrick Modiano (Paris: Gallimard, 1976), p. 27.

147. *JF*, II, p. 132.

148. This is a partial draft, probably dating from the day of Ludovic Halévy's death (May 7, 1908). Kept by Proust, it was found in the Fallois archives among the fragmentary drafts for *Swann's Way*. For his edition and his commentary, see Compagnon 2020, p. 17 sq.

149. Other Manuscripts, no. III.

150. Compagnon 2020, p. 17.

151. Other Manuscripts, no. III.

fear that he will "force her to return to the house."[152] Proust does, however, tell Daniel Halévy about one of the bad habits practiced by this "fastidious" grandfather: that of humming—in front of newcomers whom he suspected, "despite a changed name," of being "Israelites"—tunes from operas and operettas with Jewish subjects, in "a sort of figurative language" intended to make clear that he wasn't fooled. [153] In the "seventy-five folios" the grandfather is no more than his brother's stooge, and this "little eccentricity"—yet more evidence of a marked family penchant for allusion—is not mentioned. To mention it here would have been to admit the family's Jewishness and pose the question of assimilation, which Proust didn't want to do. To sidestep the issue, he transferred this habit of bad jokes ("On your guard!")[154] to the narrator's father at the expense of the womanizing uncle, and had we not known *Swann's Way*[155] it would have been impossible to detect an allusion to Jewishness from the same context. But Proust set aside the draft of the letter with an idea at the back of his mind.

It was the invention of Swann that, by clearly moving the issue of Jewishness outside the family circle, enabled him the following year to integrate the anecdote about his grandfather. But at what cost? This grandfather who retained a modicum of faith in spite of everything, who was pained by Jews changing their names (as a Bloch would do), this grandfather who was in some sense in search of lost sheep, became, in Notebook 4, against all expectation, a grandfather who, although a friend of Swann's, "did not

152. F. 1.

153. "My grandfather's memories of operas and operettas were my perpetual terror, because for him they were a sort of figurative language and easier to understand than he thought, which he used to say about people, in front of them, things that they shouldn't have heard. If he claimed that someone we'd told him about was, despite a changed name, an Israelite, then almost as soon as the [person] entered, either his face or a few pieces of information adroitly gathered, would leave him in no doubt and then he wouldn't stop humming 'Israel break your chain! Arise, display your might! Their idle threats disdain! Jehovah, God of light['] (Samson and Delilah) or 'O God of our Fathers, among us descend, hide our mysteries from evil men['] (The Jewess) or others that I've forgotten." Proust, draft of letter to D. Halévy, [May 7, 1908]. Compagnon 2020, pp. 17–18.

154. F. 63.

155. *CS*, I, p. 90: "And after cleverly asking a few more precise questions, he [my grandfather] would call out: 'On your guard! On your guard!'"

like Jews."[156] He became the anti-Semite humming *The Jewess* or *Samson and Delilah* to his grandson's "suspect" friends; a "harmless" anti-Semite, since he jokes about it afterward with Swann, who explains to him that the Christian virtues were originally Jewish virtues?[157] All the same, the scene has the feel of a U-turn in which certain family memories are being rewritten and camouflaged. Even if Proust waters down the effect slightly, by briefly turning the grandfather into a great-uncle,[158] then, in the typed version, by transporting the passage to the Catholic, sanctimonious "Combray II" and by reducing the ancestor's propensity for anti-Semitism,[159] the memorialization of Nathé Weil, for those who knew him, is paradoxical and provocative. We cannot, then, rely on the discreet role that he still played in the "seventy-five folios," while Proust distantly hints at it in his correspondence.

The Father's "Sides"

While the first chapter takes place in Auteuil, inspired by the maternal side of the family, [The Villebon Way and the Méséglise Way] unquestionably draws inspiration from Illiers and its Eure-et-Loir landscapes; in other words, the paternal side, that of Adrien Proust. Although identified once again simply as "my uncle,"[160] this appellation now no longer masks Louis Weil, but Jules Amiot, Dr. Proust's brother-in-law, who owned the Pré-Catelan garden in Illiers—a short-lived character who, in the walks along the river where the fisherman stands on the bridge,[161] would be replaced by the vague "my parents."[162] Even if the name of Illiers is not mentioned in the "seventy-five folios" any more than that of Auteuil, the rule against using place-names connected to the family history is loosened. Right away

---

156. Notebook 4, f. 46. Other Manuscripts, no. XII.

157. Compagnon 2013, lecture given March 26 at Collège de France.

158. Notebook 8, ff. 18–20 (*CS, Sketch XII*, I, pp. 681–682); Notebook 9, ff. 39–42. See above, p. 191 note 5.

159. See NAF 16733, f. 31; the following page, "24," is moved to f. 134. *CS*, I, pp. 90–91.

160. F. 28.

161. Ff. 31, 32, 33.

162. Notebook 11, f. 8; *CS*, I, p. 165.

we see the Château de Villebon, fifteen kilometers northwest of Illiers, and the "Bonneval road" to the southeast; the place-name "Méséglise," which would replace Bonneval in the second of the three versions, is fictional, but Proust changed only one letter and one accent from the village of Méréglise, close to Illiers;[163] and the name of the river that runs through it, the Loir, features in an editorial note referring to an already written fragment ("Sources of the Loir"); it would be used again in Notebook 4.[164] Proust also recycles many of the autobiographical elements already mentioned in *Jean Santeuil,* and also—for Pré-Catelan, Uncle Amiot's ornamental garden—in *Pleasures and Days* and "On Reading."[165]

After the first "chapter" of the "seventy-five folios," which, despite a few crossings-out and alterations and its obviously unfinished state, forms a fluid, continuous whole, the pages on the "ways" feel much more like rough drafts. Proust no longer hesitates to use his large double folios to sketch out ideas. There is no single, consistent version, but a series of three attempts, which we had to put back in order. They are marked by furious rewriting (ff. 33–34), the stitching together of fragments that had been written at different times (ff. 36–37), attempts at montage (ff. 32, 35), references to other pieces (f. 40), and splices (f. 41v). This is an early sign of what would become Proust's typical method in his notebooks—one of ceaseless movement.

The essential difference between this text and the older texts that mentioned walks is the desire to organize them in what Claudine Quémar, author of the first seminal study of the "ways" in the draft notebooks, called an "antithetical diptych."[166] In the "seventy-five folios," Proust contrasts the two "ways" from the first version. The family did not leave at the same time, nor from the same door, for the two walks, which "belonged to two different lands, to completely disparate days, to another side of the

---

163. "Méséglise" had already featured in "On Reading" (*SL*, p. 11); in *PM* in 1919, Proust returned to "Méréglise" (p. 162).

164. Other Manuscripts, no. XII.

165. See ff. 27, 28, 29, passim.

166. Quémar 1975, p. 240.

house that seemed [. . .] another side of the world."[167] Already Proust was
seeking what he would call "spiritual equivalents" of the perceptible,[168]
from which contrasting lessons could be drawn. Aesthetic experiences
and particular romantic feelings were grafted onto the landscapes, as was
the mystery of frustratingly obscure impressions, even if the issue of writing
had not yet been addressed.

Invention and revision went on well beyond the 1908 pages in two draft
notebooks,[169] leading to the assignment to each geographical path of an
emblematic love, allowing the two "ways" to finally become a major organizing principle: of the hero's learning and development, but first of all of
the increasingly abundant fictional material (which would further strengthen
the ways of Sodom and Gomorrah, with their initials identical to those of
Swann and Guermantes). The "lessons" that they provide in the "seventy-
five folios," and that are found at the end of "Combray II," would be further
developed. The initial separation, which governs not only the geographical
world of Combray but the social world too, is ultimately contradicted, as
we know, by the discovery that it is possible to join the two "ways": a
Swann (Gilberte) marries a Guermantes (Saint-Loup) and teaches the
stunned narrator that it is possible to "go to Guermantes by way of Méséglise, it's the prettiest path."[170] And in making Albertine die in Combray,
"on the banks of the Vivonne," in other words on the Guermantes way, and
making the hero suddenly understand that she had joined her friend Mlle
Vinteuil in Montjouvain, in other words on the Méséglise way,[171] Proust
shows us that the dynamic framework of the two "ways," put in place as

167. F. 28.

168. *TR*, IV, p. 457.

169. Notebooks 4 and 12; see the detail of this work in the notes for ff. 27–43. The division of the distinctive traits would be achieved only after several attempts. In the "seventy-
five folios," for example, Proust contrasted the two "ways" by their bridges, one of them a
"big stone bridge" (ff. 28, 35), the other a "little wooden bridge," even a simple "wooden
plank" (ff. 28, 31, 36); but they span the same river and that, despite everything, unites
them. So Proust would later get rid of one of the bridges (Notebook 4) and in the end
would move the river exclusively to the Guermantes way (Notebook 12).

170. *AD*, IV, p. 268.

171. See *Albertine disparue*, ed. N. Mauriac and E. Wolff (Paris: Grasset, 1987),
pp. 111–112.

early as 1908, at the very beginning of *Search,* would prove productive and structural until the end, strongly contributing to the "solidarity of the parts."

With the two "ways," then, Proust set up a system of organization for the world of the novel as well as an engine that would drive the story, a principle for the distribution of episodes, then of encounters and exchanges. The deep movement of the writing is in Proust's case one of reciprocal contamination and the interpenetration of developments that seem at first simply juxtaposed. So in the spring of 1909 we see him returning to the first two "chapters" of the "seventy-five folios" (which he had abandoned to work on *Contre Sainte-Beuve*) with the clear intention of making them into a single whole. Now armed (thanks to his work on *Contre Sainte-Beuve*) with the narrative framework of the woken sleeper's unfurling memories, he joins them under the banner of the fictional "Combray," appearing here for the first time;[172] in Notebook 4, the story of the walks along the "ways" written in the "seventy-five folios" is set between the two parts of the bedtime drama (part one being the usual days, and part two those exceptional days when they were visited by M. Swann or when they were returning from the "Villebon way"). And yet, in the full version of "Combray" that quickly follows in Notebook 8, the episode of the *biscotte*—which would later be transformed into the madeleine—is inserted between the bedtime drama and the resurrection of "Combray" itself; the story of the two "ways" is pushed back. Behind the unity suggested by the fictional place-name, then, Proust rediscovered, at the start of his novel—and for good—the division of the "seventy-five folios" between memories of Auteuil and memories of Illiers. That border, which permanently isolates the evening kiss, was doubled in the creation of "Combray I" and "Combray II."[173] The fictional joining of the paternal side and the maternal side never quite happened.

172. See f. 1. The name "Combray" evokes Chateaubriand (Combourg) and perhaps also Fénelon ("the swan of Cambrai"), a name dear to Proust. See also Henriet 2020, p. 52, on the subject of the château of that name in Calvados, which Proust might have visited.

173. And this occurred from the fair copy of the madeleine episode (NAF 16703, f. 6); the border would be moved at the time of the galley proofs in 1913 (*Bodmer,* from galley proof 8 to galley proof 9).

As in the first chapter of the "seventy-five folios," we are surprised to discover within those walks along the "ways" sketches of scenes that would
later migrate to other parts of the novel, yet more evidence of Proust's long
and patient work in crafting his masterpiece. So it is with the nocturnal
walks in the company of a woman, under the blue light of the moon, walks
that Proust would mention at the start of "Combray I" then delay until the
stay with Gilberte de Saint-Loup in Tansonville—without having had time
to give them their definitive form.[174] So it is with a certain "tree-lined path"
or "avenue of tall trees" seen again "in Normandy, in Burgundy,"[175] a
deeply moving passage for any reader of *In the Shadow of Young Girls in
Flower,* since Proust here gives us an anticipatory key to the memory of the
three trees in Hudimesnil that he will later so stubbornly refuse us (and
this goes back to the "preface" of *Contre Sainte-Beuve,* in late 1908).[176] The
emotion is not purely due to discovering that these might have been trees
from "Combray"—although we will perhaps take greater notice of the discreet presence of the "entrance to the path of oaks"[177] at the very end of
"Combray II"—and it is not only from finding almost the same words,
bridges between the distant eras of its genesis ("I've seen those trees before, where"; "Where had I seen them before?");[178] it is, rather, the realiza-
tion that this "recognition" itself brings no sense of completion, but
metamorphoses into a new, obscure impression, a new mystery, even deeper
and more impenetrable: "I sensed the extreme singularity of that avenue,
I sensed its inexpressible nature, I was about to express it, and I woke up.
Then the trees multiplied, it was a forest [. . .]." Isn't this the same place as
"that landscape whose individuality, at night in my dreams, would sometimes seize me with an almost fantastical power but which I could not find
again upon waking"?[179] From this place appeared women who seemed to
perform some ancestral rite in an atmosphere that was mysterious and, from
the second version onward, forbidden: "Because there really are things that

174. See f. 33.
175. Ff. 36, 37.
176. Other Manuscripts, no. VII.
177. *CS,* I, p. 183.
178. F. 37, and *JF,* II, p. 78.
179. *CS,* I, p. 183.

must not be shown to us."[180] Proust has become Nerval—perhaps the only author he couldn't pastiche—giving "to his scenes the colors of his dream," "an unreal color": those scenes, "as we fall asleep we glimpse them, we can stare at them and define their charm, but when we awake we no longer see them, we let go and before we are able to stare at them we are asleep, as if our intelligence were not permitted to see them."[181] This is precisely the dreamlike, penetrating charm of those lines from the "seventy-five folios," the expression of an anti-intellectualist credo. The pages on the "ways" are those in which the effort and the work of writing are most perceptible, those also in which, paradoxically, there is an impression of the most delicate and elusive poetry.

Traces of Reminiscences

With the exception of the dreamlike experience of the "tree-lined path," there is no experience of memory or reminiscence in the "seventy-five folios." It is all the more striking to note that the first long "piece" on the question, the one that includes the series of experiences of involuntary memory that would be shared between "Combray" and *Time Regained*—the toast and the tea, the uneven flagstone in Venice, the sound of silverware on a plate . . . —is to be found on large double pages identical to those of the "seventy-five folios." Fallois published this as Proust's "preface" to *Contre Sainte-Beuve*.[182]

From when does this piece date? Since it ends, despite its long narrative introduction, with a nod toward an argumentative essay on Sainte-Beuve's method, and does not include any allusion to the framework of a conversation with Maman, it is likely that it was developed before the first half of December 1908, when Proust, uncertain (or feigning uncertainty), was

180. F. 39.

181. Notebook 5, ff. 18 and 10; *CSB*, pp. 169, 160–161. See also Notebook 32, f. 19: "[. . .] those landscapes so beautiful that we sense we are falling asleep, as if it were forbidden for a man to look upon them while awake."

182. *CSB*, pp. 53–59; Other Manuscripts, no. VII. Fallois mentioned that these were "folios of the same format" as the "seventy-five folios" and in "identical handwriting" (*CSB*, p. 14).

consulting his friends[183] on the subject of what form his essay should take. And it must have been written after October 1908, when the translation of Ruskin's *St. Mark's Rest* appeared, in which Proust discovered a photograph that reminded him of the "unevenness of the flagstones in the Baptistery," the source of the Venetian epiphany that sparked the piece on the "shining, uneven flagstones."[184] Since there is, in the first pages of Carnet 1, from early 1908, a series of notes suggesting Proust's interest in the memory of sensations,[185] we are faced with a choice of two theories. Either he was working, in parallel with the "seventy-five folios," on an independent piece about involuntary memory, illustrating the importance of the "deep me," and he finally decided in the fall to use this as the introduction to his essay on Sainte-Beuve's critical method, or these pages on involuntary memory, in an earlier form, were part, or were planned to be part, of the "seventy-five folios." The fact that, in October or November 1908, Proust transferred them to his "Sainte-Beuve" project would mean that he was giving up on the "seventy-five folios"—in other words, temporarily, on his novel.

This second theory, the recycling theory, suggested by Françoise Leriche[186] even before the discovery of the "seventy-five folios," seems the more plausible. Several clues point toward it being correct. The first is of course the rewritten version, found in that "preface," of the experience of the "tree-lined path," in a new form accentuating the failure of recognition but again mentioning the source of the impression as being the "walks around the town where I was happy as a small child," and in particular the dream-like quality of a "forest where it was bright all night long" in an "imaginary land," "almost as real as the land of my childhood, which was already nothing more than a dream."[187] The second clue is an unpublished manuscript found in the Fallois archives, which as far as we know is the earliest ancestor of the madeleine episode. This includes the allusion to the "Breton legend" of dead souls captive in objects, the remark about the powerless-

183. George de Lauris and Anna de Noailles. See *Lettres*, pp. 465–466.
184. Carnet 1, f. 10v (*Cn*, p. 49); Other Manuscripts, no. VII; Pugh 1987, p. 111 note 3.
185. See Leriche 2012, p. 83.
186. Ibid.
187. Other Manuscripts, no. VII; *CSB* Clarac, pp. 214–215.

ness of intelligence to restore things of the past and, in a single clause, the summary of the experience of involuntary memory: "those summers [. . .] all of this had passed into a little cup of boiling tea where some stale bread was dipped," Proust ending the passage abruptly before the account leading to the epiphany.[188] This draft is written on the same large-format graph paper as four fragments that have a direct relationship with the "seventy-five folios," and that are part of their antecedent text.[189] They were all part of the same batch in the Fallois archives: their grouping in this way could date back to Proust himself, since the archives had, prior to this, been kept only in the homes of Robert and Suzy Proust.

It is, therefore, far from impossible that Proust had been planning to devote a chapter to experiences of involuntary memory in this 1908 project for his novel, which was cut short before he could insert it. The "seventy-five folios" include an account of childhood and youth accentuating the importance of feelings, emotions, perceptible experience, imagination, and dreams in accessing the world and knowledge. This account could have been crowned with a series of epiphanies on involuntary memory, demonstrating the definitive primacy of "instinct" or the unconscious over the intellect. We can imagine them as the text's grand finale.

This is only a theory, of course, and impossible to verify.[190] But there are a few clues to support it. The first is the mention in the "seventy-five folios" of "the smell of the tea I made in my Parisian bedroom in winter."[191] Immediately we think of the most famous episode of involuntary memory, already sketched by Proust when he wrote this page. The formulation "the smell of the tea" is slightly disconcerting, but it is also used in the version

188. Other Manuscripts, no. IV.

189. See the Chronology. Other Manuscripts, nos. III, V, VI; the text of the fourth is given in a note (see the Chronology).

190. And perhaps there will be resistance to the idea that Proust could, in 1908, have planned to place the reminiscences at the conclusion of his proto-novel, used as we are to seeing this as the great triumph of spring 1910, the decisive (and epiphanic) moment when he abandoned the final conversation with Maman and "officially" gave birth to *Time Regained*, with the transfer to the "final volume" of all the reminiscences already present in "Combray" (Venice, *The Country Waif . . .*).

191. F. 13.

of the "preface" and in other drafts,   [192] and even, if we look out for it, at the end of "Combray II": "[. . .] the taste—what we called at Combray the 'perfume'—of a cup of tea."[193] It is true that the drinking of tea is, in this context, an ordinary, everyday event, whereas it is presented as being unusual in all the versions of the episode. But it is likely to be echoed later in the story, and thus it could foreshadow the experience of the toasted (or stale) bread.

There is another clue in the chapter [Venice], where the tourist disappointed by the palaces he passes in his gondola laments the "moments of our life" that we do not live, in thrall as we are to "sensory perception, the tyranny of the present, the intervention of intelligence, the network of activity, the succession of selfish desires," before adding that these moments "become glorious again on the day, come at last, of the resurrection."[194] This resurrection clearly points to the resurrection of involuntary memory; in the "preface" to *Contre Sainte-Beuve*, the terms "resurrection" and "resurrect(ed)" recur constantly.[195] The verb is also present in the very first sketch found in Fallois's archive.[196] Long before Proust thought of the uneven floor in the baptistery as a vector of reminiscence, in October or November 1908, he had already intended to bring Venice back to life, and this would be, once again, a "preparation."

The third clue to a possible "postponement" of the reminiscences is an unassuming-looking passage in the first version of the "ways," where the author lists the flowers he doesn't like, including geraniums:

> . . . the boring geraniums that we walked past every time we had to give some strangers a tour of the park and whose flowers were so ordinary, so poor, so short, with a hairy leaf and a common scent, flowers that the

192. Ibid.

193. *CS*, I, p. 183.

194. F. 83v.

195. There is nothing original about this vocabulary: it is, notably, to be found in Taine's essay *On Intelligence*, the importance of which in the genesis of the madeleine episode was shown by Jean-François Perrin. See Leriche 2012, p. 81.

196. "If I had never encountered the cup of boiling tea [. . .] it is probable that that year, that garden, those sorrows would never have been resurrected for me" (Other Manuscripts, no. IV)

gardener was obsessed with, that seemed made for him alone, and that for me did not yet have a connection to any poetic idea that would revive them in my mind, make them as desirable as the strawberry plants, the periwinkles, the forget-me-nots, the asparaguses, the roses.

". . . and that for me did not *yet* have a connection to any poetic idea that would revive them in my mind, make them [. . .] desirable": how are we to read this line? In French, the italicized word is *"encore,"* which could possibly, in this context, be merely the completion of the list of disliked flowers, a reiteration of their poetic sterility ("nor did the boring geraniums . . . have a connection to any poetic idea"). But isn't it more likely that it suggests a temporary situation, in the past, opening the possibility of a reversal, a switch from disdain to appreciation? In *Jean Santeuil,* the geranium was already described as being in a similar movement of re-evaluation: it was one of those flowers "that in our childhood we were used to seeing proliferate in gardens where we didn't like them," but "which *now* we are happy to see crowning the borders of new gardens, bringing to them those beautiful, intense, musky colors *that we recognize as the persistent shine of years long past, from which period not all of those who lived then are dead, since these creatures survive, these creatures who do not remember us* [. . .]."[197] In that passage from the "seventy-five folios," then, we can, once again, discern some discreet foreshadowing.

Geraniums and Orange Trees

What may give substance to this reading is first of all the "preface" to *Contre Sainte-Beuve,* if we accept now that Proust was recycling within it a collection of reminiscences originally intended for the novel sketched out in the "seventy-five folios." Here is the first and most famous of those sketches:

I dipped the toast in the cup of tea and, in the moment when I put the toast in my mouth, and I felt the sensation of its softened matter

---

197. *JS,* p. 473. Italics are ours.

infused ~~with the smell of~~ <with a taste of> tea against my palate, I
felt a confusion of scents, of ~~roses~~ geraniums, orange trees, and a
sensation of extraordinary light, and happiness; I sat motionless
fearing ~~by~~ a single movement might stop what was happening inside
me, which I didn't understand, and still clinging to that taste of
soaked bread which seemed to produce so many wonders, when suddenly the shaken walls of my memory gave way and it was those ~~yea~~
summers that I spent in the country house I mentioned which burst
into my consciousness with their mornings dragging along with them
the whole parade, the incessant flood of joyful hours. And I remembered: all those days when I got dressed I went down to the bedroom
where my grandfather had just woken and was sipping his tea. He
dipped a *biscotte* in it and gave it to me to eat.[198]

The association of geraniums and orange trees—perhaps suggested to
Proust less by his memories[199] than by their almost anagrammatical
relationship[200]—goes back to *Jean Santeuil* in which there was already a
gardener who was both a thief and "arrogant," and who stripped the
flowers from the orange trees and grew geraniums.[201] In the "seventy-five
folios," geraniums are noted as having "a common scent" and being
"flowers that the gardener was obsessed with,"[202] and one of the reasons
for the grandmother's discontent is that the gardener "had persuaded my
uncle to let him pick all the flowers from the little orange trees at the entrance on the pretext that he wanted to make orange flower water."[203] Associated with the same disagreeable character, geraniums and orange trees
would return together at the moment when the taste of the tea mingled
with the taste of toast, only this time to delicious effect. Along with the

198. NAF 16636, ff. 1–2; Other Manuscripts, no. VII.
199. The geranium is a common flower, and Proust's two childhood homes both had an
orange grove: see Mayer 1984, p. 11; Naturel 2009, p. 834.
200. In French, both words contain the same sound (ora*nger* / *gé*ranium) and share the
same a+n sequence as well as the sound [ɔ].
201. *JS*, p. 328.
202. F. 29.
203. F. 3.

memory of the "path" or the "group of trees," they are one of the imprints left in the "preface" to *Contre Sainte-Beuve* by the "seventy-five folios."

Everything points to the conclusion that, in the first "Sainte-Beuve" notebooks, this experience of sensual rapture should still lead up to the most famous reminiscence. In a forgotten addition to one of them, Notebook 2, and in accordance with an outline straight from the "seventy-five folios," the great-uncle (quickly replaced, as we have mentioned, by a "great-aunt")[204] quarrels with the grandmother about the gardener. And then two subjects of disagreement follow, without transition: the way the gardener strips the orange trees of their flowers,[205] and the varieties of geraniums he is growing around the lawn.[206]

We don't know what the plan was for these preparations: whether they were to be final reminiscences, or whether they would be spread throughout the story, as suggested by an editorial note in the Agenda that all these reminiscences should be put "at the end," including the now familiar "smell of [. . .] tea."[207] It was in the spring of 1909—in the first draft notebook where the *biscotte* scene appeared, Notebook 8—that the real metamorphosis took place: reminiscence became an important narrative tool, a "join"[208] between the parts of the novel, Proust would say, an incident that, after the nocturnal wakings, would open up for a second time, more fully, the narrative floodgates. This is the resurrection of "all of Combray."[209] In this version, the "delicious sensation" associated with the taste of the "little *biscotte*"[210] soaked with tea is not described in other terms: the "scents of

204. See above, p. 191; Other Manuscripts, no. IX.

205. "My grandmother looked with pain at the bare orange trees whose flowers he had all torn off to make a [. . .] syrup that he sold to ~~pharmacists~~" (Notebook 2, f. 7v). See Other Manuscripts, no. IX.

206. Ibid.

207. "Don't forget violin phrase (figure) that will occur every time giving me a reminiscence. And at the end remembering one, thinking: how much time lost since Combray, I will remember them all and will tell myself their meaning (and then the complement of the smell of tea is that life is beautiful etc)," *Agenda*, f. 55v, and note 2.

208. "On Flaubert's 'style'" (1920), *EA*, p. 599.

209. Notebook 8, f. 47.

210. Ibid., f. 67.

geraniums, orange trees" have disappeared. Yet Proust did not set aside the now obsolete "preparation" that was the scene from Notebook 2: he prepared to insert it into the original typed version of "Combray"[211]—now, perhaps, in the guise of a new illustration of family dissensions. Since in the end he gave up on that scene, there was no longer any trace in *Swann* of orange trees, geraniums, or a gardener, except in passing.[212]

The arguments about the gardener between the uncle and the grandmother (later to become the great-aunt and the grandmother) would take their final form in the cruel cognac scene;[213] in the first, crossed-out version, the liquor in question was curaçao,[214] which is made from orange peel, like a humorous condensation, the essence of years of writing and rewriting, starting with *Jean Santeuil* and ending with one of the last notebooks.[215] As for the geranium, it would be associated one last time with the cup of tea and the "sensation of extraordinary light" that accompanied it in the draft of 1908. It is the mysterious scent emanated by Vinteuil's masterpiece in *The Captive:*

> Nothing resembled a beautiful phrase from Vinteuil so much as that particular pleasure which I have sometimes experienced in my life, in the presence of the steeples of Martinville for example, or of certain trees on a road to Balbec or, more simply, at the start of this book, while drinking a certain cup of tea. *Like that cup of tea, so many sensations of light,* or the bright murmurs, the noisy colors that Vinteuil sent us from the world where he composed, there paraded before my imagination, insistently but too quickly to be grasped, *something that I could compare to the perfumed silk of a geranium.* Except, while in memory that haze can be, if not intensified, at least defined by locating the circumstances that explain *why a certain taste might recall luminous sensations,* the vague sensations awakened

211. See Other Manuscripts, no. X.

212. See *CS*, I, pp. 11, 85, 87–88.

213. Ibid., pp. 11–12. On this scene, see above, p. 191.

214. "[. . .] my great-uncle, when her walk around the garden brought her close to him again, said: 'Come and stop your husband drinking curaçao then'" (crossed out in Notebook 9, f. 30v).

215. See *JS*, p. 328; Notebook 60, f. 123 (Other Manuscripts, no. III).

by Vinteuil coming not from a memory but from an impression (as with the Martinville steeples), one would have to find, *for the geranium scent of his music*, not a material explanation, but the deeper equivalent, the unknown and brightly colored celebration [. . .].[216]

In any case, Proust would memorialize the house in Auteuil, perhaps the house from Notebook 2 with its "shutters closed against the heat," with its geraniums and orange trees.[217] We can discern it in the first "Sainte-Beuve" notebook, where we find, intertwined with the memories of Venice, a memory of "going home for lunch in my uncle's cool, dark house."[218] A few months later, at the start of Notebook 4 (the notebook in which Proust, as we have noted, would recycle large parts of the "seventy-five folios"), the analysis of morning sensations on a very hot day brings the memory of an arrival "in the countryside" in a "dark, bright, and cool dining room" and an "atmosphere striped with garden smells":[219] even if the house's owner is no longer named, we recognize the uncle's house from its darkness and coolness. We recognize it too in *The Captive*,[220] where it still exists with its decor and the sensations it awakens, including "the smell of cherries in a bowl," which brings us back to one of the first impressions noted in Carnet 1, at the start of 1908: "Dining room smelling of cherry when coming in from the heat."[221] Proust effectively hands his readers the keys to this house in advance. It is, almost word for word, his great-uncle's house in Auteuil, as described in the autobiographical preface to Jacques-Émile Blanche's *Propos de peintre* in 1919.[222]

216. *P*, III, pp. 876–877. Italics are ours.
217. Notebook 2, f. 7v. Other Manuscripts, no. IX.
218. Notebook 3, f. 37v. See also ff. 35v, 38.
219. Notebook 4, f. 3. See also ff. 2v, f. 4, passim. Brun 1987, pp. 219–221.
220. *P*, III, pp. 911–912.
221. Carnet 1, f. 3 (*Cn*, p. 34). This is likely the origin of the incomplete memory in the "preface" to *Contre Sainte-Beuve*: "Walking through a pantry the other day, a piece of green cloth blocking part of a broken window made me stop dead, listen within myself. A glimmer of summer came to me. Why[,] I tried to remember. I saw wasps in a beam of sunlight, a smell of cherries on the table, I couldn't remember" (Other Manuscripts, no. VII, f. 4).
222. *EA*, pp. 572–573. For a detailed analysis of the genetic trajectory, see Brun 1987, pp. 211–241.

Hints of Sodom

While the narrator of the "seventy-five folios" does not touch upon the question of Jewishness, except to briefly indicate a character's anti-Semitism,[223] he also never mentions homosexuality. For the reader of *In Search of Lost Time*, the "seventy-five folios" might appear, from this point of view, somewhat reserved or lacking. At this stage, Proust still hadn't created the Baron de Charlus. Sodom had not been embodied, although we do catch a glimpse of Ludwig II of Bavaria and his "strange loves," then Prince Edmond de Polignac, and there is a sketch of a seductive prototype of Robert de Saint-Loup.[224]

Since late 1907, however, Proust had been fascinated by the "homosexuality trials"[225] that had been happening in Germany and which had ended with the arrest of Prince Philipp of Eulenburg, a close friend of the Kaiser, on May 8, 1908[226]—he'd even mentioned the review of the first of those trials, the Harden trial, in his pastiche of Michelet.[227] It was soon after the opening of the preliminary investigation into Prince Eulenburg that Proust announced to Louis d'Albufera that among the projects he was working on just then was an "essay on pederasty," adding in parentheses the words "not easy to publish"[228]—although it seems likely that what he meant by this was not that the subject itself was difficult to get published (because there was an explosion of articles on the question around that time)[229] but rather that it would be difficult for he himself to be the published author of such an essay. Not long after this, he wrote to Robert Dreyfus that the "forbidden article" was turning into a "short story," presumably

223. F. 81.

224. Ff. 80, 81. The phrase about Edmond de Polignac had been omitted by Fallois.

225. Letter to Robert de Billy, [circa November 9, 1907], *Corr.*, t. VII, p. 309.

226. On the Eulenburg Affair, see Vigneron 1937, pp. 69–71, 73–74, and the commentary by A. Compagnon, *SG*, III, pp. 1199–1200.

227. *Le Figaro*, February 22, 1908; *PM*, p. 27 and note 4. Murakami 2012, p. 273 sq.

228. To Louis d'Albufera, [May 5 or 6, 1908], *Corr.*, VIII, p. 113. Proust avoids the term "homosexual," which appears to him "too Germanic and pretentious" (Notebook 49, f. 60v; *SG*, III, p. 1202). The opening of the investigation into Prince Eulenburg was announced in *Le Figaro* on May 2, 1908, p. 2.

229. Vigneron 1937, pp. 71–72.

on the same subject.[230] However, until the long, apologetic piece in the 1909 notebooks—"The Queer Race," a draft of the first part of *Sodom and Gomorrah* in which he drew a parallel between the two cursed "races," the "inverts" and the Jews[231]—it is possible that Proust wrote nothing of any importance on the subject; no manuscript of the planned essay, article, or short story from the spring of 1908 has ever been found, in any case, with the Fallois archives revealing nothing new in that regard.

In July 1908, Lucien Daudet published *Le Chemin mort*, a "novel on homosexuality or pederasty"[232] that did not speak its name, and that described the influence exercised over a young man by a certain Marcel, a person of independent wealth who fancies himself an author. Proust spent a large part of the summer finding a newspaper that would accept his review (it would finally appear, pseudonymously, in *L'Intransigeant*, a newspaper edited by Léon Bailby, who was the lover of Proust's friend Albert Flament).[233] It was that same summer that Proust wrote the pages from the "seventy-five folios" on the gang of young girls seen in C. (Cabourg, undoubtedly). We can glimpse Marcel Proust in the somewhat smug character depicted "in a soft pink tie" by a journalist,[234] and who borrowed a tie of the same color from his "older brother"[235]—perhaps a nod to Lucien Daudet who, in that month of August 1908, dedicated a short story to Proust in which the hero, a rich dandy, is nicknamed by his mistress the "Prince of Ties."[236] It would be a mistake to underestimate the self-parodic element to these pages in which, as would also be the case with *In the Shadow of Young Girls in Flower*, the vanity, clumsiness, and disappointments of the

230. [May 16, 1908], *Corr.*, VIII, pp. 122, 123.

231. Notebooks 7 and 6; *SG*, *Sketch I*, III, pp. 924–928, 930–933.

232. Compagnon 2021, p. 61. Lucien Alphonse-Daudet, *Le Chemin mort* (Ernest Flammarion, 1908).

233. *EA*, pp. 550–552. On Flament and Bailby, see François Proulx, "Une lettre à Léon Bailby," *Bulletin d'informations proustiennes*, no. 48 (2018): 16.

234. L'Ouvreuse du Cirque d'Eté (Willy), *La Colle aux quintes* (H. Simonis Empis, 1899), p. 87. Column of April 12, 1898. See Leblanc 2017, p. 50.

235. F. 71.

236. "La réponse imprévue," *Mercure de France*, August 1, 1908, pp. 467–487. *Le Prince des cravates* was also the title of the short story collection published by Lucien Daudet in 1910, also mentioned by Proust in *L'Intransigeant* (*EA*, pp. 552–554).

protagonist are sources of comedy. Proust had no fear of ambivalence: he did not expect all his readers to see simple *"fillettes"* in those insolent sporty young people who played golf and straddled horses reined in by grooms. The "chattering conventicle" that they formed strongly resembles that of the "young people of Cabourg" captured in verse:

Like flocks of swallows in the autumn sky,
Fluttering their wings and chirping as they fly,
Here are gathered groups that stroll and squawk
Loudly, waving their arms as they walk![237]

Obliqueness is also the rule elsewhere in the "seventy-five folios." For these pages are filled with allusions to the outings that Proust—who had "become an 'automobile fanatic'"[238]—had taken in 1907 around Cabourg in a taxi driven by the young Alfred Agostinelli, who would become a key character in *Search*. Place-names gather memories, like passwords. The name of Bretteville, first of all, long known as that of Swann's ancestor because it was mentioned in the "Pages Written" of Carnet 1[239] and which had never provoked any commentary, is associated in the "seventy-five folios" with "Bretteville-l'Orgueilleuse."[240] A château close to that municipality in Normandy, located between Caen and Bayeux, was one of Proust's destinations in October 1907 during the trips with his driver.[241] In the 1908 pages, the name "Bretteville" becomes a synonym for punishment, since it is associated with the mother's cursory or nonexistent goodnight kiss. This symbolic instrument of separation would become Swann, but a church near Balbec would retain the epithet "l'Orgueilleuse,"[T] and it would enchant Albertine,[242] the half-confessed fictional mask for Alfred.

237. Fallois archives. See the transcription of this poem in Marcel Proust, *Le Mystérieux Correspondant et autres nouvelles inédites*, Luc Fraisse (ed.) (Paris: Éditions de Fallois, 2019), pp. 159–160 (quotation p. 160). See in this volume f. 67.

238. Letter to Antoine Bibesco, [October 1907], *Corr.*, VII, p. 296.

239. Carnet 1, f. 7v. See the Chronology.

240. F. 15.

241. The Château de Norrey: see *Corr.*, VII, p. 296, and p. 297 note 5 by Ph. Kolb.

T. English translation: "the proud" or "the arrogant."

242. *SG*, III, pp. 402–403.

In the next episode, "Robert and the goat," we might wonder why the little boy is taken to Évreux to have his photograph taken.[243] Nothing in the context explains this location (as far from Illiers as it is from Auteuil), and anyway the detail serves no narrative function; it had disappeared from Proust's next attempt at writing this episode.[244] The reason becomes a little clearer when we remember that Proust, as he told Mme Straus, "spent four or five days"[245] in September 1907 in and around Évreux, driven by Agostinelli. The mention of Évreux appears in the context of another separation imposed by cruel parents, with the victim this time being a little boy dressed as a girl. It is true, of course, that in the European bourgeoisie of the late nineteenth century both girls and boys would wear dresses, but the feminization here is excessive, at odds with all realism: an extravagant hairstyle modeled on the Spanish infanta, accessories such as mirrors and "satin bags," the comparison to "a pompous, dejected princess in a tragedy" . . . The identification with Phaedra in love is impossible to miss, at least for French readers, because Racine's verse is so familiar, but a less visible network of allusions also connects the little boy to a young Princess Esther, the Jewish wife of the Persian king Ahasuerus. Like Esther, weighed down by the "vain ornaments" that hide her true identity, the child wants to free himself from his disguise, "tearing" and "ripping" his "Asiatic gown."[246] This secret Jewishness could be an allegory (albeit a humorous one) on gay identity, with "Évreux"—but also the tender words addressed to the goat by its "little master"[247]—functioning as secret signals aimed at a few readers. In *Swann's Way*, in which the episode took the form of the farewell to the hawthorns and the brother alibi no longer existed, the separation with the "pink thorns" suggests much more crudely the dramatization of homosexual desire; this was a risky game, and the

243. F. 21.
244. Notebook 6, ff. 69v–68v; cf. *CS*, Sketch *XXVII*, I, pp. 737–738.
245. *Corr.*, VII, [October 8, 1907], p. 286.
246. "[. . .] he started violently smashing his mirrors on the ground, stamping on the satin bags, tearing out not his hair but the little bows that had been put in his hair, ripping his beautiful Asiatic gown and shouting loudly" (ff. 22–23). See notes and Mauriac Dyer 2014.
247. F. 22. In 1894 and 1895, Proust, nicknamed "pony," would call Reynaldo Hahn "little Master" or "my little master" (*Corr.*, I, pp. 345, 381–382, 396), sometimes in English (ibid., p. 326).

allusion did not escape Robert de Montesquiou; nor did Proust attempt to deny it. Quite the contrary, in fact.[248] As for the "plump face" of the "little brother"[249]—which could easily resemble (or herald?) Agostinelli's full cheeks, so beloved of Proust—we find it again in the "fat, coarse-grained face" of the girl, her hair crowned with the same infanta bow, who plays the pianola for the hero: this is, of course, Albertine.[250]

Agostinelli is also present in [Noble Names], through a series of allusions to those same outings in Normandy during the summer and fall of 1907: the trip to Falaise to stay with the Eyrague family, to Glisolles near Évreux to stay with the Clermont-Tonnerre family, the visit to the Château de Balleroy near Bayeux, and to the Sainte-Foy church in Conches, also near Évreux.[251] Narrating a nocturnal arrival to the sound of his automobile's horn, Proust paraphrases his own article from November 1907 in *Le Figaro*, "Impressions of the Road from an Automobile," in which he had praised his "mechanic, the ingenious Agostinelli"[252]—"my mechanic," writes the author of the "seventy-five folios" in the opening line of the first episode about the "ways."[253] Evoking the visit to the Château de Balleroy, he even returns to one of the more reworked drafts of that article (a draft that was also found in the Fallois archives).[254]

Already, then, Proust was taking care to secretly weave the still-hot memories of Alfred into these pages. But guilt was not far behind: it is also in [Noble Names] that we find the tirade on mothers profaned by their sons' debauches.[255] Perhaps it is preferable when Proust has fun, transforming Maman into the parodic reincarnation of Aman, persecutor of Jews.

As for the disconcerting mention, on the last page of the "seventy-five folios," of the Christ in St. Mark's, Venice, looking "effeminate, Oriental, and

248. See the letter from R. de Montesquiou, [March 22, 1912], *Corr.*, XI, p. 66, and the reply from Proust a few days later, ibid., p. 79. Mauriac Dyer 2014, pp. 159–160.
     249. F. 21.
     250. *AD*, IV, p. 70; *P*, III, p. 874.
     251. See notes for ff. 75, 76, 77.
     252. *PM*, p. 66.
     253. F. 27.
     254. See ff. 75, 76 and notes.
     255. F. 81.

bizarre, his gesture transformed into the pretention of some fat, suspect Syriot," "almost like a foolish Oriental pasha,"[256] and the surprising hierarchy of the arts that follows this, in which the narrator shows a preference for "aesthetically certain" signs produced by "those of our blood," it is best not to jump to the conclusion that Proust was making a concession to the xenophobia of the times and to a sort of misplaced artistic nationalism. True, the narrator of *Search* will admit a predilection for French Gothic, the *opus francigenum*, where "what might be fairly judged beautiful, what is of value to the heart and the mind, [is] first of all pleasing to the eye, gracefully colored, precisely chiseled, matter and form combining to create inner perfection." But that doesn't mean that one should condemn [people with] "a strange, preposterous appearance," often those whose "hair was too long, their nose and eyes too big, their gestures uncouth and theatrical": it would be "puerile to [. . .] judge them for that."[257] In the "seventy-five folios," as in this passage from *The Guermantes Way*, Proust invites us to learn to read signs in a deeper way, to see beyond the first impression, to suspend judgment, particularly when confronted with the appearance often presented, according to the narrator, by "Jews": "we must first overcome what repels or shocks or amuses us."[258] Unprepossessing appearances do not prevent the presence of invisible virtues, including here "distinction, kindness, courage, simplicity, delicacy, tact, nobility."[259] If it were not a portrait of Christ, it would be tempting to see in this "Oriental" (i.e., Semitic), "effeminate" "pasha" (i.e., one who engages in in the "Turkish vice"), the ironic, provocative, secretly apologetic self-portrait of a Jewish "invert," Marcel Proust. That, after all, is a striking end.

256. F. 86.
257. *CG*, II, pp. 702–703.
258. Ibid., p. 702. See Duval 2019, p. 66.
259. F. 86.

Notes

[An Evening in the Countryside]

This first "chapter," the longest and most complete of the "seventy-five folios," is the very first known draft of "Combray I" (ff. 1–20) and of a brief episode from "Combray II" (ff. 20–26). Although unfinished—Proust rewrote the last pages, but without a satisfying narrative join (ff. 25–26)—it forms a continuous whole (ff. 1–24) and the writing is fluid: rather than a first draft, it is most likely a montage of various preceding pieces that have not reached us, perhaps including some of the "Pages Written" listed in Carnet 1 ("Robert and the goat, Maman leaves on a trip./[. . .]/My grandmother in the garden, M. de Bretteville's dinner, I go upstairs, Maman's face then and since in my dreams, I can't fall asleep, concessions etc."; f. 7v. *Cn*, p. 43). The name "Combray" is not included: it appears in 1909 in Notebook 4 (f. 23, passim; Other Manuscripts, no. XII); it is also found in the earlier Notebook 1, but in an interlinear correction in a different ink (f. 68v; Pugh 1987, p. 122 note 29). For that reason we have not kept it, as B. de Fallois did, in the title (see above). Nor have we kept the plural: this "chapter," despite various digressions and repetitions, tells the story of one particular, decisive evening, that of Maman's abdication (ff. 1–20). A partial antecedent text, even earlier than the "Pages Written," was found in the Fallois archives (Other Manuscripts, no. III).

f. 1

1. *the precious wicker armchairs.* In the antecedent text, "summer in Auteuil," the grandmother, unlike the rest of the family, is depicted "drag[ging] her wicker armchair to the front of the garden near the lawns" (Other Manuscripts, no. III). In Notebook 1 the memory connected to those armchairs is again precisely situated: "But already my body evoked another attitude. It is no longer lying but sitting in a wicker armchair in the garden at Auteuil [. . .]" (f. 6v; Other Manuscripts, no. XI). We find them again in Combray in Notebook 4 ("We had brought in the wicker armchairs so they wouldn't get wet [. . .]," f. 24v; Other Manuscripts, no. XII). It was while rereading the typed version that Proust restored the adjective from the "seventy-five folios," which would remain in the definitive text: "But my grandmother, in all weathers, even when the rain was coming down in torrents and

Françoise had rushed the <precious> wicker armchairs indoors so that they should not get soaked, was to be seen pacing the deserted rain-lashed garden [. . .]" (NAF 16733, f. 22; *CS*, I, p. 11).

2. *verandah*. We have kept the spelling "verandah," which features in all the manuscripts from 1908 and 1909–1910 (see Other Manuscripts, nos. III, IX, X, and XII; see ff. 16–17 for Notebook 4), and until 1913 in an addition to the Grasset galley proofs (*Bodmer, paperole* added to galley proof 5, col. 1; cf. *CS*, I, p. 24).

3. *a pity not to take advantage of it*. An earlier version of the grandmother's walk in the garden is included in the Fallois archives (Other Manuscripts, no. III). This is probably a direct memory of Proust's grandmother, Mme Nathé Weil (see below): at the age of twelve, Proust wrote to her mentioning a "long walk (healthy of course)" ([just after August 3, 1883], *Corr.*, XXI, p. 542); in September 1891, a year after her death, he wrote a letter to his mother from Cabourg reminding her of "[. . .] those years by the sea when grandmother and I, pressed together, would walk into the wind, chatting" (Cattaui 1956, plate 34). After that, the scene sought its place. In Notebook 4, where Proust recycled a large part of the "seventy-five folios," he placed the grandmother's walk at the moment when Swann's voice rings out: "[. . .] each of us wondered who that could be [. . .] and we sent my grandmother as a scout since, cold as it was, she had stayed in the garden, thinking it 'a pity' to remain indoors in the countryside. On days when it rained we would see her in the empty, soaked garden walking along the paths saying: 'at last one can breathe[,]' hatless, pushing back her disheveled gray hair to feel more air and rain against her skin" (Notebook 4, f. 53, unfinished and crossed out). Next, he inserted the scene—in a version whose text is already close to the definitive text—in the middle of the walks around Combray: the rain prevents the family from walking the Méséglise road but not the grandmother from walking around the garden (Notebook 4, f. 24v; Other Manuscripts, no. XII)— by giving up on this placing, he is able to return to the Méséglise walks their "uncertain" weather: see below f. 34. At last the scene finds its place at the beginning of "Combray I," after the opening section with the bedrooms and, as here, just before the evening kiss scene (Notebook 8, ff. 14–15, and Notebook 9, ff. 30–31; *CS*, I, pp. 10–11). The walk in the garden is expanded in the present pages up to folio 6 into a moral portrait of the grandmother, of which Proust uses certain elements for the beginning of [A Visit to the Seaside] (f. 53), before dispersing or removing most of them (see ff. 3, 4, 6).

4. *my great-uncle*. The identity of this "great-uncle" is suggested by the detailed clues in the antecedent text, located "in Auteuil" at the home of an

"old uncle"—"he owned the house; we lived in his home" (Other Manuscripts, no. III)—and through cross-referencing the relatives attributed to him here (see next note, and f. 10). He is Lazard Baruch, a.k.a. Louis, Weil (1816–1896), son of Baruch Weil's second wife, Marguerite Sara Nathan, and younger brother of Proust's maternal grandfather, Nathé Weil (1814–1896). In the corresponding scene in the definitive text, the only person who calls out to the grandmother during her walks in the rain is the great-aunt, and the context is completely different (*CS*, I, pp. 11–12). The "seventy-five folios" lead us to reevaluate the importance of Louis Weil in the genesis of *In Search of Lost Time*, beyond the well-known transposition into "Uncle Adolphe" in *Swann's Way*. See the Commentary.

5. *Adèle.* This name belongs to Marcel Proust's maternal grandmother, Mme Nathé Weil, née Adèle Berncastell (1824–1890). Later, there is a mention of the great-uncle's "sister-in-law" (f. 6), and this was indeed what Adèle was to Louis Weil (see previous note). It is true that Nathé and Louis had a younger sister also called Adèle (Adèle Weil, married name Lazarus [1818–1892]): it is most likely she who is mentioned irreverently by young Marcel in a letter to his grandmother in [August 1886] (*Corr.*, XXI, p. 545, and *Lettres*, p. 64). But there is no reason to distinguish the grandmother "Adèle" of this page from the one that features in the antecedent text, where the identification of Adèle Berncastell is corroborated, without any possible doubt, by the detail that her mother was the "sister-in-law" of Adolphe Crémieux, as in real life was Rose Berncastell née Silny (see Other Manuscripts, no. III). See also f. 10. "Adèle" would be replaced by "Cécile" then "~~Octavie~~ <Bathilde>," the name that would remain into the definitive text (Notebook 2, f. 7v; Other Manuscripts, nos. IX and X; Notebook 9, ff. 30v, 32, 34). Marcel Proust's first cousin—the daughter of his uncle Georges and Georges's wife Amélie Oulman—was named after her maternal grandmother: Adèle Weil (1892–1944) died at the hands of the Nazis; her daughter, Annette Heumann, survived deportation, and died in 2020 at the age of ninety-nine.

6. *It'll be good for your new dress.* This sarcastic remark did not survive the next draft. But the uncle plays the role of the bad guy in the first version of the sadism scene, which was grafted onto the walk during the revision; Proust then replaced him with the hero's great-aunt (*CS*, I, pp. 11–12): see the Commentary.

7. *everyone else.* Two characteristics juxtaposed here would later be separated. The eccentricity, in the uncle's judgment, of the grandmother's character ("never like everyone else"), already noted in the antecedent text ("'You're too hot Adèle! It's a beautiful day Adèle!' would yell my uncle, who considered her a crank,"

Other Manuscripts, no. III), was used in Notebook 9 during the revision for the cognac scene ("she had brought to my father's family a 'mentality' so different that everybody mocked and teased her," f. 32; cf. *CS*, I, p. 11). As for the uncle's "cowardly" attempt "to gain the support of my grandfather" and everyone else due to his secret fear of being wrong, it was combined in several different forms with the reproach aimed at the grandmother of always being opposed to the rest of the family's taste: see f. 3.

8. *and sob my heart out.* This flight to "the bathroom" to escape the spectacle of the family sadism was only later, in the next part of the genesis, associated once again with the grandmother's walks around the garden. During the revisions of the future "Combray," Proust interrupted his dictation to write, on two facing verso pages, the additional cognac scene, which would in turn provoke the hero to flee (Notebook 9, ff. 30v–31v, pages then copied by his secretary in ff. 32–35). Barely indicated here, this sketch would from then on constitute the climax of the scene of the grandmother's walks (*CS*, I, pp. 11–13).

f. 2

1. *to stay in the living room an hour later than usual.* The psychological portrait of the grandmother is joined to the one from the antecedent text, which describes her as "saintlike in her gentleness" (Other Manuscripts, no. III). The way she "seemed to join in with the others' taunting of her" is repeated during the revision: "so humble in heart and so gentle," she "mocked even her own sufferings," wearing that "beautiful, self-mocking smile" (Notebook 9, ff. 33, 35; cf. *CS*, I, p. 12: "she was so humble in heart and so gentle that her tenderness toward others, and the little care that she took for her own person and sufferings, were reconciled in her expression in a smile that, unlike the smiles seen on most human faces, aimed all its irony inward"). In the pages that follow this, however, the grandmother Adèle is far from a victim.

2. *directly hit by the alluvium.* This cruel scene extends the uncle's taunts from the previous page ("It'll be good for your new dress"). In the first version, crossed out, it is the grandmother herself who is "horribly soiled," before she "horribly soiled <her plum skirt>": even though "soiled" (*crotté*) is meant in the sense of being dirtied by mud rather than feces, the text plays on the ambivalence. The scene is abridged and softened in Notebook 4, where there is no longer any reference to "the desire—unknown to her—to avoid getting mud stains on her plum skirt, which was in fact disappearing entirely under mud up to her blouse [. . .]" (f. 24v), the detail of the "blouse" being the next to disappear (Notebook 8,

ff. 14–15; Notebook 9, f. 31 and *CS*, I, p. 11). This volume also contains a line about the hem of the mother's dress, seen in a dream after her death, being "soiled": see f. 18. The grandmother's "soaked" skirts at the beach are another reminder of the theme (f. 53). On Proust's complex relationship with scatology, connected to his father's profession as a doctor specializing in hygiene and probably to his maternal grandmother's surname "Torcheux"[T] and even to his own surname "Proust,"[TT] see Leriche and Mauriac Dyer 2000, particularly pp. 92–95. One remembers, too, M. de Charlus's insulting words about Mme de Saint-Euverte, another lover of walking: "They tell me that the indefatigable old street-walker gives 'garden parties.' Myself, I should describe them as 'invitations to explore the sewers.' Are you going to wallow there?" (*SG*, III, p. 99).

f. 3

1. *everything we like is bad.* The uncle's rancorous phrase is passed first to the "great-aunt." Proust combines it with the attempt—formulated earlier here (f. 1)—to gain the support of the family on the question of the "new gardener": "she suspected that on the contrary we considered my grandmother's judgment finer than hers, and to destroy those suspicions she sought to ambush us into total disapproval of what my grandmother did. She chose a moment when, taking refuge on the verandah, or in the living room, the patio doors open to the garden, we watched it raining, and seeing my grandmother who continued to walk around the garden in the rain, she called out: Come on Cécile, come inside. But no, she can't do anything the way we do it. She's the same way with the rain as she is with everything else. *All it takes is for you or me to think something good and she has to criticize it.* Alas the only response was our silence [. . .]" (Notebook 2, f. 8v; Other Manuscripts, no. IX). The formulation is then tightened: "my great-aunt knew that my grandmother's approval was lacking. She scorned it but sought it. Unable to obtain it she tried to disparage it. 'I don't know why I bother telling you to come inside. As soon as we like something you think it's bad' she said looking at us from the corner of her eye, vainly hoping to draw from us a mass condemnation of my grandmother's opinions" (Other Manuscripts, no. X). The line disappeared at the same time as the family dispute about the "new gardener" (see below and the Commentary), but Proust would later recycle this dialogue, in April 1913 when he was adding to the scene featuring the grandmother's sisters, Céline and Flora, in the galley proofs for the first volume. Again it is the great-aunt who opposes the grandmother: "'Did you see that Swann was mentioned in

T With its similarity to the word "*torcher*," slang for wiping a bottom.
TT Similar to "*prout*," a childish word for "fart."

Le Figaro?' 'But I always told you that he was a man of taste,' said my grandmother. 'Well, of course you would say that, since you never want to have the
same opinion as *us*,' replied my great-aunt who, knowing that my grandmother
never agreed with her about anything, but not being sure that we would side with
her, wanted to extract from us a wholesale condemnation of my grandmother's
opinions, thereby forcing us into solidarity with hers. But we remained silent"
(*Bodmer, paperole* added to galley proof 4, col. 8; cf. *CS*, I, p. 22).

2. *houseleeks in the shape of a cross.* The houseleek or sempervivum (French:
joubarbe) is an ornamental succulent. Proust misspells the name on the manuscript as *joubarde* (cf. f. 29: "a lawn with houseleeks in the shape of the cross of
the Legion of Honor"—"*une pelouse avec la croix de la légion d'honneur faite en
joubarde* [*sic*]"). My thanks to Bertrand Marchal, who suggested the correct
reading. In *Sodom and Gomorrah*, Raspelière's gardener is upset by the contempt with which Mme Verdurin treats "his araucarias, his begonias, sempervivum and double dahlias" (*SG*, III, p. 309). In the handwritten version of the
passage, Proust makes the same spelling mistake: "*ses joubardes*," (Notebook V,
paperole at f. 71). Is the shape of the cross of the Legion of Honor the gardener's
tribute to the decoration received by Louis Weil (see the Commentary)?

3. *the little orange trees at the entrance.* In *Jean Santeuil*, it is clearly stated
that the gardener—the notary's gardener, at that point—was indelicate: "[. . .]
sometimes the gardener [. . .] would mercilessly attack the orange trees lined up
at the entrance in large green plant pots, standing there as motionless as organic
statues and intended, before you were found by the servants in the entrance hall,
to welcome you into the garden, stripping them of their yellowish flowers which
he stuffed into a bag so he could use them to make a liquor that he sold for profit,
thanks to the inexplicable leniency of the notary from whom he was stealing,
who, proud of his garden and completely dependent on this arrogant gardener, let
himself be persuaded that it was harmful to orange trees to let them keep their
flowers [. . .]" (*JS*, p. 328). The "new gardener" is no more honest in the versions
that followed this one: "My grandmother looked with pain at the bare orange
trees whose flowers he had all torn off to make a [*one word ill.*] syrup that he sold to
~~pharmacists~~. But since from that amount he kept one bottle that he gave to my
aunt, she was thrilled to be able to announce when she had it 'served' to visitors:
It's homemade" (Notebook 2, f. 7v; cf. NAF 16730, f. 21v; Other Manuscripts, no.
IX). In a notebook of late additions, the grandmother reproaches Mme Poussin
and her daughter, "who had [. . .] about thirty beautiful orange trees in pots, for
stripping them of their beautiful white flowers to make this liquor called: 'orange
flower'" (Notebook 60, f. 123). There is also a reference, in "On Reading," to

"the precious liquor of orange flower placed [. . .] in a glass vial" (*PM*, p. 164). As a young man, Proust wrote to his mother, from Auteuil, on [September 5, 1888]: "Grandfather has completely given up tea. Orange flower" (*Corr.*, I, p. 111). Even though there is still a mention in a draft of the "~~laboratory~~ <shed> where the gardener made his syrups" (Notebook 14, f. 48; *CS, Sketch XLIII*, I, p. 780), in the definitive text there remains only the faintest trace of these trees: "Sometimes I would be torn from my reading in the middle of the afternoon by the gardener's daughter, who came running past me like a whirlwind, knocking over an orange tree [. . .]" (ibid., p. 87). On the connection between the change to the reminiscence set off by the "toast" dipped in tea and the disappearance of the orange trees, see the Commentary.

4. *my aunt*. The change of character is forced: this "aunt" immediately inherits the qualities attributed to the grandmother Adèle in the preceding, crossed-out phrase ("~~My grandmother was generally in favor of nature, simplicity~~ [. . .]"). By folio 5 she becomes the "grandmother" again. As early as 1905's essay "On Reading" the character traits that would be attributed to the grandmother in *Search* were already being given to the great-aunt (*PM*, pp. 162–163; see also the next note); the hesitation between the grandmother and the great-aunt was already present in the manuscript of this text (NAF 16619, ff. 4–5).

5. *other worries*. It is in the "seventy-five folios" that the harmful activities of the "new gardener" are most detailed (pruning trees, mowing the lawn, stripping flowers from orange trees . . .): they would vanish by the time of the definitive text, while the character of the gardener himself would be nothing more than a faint trace ("[. . .] our garden, that undistinguished product of the strictly conventional fantasy of the gardener whom my grandmother so despised," *CS*, I, p. 85). The love of "nature," which, in the grandmother (or, briefly, here, the "aunt"), reflects her obsession with health, becomes—when transferred to the aesthetic world—a love of all things "natural," whether in gardening, cooking, or playing the piano. This trio was already present in the antecedent text of this page: "[my grandmother] loved nature, and that gardens should resemble it was one of her theories, as was not playing the piano 'dryly,' or cooking meals 'disguised' to look like other objects"—so, naturally, she abhors "the too-straight borders, the stiff flowers, the unnatural flowerbeds" (Other Manuscripts, no. III; cf. *CS*, I, p. 63). This is also found in *In the Shadow of Young Girls in Flower*, where "naturalness" is a social, even moral, quality that the grandmother finds in Saint-Loup: "[. . .] Saint-Loup made a conquest of my grandmother, not only by the incessant acts of kindness which he went out of his way to shew to us both, but by the naturalness which he put into them as into everything. For

naturalness—doubtless because through the artifice of man it allows a feeling
of nature to permeate—was the quality which my grandmother preferred to all
others, whether in gardens, where she did not like there to be, as there had been
in our Combray garden, too formal borders, or at table, where she detested those
dressed-up dishes in which you could hardly detect the foodstuffs that had gone
to make them, or in piano-playing, which she did not like to be too finicking, too
laboured, having indeed had a special weakness for the discords, the wrong
notes of Rubinstein" (*JF*, II, p. 93; cf. Notebook 28, ff. 94–93 and Notebook 70,
f. 103v). In "On Reading," there was also the "great-aunt" who displayed these
tastes (*PM*, pp. 162–163). We discover in the earliest antecedent text of this
passage (Other Manuscripts, no. II) that the character in question is Mme Santeuil the mother. On other aspects of the grandmother's love of "naturalness"
and on the style of piano-playing she prefers (which must avoid the twin pitfalls
of sentimental bombast and dryness), see f. 6; on her health obsession (here attributed to the "aunt"), see the present page and f. 53; and on the other qualities
that she prizes in society, see f. 15.

6. *to the seaside.* Theoretically, the "aunt" is still the protagonist, even if in
the previous version (Other Manuscripts, no. III) and in all the versions that came
after the "seventy-five folios" (f. 53 sq.) it is the grandmother (or, exceptionally, the
mother) who accompanies the hero on vacation. Here, as in the antecedent text,
the emphasis is on her insistence that the children spend all their time at the
beach, even in bad weather in the next version (f. 53).

f. 4

1. *our panic-stricken parents.* These disastrous outings, undertaken to see a
few "curiosities" on the way home, had already been described in the antecedent
text (Other Manuscripts, no. III). In the revision of Notebook 4, they are reduced
to a crossed-out parenthetical aside: "and having driven our parents mad with
worry the day of our return by arriving several hours later because it would have
been too sad to pass near a famous town that was on the ~~way~~ route without getting
off the train and visiting it" (f. 62). Only one sentence relating to this would remain in the definitive text: as they set off for Balbec, the grandmother wants to
follow the itinerary taken by Mme de Sévigné when she went to "L'Orient": "But
my grandmother had been obliged to abandon this project, at the instance of my
father who knew, whenever she organised any expedition with a view to extracting
from it the utmost intellectual benefit that it was capable of yielding, what a tale
there would be to tell of missed trains, lost luggage, sore throats and broken
rules" (*JF*, II, p. 7).

2. *no one could ever understand what she was talking about.* Theoretically, this is still a description of the aunt, whose letters, we are told a few lines below, were "piously kept by her daughter" (and not "Maman") after her death. The only letter from Proust's maternal grandmother that has reached us—a postscript to a letter from Marcel to his grandfather—does not correspond in any way to this portrayal, despite an allusion to Labiche (Mme Nathé Weil to Nathé Weil, [summer 1879], *Corr.*, XXI, p. 540). As for the text of *Search,* rich though it is in missives, there are none from the narrator's grandmother (nor any of his "aunts") and none, in general, based on this idea of an exaggeratedly comical system of allusions. On the other hand, the present scene should be compared with the character traits of the grandmother's sisters, as depicted in "Combray I," who are similarly prone to expressing themselves in "allusions, metaphors, riddles" to the point that nobody understands them: "my grandmother's sisters, [. . .] in their horror of vulgarity, had brought to such a fine art the concealment of a personal allusion in a wealth of ingenious circumlocution, that it would often pass unnoticed even by the person to whom it was addressed" (*CS*, I, p. 22). This character trait is illustrated almost immediately by the episode of the attempts to thank Swann for his gift of the Asti wine, unintelligible to anyone other than the great-aunts themselves (ibid., pp. 23–26, 34). This scene was a late addition, in 1913, during the correction of the galley proofs for *Swann's Way* (*Bodmer, paperole* added to galley proof 4, col. 8; galley proof 5, col. 1; cf. f. 3).

f. 5

1. *Ah! madwoman, madwoman.* "Oh! la folle! Oh! la folle! Oh! la folle!" (Molière, *L'Amour médecin,* act III, scene VI).

2. *"Dreadful doctor who does not want to be from the Académie!"* "'Nasty doctor, you don't want to be from the Académie? . . . and yet you have only one word to say . . .'" (*"Méchant docteur, vous ne voulez donc pas être de l'Académie? . . . et pourtant vous n'avez qu'un mot à dire . . ."*) (Eugène Labiche, *La Poudre aux yeux,* two-act comedy [1861], act I, scene VII). The phrase is repeated in scene X and act II, scene I. While writing about a train journey, Proust's maternal grandmother jokingly characterizes herself to her husband as the "worthy wife of M. Perrichon," another famous Labiche character (Mme Nathé Weil to Nathé Weil, [summer 1879], *Corr.*, XXI, p. 540).

3. *and can tell instantly what is wrong with it.* Machut, a character in *La Grammaire,* is a veterinarian: "Oh! I can rest easy now . . . Machut knows what he's doing . . . he has a way of looking the animals in the eye . . . he lifts up their

eyelid . . . and he tells you: 'That's a sprain! . . .'" (*"Oh! je suis tranquille . . .*
Machut connaît son affaire . . . il a une manière de regarder les bêtes dans
l'œil . . . il leur ouvre la paupière . . . et il vous dit: 'Ça, c'est une entorse! . . .'")
(Eugène Labiche, *La Grammaire*, one-act vaudevillian comedy [1867], scene
XIII). In a letter to Reynaldo Hahn in 1906, Proust had fun telling a little story
based on the titles of several Labiche plays including *La Grammaire* and *La
Poudre aux yeux* ([just after May 16, 1906], *Corr.*, VI, p. 82).

4. *"How could I be in Étampes while my spelling is in Arpajon."* Caboussat
understands that his daughter, who acts as his secretary, will follow her husband:
"Ah, no! that doesn't suit me at all! my spelling will be in Étampes while I'm in
Arpajon! It can't be!" (*"Ah! mais non! ça ne me va pas! mon orthographe serait
à Étampes et moi à Arpajon! Ça ne se peut pas!"*) (*La Grammaire*, scene XV).
Proust quoted the same passage in a letter of [March 22, 1899] to Prince Edmond
de Polignac, claiming, in the absence of his mentor Reynaldo Hahn, to be unable
to correctly express his admiration for the prince's music: "[. . .] since he's in
Hamburg, I am like that character in Labiche whose daughter wrote his letters
because he didn't know how to spell and who despairs when she wants to get
married. 'My spelling will be in Paris he said and me in Arpajon.' I should never
have written to you when he wasn't here. That's why I am stammering" (Kahan and
Mauriac Dyer 2003, pp. 18–19). But in a possibly autobiographical draft of
Contre Sainte-Beuve, the year after he wrote the "seventy-five folios," Proust uses
the quote again in a poignant context: "Maman [. . .] died while [. . .] quoting
Labiche. [. . .] 'Don't let that little one be afraid, his Maman won't leave him. It's
impossible that I'll be in Étampes and my spelling in Arpajon!' And after that
she couldn't speak anymore" (Notebook 4, f. 68v; *CSB*, p. 125). It was again
Maman who adapted the quotation in a lighter-hearted passage in Notebook 65,
where she surprised her sick son by visiting him in Querqueville: "[. . .] I endlessly kissed Maman's cold, firm cheeks as she jokingly explained to me so I
wouldn't take my illness too seriously: 'I didn't want to be in St. Cloud while my
spelling was sick in Arpajon'" (f. 15).

5. *look down on you.* This famous saying is attributed to Napoleon Bonaparte,
haranguing his troops before the Battle of the Pyramids (1798).

6. *Go hang yourself Sévigné!* The allusion to the "stupid gentleman" hides
another, because it is itself an allusion to a passage from the sketch by Eugène
Grangé and Alfred Delacour, *Le Punch Grassot, à-propos en un acte* (Paris:
Michel Lévy frères, 1858). Auguste, the owner of a bar where he makes his famous
punch, thinks he has received a letter from the "monk" who gave him the recipe:

"[. . .] (opening the letter.) Ah! it's from the good monk . . . whom I taught good manners . . . and the language of Paris . . . Let's read it. (He reads.) 'My good old man, I'm in Paris . . . I await you at La Halle, at Louis Baratte's place. It's the perfect moment to uncork a nice Burgundy.' (breaking off from reading.) Oh! Sévigné, go hang yourself! (reading again.) 'Does that suit you? . . . Get here double-quick.—I am, for life,/Your little cutie pie,/Brother Leonardo.' Quick, my habit . . . my panama!" ("*(Ouvrant la lettre.) Ah! c'est du bon moine . . . que j'ai formé aux belles manières . . . et au langage parisien . . . Lisons. (Il lit.) 'Ma bonne vieille, je suis à Paris . . . Je t'attends à la Halle, chez Louis Baratte. C'est le vrai moment de casser le cou à un joli bourgogne.' (Interrompant sa lecture.) Oh! Sévigné, pends-toi! (Reprenant.) 'Ça te va-t-il? . . . Arrive dare dare.—Je suis, pour la vie,/Ton joli trognon,/Fra-Leonardo.'/Vite mon habit . . . mon panama!*") (scene XIII; my thanks to Bertrand Marchal for this reference). "Go hang yourself Sévigné!" seems to mean, here, "Sévigné couldn't have put it better!"—we will find out later the grandmother's fascination with that famous letter-writer, Mme Sévigné: "At Mme de Villeparisis's house she had met one of his nephews and she told Maman: 'Ah, my daughter, how common he is!' and she went into ecstasies over the letters written by our servant, exclaiming: 'Sévigné couldn't have put it better!'" (Notebook 8, ff. 25–26; *CS, Sketch XII*, I, p. 685; cf. ibid., p. 20, and *CG*, II, p. 625). But everything opposes the "stupid gentleman" and the good reader, or reader of taste, who is the grandmother. See below f. 15.

7. *my grandmother*. Proust returns to the grandmother after an interval when her role had been played by the aunt (ff. 3–5). So, two characters have, by turns, been the author of those incomprehensible letters.

f. 6

1. *the Viscount and Viscountess de Bretteville*. Proust had noted in Carnet 1 among the "Pages Written": "My grandmother in the garden, M. de Bretteville's dinner [. . .]" (f. 7v; *Cn*, p. 43). M. de Bretteville (known only through the accounts of other characters) here occupies, between the narrator and his mother, the position of third wheel that had been that of Dr. Surlande in *Jean Santeuil* and that would become Swann's position from Notebook 4 onward. Apart from the fact that they both belong to the Jockey Club (f. 16; *CS*, I, p. 15), however, they are complete opposites: unlike Swann's social situation in Combray, Bretteville's, far from being unknown, is exactly what earns him an invitation from the uncle, whose vanity is emphasized here (see also f. 15); whereas Swann is all refinement and delicacy, Bretteville appears, in the only anecdote repeated about him—the

one about eggs in the salad (see f. 16)—to be a rude, discourteous character; lastly, Swann's Jewishness can be contrasted with the viscount's landed nobility: "everything in Bretteville-l'Orgueilleuse belongs to him" (f. 15; cf. f. 75: "It is still today one of the great charms of noble families that they seem to be located in a particular patch of land, that their name [. . .] is still a place-name [. . .]"). The municipality of Bretteville-l'Orgueilleuse, between Caen and Bayeux, is probably the source of the character's surname. In October 1907, Proust, during one of his automobile trips with Alfred Agostinelli, stopped nearby to visit the church in Norrey (*Corr.*, VII, p. 296). The name "Bretteville" would not survive beyond the "seventy-five folios," unlike the epithet l'Orgueilleuse, the only thing that Albertine likes in the name of a renovated church near Balbec (*SG*, III, pp. 402–403, 484; *Corr.*, VII, p. 297 note 5).

2. *his sister-in-law.* In other words, the grandmother Adèle: affection shows through the squabbles.

3. *bouquets in all the vases.* These bouquets are mentioned a little farther on: see f. 10. On other indelicacies on the part of the gardener and their antecedents, see above f. 3.

4. *when playing Chopin's* Polonaise. In *Sodom and Gomorrah*, old Mme de Cambremer, who "had learned simultaneously to write and to play Chopin's music," seeks in her correspondence to "redeem the monotony of her multiple adjectives by employing them in a descending scale," but the narrator "changed [his] mind as to the nature of these diminuendos," seeing in them ultimately a sign of the same "depravity of taste" committed by Sainte-Beuve (*SG*, III, p. 473; cf. p. 336).

5. *can only harm children.* These snatches of dialogue recall the words of Mme Santeuil the mother, taken up by the great-aunt in "On Reading": "'She might have many more fingers than me but she lacks taste, playing that simple andante with such emphasis.' 'She might be a brilliant woman with many qualities but it shows a lack of tact to talk about oneself in such circumstances.' 'She might be a very skillful cook but she doesn't know how to make steak and potatoes.'" (Other Manuscripts, no. II; *PM*, p. 163). See also f. 15, and on the grandmother's character, f. 3.

6. *pulled at a rose to make it look more casual.* This gesture would be included again from Notebook 4 onward, when the bell is rung to announce Swann's arrival: sent out as a scout, the grandmother is "always happy to have an excuse to

walk through the garden and to surreptitiously rip out a stake from the rosebush to make the roses look a little more 'natural'" (Notebook 4, f. 52v; *CS*, *Sketch IX*, I, p. 669, and var. *a;* ibid., p. 14). Suddenly the incident of the knocked-over vase, which is associated here with the grandmother's gesture, was available for other contexts: see the next note.

7. *it wouldn't be such a bad thing.* This incident of the knocked-over vase and the grandmother's indifferent reaction prefigure Bloch's clumsiness during the tea party at Mme de Villeparisis's house: "Bloch rose and in his turn came over to look at the flowers which Mme de Villeparisis was painting. [. . .] Bloch wanted to express his admiration in an appropriate gesture, but only succeeded in knocking over the glass containing the spray of apple blossom with his elbow, and all the water was spilled on the carpet. [. . .] To cover his shame with a piece of inso- lence, [he] retorted: 'It's not of the slightest importance; I'm not wet'" (*CG*, II, pp. 512–513 and p. 512 note 2).

8. *as I left her and went up to my bedroom.* We find here the resumption of some of the "Pages Written" listed in Carnet 1: "My grandmother in the garden, M. de Bretteville's dinner, I go upstairs [. . .]" (f. 7v; *Cn*, p. 43). This is the begin- ning of a long piece of writing about the evening kiss, juxtaposing the experience of "every night" (ff. 6–9) with the even more painful experience of "that night" when the family has a guest to dinner (ff. 7, 9–20). Even if this rediscovered ver- sion from 1908 has left its trace in all the later versions (Notebooks 4, 6, and 8), it differs profoundly from them in its repeated allusions to Maman's death: see ff. 17–19; the Commentary. In Notebook 4, the bedtime drama is aggravated by two circumstances: "the evenings when we had walked the Villebon way and the evenings when M. Swann came to dinner" (f. 25, cf. ff. 43–44); the walking of the "ways" even precedes Swann's arrival (ff. 25–44; Other Manuscripts, no. XII). This arrangement would prove temporary, but the walks along the Guermantes way remained associated with the loss of the evening kiss: "[. . .] as was the rule on days when we had taken the Guermantes way and dinner was in consequence served later than usual, I should be sent to bed as soon as I had swallowed my soup, and my mother, kept at table just as though there had been company to dinner, would not come upstairs to say good night to me in bed" (*CS*, I, p. 180). In Notebook 6, Proust restricted the story to the night of Swann's visit, but ex- panded it with two important scenes: the father's permission for his mother to stay with the narrator in his bedroom, and her reading of George Sand (ff. 43–51; *CS*, *Sketch X*, I, pp. 673–677). The episode, thus embellished, was integrated into the more polished story of the future "Combray" in Notebook 8; there, it was given back its full scope, with Proust drawing liberally from the "seventy-five

folios" (Notebook 8, ff. 13–17, 30–45; *CS, Sketch XII,* I, pp. 679–680, 687–694): see the notes for the following pages. For an antecedent text, see Other Manuscripts, no. III.

f. 7

1. *"la rosse."* Literally meaning "a horse with no strength or vigor" (Dictionnaire Littré), *"rosse"* is used here in its figurative sense of a "nasty, malevolent person who enjoys tormenting and seeks to harm" (TLFi).

2. *He had already decided in any case that he would let his guest believe her mad.* When the father replaces the great-uncle, the violence of the reaction triggered by the grandmother is somewhat toned down, and is expressed (as here in the preceding phrase) in a "whisper." At another point in the bedtime drama, there is a digression about the books she wanted to give her grandson for his birthday: "Grandmother, believing that works of genius, however daring, could do no more harm to a child's mind than the forces of nature, including rain, could do to his body, had bought me Musset, George Sand, and Rousseau, prompting my father to whisper: 'She must be mad!'" (Notebook 8, f. 44 [cf. f. 43v]; cf. *CS, Sketch XII,* p. 694; ibid., p. 39). Cf. f. 15.

3. *my torture.* The term, if not the idea, recurs like a leitmotif: a little farther on, it is associated with maternal cruelty and extended by the image of the condemned man begging for mercy (f. 7); the "theater" of "nightly torture" is the staircase, the "labyrinth of sufferings" (f. 11) that "could not have been crueler [. . .] to climb if it had led to the guillotine" (f. 10); the bedroom is the "prison," and the bed "the prison inside my prison" (ff. 11, 12); the end of the torture finally appears in folio 16. Proust then uses the term more sparingly: with one exception, it is thereafter found only at the beginning of the piece (Notebook 4, f. 23; Notebook 6, f. 43; Notebook 8, ff. 13–14). In Notebook 8 the metaphor is extended into a more coherent image: "Finally I had to go upstairs like a prisoner to the guillotine, I had to close the cell door of my prison by closing the shutters of my bedroom, dig my own grave by pulling back my bedcovers, wrap myself in the shroud of my nightshirt. But before burying myself in my bed [. . .] I wanted to make one last escape attempt" (f. 35; *CS, Sketch XII,* I, p. 689; cf. ibid., p. 28). In the antecedent text, the narrator had already compared himself to "a man condemned to death" (Other Manuscripts, no. III). The expression in the definitive text, "the torture of going to bed," like the new introduction ("my bedroom became the fixed point on which my melancholy and anxious thoughts were centered"), was not written until 1913, on the proofs (*Bodmer,* galley proof 2, col.

2 and 3; *CS*, I, p. 9). In Notebook 9, the behavior of the great-uncle (then the great-aunt) toward the grandmother, in making her husband drink, is also described as "torture" (Notebook 9, f. 30v; *CS*, I, p. 12).

f. 9

1. *I always tried to lure Maman into another room.* See the antecedent text of this scene: "Often I would find an excuse to call Maman to the stairs or to the parlor" (Other Manuscripts, no. III).

2. *I would beg her not to be angry.* This passage (which begins on folio 7, Proust having forgotten to write on folio 8) is then divided between "ordinary" days (for the "Host" kiss, the anxiety caused by the brevity of the long-desired moment, the nervous pleas to return: *CS*, I, p. 13) and the day of Swann's visit (for the anxious anticipation of the goodnight kiss and the unwittingly cruel words spoken by the father—replacing the uncle—and the grandfather: *CS*, I, p. 27). But Maman's "cruel" face is no longer mentioned. The comparison of the kiss to a Host, corrected here to "one of those modern scientific Hosts," a "narcotic pill," is taken up again in Notebook 4 (ff. 24–25; Other Manuscripts, no. XII) and in Notebook 8 (f. 16; *CS, Sketch XII*, I, p. 680), but is restricted to the "act of Communion" on the Grasset galley proofs (*Bodmer,* galley proof 3, col. 1; *CS*, I, p. 13).

3. *by the sound of the bell.* Still absent from Notebook 6 ("it was the hour when M. Swann would ring"), the distinction between the two different kinds of bell—the "large and noisy" *carillon* for the servants and the "timid, oval, gilded" *sonnette* for visitors—was first made in Notebook 8 (f. 17; *CS, Sketch XII*, I, p. 681; cf. *CS*, I, p. 14).

f. 10

1. *her blue summer dress.* The description of the dress is picked up again in Notebook 4, where a marginal addition reads: "a garden dress, of blue muslin with straw tassels" (f. 23; Other Manuscripts, no. XII). Cf. *CS*, I, p. 13.

2. *"come on Jeanne this is ridiculous."* This is the only time, to our knowledge, that the real first name of Marcel Proust's mother—Mme Adrien Proust, née Jeanne Weil (1849–1905)—appears in the bedtime drama scene, or even in any fictional manuscript by Proust, and it is notable that it does so just after the appearance of Jeanne's own mother, Adèle Weil née Berncastell (see above f. 1).

The father's criticisms have already been suggested without being precisely attributed: "because I was not allowed to kiss her several times, such a thing being considered ridiculous" (f. 7). A similar statement appears in the antecedent text: "because if I kissed her several times Papa would say to me: come on now no ridiculous scenes and Maman would turn away" (Other Manuscripts, no. III). It was this first formulation that—after "absurd sentimentality" becoming "ridiculous 'shows of sentiment'" (Notebook 9, f. 69)—Proust finally returned to in the 1913 proofs: "No, no, leave your mother alone. You've said good night to one another, that's enough. These exhibitions are absurd. Go on upstairs" (*Bodmer*, galley proof 5, col. 4; *CS*, I, p. 27). In Notebook 4, the excuse is medical: "Maman, so as not to annoy my father who thought that letting children get used to kissing their parents only perpetuated their neuroses, withdrew her face almost immediately" (f. 45; Other Manuscripts, no. XII).

3. *permission to leave her and to accompany me.* This expression is kept until the definitive text: "[. . .] against my heart, which wanted to go back to my mother because she hadn't, with her kiss, given it permission to follow me" (*CS*, I, p. 27).

4. *control my anguish while I stayed downstairs.* Here begins a long description of the protagonist's painful, pensive wait before he goes up to his bedroom, first in the parlor (f. 10), then at the foot of the stairs (ff. 10–12), a wait that ends with his stratagem of the letter to Maman and its failure (f. 12). In Notebook 6, this wait was abbreviated ("I returned to the parlor before dinner was served. We stayed at the table until bedtime, and then I had to go upstairs [. . .]" f. 43; *CS*, *Sketch X*, I, p. 673), and the narrative modified: the hero did not write the note for Maman until he was already up in his bedroom, which would remain the case until the definitive text (ibid.). In Notebook 8, Proust reintroduced this waiting time from the "seventy-five folios," first the mention of the "wretched staircase" (f. 33, see below), then the passage into the parlor, but it was after the hero had been upstairs once and then gone back down: "So that I wouldn't go downstairs near 'company,' I was allowed to stay up until nine o'clock without going to bed and I could even return to the parlor when they had 'gone through to the dining room.' Which I did. And sensing that I still had an hour before the dreadful moment of bedtime, I forced myself not to think about it. I looked at the flowers <in the vases on the card table> that the gardener, lacking any feeling for nature, had placed there in tight, heavy bouquets, I listened to a piano melody coming from a nearby house. But the soul of someone whose thoughts are turned inward is convex, like the look in his eyes, and no feeling from without can penetrate it. I forced myself to remember the most beautiful verses I knew, but they left all their charm and joy outside before entering my mind. And at last it was time to go

upstairs [. . .]" (Notebook 8, ff. 34–35; cf. *CS, Sketch XII*, I, p. 689). This outline was farther elaborated during the revision (Notebook 9, f. 73), but, presumably because of all the comings and goings on the stairs, the entire passage was cut from the 1913 proofs (*Bodmer,* galley proof 5, col. 5).

5. *to the guillotine.* See above f. 7.

6. *green wood-paneled door.* Proust tries out various formulas for this, from version to version: the "green wood-paneled door" becomes the "green wooden trellised door" (Notebook 6, f. 43)—but "ask Auguste," he adds (see f. 12)—then the "green-painted wooden fencelike door from the entrance hall" (Notebook 12, f. 36), and lastly "the latticed door which led from the hall" (Notebook 9, f. 89; *CS,* I, pp. 34–35). See ibid., *Sketch X,* p. 673 (Notebook 6) and *Sketch LIV,* p. 827 (Notebook 12).

7. *that odor of varnish on the staircase.* This hated "odor of varnish on the staircase" is added to here by the smell of vetiver in the bedroom, on folio 13. Proust rewrote it in Notebook 8, removing the "struggle to breathe" that is mingled here with the hero's toothache, but keeping the trace of "this young girl we were trying to lift up": "That wretched staircase, which I climbed so sadly every night, emitted an odor of varnish that had in some way absorbed my sorrow, fixing it and making it perhaps even crueler to my sensibility because in that olfactory form my intelligence could no longer intervene to save me. When we sleep and a toothache becomes in our mind a young girl whom we are desperately trying over and over to pull from the water, or like a sentence of philosophy that we endlessly repeat to ourselves, it is a great relief when we are woken and our intelligence can untangle the toothache from all these mirages of drowning girls and syllogisms. But it was the opposite of relief, a worsening of my toothache, that I felt when it oppressed me in the subtle, deceptive form of the odor of varnish on the staircase" (ff. 33–34; *CS, Sketch XII,* pp. 688–689). Cf. Notebook 9, f. 72 and *CS,* I, pp. 27–28.

f. 11

1. *the torturous evening climb.* See above f. 7.

2. *"against the heart."* This is a play on words: *"à contrecoeur"* is the French expression for "reluctantly," but with the words separated and placed inside quotation marks, as here, its source meaning—"against the heart"—is emphasized. "I had to climb each step of the stairs against the heart, as they say" (Notebook 8,

f. 33; "in the words of the beautiful expression," Notebook 9, f. 71; "as the saying is," NAF 16733, f. 53; *CS*, I, p. 27).

3. *an impression of pain.* This description of the way the nightly torture bleeds into the happy impressions of the day was not retained. In Notebook 4, Proust introduced the opposite idea—of a watertight border between the different states, euphoric or pained, that the hero goes through during the course of a single day, undoubtedly influenced by his reading of Nerval, as a note in Carnet 1 from the fall of 1908 attests: "Sylvie. the 2 states (pleasures day, sadness of losing Maman evening [. . .])" (Carnet 1, f. 13; *Cn 1908*, p. 149 note 110; *Cn*, p. 54). The contrast is shown in the context of the walks along the Guermantes way, with their late returns synonymous with the loss of the evening kiss: "But what distinguished Garmantes above all for me was that the days when we went walking along that 'way,' since we came home late we would be sent to bed almost immediately after we had finished our soup and that on those evenings Maman would not go upstairs to tell me goodnight in my bed. All day long during the walk I thought about the Countess of Garmantes or about water lilies, as if I didn't have that apprehension for the evening. But on the way home when night started to fall, my anxiety took hold of me. And so it was on the Garmantes way that I learned to distinguish within myself those distinct, almost opposed states that succeed one another in my life, even in each day, when the sadness returns at a certain hour with the regularity of a fever, and during which what was desired, feared, accomplished in the different states appears almost incomprehensible" (Notebook 4, ff. 43–44; Other Manuscripts, no. XII; see also above f. 6). This discovery survived the narrative separation of the evening drama and the walks. The thought was then developed in Notebook 26 (ff. 6–7; *CS, Sketch LV*, I, p. 833; ibid., pp. 180–181). For the influence of Nerval, see also Notebook 5, f. 14, about his novella *Sylvie:* "it's the memory of a woman he loved at the same time as another, who dominates certain hours of his life and who every night takes him back at a certain hour" (*CSB* Clarac, p. 237).

f. 12

1. *to come and talk to me when dinner was over.* In *Jean Santeuil,* Jean hardly dares ask Augustin, "the old servant," "to go and fetch Maman" (*JS*, p. 206). The stratagem of the letter appears here, but it is the only version in which the hero has the idea before going upstairs to his bedroom (see above f. 10). When Proust resumes this "ruse" in Notebook 6, the "old maid" of the present page has already been replaced by Françoise, and Auguste by the "manservant" (Notebook 6, ff. 43–44; *CS, Sketch X*, I, pp. 673–674). The first considerations on the "subtle

code" that Françoise obeys are in Notebook 8 (ff. 35–36; *CS, Sketch XII*, I, pp. 689–690; cf. ibid., pp. 28–30). On Auguste, see the next note.

2. *Auguste.* See also the antecedent text: "[. . .] they would soon tell the man-servant: Auguste, serve coffee in the garden" (Other Manuscripts, no. III). The most obvious reference here is to Auguste Sauton, Louis Weil's manservant at Auteuil, to whom Uncle Louis left the sum of 10,000 francs in his will (with an-other 10,000 for Auguste's wife) (Duchêne 2004, p. 681). The "old servant" of the Santeuil family, Augustin, the protagonist of the bedtime scene, was also prob-ably inspired by him (*JS*, pp. 206–208, 210); Mme Proust jokingly calls him "Octave" in a letter to her son ([August 14, 1890], *Corr.*, t. I, p. 152). In Notebook 6, at the start of the shortened version of the bedtime scene, Proust writes a note to himself suggesting that he ask this manservant about the door in the entrance hall at Auteuil: "the ~~antechamber~~ <entrance hall> with a green wooden trellised door (ask Auguste)" (f. 43; see above f. 10; cf. *Corr.*, VII, letter no. 153). Proust noted the Sautons in the family address book: "Sauton [(]M. and Mme Auguste) rue Brey 11" (private coll.). Their surname was given to a family in Combray (Notebook 10, f. 35; *CS*, I, p. 57).

3. *prison.* Cf. f. 7, and *CS*, I, p. 28. "The bedroom was the prison, but the bed was the grave," said Jean Santeuil when he arrived without Maman at the Hotel des Roches-Noires in Trouville (*JS*, p. 358). See also f. 13.

f. 13

1. *an extension of my gaze.* Proust used this formula again to describe the hotel room upon his hero's arrival in Querqueville: "I no longer had around me those things fully permeated by us through seeing them daily and through habit, those things that surround us like friends, or like an extension of our body [. . .]" (Notebook 65, f. 10v). An editorial note at the foot of the page added: "maybe put here the other piece on the sound of the clock etc."

2. *to think about the smell of the tea I made in my Parisian bedroom in winter.* In *Contre Sainte-Beuve* and "Combray," where the reminiscence sparked by the toast or the madeleine dipped in tea occurs on a cold winter day, the drinking of tea is, by contrast, an exceptional event: "a cup of tea, which I never drink" (Other Manuscripts, no. VII), "[. . .] offered me some tea, a thing I did not ordi-narily take" (*CS*, I, p. 44). But in the "preface" to *Contre Sainte-Beuve*, it is the "smell" of the tea, corrected to its "taste," that first causes the delicious confu-sion: "when I put the toast in my mouth, and I felt the sensation of its softened

matter infused ~~with the smell of~~ <with a taste of tea> against my palate, I felt a confusion [. . .] suddenly the shaken walls of my memory gave way" (NAF 16636, ff. 1–2; Other Manuscripts, no. VII). The "smell of [. . .] tea" is also associated with a "memory we try to bring up" in a later editorial note from Notebook 26 (f. 12v); we also find it in the 1906 Agenda: "the complement of the smell of tea is that life is beautiful" (*Agenda*, f. 55v and note 3). In "Combray," smell and taste would become synonymous: "[. . .] the taste— . . . what would have been called at Combray the "perfume"—of a cup of tea" (*CS*, I, p. 183).

3. *that little dose of vetiver.* In 1909, Proust removed this inhospitable little room from the bedtime drama scene and inserted it in the reverie of bedrooms at the beginning of "Combray," but without specifying which place or which situation it was connected to (Notebook 8, ff. 7–8 and 6v; *CS, Sketch IV*, I, pp. 656–657). It began to feature at the end of the enumeration from the revision stage onward (Notebook 9, ff. 12–14; cf. *CS*, I, p. 8). We find that bedroom again when the hero and his grandmother arrive at the seaside hotel, where the story is first reduced to a brief notation, an aide memoire for something to be written in full later: "I was ill when we left, we stopped en route to visit Caen, we did not arrive until very late at night, [and] when opening the door of the pyramidal bedroom [. . .]" (Notebook 12, f. 49; Other Manuscripts, no. XIII). It was in Notebook 32 that the description was fleshed out with the reintroduction of elements of decor (ff. 29–30, 29v; cf. *JF, Sketch XXXI*, II, p. 897). See also Notebook 70, ff. 34–36, and *JF*, II, pp. 27–28. This inhospitable bedroom, first humanized by the arrival of the loving grandmother and ultimately tamed by habit, becomes much later the setting for "Intermittences of the Heart" (i.e., the grandmother's resurrection) (*SG*, III, pp. 148, 152 sq.). Certain elements of its decor, absent from the present page, were connected to memories of Mme Proust. See the Commentary.

4. *Eugénie.* The likely reference here is to Eugénie Lémel, Mme Proust's chambermaid, even though she is not mentioned before 1890 in the correspondence we possess (letter from Mme Proust to Marcel Proust, [April 28, 1890]. *Corr.*, I, p. 141). In *Jean Santeuil*, "Eugénie," Jean's chambermaid, appears only once, also in a scene of distress in an unfamiliar bedroom (*JS*, p. 357).

f. 14

1. *my heart began to beat intolerably.* Nothing would remain of this mantilla scene. Despite the denial—"Maman (whom Papa always made the happiest of women)"—the narrator adopts the same behavior here as when his grandmother was the target of the uncle's sarcastic remarks: then, he "frantically cover[ed] her

with kisses to console her" (f. 1); here, he feels the "irresistible need to kiss [his mother] to console her." In both cases, the female relative—the mother, the grandmother—is the victim of her own male relative's cruelty. In *Sodom and Gomorrah*, it is the hero who reproaches himself after his grandmother's death for "a few impatient wounding words" toward her: "it was I whose heart they were rending, now that the consolation of countless kisses was forever impossible" (*SG*, III, p. 156).

2. *to go to her bathroom*. The "immense joy" prompted by this decision to wait for Maman becomes, in Notebook 6, "a great joy," "a profound joy" (f. 45; *CS, Sketch X*, I, p. 674), and from Notebook 8 "bliss" and even "an extraordinary exultation" (f. 37; *CS, Sketch XII*, I, p. 690; ibid., p. 32). But, in those two notebooks, the account was shortened; the scene that follows here, namely the new dispute between the uncle and the grandmother, disappeared. See also f. 16.

f. 15

1. *a lively discussion between my uncle and my grandmother*. This "lively discussion" between the uncle and the grandmother about M. de Bretteville and the meaning of "distinction" (ff. 15–16) was not taken up in the following versions of the bedtime drama, in which only the conversation between the parents was kept (see below f. 17). There was no longer any reason for it, since the new nocturnal visitor, Swann, was so tactful and artistic in his tastes that he received the grandmother's approval. Elements from this page, however, did survive in other contexts: see below and f. 16.

2. *he might have many more horses than I do*. Proust uses the same template for the sentence as he used in an analogous situation in "On Reading," itself based on a scene from *Jean Santeuil:* "From the first mouthful, the first notes, the first words, [my great-aunt] had the pretension of knowing if she was dealing with a good pianist, a good cook, or [. . .] a tactful, well-raised person. '*She might have many more fingers than me* but she lacks taste, playing that simple andante with such emphasi.'" (*PM*, p. 163; Other Manuscripts, no. II; italics are ours).

3. *Bretteville l'Orgueilleuse*. See above f. 6.

4. *"My word she's mad!"* After *"la rosse,"* this echo of the insult "She must be mad!" (f. 7) is exacerbated a few lines on with "she's rabid." See later in "Combray": "'Mme Amédeée is always the exact opposite of everyone else,' said Françoise, not unkindly, refraining until she should be alone with the other servants from stating her belief that my grandmother was 'slightly batty'" (*CS*, I, p. 101).

5. *considered "extremely distinguished."* In Notebook 8, Proust returned to the grandmother's ideas of "distinction" by associating her with the other quality she prized above all, "naturalness" (cf. Notebook 6, f. 71v; *CS, Sketch XXVII*, I, p. 736, and ibid., p. 63). Mme de Villeparisis tries to persuade her to rent an apartment close by: "and my grandmother came back each time filled with enthusiasm for those wonderfully 'natural' gardens that nobody looked after, and also by a florist [. . .] who was the best of men, the most distinguished man she had ever met. Because for my grandmother, distinction was something entirely independent of social rank"; in the same way, she goes into ecstasies about the letters worthy of Sévigné written by "our servant" (Notebook 8, ff. 25–26; *CS, Sketch XII*, I, p. 685; cf. f. 5). In 1913, on the galley proofs for the first volume, the florist became a tailor, and the letter-writing servant—who duplicated the tailor's daughter, newly created during the revision (Notebook 9, f. 60)—disappeared: see *Bodmer,* galley proof 4, col. 4; *CS,* I, p. 20.

6. *to leave his entire fortune to my grandmother.* This passage might lead to the impression that the uncle and the grandmother are, in this story, more like brother and sister than brother-in-law and sister-in-law (see f. 1). Louis Weil, who died a childless widower, in any case proved his generosity with the contents of his will, which distributed his fortune among various members of his family, his principal heirs being his nephews Georges Weil and Jeanne Proust, the children of his brother Nathé and his sister-in-law Adèle (Duchêne 2004; this author did, however, mistakenly state that Louis and Nathé were half brothers).

f. 16

1. *member of the Jockey Club.* Being a member of the highly select Jockey Club was the only thing M. de Bretteville had in common with Swann (Notebook 4, f. 54; *CS, Sketch IX*, I, p. 669; cf. ibid., p. 15). See above f. 6.

2. *eggs in the salad.* This absurd idiosyncrasy of Bretteville wasn't lost. In 1909, when the reasons for the grandmother's approval of the friendship between Montargis (the future Saint-Loup) and her grandson were delineated, they included not only "naturalness," but "the politeness of a young man in whom she would prefer a flaw to the overly affected manners of someone like M. de Prémisy de Blanqueville who had persuaded my great-aunt, to my grandmother's silent fury, to stop serving quartered eggs in the salad because this was not done among polite society in Blois" (Notebook 28, ff. 94–93; cf. above f. 3). Here once again we find the transposition of the uncle into a great-aunt (cf. f. 1, and the Commentary). After this, all traces of the quarrel in the present chapter, and in particular of "M. de Prémisy de

Blanqueville," the final avatar of M. de Bretteville, would be erased: in Balbec, the wives of the Grand Hotel regulars would "put up their glasses and stare at us, my grandmother and myself, because we were eating hard-boiled eggs in salad, which was considered common and was, in fact, 'not done' in the best society of Alençon" (*JF*, II, p. 37). In Notebook 70 (f. 51) and the extract of *In Search of Lost Time* published in the *Nouvelle Revue française* in June 1914 (p. 942), the "society" in question was not that of Bayeux, Blois, or Alençon, but Nantes.

3. *and tenderly kissed it.* This scene showing the hero's jubilation was kept only in Notebook 8, where it followed—instead of preceding, as here—the brief dialogue between the parents before they go upstairs: "I was in such a joyous mood that those insignificant words rising up from the garden enchanted me. I kept repeating Zut, Zut, Zut, Zutiflor with the same intoxicated accent as if these words had contained some deep, delicious truth. I jumped about alone in my bedroom, I smiled at my mirror and, not knowing on whom to pour out my tenderness and joy, I grabbed my own ~~hand~~ <arm> and ecstatically planted a kiss on it" (f. 37; cf. *CS, Sketch XII*, I, pp. 690–691). The interjection that would become the quadruple "Zut" of *Swann's Way* appeared in Notebook 26 (ff. 9v–10v; *CS, Sketch LV*, I, pp. 835–836), in the entirely different context of an artist's powerlessness to convey obscure impressions (*CS*, I, p. 153).

f. 17

1. *fond of the ortolans.* The conversation between the parents was kept in the following versions, but shortened, while the lavish menu (fillet of duckling, lobster, ortolans, banana salad, etc.) was reduced but kept changing: in Notebook 6, ice cream and chocolate cookies (f. 45; *CS, Sketch X*, I, p. 674); in Notebook 8, lobster and ice cream (f. 36v; *CS, Sketch XII*, I, p. 690); and in the definitive text, lobster and coffee-and-pistachio ice cream (*CS*, I, p. 33). On the "*demoiselles de Caen*,"[T] crossed-out here and replaced with a single lobster, see *SG*, III, p. 293 and note 2.

2. *my mother went with my father into their bedroom.* This is one of the main differences of this version: the father does not yet play the decisive role that will become his the following year, and for the first time in Notebook 6 (ff. 45–47; *CS, Sketch X*, I, pp. 674–675; Notebook 8, ff. 38–40; *CS, Sketch XII*, I, pp. 691–692, and ibid., pp. 35–37). Everything happens here between the mother and her son.

T Small lobsters from Normandy.

3. *She was in a white canvas bathrobe, her beautiful black hair hanging loose.*
We find the same vision in the notebooks for *Contre Sainte-Beuve*, but associated
with the morning of the *Figaro* article: "[. . .] before going back to bed, I wanted
to kiss Maman and find out what she'd thought of the article. I found her sitting
in her bathroom, her long black hair spread over her batiste bathrobe." (Notebook 1, f. 2); "[. . .] Before going back to bed, I wanted to find out what Maman
had thought of my article. [. . .] Maman was sitting in front of her bathroom
mirror, in a long white bathrobe, her beautiful black hair spread over her shoulders" (Notebook 2, f. 25v; *CSB*, p. 105). On Maman's beauty, see also Notebook 2
("the sublime lines of her Jewish face," f. 6; *CSB*, p. 128).

4. *a face of adorable purity.* We find here the scenes from the list of "Pages
Written" in Carnet 1: "My grandmother in the garden, M. de Bretteville's dinner, I
go upstairs, Maman's face then [. . .]" (f. 7v; *Cn*, p. 43). See also the next note.

5. *that the artist wipes away with a finger.* This is, along with the antecedent
text from the Fallois archives (Other Manuscripts, no. III), the only known version of the bedtime drama in which the death of "Maman" is mentioned, in terms
moreover that directly—and in places textually—prefigure the grandmother's
death at the start of the second part of *The Guermantes Way.* There, again, we
would find the "funeral couch," the face "from which had vanished the wrinkles,
the contractions, the swellings, the strains, the hollows which pain had carved on
it over the years," the mention of the "purity" and "innocent gaiety" of youth
(*CG*, II, pp. 640–641). A letter from Proust to Anna de Noailles the day after his
mother's death is enough to suggest the fictional transposition: "She died at fifty-
six but she looked thirty, since she had lost weight during her illness, and especially since death had given her back her youth before all her sorrows. She didn't
have a single white hair" ([September 27, 1905], *Corr.,* V, p. 345; see also *CG*, II,
"Notice,", p. 1673). In the spring of 1910, when Proust was writing the episode of
the grandmother's final illness and death in Notebook 14, he resumed and expanded the present passage: 'My grandmother's face had become, so to speak, her
true face, the one I had ~~hardly~~ <never> not known, relieved of life and of all that
life had inflicted upon it: the impasto, the lines, the furrows of pain. On the funeral bed where she lay as in her grave, it seemed that death—like those early
medieval sculptors who, before the advent of realism, represented death in repose
in the guise of a young woman—had given her the effigy of her youth. It was her
as she had been in the portrait at my uncle's house, on the day of her engage-
ment, her face radiant with purity and submissiveness, but also with hope and a
desire for happiness that life had disappointed even before I knew her, and whose
final remnants I had destroyed. So she had entered her husband's house, cheerful,

with her young girl's dreams, believing in happiness, but infinitely pure and submissive, ready to serve her husband. And it was that purity and submissiveness
that, when she understood that happiness was not for her and when it was replaced by the painful desire for happiness for us that we did not fulfill, was
transformed in turn to that abnegation, that suffering which I had always seen
upon her face, which had aged her, which had impasted her cheeks, hardened
her features, dug those furrows under her eyes. Life had given her all of that, and
now it had taken it away. In her virginal purity, a smile of hope upon her lips, still
and submissive, my grandmother looked ready to begin life again, ready for a
new cortege to lead her to her husband" (Notebook 14, ff. 85–85v; cf. *CG, Sketch
XXV*, II, p. 1210). See also f. 18.

f. 18

1. *I started running after her.* Like the sudden appearance of the dead Maman's face (f. 17), this long account is unique among the versions of the bedtime
drama; and as with the fleeting vision of the "funeral bed" on the previous page,
the subject would later become the grandmother. Proust had noted at the start of
Carnet 1, in the first months of 1908, three brief accounts of dreams of his dead
relatives (ff. 2, 3v, 4; *Cn*, pp. 31–32, 36). This dream was not among them. It
could date from July 17 or 18, 1908, when Proust was traveling to Cabourg:
"*Maman rediscovered during journey, arrival in Cabourg*, same room as in Evian,
the square mirror!" (Carnet 1, f. 5v; *Cn*, p. 39; italics are ours). When the note of
the "Pages Written" in Carnet 1 mentions "Maman [. . .] in my dreams" (f. 7v;
Cn, p. 43), it is a reference either to different dreams or to a different version of
the present dream (see the Chronology). During the first months of 1910, in Notebook 65—a notebook focused on the character of the grandmother in Querqueville (the future Balbec), where she is sometimes replaced by Maman—the
four dreams are recounted one after another (ff. 39–42, 41v, 42–44), following
the first version of "Intermittences of the Heart." The present posthumous
dream appears there "on a train," without any further detail. The character's
physical degradation is exacerbated by a "splash of mud" that recalls the grandmother in the garden (see above, f. 2); the bitterness and the guilt felt, respectively, by the mother and the son are amplified; lastly, the blank that follows the
interruption of the passage on the present page—"I started running after
her/"—was echoed in Notebook 65 by the paralysis that strikes the dreamer, the
powerless spectator of a cruel vision (Notebook 65, ff. 42–44; Other Manuscripts, no. XVI). A few months after this, in late 1910 or early 1911, Proust reworked this dream again in very similar terms when the hero, just after having an
adventure with Mme Putbus's chambermaid, leaves Venice by train with his

mother (Notebook 50, f. 19, then Notebook XV, unstuck undersides[1] from ff. 12 and 11; *SG, Sketch XIII,* III, pp. 1033–1034 and p. 1033 var. *a*). The term "soiled" (*crotté*) from the present page, which had disappeared in the Notebook 65 version, was reintroduced: "She had ~~dirtied~~ <soiled> her dress, almost lost an ankle boot" (Notebook 50, f. 19). During the war, Proust moved this dream again, situating it this time during the second stay in Balbec (Notebook V, ff. 136–138 and Notebook VI, f. 1), but without ever again placing it among the dreams in "Intermittences of the Heart" (on which, see *SG,* III, pp. 157–179, 175–176): nevertheless, this chapter ends with the reminder of the soiled grandmother (ibid., p. 177). In the end, the dream disappeared altogether: during the revision of the typed notebooks of the second part of *Sodom and Gomorrah,* in 1922, Proust replaced it with a long, recently written scientific essay on deep sleep (*SG,* III, p. 368 var. *a* [pp. 1553–1554], and p. 379 note 1), leaving it out of the definitive text. But the "dark roads of sleep and dream" from the present page, by way of the "dark archways of that other world which is the realm of sleep" from Notebook 65 (f. 38v), can still be traced in the "sombre portals" of "Intermittences of the Heart" (*SG,* III, p. 157).

f. 19

1. *you'll wake your father.* In the next version, the one in Notebook 6, we find the same scene but in a very different context, since the vision of Maman's face (f. 17) and the account of the dream (f. 18) have disappeared, and the father—who in the present version has gone back into the parents' bedroom (f. 17)—bursts out again: "[. . .] soon I heard Maman's dress as she came upstairs to close the window, I saw her light, then I saw her and I rushed toward her. At first she didn't understand what I was doing there so late, then as understanding dawned her face contracted with anger and she didn't even want to speak to me because I had done one of those things for which I was punished by silence, but she heard my father coming upstairs and, faced with the imminent danger, wanting to avoid upsetting my father, she told me in a shaking voice: 'Get away now so at least your father won't see you, and never do this again.' But I repeated come and say goodnight to me. I was probably terrified by my father's light as it came toward the hallway but this was also a kind of blackmail; I sensed that Maman, to avoid me staying out there another second longer and my father seeing me, would say

---

1. Often, when Proust wished to move a piece of writing, he would remove pages from his notebooks and stick them to other pages. But sometimes the cut and pasted page had writing on both sides, and when the glued part was unstuck by the Bibliothèque nationale de France, this allowed what was written on the underside to be read.

to me: quickly back in your room, I'm coming. And once she was there, we would see. But it was too late and my father was standing before us" (Notebook 6, ff. 45–46; *CS, Sketch X*, I, p. 674, and ibid., p. 35).

2. *in her grave.* This is the third and final allusion to Maman's death. See also ff. 17 and 18.

3. *for the first time Maman had been defeated by life.* In this version as in *Jean Santeuil* and its antecedent text (Other Manuscripts, no. I), it is the mother alone who makes the decision to stay with the child in his bedroom. But it is the father who, against all expectations, gives her the signal to go with their son in the version from Notebook 6 (ff. 46–47; *CS, Sketch X*, I, p. 675, and ibid., pp. 35–37). In the antecedent text of *Jean Santeuil*, the servant's visit and the feeling of exoneration are already mentioned, though neither is present in *Jean Santeuil*. From Notebook 6, we find all the elements of the present version: the servant's question, Maman's words of explanation, the joy of exoneration quickly spoiled by the sadness of having made Maman feel "defeated by life" for the first time (Notebook 6, ff. 47–48; *CS, Sketch X*, I, pp. 675–676; Notebook 8, ff. 41–42; *CS, Sketch XII*, I, p. 693, and ibid., pp. 37–38). See also f. 20.

f. 20

1. *a first abdication.* The verb "concede" appeared on the previous page, but in a negative sense, and associated with a Freudian slip, as if intransigeance was always masculine, a trait of the father or the doctor: "[. . .] to have a son worthy of her hopes, to whom *he* would concede nothing that might be bad for him" (italics are ours). In Notebook 6 we find the pairing "painful concession" and "first defeat" (f. 48), and in Notebook 8 "first concession" and "first abdication" (f. 43): the three terms feature in the present version, which contains the scenes from the "Pages Written" listed in Carnet 1: "I go upstairs, Maman's face then and since in my dreams, I can't fall asleep, concessions etc. [. . .]" (f. 7v; *Cn*, p. 43). See *CS*, I, p. 38.

2. *little idiot, little canary.* In Notebooks 6 and 8 and from then until the final text, we also find the intensification of the child's tears under the effects of guilt, Maman's efforts to suppress her tenderness, and the affectionate little nicknames she calls her son (Notebook 6, ff. 48–49; *CS, Sketch X*, I, p. 676; Notebook 8, f. 43; *CS, Sketch XII*, I, pp. 693–694, and ibid., p. 38). A little farther on, Proust glosses the meaning, here, of *jaunet* (literally: "yellowish"): the translation reads "So my little canary," but in French the line is *"Alors c'est mon jaunet (serin),"*

with *serin* being the French word for canary (see also f. 21). We find these little names in the long, intimate scene between Maman and her adult son in *Contre Sainte-Beuve*, when his article appears in *Le Figaro* ("my idiot," "little idiot," "my little canary," Notebook 2, ff. 24v, 22v). "A letter as *jaunette* as possible, I warn you," Proust writes to his mother, before telling her about his schedule and his physical troubles ([September 21, 1904], *Corr.*, IV, p. 279). See also, farther on, "my wolf," f. 25.

3. *when they are grumpy.* Even if Maman is "fully in control" of herself by the end of the episode, her capitulation marks the start of a new era: "henceforth . . ." The confession of her preference for her son when he is "grumpy" can also be read as the conclusion of the bedtime scene, rather than a scene that is repeated. From Notebook 6 onward, Proust lengthened the intimate scene in the child's bedroom with the description of Maman reading George Sand's pastoral novels, the apotheosis of the communion between mother and son (Notebook 6, f. 49 sq.; *CS, Sketch X*, I, pp. 676–677). It was then that the phrase about Maman being "admirably practical" was adapted to its new context: "She wasn't in a rush to go to bed, because with her great intelligence she was more realistic than my grandmother and now that we had done something out of the ordinary at least wanted me to fully savor my pleasure, and the good—mingled with the great harm—it might do me. She was one of [those people] who even while sticking to their principles [can] recognize the moment when they must be bent, and who while forbidding narcotics can recognize the moment when the suffering becomes worse than the morphine and do not let you suffer pointlessly; and I think that even without the fear of angering my father when she saw me on the stairs she would have entered my bedroom, and that she was almost as happy as I was about her sudden decision" (Notebook 6, f. 50; cf. *CS, Sketch X*, I, p. 677).

4. *I would join them a little later with my father.* Here begins an episode of just over five pages (ff. 20–26) that explores through other examples the treatment of the theme of attachment and separation: in a comic register, with the (unfinished) anecdote of the goat (ff. 20–24), and in a serious register, with the scene of Maman's departure, which provides (although without a satisfying join) the conclusion that had been missing to what came before (ff. 25–26). Proust drew from this an important but shorter episode: the farewell to the hawthorns in "Combray" (*CS*, I, p. 143; see below ff. 21–23). The contents of these two juxtaposed pieces correspond to the very first note on the list of "Pages Written" in Carnet 1: "Robert and the goat, Maman leaves on a trip" (f. 7v; *Cn*, p. 43). But this mention most likely refers to drafts prior to the "seventy-five folios," now lost (see the Chronology).

f. 21

1. *worthy of Leonidas.* The first use of *"jaunet"* in this sentence was deleted by Fallois, who indicated: "Lacuna in the manuscript" (*CSB,* p. 292). Of course, it could simply be a mistake on Proust's part. But it could also be seen as a play on words by Maman on two meanings of *"jaunet"*: a *jaunet* is a canary (*serin*—see f. 20) but it is also "a small gold coin, in particular a louis d'or or a napoléon" (TLFi). In that case, Leonidas's "yellow face" would be a medal-like face, looking stern and impassive, something the "little canary" would do well to imitate by being more stoical. Leonidas was the heroic Spartan king who sacrificed himself to save his homeland at the Battle of Thermopylae; Maman alludes elsewhere to this battle reported by Herodotus in the seventh volume of *Histories* ("Tell Sparta," *JF,* I, p. 507). This is a pseudo-quotation from Plutarch, whose *Life of Leonidas* is lost. See also f. 25.

2. *in Évreux.* We don't know the starting point for this little family trip: even if a memory of Illiers takes shape later (see below), Évreux, the capital of the Eure département in Normandy, is almost a hundred kilometers away—and the same is true for Auteuil. We should probably see in this name, as elsewhere in this chapter (f. 6) and in [Noble Names] (ff. 75–77), the trace of the excursions Proust took in 1907 in Normandy in a car driven by Alfred Agostinelli, notably in September around Évreux, where he told Mme Straus he had "spent four or five days" ([October 8, 1907], *Corr.,* VII, pp. 286, 287, 288). Returning to this scene in 1909 in a notebook for *Contre Sainte-Beuve,* Proust situated it in Combray, close to Chartres (because, let us remember, Combray was not moved to the Champagne region until the 1919 edition of *Swann's Way*): "[. . .] on the contrary, I never saw the steeples of Chartres without feeling sad, because it was often to Chartres that we went with Maman when she left Combray before us. And the inexorable form of those two steeples appeared to me as terrible as the train station. I traveled toward them as toward the moment when I would have to say goodbye to Maman, feeling my heart shake inside my chest and detach itself from me to follow her and come back alone! I remember one especially sad day when Maman took my brother with her: the car was supposed to drive us from Combray to Chartres and it was a long way. They had [wanted] to have my brother's photograph taken in the morning, before he left" (Notebook 6, ff. 69v–68v; cf. *CS, Sketch XXVII,* I, pp. 737–738). Since this little fragment seemed to precede a reworking of the goat episode, Fallois used it as a partial introduction in his edition (*CSB,* p. 291). But in the first (brief) rewrite of the scene, the hero took the place of the vanished brother and the hawthorns replaced the goat (Notebook 29, f. 72v; *CS, Sketch LXII,* I, p. 860). See next note, passim.

3. *big white bows stuck to it like the butterflies of Velazquez's infanta.* Proust may have had in mind the portrait of the Infanta Maria Theresa (1652), or that of the little Infanta Margarita (circa 1653), both at the Louvre, the latter reproduced in a work from his favorite collection, "Les grands artistes" (Elie Faure, *Velazquez* [Paris: Henri Laurens, 1904], p. 85). The comparison disappeared from the first developed rewrite of the scene in which the hero replaced his brother ("[. . .] my hair had been curled and I'd had to wear a new hat," NAF 16703, f. 51); later, on the corrected typed version, came the "hair curlers" (NAF 16733, f. 213), replaced by "curl papers" (*papillotes*)[2] when the extract "White Thorns, Pink Thorns" was published in *Le Figaro* (March 21, 1912), with the latter vaguely recalling the "butterflies" (*papillons*) of the present passage. During the war, Proust partially reused the image from the "seventy-five folios" in the portrait of Albertine at the pianola: "And as she played, of all Albertine's multiple tresses I could see but a single heart-shaped loop of black hair clinging to the side of her ear like the bow of a Velazquez infanta" (*P*, III, p. 874; see also *Cahier 53*, 2012, f. 163 note 2 and f. 167 note 7).

4. *the small copse in the center of which was the cirque where the horses were tied so they could bring up water.* Compare with *Jean Santeuil:* "In the park, near the enclosure wall, in a place where Jean almost never went, there was a stone cirque in a clearing with a pump in the middle to which the horses were attached now and then so they could slowly turn around it and bring up the water" (*JS*, p. 305; see also p. 322: "[. . .] a carousel where one of M. Santeuil's father's horses, by turning it around, could bring water up from the canal below"; cf. *PM*, p. 168). This water wheel, redolent of North Africa, connects the scene to the Pré-Catelan in Illiers, the work of Proust's uncle Jules Amiot, who made several trips to Algeria where his children had moved (see Naturel 2009, p. 834). On that ornamental garden, see below ff. 27 and 28. The setting of the rewritten scene, in "Combray," is the "steep little path near Tansonville" (*CS*, I, p. 143).

f. 22

1. *caressing an animal.* Philip Kolb compared this remark to a letter sent by Proust in early 1908 to Auguste Marguillier, editorial secretary of the *Gazette des beaux-arts:* "[. . .] would it be possible for you to send me provisionally a few of your English engravings, particularly those where an animal is shown next to a person or persons? I don't know if they would be what I'm looking for, but per-

2. In French, *"papillote"* also instantly suggests Jewish sidelocks or sidecurls.

haps I would take one or two of them if the format isn't too small" (Kolb 1956, p. 751; [just before January 8, 1908], *Corr.*, VIII, p. 25 and note 10). This letter, then, would have coincided with the writing of "Robert and the goat." According to Kolb, Proust also read a book mentioned in the *Gazette des beaux-arts* in December 1907, *La Peinture anglaise des origines à nos jours* ("English Painting from Its Origins to the Present Day") by Armand Dayot (Paris: Lucien Laveur, 1908; Kolb 1956, p. 754). In that work there are two portraits by Joshua Reynolds showing little girls with their dog (pp. 17, 38): charming scenes, but somewhat insipid and idyllic, in obvious contrast to the present scene with the little boy sobbing and tearing at his clothes.

2. *and gather'd o'er my brow these clustering coils*. A quotation from Racine (*Phèdre*, act I, scene III, vv. 159–160; translated by Robert Bruce Boswell). In the tragedy, these are almost Phaedra's first words, as she tries to conceal her love for Hippolytus: "Ah, how these cumbrous gauds / These veils oppress me! What officious hand / Has tied these knots, and gather'd o'er my brow / These clustering coils? How all conspires to add / To my distress!" The quotation continues a little farther on with verse 158: see f. 23. When rewriting the scene for the typed version of "Combray" in 1911, Proust used this verse again, paraphrasing it in an unfinished addition: "[. . .] my mother found me in tears on the little path bidding farewell to the hawthorns and like a tragic princess oppressed by those vain ornaments <to whose brow some officious hand had tied the knots that gathered the clustering coils> stamping <my feet> on my ~~new~~ hat [. . .]" (NAF 16703, f. 51; cf. *CS*, I, p. 143).

3. *My sweet sister of angels*. Paraphrased quotation of the lyrics to a song by August Heinrich von Weyrauch, wrongly attributed to Schubert, translated into French by Émile Deschamps (see *CG*, II, p. 666 and note 1). It is reused in this volume (f. 43) and in the next part of the genesis, in the context of romantic disappointment, usually in a self-deprecating tone: see f. 43.

f. 23

1. *shouting loudly*. This violent tantrum might have an autobiographical root ("my brother, though infinitely tender toward me [. . .] is not always very pleasant with other people," Proust wrote to Gallimard on [September 21, 1922], *Corr.*, XXI, p. 484). But above all it has a symbolic function, concealing as it does a series of allusions to another Racine play, *Esther*. The three verbs used to show acts of violence in this scene—stamping ("stamping on the satin bags"), tearing ("tearing out [. . .] the little bows that had been put in his hair"), and ripping

("ripping his beautiful Asiatic gown")—suggest two scenes from *Esther:* the queen's prayer when she is forced to conceal her Jewishness from her husband Ahasuerus ("This headband, which I must wear in public,/Alone, in secret, I stamp it under my feet"), and the lamentation of the chorus of Israelites persecuted by Ahasuerus's minister, Aman ("We tear and rip at all these vain ornaments/That adorn our head"). See Racine, *Esther,* act I, scene IV, vv. 278, 280, and scene V, vv. 309–310, repeated in vv. 314–315. In this context, the choice—otherwise incomprehensible—of the epithet "Asiatic" to describe the boy's gown becomes clear: in *Esther,* Ahasuerus and the Persians are counted among the "peoples of Asia" (*Esther,* act I, scene III, v. 214). See *CS,* I, p. 143 (for a reading of this passage as a comic allusion to the Jewish holiday of Purim, see Mauriac Dyer 2014) and the Commentary.

2. *Ah, how these cumbrous gauds, these veils oppress me!* In this phrase, which was omitted by Fallois (*CSB,* p. 295), Proust completes the quotation from *Phèdre* begun on the previous page (f. 22): "Ah, how these cumbrous gauds/These veils oppress me! What officious hand/Has tied these knots, and gather'd o'er my brow/These clustering coils?" (act I, scene III, vv. 158–160). Those "cumbrous gauds" (or "vain ornaments," which would be a more literal rendering of the French "*vains ornements*") are also associated by Racine with Queen Esther ("I prefer ashes to these vain ornaments," *Esther,* act I, scene IV, v. 281) and with the chorus of Israelites ("We tear and rip at all these vain ornaments," ibid., scene V, vv. 309, 314), in the two scenes implicitly evoked a little earlier: see previous note.

3. *and he started to sob.* These reproaches are reminiscent of Jean's when he is leaving Éteuilles, when his mother throws away the "large bundles of hawthorns and snowball flowers" that they had been given: "And Jean wept at being separated from those dear creatures that he would have liked to take with him to Paris, and at his mother's meanness" (*JS,* p. 326).

f. 24

1. *the goat should be taken back.* This tragicomic and possibly autobiographical episode was not included in any later versions.

2. *to make them miss the train.* This desire to make his parents miss the train echoes the earlier suspicion that Robert had hidden "so that he could get his revenge by making Maman miss her train" (f. 21); farther on, the aggressive urges shown by "Marcel" eclipse his brother's with their violence.

3. *We had to.* This unfinished sentence was not included by Fallois (*CSB*, p. 296). Proust left the rest of the page blank.

f. 25

1. *poultry course, salad, and dessert.* Proust continues writing on a new bifolio without having completely filled the previous one. Despite sharing the same narrative outline—Robert and his goat, Maman's departure by train—the new piece does not fit perfectly with the previous one, as if Proust was not really concerned about the continuity of the story: while "time was short" in the previous scene (f. 23) and they had to rush to the station so as not to miss their train, here the family calmly goes home to eat lunch before the departure.

2. *my brother yelled.* Coming after the first names of the grandmother and the mother—Adèle (ff. 1, 3, 5) and Jeanne (f. 10)—this "Marcel" (as well as "Robert" in Carnet 1, f. 7v) puts this chapter firmly in a register that is, if not autobiographical, at least autofictional. "Marcel" and even "Marcel Proust," a journalist publishing articles in *Le Figaro*, was still present in a notebook for *Contre Sainte-Beuve* (Notebook 2, ff. 33v, 23v, while "Robert" is also named in f. 21v); "Marcel" and "Monsieur Marcel" would also be found (though for the last time) in the reworking of the bedtime drama (Notebook 6, ff. 47, 48; *CS, Sketch X*, I, p. 675) and in the portrait of Françoise (Notebook 5, ff. 28, 32; *CG, Sketch IV*, II, pp. 1036, 1038). Several years later, Proust reintroduced his first name in additions to the manuscripts of the Albertine episode: "Albertine to me My darling Marcel" (Notebook 61, f. 71); "But when she woke she had said to me: 'My Marcel' 'My darling Marcel'" (Notebook VIII, f. 39); "[. . .] she half-opened her eyes and said to me in a surprised voice—it was already night, after all—'But where are you going like that, Marcel?' then fell back asleep" (Notebook IX, *paperole* at f. 14); "My darling, dear Marcel, I'm coming [. . .] What ideas you have! Oh Marcel, you're such a Marcel!" (ibid., f. 34). In each case, however, Proust later removed the mention of his name by Albertine, except in the final passage, but just before this he had interrupted his revision of the typed version of *The Captive* (*P*, III, pp. 583, 622, 663; Mauriac Dyer 2006, pp. 72–75).

3. *since the previous evening she appeared to understand my sorrow, to take it seriously.* This line makes clear that Maman's attitude has changed, and creates a clear dramatic progression between the bedtime scene and "Robert and the goat." It is one of the elements that prevents us identifying the "seventy-five folios" in the list of "Pages Written," where these episodes are not joined and "Robert and the goat" is placed first (see the Chronology). It should be noted that,

in the Fallois edition, "since the previous evening" (*CSB*, p. 296) did not refer back to any narrative event.

4. *in difficult circumstances.* After the Spartan king Leonidas (f. 21), Maman cites the example of the Roman consul Regulus, hero of the Punic War, who did not hesitate to sacrifice himself to honor his word to the Carthaginians (see Cicero, *De Officiis*). The wildly disproportionate analogies were intended to edify the little boy ("what I thought was a source of sorrow was nothing of the kind"). As with the previous quotation, this one is made up. Proust uses it again when the present separation is repeated, only in reverse, in the scene where the hero leaves for Querqueville (Balbec) with his grandmother, but without Maman: "These were the last moments. My eyes were full of tears. In a tender, jocular tone, she told me: '<If you are no Roman, show yourself worthy to be one> Regulus in grave circumstances . . .'" (Notebook 65, f. 9). The Corneille quotation ("If you are no Roman . . ." *Horace*, v. 483), which was connected to the death of Maman in Notebook 4 (f. 68v; *CSB*, p. 125), would afterward disappear completely. See *JF*, II, p. 11.

5. *my wolf.* Another affectionate nickname, used from Notebook 2 onward (ff. 44v, 25v [*CSB*, p. 105], 21v, 20v); see also Notebook 6, ff. 8 (*CSB*, p. 299), 49 and 51 (*CS*, *Sketch X*, I, pp. 676, 677). Mme Proust frequently called her son this: see *Corr.*, I, pp. 113, 131, 137, IV, p. 299, and in particular the letter of [October 21, 1896] about a telephone call: "Hearing the poor wolf's voice—the poor wolf hearing mine!" (ibid., II, p. 142, see also p. 141). See also f. 20.

6. Sursum corda. "Lift up your hearts." The formula is spoken during Mass at the start of the preface of the Eucharistic Prayer, but it had passed into common parlance, which explains why Jeanne Proust, who never converted to Catholicism, might quote it. A letter in which Proust tells her his news shows that the expression was part of their private language: "You see that the *Sursum* is still up" ([September 16, 1896], *Corr.*, II, p. 124).

f. 26

1. *something of me went away too.* Cf. f. 10: "my heart could not come with me and had stayed close to Maman who had not with her usual kiss given it permission to leave her and to accompany me." This torn feeling was developed in Notebook 6, at the "moment when I would have to say goodbye to Maman, feeling my heart shake inside my chest and detach itself from me to follow her" (Notebook 6, f. 68v; *CS*, *Sketch XXVII*, I, pp. 737–738). These two pages (ff. 25–26) were published under the title "Separation" in the first volume of the *Bulletin de la*

Société des Amis de Marcel Proust et des Amis de Combray, in 1950 (pp. 7–8), in other words four years before Fallois used them in *Contre Sainte-Beuve.*

[The Villebon Way and the Méséglise Way]

The present chapter is the most developed section of the "seventy-five folios": there are three versions (with the third itself including pages written at different times). Having been at some point moved out of order, these pages were reordered for the present edition. Their theme appears in the list of "Pages Written" in Carnet 1: "The Villebon way and the Méséglise way [. . .] What I learned from the Villebon way and the Méséglise way" (f. 7v; *Cn*, pp. 43–44); however, those were probably intermediary stages in the chapter's development (see the Chronology). The walks along the "ways" were the subject of many drafts in the early rough notebooks, Notebook 4 then Notebook 12 (1909); the shorter version from Notebook 26, most likely an intermediary draft, is more concerned with the literary affinities of each "way," a dimension practically absent from the "seventy-five folios," with only one brief exception (see f. 29). See Notebook 4, Other Manuscripts, no. XII; Notebook 12, *CS, Sketch LIV,* I, pp. 814–830; *Cahier 26,* 2010, ff. 1–8 and their notes, and "Introduction," p. xxiv sq.

f. 27

1. *I was surprised to be told by my mechanic.* When he transposed this passage in Notebook 4, Proust chose the term "driver" (f. 37; Other Manuscripts, no. XII). He uses "mechanic" about Alfred Agostinelli, whose services he began using in the summer of 1907, in "Impressions of the Road from an Automobile" (*PM,* pp. 64, 66–67, 68).

2. *Château de Villebon.* The Château de Villebon is on the banks of the Loir, about fifteen kilometers northwest of Illiers, roughly midway between Chartres and Nogent-le-Rotrou. Built in the fourteenth century, it was reconstructed in the seventeenth century by the Duke de Sully (Quémar 1975, pp. 241–242; Abbé Joseph Marquis, *Illiers* [Chartres, 1904] [republished 1907], p. 12).

3. *in the land of dreams.* In Notebook 4, Proust uses the phrase "the paradox of a realized ideal" to describe that moment when "a thing known only through the imagination [. . .] by a sudden volte-face appears before your eyes": "But I

who as a child never knew more of Garmantes than the 'Garmantes way,' for whom Garmantes was only the almost ideal extremity of that famous way, something mysterious like a cardinal point, the day when lost after a long day in an automobile in a place I didn't know, my driver told me that if we took the first road to the right we would arrive [in] Garmantes, it was absolutely as if he were telling me that if I took the first path to the left and then the second to the right I would fall right into my youth or my first love" (Notebook 4, ff. 37–38; Other Manuscripts, no. XII). This discovery was at the time placed toward the end of the piece, between the discovery of the "Sources of the Loir" (Notebook 4, f. 35) and—"although years later"—the discovery that "the Méséglise way and the Garmantes way were not as irreconcilable" as the hero "used to think" (Notebook 4, f. 42). In the next version, on the other hand, as in the present folio, it features almost at the beginning of the walks: "And when a few years ago lost during an automobile journey in an unknown region[,] a farmer whom I asked to tell me where I might stop nearby told me: follow the road for ten minutes, the second avenue of oaks to your left will lead you to Guermantes, it was as if he'd told me, continue straight on[,] take the first left and to your right you'll find your past, your youth; you will touch the intangible, you will reach the unreachable distance of which no one on earth ever knows more than the direction, the 'way'" (Notebook 12, f. 17; *CS, Sketch LIV*, I, p. 815). It was while rereading the typed version of the first volume that Proust removed this discovery at this point of the story (NAF 16733, f. 198): he detached it completely from "Combray" and from the context of an automobile journey, and situated it during the walks at Tansonville in the company of Gilberte, who had become Mme de Saint-Loup, at the end of the hero's development (Notebook XV, f. 70; *AD*, IV, p. 268). Cf. f. 40. In the version of these walks in *Contre Sainte-Beuve*, the woken sleeper remembers a church and a château "that I had only ever known by name and which it seemed to me should only be found on a map of Dreams" (Notebook 1, f. 58v; *CS, Sketch III*, I, p. 652).

4. *surrounded by real places.* In the following manuscripts of the "walks," the surprise of learning that it is possible to reach the "Sources" of the Loir or the Vivette is compared to the surprise of the "Roman" or the "pagan" discovering the geographical existence of the entrance to Hell (Notebook 4, f. 35, Other Manuscripts, no. XII; Notebook 12, f. 33; cf. *CS*, I, p. 169, and *EA*, pp. 416–417).

5. *the road to Bonneval.* The municipality of Bonneval, which to our knowledge is not mentioned anywhere else in Proust's manuscripts nor in his correspondence, is located about twenty kilometers southeast of Illiers, on the banks of the Loir, geographically opposed to Villebon, to the northwest. This is the first clue that Proust intends to contrast the two walks. He would never again mention

"Bonneval" after this page, replacing it with the fictional name "Méséglise," based on Méréglise, a small municipality a few kilometers west of Illiers.

6. *the afternoon at the park*. The park in question can be identified as the Pré-Catelan, the estate in Illiers belonging to Marcel Proust's paternal uncle, Jules Amiot (see "the park that we had outside the town" in f. 33). Proust distinguishes it from the "small garden on the edge of town belonging to my uncle," although the model was most likely the same for both (see f. 28). With the Loir running through it, the Pré-Catelan was located southwest of the village, in other words quite close to the Bonneval road. We encounter it frequently in the pages that follow, where it is connected to the Méséglise way (ff. 31–32, 33–34, 35–36); it passes through "the Villebon way" in Notebook 4, and is split into two under the form of "M. Swann's park." (Notebook 4, f. 30; Other Manuscripts, no. XII): only this last would remain, definitively located on the Méséglise way (Notebook 12). Proust had already mentioned this "park" in *Jean Santeuil* (pp. 295–296, 322 sq., 329–330, 333–335, 367–368), sometimes called the "meadow" (pp. 280, 304), the "garden" (p. 322) or "les Oublis" (pp. 308, 327; cf. "The Confession of a Young Girl," *PJ*, pp. 85–86). In "On Reading" (1905) there is also a fairly long description of afternoons "at the park" (*PM*, p. 168). See Quémar 1975, p. 243.

7. *the white wooden wickerwork door*. In other words, it was made from willow.

8. *the bells ringing to bless the fruits of the earth*. All these features, obviously based on memories of the Pré-Catelan in Illiers, are also found in Proust's earlier writings: the departure for the rest of the walk around five o'clock (*JS*, p. 327), the asparagus plant (ibid., pp. 322, 330), the "louvered door" or the "white gate that was at the 'end of the park' higher up" (ibid., pp. 322, 330; *PM*, p. 168), "and beyond, the fields of cornflowers and poppies" (ibid.; *JS*, p. 330). See below f. 31. The expression "the fruits of the earth" (i.e., the harvests) had already been mentioned in "On Reading": "It was not the thundering bells that were heard on our return to the village [. . .] exploding our eardrums in the square 'for the fruits of the earth'" (*PM*, p. 169). We find it in the notebooks on the "ways" that came after this (Notebook 4, f. 26, Other Manuscripts, no. XII; Notebook 12, f. 23v), and in the novel itself, where it is mentioned by Françoise; but as the Pléiade edition note makes clear, the bells for the harvests were rung on Rogation days, leading up to Ascension (*CG*, II, p. 325 and note 1). By placing the bells "for the fruits of the earth" at sunset as he does in the "seventy-five folios" and in all the drafts that followed it, Proust seems to be confusing them with the everyday evening bells, the angelus bells, mentioned here on folio 32 ("the angelus bells on the way home").

9. *another life.* The departure "after lunch" and in good weather for the Villebon road; a later departure toward Bonneval, with the sun setting over the fields;
the inaccessible nature of the end points of the two "ways": these traits barely
altered after the "seventy-five folios." The same is true for the phrases used to
designate the doors taken for each walk: "from the back of the house" for Villebon, but "from the hall" for Bonneval, a distinction that remained in the definitive text (*CS*, I, pp. 132, 133, 163).

f. 28

1. *I made no connection between them.* "Two different lands," "completely
disparate days" with "no connection," "another side of the house that seemed to
me another side of the world" . . . this is the first appearance in Proust's manuscripts of the opposition that would structure the descriptions of the walks. It was
still, in part, dependent on the geography of Illiers, because there really were
two dissimilar bridges over the Loir: the Saint-Hilaire bridge, which was a "big"
(f. 28) or "broad" (f. 35) "stone bridge," particularly in comparison to the modest
bridge known as "the Plank" or "the Big Plank" farther downstream, east of the
Pré-Catelan, here referred to as the "little wooden bridge" (ff. 28, 31) or a simple
"wooden plank" (f. 36). Proust accentuates the distinction, describing the first
bridge as spanning "almost a little town river" (f. 28), a "broad, deep river" (f. 35),
and the other a "sleepy trickle of water" (f. 28), a river "as thin as a thread"
(ff. 31, 33), a "thin trickle of water" (f. 36). Despite this double contrast, however, the
river serves as a link between the two walks: presumably aware of this difficulty,
Proust removed one of the two bridges during the first rewrite of the scene in
Notebook 4, keeping only the smaller one, an "old wooden bridge (not much more
than a plank with a rope running above one side of it like a railing)" (Notebook 4,
f. 27; Other Manuscripts, no. XII). It was in the next notebook that the river was
definitively attached to only one "way," the Guermantes way (Notebook 12, f. 27;
CS, Sketch LIV, I, pp. 822–823; ibid., p. 164). On the other hand, Proust takes
liberties with the topography of Illiers. It is highly unlikely, for example, that
from the Amiot house, one would take—when heading toward Villebon (i.e.,
northward)—the detour of crossing the Loir on the Saint-Hilaire bridge, which
would mean going west: it would make more sense to go via the Calvary, an itinerary that, in the last version of the "seventy-five folios," was combined with this
one (see f. 36; Quémar 1975, map facing p. 241, and p. 248 note 3).

2. *a small garden on the edge of town belonging to my uncle.* This uncle, who
is reminiscent of the "gardener" and "horticulturist" uncle in "On Reading"
(*PM*, pp. 161, 162), was probably modeled not on Louis Weil but on Jules Amiot,

husband of Adrien Proust's sister Élisabeth, who was the inspiration for Aunt Léonie. This "garden," at once an ornamental garden, orchard, and vegetable garden, partly corresponds to the description of the Pré-Catelan, on the south-western edge of Illiers (Larcher 1960, p. 242; f. 27). But since, if you left that garden, you emerged "directly [on] 'the Villebon road'" (i.e., to the north), Proust praised its "wonderful" plants, which distinguished it from the boring vegetation of the "park," which was linked to the other walk, on "the Bonneval road" (f. 27). So, if it was the Pré-Catelan, then at this point it was split in two.

3. *countless butterflies with pale blue wings.* From the description, the only elements that survived into the next stage were the strawberries and the butter-flies, and even then only in a metaphorical sense, to describe the Loir's aquatic plant life, transplanted to the Villebon/Garmantes way: "Here and there on the surface in red flashes like strawberries were the smooth flowers of scarlet water lilies [. . .]. One corner appeared to be reserved for common species, [. . .] while elsewhere, pressed together as if in a floating flowerbed, garden pansies seemed to have fluttered down like butterflies to reveal their bluish, glazed wings [. . .]" (Notebook 4, ff. 33–34; *CS, Sketch LIII,* p. 809; ibid., p. 167).

f. 29

1. *None of the boring geraniums.* This is the only occurrence of the word "ge-raniums" in the "seventy-five folios," but Proust would return to them later, as-sociating them with orange trees (Other Manuscripts, nos. IX and X; cf. *JS,* p. 328): most likely as a way of preparing, as may also be the case here, the impressions felt at the moment of the reminiscence sparked by the toast dipped in tea (see the Commentary). In *Search,* a sensual connotation is attached to the geranium, linked to the complexion of the young girls in Balbec (*JF,* II, pp. 148, 186, 297) and to Albertine's laughter (*SG,* III, p. 191).

2. *Musset's* Merle blanc. Alfred de Musset, *Histoire d'un merle blanc* (1842) ("The Story of a White Blackbird") is a fable that begins: "How glorious but how difficult it is in this world to be an exceptional Blackbird!" Proust wrote to Henry Bordeaux [just after April 16, 1913]: "my favorite childhood book was Alfred de Musset's *Merle blanc,*" and passages from that story were "the daily litanies, misunderstood but adored, of my eighth year" (*Corr.,* XI, p. 142).

3. *Saintine's* Picciola. The popular novel *Picciola* (1836) by Joseph-Xavier Boniface a.k.a. Saintine (1798–1865) is a sentimental story about a prisoner saved from despair by his devotion to the flower that grows inside his cell.

4. *about a moon*. Proust might have finished this sentence with the following idea: "The other gardens resembled Mérimée's *Colomba* or Musset's *Merle blanc*, which I liked far less than Saintine's *Picciola* because no sooner did he talk about something beautiful that I liked, about a moon" . . . than he (Musset) started saying something comical. Indeed, there are several parallel passages. Jean Santeuil "prefer[red] Saintine's *Picciola* to Mérimée's *Colomba* in which at any moment a joke would come along and interrupt his pleasure in the vague poetry of the images" (*JS*, pp. 307–308). Writing notes on Monet, Proust remarked on his desire for a "complete vision" that would not be "interrupted by things [he] didn't like": "When we are children and we search in books for the moon and the stars, the moon in *Picciola* delights us because it is a sparkling star, and in *Colomba* it disappoints us because it is compared to a wheel of cheese, and a wheel of cheese seems vulgar where the moon appears divine. And in Musset's *Histoire d'un merle blanc*, while he is telling us of white wings and a pink beak and droplets of water we are captivated, but as soon as the blackbird says: 'Madame la Marquise' to the dove, those men and those women—representing life for us, which is ugly, which for us is not poetry—those people bother us and rob us of our wonder" (*EA*, p. 677; NAF 16636, f. 88v). According to the narrator of Notebook 26 (1909), when he was a child, a "joke [. . .] mingled" with the description of the moon in *Colomba* "immediately prevented [him] from seeing the shining star" whereas "certain phrases in *Picciola* enchanted" him (f. 4). See also Notebook 64, f. 4.

5. *notary's garden*. We find this garden one last time, and more briefly, on folio 36. In *Jean Santeuil*, during the walks in Éteuilles toward Les Oublis (i.e., toward the park), a "notary's garden" showed similar traits: "We passed the notary's metal gate. Through the gate we could see an elm-lined driveway disappearing toward the house [. . .]. On either side of the gate, enclosing the property, was an old wall with clematis hanging from it. We spotted an enormous pink hawthorn bush [. . .]" (*JS*, p. 327). It was also in this garden that the gardener stripped the orange trees of their flowers and grew "magnificent geraniums" (ibid., p. 328; cf. f. 3).

6. *houseleeks in the shape of the cross of the Legion of Honor*. See f. 3.

f. 30

1. *smashed strawberries*. Proust had devoted a lot of space to the hawthorn in *Jean Santeuil*, in which his childhood love for the flower was already expressed: the gift of a branch brought to Jean (at the time by his mother) when he was ill,

the flower's ornamental function in churches, and, lastly, the distinction between its two colors and the culinary comparison that favors the pink thorn (*JS*, pp. 331–332). In "Combray," the motif of the hawthorns, now located on the Méséglise way and connected to Mlle Vinteuil and Gilberte, would be considerably expanded (*CS*, I, pp. 110–112, 136–138, 143); and it is when he sees them stripped of their flowers in Balbec that the narrator remembers his mother's gift: "They came to see me, too, at Combray, in my room; my mother brought them when I was ill in bed" (*JF*, II, p. 275). Meanwhile, after the "cousin" of the present page, it was Mme Goupil who brought them to him (Notebook 12, ff. 96v, 98v; Notebook 29, f. 70; Brun 1984, pp. 219, 221, 229–230).

2. *with all its colors.* In Notebook 4, the artist disappears completely, as does the composer's name, and the comparison evolves; it is no longer a question of moving from score to interpretation, but from one single instrument to several: "[. . .] it was on the Garmantes way that I began to love hawthorns, then with an even greater joy, with an extra color, pink hawthorns, like loving a piece played on the piano then hearing it with a full orchestra" (f. 41; Other Manuscripts, no. XII; cf. Notebook 29, f. 71v; Brun 1984, p. 232). Likewise, in Notebook 12 where Watteau replaces Vermeer, it is no longer a question of moving from the reproduction to the original painting, but of discovering "another Watteau, as beautiful, more beautiful still, of being the same while being different" (f. 98v; cf. Notebook 29, f. 70v; Brun 1984, pp. 221, 231). During the revision, Proust went back to the idea of a movement from the "reproduction" to the original, which became, in 1913, the movement from a "sketch" to the painting (NAF 16703, f. 40; *Bodmer*, galley proof 22, col. 8; *CS*, I, p. 137).

3. *like later the leaf of an apple tree.* See this passage from a verso in Notebook 12, attached to the Méséglise way, which would not make it into the definitive text: "Every leaf, every blossom on an apple tree would intoxicate me with its perfection, exceeding my expectation of beauty. But at the same time I sensed that within me there was an unspoken beauty that responded to this, and which I wished I could speak and which would have been the reason for the beauty of the apple tree's blossoms. I forced myself to try and grasp what I could feel[,] to bring it into the light, I hung back to be alone, I put my hands over my ears and used them as blinkers so that all I could see was my apple tree blossom then, tired, I gave up and ran to catch my uncle" (f. 24v; *CS*, *Sketch LIV*, I, p. 820).

4. *but in my brain.* Although a similar kind of frustration remained attached to the hawthorns in *Swann's Way*, with the flowers offering "the same charm in inexhaustible profusion, but without letting me delve any more deeply, [. . .] the feeling

they aroused in me remain[ing] obscure and vague" (*CS*, I, pp. 136, 137), we can recognize in the present passage a distant antecedent of the various "impressions" felt by the young hero on the Guermantes way, "which seemed to hide behind the veil of the visible world" something "that despite all my efforts I could not manage to discover" (*CS*, I, p. 176). Here, it is not yet writing that is at question, but a pleasure that mobilizes the individual and demands its deeper exploration ("the promise of a particular happiness," "to try to understand what it was that I liked so much about it," "intuiting from the pleasure it gave me"), in search of what is hidden *under* the image. In Notebook 26 the term "impression" was used in the context of the lessons learned from the Méséglise way, although it was not only the image of the hawthorn that was listed: "Suddenly while an image passed in front of my eyes or inside my mind, I thought of a particular pleasure, of a sort of depth, that there was something *under* it, a deeper reality. I didn't know what. I preciously guarded the image in my mind, I walked carefully as if afraid that it might fly away. Sometimes I convinced myself that it was only at home in front of my paper that I could open it safely and discover its intellectual contents. It was a steeple that I had seen pass in the distance, a sage flower, a young girl's face. I sensed that beneath lay an impression, and I returned to the house with my living impression hidden under that image [. . .]" (Notebook 26, f. 15; see also Notebook 11, ff. 13–14, quoted by Brun 1979, pp. 33–34). These impressions are called "obscure impressions" by the narrator of *Time Regained* and are distinguished by him from reminiscences in that they hide "not a sensation dating from an earlier time, but a new truth" (*TR*, IV, p. 456).

f. 31

1. *"the Villebon road, the Villebon way."* Here begins the second version of the walks (ff. 31–32), which Proust quickly gave up. The term "way" appears here for the first time attached to a place-name, in quotation marks as if to suggest a local expression. The "Méséglise way" replaces the "Bonneval road" and, unlike the previous version, occupies most of the story, which ends abruptly at the threshold of the "Villebon way" (or mentions only the return from it, with the introduction of the character of the great-aunt). So here we do not find the uncle's "garden" (which disappears for good) nor the notary's garden (which makes a fleeting reappearance in the next version, see f. 36), nor any development of the hawthorns.

2. *"the Méséglise way"* and *"the Villebon way."* We have restored the deleted passage: "and the Villebon way" is crossed out in the manuscript. The fundamental opposition between the ways is still being sought in the next version from the "seventy-five folios": "For a long time I knew Villebon only by these words:

'the Villebon road, going the Villebon way,' as opposed to the 'other' walk, the Meséglise road, the Meséglise way" (f. 33). In Notebook 4, Proust returned to his initial formulation: "For walks in Combray, there was the Meséglise way and the Villebon way" (f. 25; Other Manuscripts, no. XII); in Notebook 12, it became fixed: "Because there were two 'ways' around Combray for walks, and they were so opposed that we did not leave home by the same door when we went on one of the ways or the other, the Meséglise way and the Guermantes way" (f. 16; *CS, Sketch LIV*, I, p. 814; cf. ibid., p. 132).

3. *a sunken path of hawthorn that ran up alongside the park.* We recognize here the ancestor of the "steep little path" of hawthorns near Swann's park, the "little path leading up to the open fields" (*CS*, I, pp. 136, 143). The hawthorns are now associated with the park—in other words, with Meséglise—unlike the previous version (ff. 29–30); but this would prove a short-lived change, with it returning to the "Villebon way" in the version after this (f. 40).

4. *The "Meséglise way."* In "On Reading" (1905) and the preface to the translation of *Sesame and Lilies* (1906), Proust had already used the fictional place-name "Meséglise" (which he would modify to "Méréglise" in *Pastiches et mélanges*): "[. . .] long before lunch there began to arrive in the dining room all those who, being tired, had cut short the walk, had 'gone via Meséglise'" (*SL*, p. 11; cf. *PM*, p. 162). In all of the present pages—with the exception of the bottom of folio 34, and that perhaps is a Freudian slip—Proust adopts the spelling "Meséglise." It is also "Meséglise" that we read in Carnet 1 when he draws up the list of "Pages Written" (f. 7v), even though the currently published editions change it to "Méséglise" (*Cn 1908*, p. 56; *Cn*, pp. 43, 44). The two spellings coexist in the notebooks, sometimes even on the same page (Notebook 63, f. 60), until the typed version where "Méséglise" becomes the standard spelling (NAF 16733, f. 198 sq., 214 sq., passim). See also Quémar 1975, p. 240 note 1.

5. *Such was the entrance to the "Meséglise way."* The rapidly narrated walk on this page again transposes quite faithfully the journey that the Proust family might have taken in Illiers to reach the Pré-Catelan: to get there, they had to cross the Loir on the bridge known as "the Plank," then walk alongside the river on the towpath (below, f. 34) before coming out above the park in the fields of Méréglise (see Quémar 1975, pp. 244, 257; above, ff. 27, 28). So, in a clearer way than in the previous version, two types of landscape coexist here, on the Meséglise way—the landscape of fields and the river landscape—a disconcerting idea for the reader of the definitive "Combray," in which each of these landscapes is characteristic of one of the "ways" (*CS*, I, p. 133). All the descriptive

elements in this version (ff. 31–32) would be reused in the next—highly polished—
version: the later and briefer nature of the Méséglise walk, associated with bad
weather (f. 34), the different doors taken depending on which "way" was being
followed (f. 33), the villagers encountered on the journey toward Méséglise (the
gunsmith, the grocer, the fisherman, f. 33), the bottles used to catch tadpoles in
the river and the fragrant lilac near the gate to the park (f. 34), the fields and
what lay beyond, out of reach (f. 35), and the "strangers" who came on Sundays
from Méséglise (f. 35).

f. 32

1. *"strangers" who came from beyond Méséglise.* We can recognize a brief antecedent text to this walk in an untitled piece written on a loose sheet that narrates,
in the first person, some springtime impressions of the countryside: "The days
were already hot. After lunch, a short walk was enough. If there was a breath of
wind we might try, despite the sun, to reach the small wood more than a league
away which was in the next canton. When you were young, you could never go
that far. And you dreamed of the lives of the men in that other land who came
sometimes on Sundays to our little town, with unfamiliar looks and ways under
their wide-brimmed hats and headdresses [. . .]" (*EA*, p. 416; cf. "On Reading,"
PM, p. 168: "[. . .] villages that had other names, the unknown"). See also f. 40.
After that "small wood more than a league away which was in the next canton,"
the particularity of the limits of the Méséglise way, where its landscape of fields
began to change, seems to be "little oak woods that could never be reached"
(f. 27), echoed here by "thickets of trees," and then "at the very end [. . .] a small
thicket of trees" (f. 35). It was in this landscape, apparently, that Pinsonville—the
future Roussainville—would be located: "In our walks of the Méséglise way we
left behind us to the left a small, sloping path lined on both sides by a few trees
that gradually thickened as they shrank into the distance, forming, in a hollow on
the horizon, a real little wood, with the steeple of Pinsonville rising above it [. . .]"
(Notebook 7, f. 25; *CS, Sketch LXV,* I, p. 871; see also Notebook 12, f. 24; *CS,
Sketch LIV,* I, pp. 820–821). Cf. *CS,* I, p. 148: "[. . .] the climate of Méséglise
was somewhat wet, and we would never lose sight of the fringe of Roussainville wood beneath whose dense thatch of leaves we could take shelter."

2. *Maybe put here.* This editorial note—one of the few in the "seventy-five folios" (see also ff. 40, 77)—suggests inserting the lessons learned from the Méséglise "way" at the end of this walk: quickly listed here at the top of the folio (the
only addition of this type in the "seventy-five folios"), probably copied from a
preparatory manuscript that has not reached us, they would have been separated

from the lessons learned from the other "way." Proust starts to put this plan into action in the next version (f. 35), before changing his mind. In the definitive text, he would intertwine the lessons of the two "ways" and place them—from the "seventy-five folios" onward—at the end, as a coda (ff. 40–41).

3. *as abstract as the North or Spain.* Proust expresses here, more clearly than in the previous version, one of the essential differences between the "ways": Meséglise, while inaccessible, retains a geographical reality ("the horizon") whereas Villebon is an abstraction (a cardinal point, a "place-name"). Cf. *CS*, I, pp. 132–133. This distinction is blurred in Notebook 12, however: "Throughout my adolescence Guermantes, like Meséglise, appeared to me only as the endpoint, more ideal than real, of a 'way,' something like the horizon line, like the Orient, like the North Pole" (f. 17; cf. *CS, Sketch LIV,* I, pp. 814–815).

4. *that it wouldn't rain.* This father preoccupied by the weather prefigures the father at the start of *Swann's Way* with his enthusiasm for meteorology (*CS*, I, p. 11). See also ibid., p. 163: "[. . .] when my father had invariably received the same favorable responses from the gardener and the barometer, one of us would say at dinner: 'Tomorrow, if the weather holds, we'll walk the Guermantes way.'"

5. *the scent of lilac.* Paradoxically, Proust begins his narration of the walk toward Villebon by listing the characteristics of the other walk that would not be encountered. Was this why he abruptly stopped writing, and why he crossed out "and the Villebon way" on the previous folio (see f. 31)?

f. 33

1. *the Meséglise way.* The start of the third and last version, which despite being unfinished is also the most developed version, integrating some already written fragments. On the opposition of the "ways," see above f. 31.

2. *it's only a tiny little leg of lamb.* Proust integrates the corrections from the previous version (f. 31) here, and adds to the short scene involving the great-aunt by introducing the character of Félicie, the archetype of Françoise (cf. *CS*, I, p. 132). Once again, a first name in the "seventy-five folios" can be linked to the author's biography: Félicie Fitau was the Proust family's cook and Mme Proust's chambermaid. Frequently mentioned in the correspondence between mother and son, she appears in several drafts subsequent to the "seventy-five folios," notably in the conversation with Maman in Notebook 2 (ff. 45, 25v sq.; cf. *CSB*, pp. 105–106, passim; see also Carnet 1, ff. 11v, 36v, 44v; *Cn,* pp. 51, 95, 108). A conversation

in Notebook 5 vaunts her culinary talents: "Through the half-open door I heard Maman saying: 'What if we served a nice leg of lamb? They're so tender and juicy and it's been a long time since we had one. And you know you're so good at getting it right, making sure it's not too well-done. The last one you cooked was delicious.' The moment when Félicie fixed Maman's hair was also the moment when they discussed the dinner menu" (f. 104; cf. *CS, Sketch XXI*, I, p. 726). Félicie Fitau had recently left Proust's service, in July 1907 (*Corr.*, VII, p. 213).

3. *along a side road.* In the previous version (f. 31), this phrase adds to the idea of the impossibility of joining the two ways: the thought of a "side road" running between them remains "incomprehensible." In Notebook 4, it becomes a dramatized discovery, contrasting the present with the past: "Years later [. . .] we came back [with Mme de Guerchy], 'retaking' the Garmantes way. Because I learned then that the Meséglise way and the Garmantes way were not as irreconcilable as I used to think and that we could leave the Meséglise way and take a shortcut via Garmantes. But in the years that I am talking about, joining the Garmantes way and the Meséglise way appeared to me as impossible as bringing the East close to the West and placing them next to each other" (Notebook 4, ff. 42–43; Other Manuscripts, no. XII). In Notebook 12, the same discovery is entrusted to the farmer who has just revealed that it is possible to reach Guermantes: "This same farmer taught me something else that I found equally troubling: that it was possible to go to Guermantes 'by way of Meséglise,' which makes me think now that Meséglise and Guermantes were not as absolutely opposed and irreconcilable as I believed throughout my childhood. So that the idea of going 'by way of Meséglise' when you were walking the Guermantes way, or vice versa, seemed to me as nonsensical as going by way of the north on your way to the south" (Notebook 12, f. 18; see *CS, Sketch LIV*, I, p. 815; cf. Notebook 63, ff. 61–62). But in the end Proust left only, at the start of the long piece about the walks in "Combray," the phrase about his childhood beliefs: at the stage of the typed version, the discovery of the road between the two ways was crossed out (NAF 16733, recto of unpaginated folio preceding f. 200; cf. *CS*, I, p. 133 var. *a* [p. 1164]). Like the discovery that it was possible to reach Guermantes, it was in the end completely detached from "Combray" and placed—much later in the narrative—in the mouth of Gilberte (by now Mme de Saint-Loup) during one of their walks at Tansonville: "Gilberte told me: 'If you like, we could go out one afternoon and we could go to Guermantes by way of Meséglise, that's the prettiest way,' a sentence that overturned all the ideas of my childhood and taught me that the two ways were not as irreconcilable as I had believed" (Notebook XV, ff. 70–71; *AD*, IV, p. 268; see also ff. 27 and 40). But it is likely that this version would have been rewritten, had Proust been able to oversee the publication of the

final volumes. On one hand, the discovery about the "ways" had been prepared, even anticipated, during the automobile trips with Albertine around Balbec, where it had been put in the mouth of the "mechanic" (inspired by Alfred Agostinelli?): all the villages in the vicinity, "prisoners hitherto as hermetically confined in the cells of distinct days as long ago were Méséglise and Guermantes upon which the same eyes could not gaze in the course of a single afternoon," were now "delivered" by the car's speed (*SG*, III, pp. 385–386; cf. Notebook VI, f. 13; the rest can be found in *Reliquat* NAF 27350[1], f. 10). On the other hand, the rewriting, in 1922, of the Albertine episode weakened this scene, the young woman's death "on the banks of the Vivonne" making the discovery that it was possible to join the two ways more tragic by suddenly bringing together the Vivonne, from the Guermantes way, and Montjouvain, from the Méséglise way; everything that preceded the scene with Gilberte in Notebook XV had been "removed" by Proust in order to be reworked (see on this subject N. Mauriac Dyer, *Proust inachevé: Le dossier "Albertine disparue"* [Paris: Honoré Champion, 2005], pp. 153–155).

4. *To go toward Méséglise.* There are a lot of changes and corrections on this page and the next. Proust is working in much greater detail on his text, perhaps because he was now satisfied with the overall framework of the piece. The opening of the section on the Méséglise walk begun in the previous version (f. 31) here receives three treatments in two pages (the second, in the upper part of folio 34, not having been crossed out). They still leave by rue de l'Oiseau bleu, but already the name of "rue du Saint-Esprit" appears immediately afterward, and it would end up replacing the former in Notebook 12 (f. 18; cf. *CS*, I, p. 133). Here, the grocer, "head bare" and "carrying sugar-loaves" in a stage of the next version, is still "bare-headed outside his door, his head like a sugar-loaf with a pencil in one corner" (Notebook 4, f. 27); his surname (or nickname), "Monsieur Orange," which appeared in the previous version (ff. 31, 32), is again mentioned in Notebook 68 (f. 38v) and inspires the "Borange's grocery" of the definitive text, where the hero stocks up on books and stationery (*CS*, I, p. 83). It is made clear here, for the first time, that the fisherman in the straw hat, whom the uncle knows, is not someone the narrator knows (see also Notebook 1, f. 65v: "he would wave to my uncle who must have known him and who signaled to us not to make any noise and yet I never knew who he was"; Notebook 4, f. 28: "I never knew who that fisherman was"; Notebook 12, f. 19: "he was perhaps the only person in Combray whose name I didn't know, about whom I knew nothing beyond his ostensible occupation"; Other Manuscripts, nos. XI and XII; *CS, Sketch LIV,* I, p. 815; ibid., p. 165). For the description of the lilac and the bottles placed in the river by "kids," see below, notes to f. 34.

f. 34

1. *and lastly, walking alongside the river.* Proust joined this page to the previous one, but did not cross out the nine-line transitional section.

2. *the scent of the big lilac bush.* The personification of the lilac, here relatively ambiguous (*lilas* is a masculine noun in French, but the "shivers" and the "supple waist" suggest femininity), is made explicit in the following versions: in Notebook 1, the lilacs are compared to "attractive, affected old ladies" (f. 66v; Other Manuscripts, no. XI), in Notebook 4 to "women of a certain age attending a garden party" and to "female relatives M. Swann had asked to be friendly" (f. 30; Other Manuscripts, no. XII), but in Notebook 12 they became "young houris from Persia" (f. 20v; *CS, Sketch LIV,* I, p. 818), exciting the adolescent's desire (ibid., p. 134), and recalling the "svelte Scheherazades" of "Persian blood" in *Jean Santeuil* (*JS,* p. 325)—when young Jean sees the lilac in his grandfather's garden, he puts his "arm around the bush and pulls its scented face toward him," then "ceasing to hold its delicious face against his own [. . .] cannot help watching the graceful way the weightless, adored face throws itself back and, still beautiful and pure, now stands motionless, leaning graciously over the leaves that surround it" (*JS,* p. 323; cf. pp. 278, 280). In Notebook 1, the bush is associated with the masturbation scene: "Finally an opal jet arose, in successive surges [. . .]. At that moment I felt a sort of tenderness surrounding me, it was the scent of lilac that in my excitement I had ceased to notice and which reached me, as on all those days when I used to go and play in the park outside the town, long before I had even spotted from a distance the white gate near which they swayed in the wind* on their flexible waists like attractive, affected old ladies, and shook their feathered heads" (f. 66v; see Other Manuscripts, no. XI). This lilac would perfume a certain "little room with its scent of irises" until the corrected proofs of *Swann's Way,* when it was replaced by a "wild currant" bush (*CS,* I, p. 13).

3. *on the little towpath.* This was the name for "the path that, to the southwest of Illiers then to the west, leads across the Pont-Vieux to the Pré-Catelan" (i.e., over the little wooden bridge known as the Plank) (Quémar 1975, p. 245).

4. *where the bottles are put into the current by kids to catch fish.* Within a few pages, we find here five early stages of the famous passage in "Combray" about the "glass jars [. . .] in the Vivonne" (*CS,* I, p. 166; Lejeune 1977). The first version features only the kids filling their bottles with tadpoles and minnows (f. 28). In the second version, Proust introduces the tadpoles' dual movement of gathering and scattering (f. 31). In the third, which is just a brief, crossed-out opening

(f. 33), there appears the idea of the coolness of the bottles. The fourth brings together all these elements for the first time, completing the idea of coolness with the comparison to the set table and introducing "supersaturation" (f. 34). The fifth, on the same page, combines the previous states into the first finished version; it is rendered more complex by two new elements: for the bottles, the idea of the water that simultaneously fills and surrounds them (which will give rise, in Notebook 4, f. 29, to the image of "alliteration"); for the tadpoles, the idea of their being "held in solution" by the "supersaturated water" prior to their "gathering" (f. 34)—from Notebooks 4 (f. 30) and 12 (f. 20) onward, there would no longer be any mention of "gathering" but of "crystallization," a term that already featured in the piece on the Sources of the Loir that predated the "seventy-five folios" (*EA*, p. 416). But before reworking this passage within the walks along the "ways" in Notebooks 4 (ff. 29–30; Other Manuscripts, no. XII) then 12 (ff. 19–20; *CS*, *Sketch LIV*, I, pp. 817–818), Proust recycles it at the end of the masturbation episode, just after the scent of lilacs (see above): "the scent of lilac coming out to welcome us on the little path that runs above the river, where the bottles are put into the current by kids to catch fish, giving a dual idea of coolness because they contain not only water as on a table where they give the impression of a crystal, but are contained by it and, receiving from it a sort of liquidity, where around little breadcrumbs that we tossed in there gathered in a living nebula the tadpoles held in solution in the water and invisible the instant before" (Notebook 1, ff. 66v–65v; Other Manuscripts, no. XI).

5. *Its climate was quite rainy.* Cf. above, f. 31: "The 'Méséglise way' was open-air, immense, and it would rain sometimes because, since it was the shorter walk, we reserved it for uncertain weather." The family is more circumspect in the next version, in Notebook 4: "If on the contrary it looked like rain, we didn't go on the Méséglise road and as soon as we felt the first drops we went home. We read in the living room. We had brought in the wicker armchairs so they wouldn't get wet and in the empty rain-whipped garden all we could see was my grandmother [. . .]" (f. 24v; cf. ff. 26, 27; Other Manuscripts, no. XII). The nuance thus attached to walking toward Méséglise seems connected to the need to find a place for the grandmother's walks around the garden. When, in Notebook 8, Proust finally situated this scene at the beginning, still uncertain, of "Combray," after the nocturnal wakings (ff. 14–15), the contrast of the climates associated with the two walks was clearly expressed: there were "walks around town [. . .] for fine weather, and walks for uncertain weather" (Notebook 8, f. 12). By Notebook 12, which followed on from Notebook 8, the threat of rain was no longer an obstacle to a walk on the Méséglise way ("we went out [. . .] even if the weather was overcast because it wasn't far," f. 18), whereas they would "risk" the Guermantes way

"only on sunny days" (f. 25): "And because of that fine weather, this land of Guermantes, already so different from the land of Méséglise [. . .]" (f. 25; *CS*, *Sketch LIV*, I, pp. 815, 821). In the published version, they walk toward Méséglise "even if the sky were clouded over" (*CS*, I, p. 133), while for walks on "the Guermantes way," they "must first make sure of the weather" (ibid., p. 163). In the end, Proust returned to the principles outlined in the present ff. 31 and 34: "Since the Méséglise way was the shorter of the two that we used to take on our walks round Combray, and *for that reason was reserved for days of uncertain weather*, it followed that the climate of Méséglise *was somewhat wet* [. . .]" (NAF 16703, f. 57, passage dictated to a copyist [italics are ours]; cf. *CS*, I, p. 148).

f. 35

1. *But we never went that far.* After this sentence, Proust continued by implementing the plan laid out in the editorial note from folio 32 (i.e., beginning to develop the "lessons" learned from the Méséglise way). This passage was later crossed out: "It was on the Méséglise road that I began to pursue cornflowers, poppies[,] those two scarlet wings held together by some bitter-smelling black glue which yet fly so quickly away in the wind; back then, I disdained the purple fleece of the clover; it was on the Méséglise road that I began to notice the black shadows that the trees made move around their feet, to feel a tenderness for the wide white blossom of the apple tree that even today cannot be fooled by the sight of any similar flower. It was coming back on the Méséglise road in the evenings that I learned what a sunset was, that I noticed that a fragile white moon would sometimes flit through the afternoon sky, perhaps in pursuit of business unknown to us because it was not yet time for her to play her role; for now she was still dressed in her ordinary clothes, discreetly watching her colleagues from the wings, a few hours prior to her entrance." But Proust did not write here about the nocturnal walks mentioned in the folio 32 note ("It was in those fields of Méséglise that twelve years later I felt the thrill of going out after everyone else when the moon was already in the sky, seeing sheep blue in the moonlight, etc."), which he would finally place on the other way (see f. 41). The off-duty moon that Proust develops here—after the simple "pale crescent moon" of folio 32— would not be mentioned again until Notebook 4 ("It was on the Méséglise way that I first noticed the beautiful round shadow made by apple trees in sunlight, and that the white moon, not yet wearing make-up, would sometimes pass through the sky in the middle of the day, like an actress in her street clothes during a rehearsal where she has no part to play," f. 41; Other Manuscripts, no. XII). In Notebook 12, this vision would be associated with the returns from the walk, and no longer with the lesson of the "ways" ("The sun was starting to set[,]

we retraced our steps. The white moon like a cloud would sometimes flit through the afternoon sky, but furtively, in her street clothes, like an off-duty actress who watches her colleagues from the wings for a moment, waving her hand as if to say: pay no attention to me," f. 23v; cf. *CS, Sketch LIV*, I, p. 821). In the definitive text, as if Proust had returned to the type of montage planned in the "seventy-five folios" (see f. 32), the sentence about the moon follows, in a new paragraph, a stray first "lesson" learned from the Méséglise way ("It was on the Méséglise way that I first noticed [. . .]," *CS*, I, p. 144). In the version from Notebook 26, inserted between those of Notebooks 4 and 12, the "white moon like a cloud" seen "flitting past in the middle of the afternoon" is associated, briefly, with the Guermantes way at the start of the lessons learned from the "ways" (*Cahier 26*, 2010, f. 1 and note 2; see also pp. xxiv, xxvii).

2. *as abstract as a cardinal point.* This opposition had already been announced on folio 32, but its two ends were separated by the long parenthesis of the editorial note on the lessons learned from the Méséglise way ("Méséglise remained as mysterious as the horizon. [Maybe put here [. . .]] But Villebon was just as distant, as abstract as the North or Spain"). In the present folio, while faithfully sticking to the framework of the previous version, Proust inserted those lessons ("It was on the Méséglise road that I began to [. . .]") before starting to set out the opposition ("Méséglise remained as mysterious as the horizon. But Villebon"). He then crossed all of this out and started again with that sentence a little farther down the page: "And for me Méséglise ~~remained~~ <was> as mysterious as the horizon. But Villebon was as abstract ~~as the East or the N~~ as a cardinal point." See also f. 32.

f. 36

1. *as if born from the warm air.* For the walk along the Villebon way, Proust retraces the steps already listed in the first version: leaving by the "garden" door usually reserved for tradesmen (cf. ff. 27–28), crossing the river over a "broad stone bridge" (cf. f. 28), so different from the "wooden plank" that led to the park (ibid.), and finally the notary's garden (cf. f. 29), which loses its hawthorn bush, now moved to the countryside at the edge of town (see next note). The uncle's garden also disappears from this version (cf. ff. 28–29).

2. *We passed the Calvary.* Proust again seems to have the topography of Illiers in mind: to reach the Villebon road from the Amiot house, one really does pass the Calvary before joining rue de Courville (see Quémar 1975, map facing p. 241). In the manuscript, we can read a first version that was then crossed out:

"You climbed a hill called the Calvary then <the town was over,> you went through a series of sunken paths lined with white hawthorns, pink thorns and dog roses. You arrived ~~under a high arch of trees~~ in a long endless path of trees; on both sides, farms enclosed by apple trees, then the enclosures ended and there were more and more trees. It became a forest, the path climbed, and soon on both sides, in gaps between trees you could see deep blue valleys between steep hill-sides, the path turned again and." The interruption can be explained, retrospectively, by the fact that Proust was creating a sort of compressed version here, with the intention of writing it at greater length afterward, which he did in two successive versions: the farm village after the Calvary and its hawthorns (f. 36), the "path" or "avenue" of trees (ff. 36, 37, 39), the landscape of "blue valleys" (ff. 37, 39), followed by a "vast plain" (ff. 37, 39), the final element that was not included in the compressed version.

3. *that seemed to know where it was leading.* The page was not completely filled, and Proust drew a line connecting it to the next one. See the manuscript.

f. 37

1. *that gave the impression it knew where it was leading.* The join between the two pages is imperfect—"Then a tree-lined path that seemed to know where it was leading" (f. 36)/"We took a sort of avenue of tall trees that gave the impression it knew where it was leading" (f. 37)—suggesting two independently written passages. It is likely that the present bifolio was written before the previous one. The writing ends abruptly on the first page in the middle of a sentence, while folio 38 remains blank: it would begin again on a new bifolio (ff. 39–40), which would provide a new beginning for the piece: "Before reaching what was actually the Villebon road we took a sort of wide avenue of trees that seemed to know where it was leading" (f. 39).

2. *I've seen those trees before, where.* The reader of *In Search of Lost Time* immediately recognizes here an impression akin to the impression felt by the hero during a horse-drawn carriage ride with Mme de Villeparisis near Balbec, when he sees the trees in Hudimesnil: "Where had I seen them before?" (Notebook 70, f. 123v; cf. *JF*, II, p. 78: "Where had I looked at them before?"; Proust changed "*voir*" to "*regarder*" quite late, during the Gallimard proofs [Rés. M Y^2 824, p. 232]). But the difference between the two scenes is complete. Here the "avenue of tall trees" is immediately placed in a geographical context—the walk along the Villebon way—before the experience of remembering is described ("since then, seeing similar trees in Normandy, in Burgundy") and the mystery

instantly solved: "And then I remembered, it was the avenue we took as we were leaving town to go on the Villebon road" (f. 37). In the draft of *Young Girls* as in the definitive text, the memory or the pseudo-memory appears first and remains entirely mysterious. But—a sign of the importance or the persistence of the 1908 text—the first hypothesis to be cast aside in the finished version was precisely that of the solution provided in the "seventy-five folios": "Where had I seen them before? ~~Nowhere Such a path~~ there was no place ~~on the Gue~~ around Combray or on the Guermantes way, nor ~~anyw~~ on the Méséglise way where such a path opened up like that." (Notebook 70, f. 123v; cf. *JF*, II, p. 78: "Where had I looked at them before? There was no place around Combray where a path opened up like that.") Moreover, while Proust seems to have quickly decided to remove this experience of incomplete recognition from the context of the walks along the "ways," since it does not feature in Notebook 4, its background remains as it does in Notebook 12, still associated with the Garmantes/Guermantes way, but now with the way home: "the path of trees by which we returned to Combray along what used to be the Calvary and was now the racecourse [. . .]" (Notebook 4, f. 35; *CS, Sketch LIII*, p. 810), "a sunken path shaded by oaks," "this long path under an arch of oaks," "the path of trees that leads to what used to be the Calvary" (Notebook 12, ff. 35, 36v; *CS, Sketch LIV*, I, pp. 826, 827). This trace remained even in the definitive text, on the walks home along the Guermantes way: "[. . .] to return to Combray, we need only turn down an avenue of oaks" (*CS*, I, p. 180). It is for this "entrance to the path of oaks" that the narrator, at the end of "Combray II," expresses a longing: "what I want to see again is the Guermantes way as I knew it, with the farm that stood a little apart from the two neighbouring farms, huddled side by side, at the entrance to the oak avenue; [. . .] that whole landscape whose individuality grips me sometimes at night, in my dreams, with a power that is almost uncanny, but of which I can discover no trace when I awake" (*CS*, I, p. 183). It should be noted that the phrase reiterates the dreamlike climax that dominates the present passage and its immediate rewrite (f. 39). Moreover, the mysterious vision from Notebook 70—"three trees that seemed to mark the entrance to a shaded path" (f. 122v; cf. *JF*, II, p. 77)—reuses elements that appeared in Notebook 12, namely the adjective "shaded" and the grouping of three elements: "a sunken path *shaded* by oaks" (f. 35), "the *single farm opposite two farms,* the path of trees that leads to what used to be the Calvary" (f. 36v; italics are ours). On these connections between the trees in Hudimesnil and the path in Combray, see Boucquey 1992, pp. 148–163, and 1999, p. 99.

3. *that avenue.* In the first draft, on folio 36, what was being described was "a high arch of trees," "a long endless path of trees," then "a path of trees." Here it is "a sort of avenue of tall trees," then "a sort of wide avenue of trees" (f. 39), but

the term "avenue" is used here for the only time among all the drafts at our disposal. The word "path" predominates, and is used again on folio 39 ("the path of
trees"), later in the version of the "preface" to *Contre Sainte-Beuve* ("a path o[ ],"
NAF 16636, f. 4; Other Manuscripts, no. VII), then in Notebook 4 ("the path of
trees," f. 35), and Notebook 12 ("this long path under an arch of oaks," "the path
of trees that leads to what used to be the Calvary," ff. 35, 36v). This is also the
case in Notebook 70: "three trees that seemed to mark the entrance to a path
inserted in the middle of these places" (f. 123), "three trees that seemed to
mark the entrance to a shaded path" (f. 122v; cf. *JF*, II, p. 77). We also find the
term in a passage intended to recall the episode: "[. . .] another day at Balbec, in
Mme de Villeparisis's barouche, when I strove to identify the reminiscence that
was suggested to me by an avenue of trees" (*CG*, II, p. 836), and elsewhere there
is a vaguer mention of the memory of "a line of trees" (*P*, III, p. 765), of "certain
trees along a road" (ibid., p. 877), and of "the sight of trees" (*TR*, IV, p. 445).

4. *I woke up*. The shift toward mystery first occurs in this version, in which we
see the perspective alter: the elucidated memory is succeeded without transition
by the return of the image in the world of dreams, where the familiar avenue acquires an "extreme singularity" that can never be fully grasped. See also f. 39.

5. *a few white clouds had been left*. Proust brings another passage to an abrupt
end. The rest of the bifolio is blank. The characteristics of that "vast plain," like
the forest and the valleys before it, are described in the next version, on folio 39.
The sentence left unfinished here is completed: "[. . .] white clouds left on the
sides" (f. 39).

f. 39

1. *Before reaching*. This new version continues the shift in perspective begun
in the previous one: the avenue of trees, even if it is well-known and clearly
located—"before reaching what was actually the Villebon road"—harbors a
"mysterious singularity," which, unlike that of places visited during "useless"
journeys, remains, eluding the grasp of the dreamer just as it does the waking
man: it is, then, a form of obscure impression that requires exploration. While
this aspect remains in the version in Notebook 70 (1912) and then in the definitive text, the experience there is singular and based on the initial absence of
recognition, so much so that the feeling of a possible reminiscence is added to
the obscure impression (Notebook 70, ff. 122v–125v; *JF*, II, pp. 76–79). In the
"preface" to *Contre Sainte-Beuve*, where the experience is repeated, only the
unelaborated reminiscence is emphasized: "So many times friends have [seen]

me stop like that during a walk by a path of[ ] that opened up before us or by a group of trees, asking them to leave me alone for a moment. It was in vain, even if sometimes to regather my strength afresh for my pursuit of the past I have closed my eyes, thought of nothing, then abruptly opened them, hoping to see again those trees like the 1st time[,] I still didn't know where I had seen them. I recognized their shape[,] their disposition, the line they drew seemed traced from some mysterious beloved drawing that trembled in my heart. But I couldn't say more[;] they themselves from their nave and passionate attitude seemed to express their regret at not being able to speak to me, to tell me the secret that they sensed I couldn't untangle' (NAF 16636, f. 4; Other Manuscripts, no. VII). Moreover, that "preface" also contains traces of the avenue leading to the Villebon road, as well as the dreamlike atmosphere that dominates this episode in the "seventy-five folios": "Was it ~~in hell~~ in the walks around the town where I was so happy as a small child, was [it] only in that imaginary land where later I dreamed of Maman so ill, by* a lake, in a forest where it was bright all night long, a land only dreamed but almost as real as the land of my childhood, which was already nothing more than a dream, I didn't know" (ibid., f. 5).

2. *invisible tasks.* Should we see, in these "women half-hidden in the shade busy at invisible tasks," which recall the "women mysteriously in the shade, with only their faces illuminated" of the previous version, an anticipation of the "<~~Shakespearean~~> witches or norns" from Notebook 70 (cf. *JF*, II, p. 78)? Or are they closer to the sick mother from the version in *Contre Sainte-Beuve*, who inhabits the narrator's dreams? (See previous note.)

3. *things that must not be shown to us.* There can be no doubting the influence of Nerval on the tone of this episode, in both successive versions. The way the narrator experiences it and is, each time, frustrated in his attempt to grasp the mystery—either because he's woken as he's falling asleep or daydreaming, or because he suddenly falls asleep—prefigures the experience Proust described in 1909 when reading *Sylvie:* "So what we have here is one of those scenes in unreal colors that we do not see in reality, that cannot be evoked by words, but that we sometimes see in dreams [. . .]. Sometimes as we fall asleep we glimpse them, we can stare at them and define their charm, but when we awake we no longer see them, we let go and before we are able to stare at them we are asleep, as if ~~we should not~~ our intelligence were not permitted to see them. The beings themselves that are in such scenes are beings [from] dreams" (Notebook 5, f. 10; cf. *CSB*, pp. 160–161; *CSB* Clarac, p. 235). Note that "as if ~~we should not~~ our intelligence were not permitted to see [those scenes]" echoes "Because there really are things that must not be shown to us."

4. *the forest of Barbonne*. Proust may have had in mind here the forest of La Traconne, west of the municipality of Barbonne, in the Marne département: Barbonne is located about thirty kilometers from the Château de Réveillon, where he stayed, with the château's owner Madeleine Lemaire, in 1894 and 1895. There remains a memory of that "forest of Barbonne" in the woods or forest "of Arbonne" through which Mme de Villeparisis's carriage travels during their rides around Balbec: "Sometimes to please my grandmother she would ask the driver to cut through the woods of Arbonne [. . .]" (Notebook 70, f. 105v; *JF*, II, p. 68 var. *a*). In Notebook 70 we also find this journey "on the way home," just after the passage on the trees in Hudimesnil (f. 126v).

5. *fat white clouds left on the sides like farm tools in the furrows*. Proust returns to this motif of the "vacant sky" in Notebook 1 (f. 65v: "at the hour when even the bells and the clouds were strolling idly through the empty sky"), and in the two notebooks of walks: "It was in those vacant hours of the first afternoon when even the sky is empty, except for a scrap of cloud or a sound of bells [. . .]" (Notebook 4, f. 29; Other Manuscripts, no. XII), "It was at those vacant hours of early afternoon when the sky, empty like the fields, but for a cloud, a bird, a sound of bells going hardly any faster [. . .]" (Notebook 12, f. 19; cf. *CS, Sketch LIV*, I, p. 816).

f. 40

1. *What a magnificent view*. A "deputy" who was a "regional maps" enthusiast was a minor character in *Jean Santeuil:* "[. . .] the office belonging to the deputy [where] Jean had accompanied his father on so many dreary visits" (*JS*, p. 476). We find him in Notebook 14, with his office "decorated only with old eighteenth-century maps of Combray" (f. 55). Here his perception of the landscape, limited to a sort of picture-postcard realism, clashes with the narrator's own dreamlike, impressionistic perception. Proust seems to want to illustrate—or briefly note for a future illustration—the phenomenon of the noncorrespondence of impressions: it is, then, a note for a new stage in the hero's aesthetic development. Such an idea was already present in *Jean Santeuil:* "And what the philosophers say, that each of the little joys, the simplest events of that past, were not experienced by others the way they were by us, that we couldn't feel what they felt nor vice versa, this idea which sometimes gives to those who think about it such a sad feeling of isolation, shouldn't it ultimately give our past a unique character that, for us, turns our memories into works of art that no artist, however great, could possibly imitate, that he could only pride himself on encouraging us to contemplate within ourselves?" (*JS*, p. 319). In Notebook 26, this discovery of the gap between his own impressions and those of others is the subject of a comic scene during the walks

along the Méséglise way (*Cahier 26*, 2010, f. 12 and note 3). As for the character of the "deputy," whose remark stuns the narrator, we might connect him to the parish priest in Combray who boasts of the "view" to be enjoyed from the belfry of his church: "But what is unquestionably the most remarkable thing about our church is the view from the belfry, which is full of grandeur" (NAF 16703, f. 22; *CS*, I, p. 104).

2. *Sources of the Loir.* This editorial note brings an abrupt end to the walk along the Villebon way, begun on folio 35. After "Villebon" and "Bonneval," the "Loir" is the third and last place-name from the Illiers region to be found in these pages; the river, elsewhere anonymous in the "seventy-five folios," would take its own name in Notebook 4 before, in later notebooks, being given the fictional appellations the Gracieuse, the Vivette, and lastly the Vivonne (see *Cahier 26*, 2010, f. 5 note 1). Proust could be thinking of the version of "Sources of the Loir" that is featured at the end of the piece, already mentioned, which gives a first-person account of the narrator's impressions of the countryside (see f. 32); he already used it to describe the tadpoles in the river (see f. 34): "I remember as a small child being taken one day to the sources of the Loir. It was a sort of <small> rectangular washhouse where a thousand little fish would gather like a quivering black crystallization around the tiniest bread crumb thrown into the water. Around the washhouse was the hard, solid road and not the faintest trace of water or the Loir. And yet it was here, the Sources of the Loir, which ran invisible alongside the road for two leagues before joining, in Illiers, the broad and gracious river. So I could not understand how this little washhouse—at the bottom of which I could see little drops of water bubbling up above each other in little trees of air like those you see in aquariums where the water is constantly freshened—could be the sources of the Loir. But the absence of all connection between [the Loir and] this little washhouse with laundry hanging from its edge which I was not allowed to touch only made that place more mysterious to me and in fact gave it that incomprehensible character which should be attached to the origin of a natural lifeform. So for me that water spouting in distinct drops at the bottom of the tadpole-filled washhouse was the Sources of the Loir in a way as abstract, almost as sacred as <a certain figure> might be the River for the Roman. And I vaguely imagined that the women coming there constantly to wash their laundry had chosen this place in preference to all others because of its illustrious and sacred character" (text revised from the facsimile of the manuscript, Sotheby's, "Livres et manuscrits," coll. Marie-Claude Mante, sale of May 24, 2018, lot 160, online; cf. *EA*, pp. 416–417). In Notebook 4, Proust placed this visit to the Sources of the Loir at the end of the walk along the Villebon/Garmantes way (at a time when it was given the characteristics of the Méséglise

way), but in an abbreviated form: "One day we went as far as the Sources of the Loir. I saw only a sort of square little washhouse with a few bubbles bursting at its surface. And I leaned down in surprise over that washhouse where that immaterial and immense thing was: the Sources of the Loir, as a Roman might have leaned over the [ ], where the gates of Hell are located. Such was the 'Garmantes' way" (f. 35; Other Manuscripts, no. XII). In Notebook 12, the visit was inserted toward the end of the walks along the Guermantes way, but was no longer described as being part of the narrator's childhood: "I who for so many years had followed the banks of the Vivette as we walked along the Guermantes way, had heard people talk about the 'Sources of the Vivette' as an almost abstract place[,] was as surprised to learn that these 'Sources' were located at a certain spot, at a certain distance from a real town, as a pagan would have been to learn that the Gates of Hell were near this or that town, and one day I was taken to see the Sources of the Vivette. Being told as I stood in front of a square washhouse where a few bubbles were rising, that these were the sources of the Vivette, being forced to accept such an immense, ideal conception in a sight so meagerly material, was as tiring as entering Rome and thinking: This is Rome, or being shown an elderly gentleman in a bowler hat [. . .], it's Victor Hugo. I stood there confused, in that saddened state of surprise that strikes us when we must think at once[,] in other words make one single thing[,] of a thing imagined and a thing seen" (Notebook 12, ff. 33–34; *CS, Sketch LIV*, I, pp. 825–826; see also the version gathered from Notebook 11, f. 11; *CS, Sketch LXVII*, I, p. 877). In the end, the disappointment was delayed until the trip to Tansonville to stay with Mme de Saint-Loup, where it was inserted between the two discoveries linked to the "ways" (Notebook XV, f. 70; *AD*, IV, p. 268; cf. ff. 27 and 33). Like, earlier, the frustrating hawthorns and the evanescent "path of trees," the insignificant-looking "Sources of the Loir" were part of an aesthetic development that took place mostly on the "Villebon way." The last milestone on this journey is, here, the lesson of the "ways." See also f. 51.

3. *It is probably due to the walks along the Méséglise way.* The lessons of the "ways"—as noted at the end of the list of "Pages Written" in Carnet 1: "What I learned from the Villebon way and the Méséglise way" (f. 7v)—were absent from the first version (ff. 27–30). In the second, Proust introduces them at the end of the Méséglise walk, but only for that "way," in a marginal addition that reads like a plan (f. 32); he develops it at the same point in the story in the present third version, before deleting it (f. 35). And it was ultimately here (ff. 40–41) (i.e., at the conclusion of the account of the walks along the two "ways") that he placed the lessons, intertwining them, but beginning once again with the Méséglise way. A sort of meditation on the "ways" also features almost at the end of "Combray

II" in *Swann's Way* (*CS*, I, pp. 180–183), after the addition of numerous episodes, during the genesis of the book, to the story of each walk.

4. *the two red wings of a poppy*. Proust begins with the flora characteristic of each "way": for Méséglise, that means poppies, cornflowers, clover, and apple trees. See above, f. 35, the previous crossed-out version: "It was on the Méséglise road that I began to pursue cornflowers, poppies[,] those two scarlet wings held together by some bitter-smelling black glue which yet fly so quickly away in the wind; back then, I disdained the purple fleece of the clover" (f. 35). For previous mentions of poppies, see "The Confession of a Young Girl," *PJ*, p. 89; *JS*, pp. 301, 330, 461. See also Notebook 4, f. 40: "It was on the Méséglise way that I first fell in love with cornflowers and poppies, apple tree blossoms, and that there was for me between those flowers and the flowers sold by florists the same difference as between the Méséglise way and a pretty foreign landscape [. . .]" (Other Manuscripts, no. XII), and Notebook 12, f. 37 (*CS, Sketch LIV*, I, p. 828). In *Swann's Way*, the flora characteristic of Méséglise is also remembered at the moment of the "lesson" of the "ways": "The Méséglise way with its lilacs, its hawthorns, its cornflowers, its poppies, its apple-trees [. . .]" (*CS*, I, p. 182); but the mention of the poppy was placed during the walk (ibid., p. 137).

5. *my even deeper tenderness for the hawthorn*. Proust moves on to the flora emblematic of the Villebon way. The declaration of love for the hawthorn is no longer attached, as in the first version, to the "notary's garden" (ff. 29–30), which is now only mentioned in passing (f. 36). The bush was still associated with the Villebon/Garmantes way in Notebook 4 ("But it was on the Garmantes way that I began to love the hawthorn, then with an even greater joy, with an extra color, the pink thorn [. . .]," f. 41), before being placed definitively on the Méséglise way starting in Notebook 12, where the two types of landscape were divided: "Such was the Guermantes way. The Méséglise way, all in fields high above the town with cornflowers, poppies, apple tree blossoms and hawthorns as far as the eye could see, always did something very different for me [. . .]" (f. 37); "If I were given vast lands with no poppies, no cornflowers, no apple trees, no hawthorns, I wouldn't want them, because I wouldn't feel surrounded by nature. The Guermantes way fixed forever the different but equally necessary features of another part of what is for me the image of happiness. While I can no longer conceive of nature without hawthorns, I can also no longer conceive of it without rivers" (f. 38). See also *CS, Sketch LIV*, I, p. 828.

6. *the months of Mary at the church*. The association of the hawthorn with the rite of the Virgin Mary in May had already been made in *Jean Santeuil* (pp. 331–332,

335), which also features other flowers in that role (pp. 320, 326). The Catholic theme, begun above (the hawthorn as "a wonderful adornment for an altar," f. 29), blooms fully in Notebooks 12, 29, and 14 (see Brun 1984, p. 217 sq.). See *CS*, I, pp. 110–112 ("It was in the month of Mary that I remember having first fallen in love with hawthorns. [. . .]") and pp. 136–138 ("[. . .] ready for the "Month of Mary" of which it seemed already to form a part, it glowed there, smiling in its fresh pink garments, deliciously demure and Catholic").

f. 41

1. *pale blue silk forget-me-nots.* Even though the uncle's "small garden" (f. 28) has disappeared from this version, we do find here its strawberries and cherries, its periwinkles and forget-me-nots. Proust seems to have kept almost nothing but the metaphor of "agate cherries," which he developed in a description of the house's interior at the start of Notebook 4 (ff. 2v, 3, 4, 8; *P, Sketch XVIII*, III, pp. 1171, 1172); it made its way into the preface to Jacques-Émile Blanche's *Propos de peintre*, where the Auteuil of Proust's childhood was evoked: "[. . .] the dining room with its frozen, transparent atmosphere like an immaterial agate veined with the smell of cherries" (*EA*, p. 573; cf. *P*, III, pp. 911–912).

2. *as in a house without furniture.* "[T]he black shadows at the feet of apple trees" (cf. "the black shadows that the trees made move around their feet," f. 35) is the sole stable element in this enumeration. See Notebook 4, f. 41 ("the beautiful round shadows made by apple trees in sunlight"; Other Manuscripts, no. XII), Notebook 26, f. 1 ("the round shadows made by apple trees on a sunlit field"), and *CS*, I, p. 144 ("apple-trees which cast upon the ground, when they were lit by the setting sun, the Japanese stencil of their shadows"). We find these apple tree shadows on the Guermantes way in Notebook 12 ("avenues of apple trees whose foliage cast Japanese shadows on the illuminated ground," f. 35; *CS, Sketch LIV*, I, p. 826).

3. *a pleasure different from that of walking all day long and going home at night.* The opposition between yesterday's pleasures and today's was continued in the story of *Contre Sainte-Beuve*, but it was placed during the narrator's nocturnal wakings, without any further mention of the "ways": "Because years have passed since I lived at my grandparents' house. Now we do not dine until nine in the evening, after the walk for which we leave at the hour when long ago I used to come home. It was a pleasure when we saw the setting sun make a red stripe behind the château to hurry home to find the lamp lit and dinner served. It is also a pleasure, of a very different kind, at that same moment of preparing to go out,

walking through the village [. . .]" (Notebook 1, ff. 60v–59v), "The pleasure of returning to the château when the château stands out against the red sky, when the water in the ponds is red too, and reading for an hour by lamplight before eating dinner at seven o'clock, was followed by a more mysterious pleasure: we set out after nightfall [. . .]" (Notebook 1, ff. 61–60; Other Manuscripts, no. XI). In the reworking of the walks along the "ways" in Notebook 4, Proust once again opposed the two eras, with the landscape with the setting sun then associated with the Méséglise way: "It was on the Méséglise way that I first noticed the setting sun, that I knew the sweetness when the sky was red between the trees, associating that redness with the idea of the kitchen stove, and of going home early, when the day ended, before the usual time so that I could read before dinner. But a curious thing: the Méséglise [*sic*] way one day taught me a completely opposed pleasure. Years later I was with Mme de ~~Forcheville~~ <Guerchy> of whom I will write more later and we would leave Combray at the hour when I used to come home" (f. 42, passage ends there; Other Manuscripts, no. XII). In Notebook 26, the walks are made with some unidentified friends: "A peculiar thing: while it was on the Méséglise way that I first felt the sweetness of a life of daily routine, going home to read every day before dinner as the sky above the trees on the Calvary was a strip of scarlet that I associated with the comfortable feeling of being hungry already and, with the air growing cool, the idea of the kitchen stove [. . .], it was also on the Méséglise way that I learned, years later, on vacation with some friends I didn't know before, the sweetness of a life without routine, of going out at an hour when back in Combray I would already have finished eating dinner" (Notebook 26, ff. 7–8). During the revisions of the future "Combray," this firmly established opposition left the lesson of the "ways" and was moved to the opening of the novel, when the sleeper awakes and thinks he's "at Madame de Villeparisis's house in the countryside": "I must have overslept during the nap I always take after coming home from my walk with Madame de Villeparisis, before putting on my frock coat. Because years have passed since Combray, where we came home every evening at sunset and where we went to bed after dinner. It is another life, another kind of pleasure that we enjoy at Madame de Villeparisis's house, going out only at night, silently following in the light of the moon those paths where I used to play in sunlight [. . .] while in Combray, when we returned home late, it was shades of red from the setting sun that I saw in the glass pane of my window[,] reflections of the strip of crimson that stretched over the little black woods of the Calvary" (Notebook 9, ff. 9–10; cf. *CS*, I, p. 7). As for the landscape of the setting sun, it is no longer included during the lesson of the "ways," but just before the narrator introduces those ways, on his return from the walks toward Guermantes: "We always came home early from our walks so we could pay a visit to my Aunt Léonie before dinner. At the start of the season when the day ended early, when we arrived on rue du St. Esprit we could still see the sunset reflected in the windows of the house and a strip of crimson on the brow of the Calvary woods that was reflected farther off in the pond, a redness that often accompanied a biting cold, associated I know not why in my mind with the redness of the oven above which the chicken was roasting, offering the pleasures of fine food, the promise of warmth and rest, after the poetic pleasures of the walk" (Notebook 63, ff. 58–59; cf. *CS*, I, p. 131).

4. *going out for a walk at night.* In the editorial note on folio 32—as in the previous, deleted version, of this folio 41—these nocturnal walks are located not on the Villebon way but the Méséglise way: "It was in those fields of Meseglise [*sic*] that twelve years later I felt the thrill of going out af[ter] everyone else when the moon was already in the sky[,] seeing sheep blue in the moonlight, etc." This would also be true in Notebooks 4 and 26 (see previous note). While these walks were subsequently mentioned at the beginning of the novel (*CS*, I, p. 7 and previous note), they were not described in detail until much later, during the stay in Tansonville at Mme de Saint-Loup's (Notebook XV, ff. 69, 70, 72; *AD*, IV, pp. 267, 268–269). In those walks with Gilberte, we still recognize the changing backdrop of "deep valleys" and "hillsides" characteristic of the first Villebon (ff. 37, 39, 40), as well as the dreamlike atmosphere: "While we walked, I saw the country changing; I had to climb hillsides, then the land sloped downward," "As we descended into the mystery of a deep valley painted with moonlight [. . .]" (Notebook XV, ff. 70, 72; *AD*, IV, pp. 267, 268–269). The "sheep blue in the moonlight" also remain throughout all the versions: here "lines of sheep with bluish fleeces" under the moon, they became in Notebook 1 "the blue triangular moving mass of sheep returning home in moonlight" (f. 59v) or the "the irregular bluish moving triangle of sheep returning home" (f. 59; Other Manuscripts, no. XI), which is almost exactly the same as that in Notebook XV (f. 69; *AD*, IV, p. 267). Lastly, we find in the present page the only occurrence of a "Duchess of Villebon." Her role would be taken successively by the "lady of the château" in Réveillon (Notebook 1, f. 59; Other Manuscripts, no. XI), "Mme de ~~Forcheville~~ <Guerchy>" (Notebook 4, f. 42; Other Manuscripts, no. XII), and lastly Gilberte, "Madame de Villeparisis" briefly taking her place at the start of the novel (Notebook 9, ff. 9–10). Gilberte might be the symbol of the ambiguity of these nocturnal walks, which belong alternately, in the book's genesis, to each of the "ways."

5. *who could not be mentioned.* In Notebook 1, there would no longer be any mention of forgetting the dead: "[. . .] as we descended into the mystery of a deep valley painted with moonlight we would stop for an instant my companion and I before descending into that opal chalice and the lady indifferent spoke one of

those words in which I saw myself suddenly placed unwittingly and seemingly forever in her life, where I hadn't believed I could enter, and from where the next day when I left the château she had already expelled me" (f. 58v; Other Manuscripts, no. XI). The tone was then further softened in favor of Gilberte: "As we descended into the mystery of a deep, perfect valley painted with moonlight, I stopped for a moment [. . .]. Gilberte then, a woman of the world taking advantage of a momentary silence, spoke certain words, perhaps simply out of the graciousness of a hostess who regrets that you will soon be leaving and who would have liked to show you more of this land which you seem to love, expressing her feelings with such simplicity and seriousness as to make you believe that you hold a place in her life that no one else could ever take." (Notebook XV, f. 72; cf. *AD*, IV, pp. 268–269). That indifference to the dead was instead ascribed to Mme Verdurin (perhaps inspired by Madeleine Lemaire, the lady of the Château de Réveillon, in the background to the present passage): "Mme Verdurin, like most people who move in society, simply because she needed the society of other people, never thought of them again for a single day as soon as, being dead, they could no longer come to her Wednesdays or her Saturdays, or drop in for dinner. And it could not be said of the little clan, akin in this respect to every other salon, that it was composed of more dead than living members, seeing that, as soon as you were dead, it was as though you had never existed." (*SG*, III, p. 288).

f. 41v

1. *To return to the time when.* Proust rarely uses verso pages in the "seventy-five folios." This one is a sort of complement to the preceding page, quite abruptly introduced but, as with all these pages, largely retained in the next stage of the novel's development. It would seem that the introduction of a female character, the Duchess of Villebon (f. 41), had encouraged Proust to explore a romantic storyline. He does the same thing for each "way," as an appendix to their "lessons," albeit the storyline for the Villebon way is considerably longer.

2. *unite our thoughts, song of bells.* The theme of the wind as messenger proved highly productive. First it was taken up in Notebook 4, in the series of memories sparked by smells, including an automobile's "delicious smell of petroleum" (f. 18), for an anonymous woman: "All morning, I remember, the walk through those fields in the Beauce took me away from her; she had remained ten leagues away, and occasionally a strong wind would bend the wheat in the sunlight and make the tree branches shiver. And in this wide, flat land where even the most distant lands seemed the endless continuation of the same place, I sensed that this wind was coming in a straight line from the house where she was

waiting for me, that it had grazed her face before coming to me, encountering nothing on its journey between us except those vague fields of wheat and corn-flower and poppies that were like one single field at each end of which we would have stood and tenderly waited, at a distance too far for our eyes to meet but which a gentle breeze could cross like a kiss blown from her to me, like her breath which reached me, and which the automobile would quickly traverse when the time came for me to return to her" (Notebook 4, f. 19; *P, Sketch XIX,* III, pp. 1175–1176). Later in the same notebook, during the walks along the ways, the beloved woman was now (and would remain in this context) Mlle Swann, and the wind from Meséglise opposed to the Garmantes telegraph: "On the Meséglise way, when I knew that Mme Swann had gone with her daughter to Chartres I felt the sweetness of being on that same rolling plain where she herself was, leagues away. Occasionally a breath of wind would pass, bending the wheat, and I thought that it was the same breath of wind that had passed over her[,] that nothing had stopped it and that at the moment when it came to my lips I told myself: she told it, take him my kiss. But on the Garmantes way when we had long ago left behind her estate on the main road it was the quivering telegraph wires that would bring a telegram from her. I would find it when I got home, I arranged each sentence then frightened at the idea etc." (Notebook 4, f. 38; Other Manuscripts, no. XII). In the next version, in Notebook 12, Proust combined the memory of Gilberte with an observation on love affairs in general: "It was on the vast rolling plains of the Méséglise way that I felt the great sweetness of thinking about Mlle Swann, who was in Chartres, so many leagues from me: nothing separates us, and if my vision were more powerful I would see her. And when the great warm wind arrived, bending the wheat and touching my cheek, I thought: it is coming in a straight line from Char-tres, this breath of air that is even now touching my cheek came from Chartres, it could bring me news of her, and perhaps when she felt it leaving her she told it: Kiss him for me. Far from me but in the same field, I felt she was still with me. Ever since, when sensing that it was necessary not to stay too long with a woman I loved [. . .], when I left her for the whole day [. . .], I would order the driver to stop, then sit on the embankment of a field and, staring out at a distance that my eyes could not see, wait for that great wind which nothing had stopped since it left her, bending the stalks of wheat one after another like a wave crossing thirty leagues. But on the Guermantes way when I came from the main road, hearing the telegraph wires humming I would think: Mme de Guermantes has seen me, she has asked about me [. . .]" (Notebook 12, ff. 40–42; *CS, Sketch LIV,* I, pp. 829–830). The "telegraph wires" on the Vil-lebon way appeared first in the present page. See *CS,* I, pp. 143–144.

3. *a small house that looked remote from everything.* In Notebook 4, the men-tion of the isolated house came straight after the passage about the Meséglise wind

and the Garmantes telegraph, but the physical description of this part of the river had disappeared: "At some meander of the Loir, sometimes isolated from everything by the woods that surrounded it, was a little house. I thought of the sadness of going to end one's days in a place unknown to she whom I loved, where I would myself be unknown, accepting the thought: I have voluntarily distanced myself from everything that would have allowed me to see her again, from those who could speak to me about her, perhaps speak to her about me. I will no longer know anything but these water lilies and this hedge, I will no longer be known to anything but this little door that rings for a long time when you open it. Nobody will see me beyond this path, I will not see any farther than that moored boat. And at the window there appears a woman with a sad face, of a delicacy that is not from these parts, who must have come here to end, to renounce her life. I would like to do the same thing, but by the second evening I would be crazy, I would leave. And yet if one wishes to know the land, in that great anxiety that we have to be what is not us, to marry the land, to taste the secret life of those who inhabit it, wouldn't it be by becoming an inhabitant, by being the castellan of that castle lost in the woods, by becoming a citizen of this hamlet, by paying taxes to the collector of Garmantes? But no! It's impossible, we never inhabit a new home. Like the snail we carry our home around with us, our atmosphere, our past, our habits. In a few days the little house on the Loir will be full of me, it is this country that will become my residence, it isn't me who will become its inhabitant, it will not leave its mark upon me, it will be I who leave my mark upon it. Despite myself I would spread out on the ground this carpet that I carry out around with me like a street performer and I would not know the smell of the earth" (Notebook 4, ff. 38–40; Other Manuscripts, no. XII). The image of the snail, and the theme of the impossible journey, come from the portrait of the dowager on vacation at the seaside (see below, f. 58). In the next notebook as in the definitive text, all allusions to the narrator's desire to withdraw from society were removed: "Sometimes at a bend in the Vivette, by the water, surrounded by woods, we would come across a 'pleasure house,' remote and isolated, with a view of the plants in the river, the passing water, and nothing else in the world. A young woman whose face and elegant dress were not from those parts and who had presumably gone there, in the popular expression, to bury herself away, to taste the bitter pleasure of feeling that her name, and particularly the name of the man she couldn't have, were unknown there and always would be, to know that on the rare occasions when she might hear voices behind the trees on the riverbank before seeing the people's faces, she could be sure that the passers-by had nothing in their past or in the future that had been marked by that ungrateful man's presence, and that he had no notion of their existence, and to be certain that when she went outside for the melancholy diversion of a walk, chance could

not put him on the same path and she would return from the walk with vacant
eyes, a tight smile, her heart resigned forever, and before dinner she would remove from her noble hands that he would never see again those long and uselessly beautiful gloves" (Notebook 12, f. 30v; *CS, Sketch LIV*, I, p. 824; cf. ibid.,
pp. 168–169). The Balzac-esque nature of this situation (*The Deserted Woman*)
was emphasized (ibid., p. 169 note 1).

4. *that could give me joy.* This idea of the sterility to be found in waiting for a
love letter that one has already imagined was reworked in Notebook 2, during the
internal monologue that follows the publication of the article in *Le Figaro:* "[. . .]
in times past when I was hoping for a letter from my mistress I would write in my
mind the letter I would have liked to receive. Then, knowing that it wasn't possible, since chance is not so magnanimous, that she would write to me just the
way I'd imagined, I stopped imagining so as not to exclude from possibility what
I had imagined, so that she might write me that letter. Even had she by chance
written that letter to me, it would have given me no pleasure, because I would
have felt I was reading a letter that I myself had written" (ff. 32v–31v; *AD,
Sketch XII.4*, IV, p. 676). In Notebook 12, the theme of the dreamed letter was
reworked in the same context as in the "seventy-five folios," but without the narrator drawing the same lesson from it: "[. . .] on the Guermantes way when I came
from the main road, hearing the telegraph wires humming I would think: Mme de
Guermantes has seen me, she has asked about me, she has repented of her
mockery, she will love me, she wanted to send me a letter, that is what she is
doing at this very moment, she will be in Combray before us, that is what she will
tell me, and I would reformulate this letter several times until it said precisely
what I wanted it to say" (Notebook 12, f. 42; *CS, Sketch LIV*, I, p. 830). Ultimately, it is in Paris, after Gilberte has announced that she will no longer be
going to the Champs-Élysées, that the hero hopes to receive from her the letter he
dreams about, before realizing the absurdity of his desire (Notebook 20, ff.
40–41; Notebook 24, ff. 21–22; *CS*, I, pp. 401–402).

f. 43

1. *"Reproaches are no use."* The beginning of the second verse of "Petit cha-
grin" ("Little Sorrow"), a song for voice and piano by Paul Delmet (1900), inspired by Maurice Vaucaire's poem "Petite peine": "I. The tenderest words will
never/Tell you how much I love you,/My young mistress!/I spoke so much to
move you/When in your eyes I wished to see/Holy intoxication./II. Reproaches
are no use,/Especially when made from afar,/When made alone;/But thinking
about the days we spent/Together and the kisses we sent,/I am consoled." ("Petite

peine," in *Les Gaîtés du Chat Noir*, preface by Jules Lemaitre [Paris: Ollendorff, 1894], pp. 14–15.) "The poor and very kind Maurice Vaucaire was for Marcel always a particular target, a kind of whipping boy" (René Peter, *Une saison avec Marcel Proust: Souvenirs* [Paris: Gallimard, 2005], p. 54).

2. *"Farewell the voices of strangers."* The younger brother of "Marcel," upset at being separated from his goat, has already sung this lied by A. H. von Weyrauch wrongly attributed to Schubert (see above f. 22). In the next part of the novel's genesis we would also hear it in some rather theatrical and ridiculous situations, when the hero sank into self-pity at having to give up a love affair. So, with Gilberte: "[. . .] the patisserie where, when Simone told me that Gilberte had been mocking me, I resolved never to see her again, where my love ended, but where I soothed that end by singing this line from S[c]hubert: Farewell the voices of strangers Are calling you far from me, My sweet sister of angels, and where having been struck by the sound of my voice I took pity on that poor betrayed child who was singing and sobbing so loudly that Françoise let me inside and gave me a croissant at a time when we were not allowed to eat, more than two hours before teatime, which consoled me a little by showing me that my unhappiness was exceptional and understood" (Notebook 64 [1909], f. 12); or when he had to give up Andrée (ibid., f. 73v) or Mme de Guermantes (Notebook 41 [1910], f. 16; *CG, Sketch XVIII*, II, p. 1161; ibid., p. 666). The tone was darker at the moment of Albertine's departure, in a notebook from 1913: "Don't forget that after this separation I go to the pianola where she sat and I play a S[c]hubert melody: a Farewell she had played: 'Farewell the voices of strangers are calling you far from me'" (*Cahier 71*, 2009, f. 103v and note 5). But this editorial note was not pursued. Proust mistakenly wrote here: "Farewell the voices of strangers are calling me far from me."

3. *it made five, four stars.* This children's game was taken up again in Notebook 4 with regard to Mlle Swann: "The first stars were already out when we came home late from the Garmantes way and I thought that she could see them at the same time, in Chartres, or even in Paris to where she must have returned. If I saw three at once, she was thinking of me! But I only saw two. But two and my desire made three. She was thinking of me" (f. 40; Other Manuscripts, no. XII). We find an echo of this in Doncières, when the hero is in love with the Duchess of Guermantes, with a memory of Gilberte: "I would look up at the sky. If it was clear, I would say to myself: 'Perhaps she is in the country; she's looking at the same stars; and, for all I know, when I arrive at the restaurant Robert may say to me: "Good news! I've just heard from my aunt. She wants to meet you, she's coming down here."' It was not the firmament alone that I associated with the

thought of Mme de Guermantes. A passing breath of air, more fragrant than the rest, seemed to bring me a message from her, as, long ago, from Gilberte in the wheatfields of Méséglise. We do not change; we introduce into the feeling which we associated with a person many slumbering elements which it awakens but which are foreign to it" (*CG*, II, p. 418). The passage had been prepared in Carnet 2, ff. 28v, 29v (*Cn*, pp. 194–196).

4. *"I love you."* Just below these final words, sideways on, Proust drew the outline of a church. He ends his account here, leaving the rest of the bifolio blank along with the next three bifolios (ff. 45–50), which reached us nested between folios 43 and 50.

f. 51

1. *to the Sources of the Loir.* Proust does not develop this phrase, which corresponds to the editorial note from folio 40. See *loc. cit.*

2. *one day you must come to Villebon.* This mysterious "Madame de C." could be the lady of the Château de Villebon, since she seems to be inviting the narrator and his mother there. However, we also encountered a "Duchess of Villebon" a little earlier (f. 41). From Notebook 4 onward, the "Countess of Garmantes" becomes a distant, inaccessible figure (see ff. 34–35, 41–42, 44; *CS, Sketch LIII*, I, pp. 809, 813–814). This is the only mention of "Maman" in this chapter.

[A Visit to the Seaside]

Bernard de Fallois had entitled all the material in folios 53–74 "The Young Girls," after the title of the definitive text. But in the manuscript the description of the hotel and its guests (ff. 53–65) is clearly separated from the encounter with the *"fillettes"* (ff. 67–74): we have made them two distinct chapters, particularly since they must be from two different vacations, given that the hero is accompanied by his grandmother in the first and by his mother in the second. Moreover in the manuscripts, until 1913, the meeting with the *"fillettes"* did not take place during the first visit to Querqueville/Balbec: see f. 67.

f. 53

1. *the months that have just passed.* This phrase clearly indicates that Proust originally intended these pages—which he wrote in Cabourg during the summer of 1908 (see the Chronology)—for a quick publication: pegged to a certain date, they

could have served as a feature for the *rentrée* (the end-of-summer return to work and school) in a newspaper whose readers would have had the free time and the financial means to have gone off on vacation—*Le Figaro*, for example. See also f. 78.

2. *of cold and rain.* This detail of outings taken even in bad weather had not been mentioned before among the grandmother's health-obsessed idiosyncrasies (cf. f. 3). It would be kept, along with its harmful consequences, in the next stage of the genesis: "it was always to my grandmother that we were entrusted during those months, and we always returned home with sore throats because she believed that air and water never did any harm" (Notebook 4, f. 62; Other Manuscripts, no. XII); "I generally got sore throats there, because to be in direct communication with the sea, she made me spend the whole day with my feet in the water, and as soon as we were inside she opened all the windows" (Notebook 12, f. 42v; Other Manuscripts, no. XIII).

3. *"going through the motions."* The grandmother's complete indifference to social niceties while on vacation was only hinted at during the first chapter (f. 3). The presence of a "best friend" has been crossed out here, but the role would be played by Mme de Villeparisis from Notebook 4 onward: "From the day of our arrival my grandmother had spotted Swann and also an old marchioness of Villeparisis with whom she had been at Sacré-Coeur [. . .]. But my grandmother had pretended not to see them [. . .] because any time given to people would have been so much time taken away from the famous 'sea air,' which we had to breathe from morning until evening. As for the other people in the hotel, I don't think my grandmother could have told you after a month what they were like. The thought that one might take an interest in someone one didn't know was something she could not understand and that she considered the very depths of vulgarity" (ff. 63–64; Other Manuscripts, no. XII). In the definitive text, the danger could also come from Legrandin and the emphasis was on her health obsession: "My grandmother, who held that when one went to the seaside one ought to be on the beach from morning to night sniffing the salt breezes, and that one should not know anyone there because visits and excursions are so much time filched from the sea air, begged him on no account to speak to Legrandin of our plans; for already, in her mind's eye, she could see his sister, Mme de Cambre-mer, alighting from her carriage at the door of our hotel just as we were on the point of going out fishing, and obliging us to remain indoors to entertain her" (*CS*, I, p. 128); "She was free [. . .] to rejoice in the thought that never, when the time came for us to sally forth to the beach, should we be exposed to the risk of being kept indoors [. . .] since we should not know a soul at Balbec, Legrandin having refrained from offering us a letter of introduction to his sister" (*JF*, II, p. 7).

4. *of my brother and myself.* From Notebook 12 onward, the brother would disappear from this seaside visit: the cutting of "us" takes place in folio 42v (see Other Manuscripts, no. XIII). We find this brother even a little later in the account, but he is described as being the narrator's "older brother" (f. 71).

5. *looking at the sunlight on the sea.* Should we see in this line the first hint of Baudelaire's "Sun's rays upon the sea" ("Autumn Song," v. 20) that the hero seeks in Balbec? (*JF*, II, p. 34; on this famous passage, see Compagnon 1989, p. 192 sq., and Matthieu Vernet, "Mémoire et oubli de Baudelaire dans l'œuvre de Proust" [doctoral thesis, University Paris-Sorbonne, 2013], pp. 330–370). The context is the same: the hero and his grandmother are in the hotel dining room, and the grandmother opens the patio door at an untimely moment (see next note).

6. *so we can get back to the sea.* This is the first known version of the grandmother's whim. In Notebook 4 the scene was shortened and above all dramatized, with her inconsiderate action leading to the family being ejected from the hotel: "[. . .] we were in the same hotel as Swann or rather we had been there to start with because, my grandmother thinking it 'a pity' to have the windows closed at the seaside, demanded that the patio door of the dining room be left wide open, despite the complaints of other people whom she did not want to hear and one stormy day when they had closed the windows despite her, she tried to open them again herself while the waiter's back was turned, the glass smashed and they showed us the door" (Notebook 4, ff. 62–63; Other Manuscripts, no. XII). Proust extended the motif: the grandmother's blithe indifference to the trouble she causes ("[she] would laugh about this a lot") became a martyr's smile ("[she] would open the windows every day during lunch and smilingly brave the insults of various 'families' with the smile of Saint Blandina among the lions, lost in ecstatic contemplation of the paradise of health and vigor to which the famous 'air' would allow us entry," ibid., f. 64). In the definitive text, the scene occurs only once (*JF*, II, pp. 34–35).

f. 54

1. *a few other people.* This phrase is the transition preceding the portrait of the dowager (ff. 54–58). It was rewritten at the start of Notebook 31, which followed on from Notebook 4 where the narrator had listed (ff. 64–65) the prestigious hotel guests avoided by the grandmother (Swann, Mme de Villeparisis) when they could have been used to "place" him with the young girls he desired: "All this reality that my grandmother's natural elevation prevented her from even perceiving and in the grips of which my undoubted vulgarity left me disarmed, I realized then how many

people for other reasons elude it" (Notebook 31, f. 1). So, by 1909, everything was ready for a reprise of the portrait of the dowager, and even of the group of four friends; this, however, did not happen for a long time afterward: see next notes.

2. *distorted impressions.* In 1910, Proust planned to place the pages following the line about "the dowager, my grandmother, the Monsieur and his mistress" (Notebook 69, f. 7; Other Manuscripts, no. XV) at the beginning of "Swann in Love": see f. 62. He did not in the end do anything of the kind, but a trace would remain of this phrase, which here introduces the remainder of the portraits: Swann was "unlike so many people who, either from lack of energy or else from a resigned sense of the obligation laid upon them by their social grandeur to remain moored like house-boats to a particular point on the shore of life, abstain from the pleasures which are offered to them outside the worldly situation in which they remain confined until the day of their death, and are content, in the end, to describe as pleasures, for want of any better, those mediocre distractions, that just bearable tedium which it encompasses" (*CS,* I, p. 189). When Proust reworked this passage in 1912 in the typed version of the future "Place-Names: The Place," it was the "notary's wife and the barrister's wife" at the Grand Hotel in Balbec who were now their own victims: they "wished to show, as everybody does, that while there may have been certain things that they lacked [. . .] it was not because they couldn't have them but because they didn't want them. But the sad thing was that, in seeking only to convince others of this, they had ended up convincing themselves. And it was the suppression of all desire, all curiosity for forms of life that one does not know, the hope of being liked by new people, the effort made to be liked, replaced in these ladies by simulated disdain, by feigned cheerfulness, that had the drawback of making them mask their displeasure as contentment and constantly lie to themselves: two reasons why they were unhappy" (NAF 16735, f. 213; Other Manuscripts, no. XVII; cf. *JF,* II, p. 38).

3. *at a table close to ours.* It is never stated here that the "old lady" who surrounds herself with her servants and knows "the Duchess of T." is from a noble family herself. This, however, was the role that would later be played by Mme de Villeparisis; in retrospect, this passage (ff. 54–58) is probably the first stage in the development of her character. In Notebook 4, while the "old marchioness of Villeparisis with whom [the grandmother] had been at Sacré-Coeur" appeared at the seaside, there was as yet no portrait of her; at the beginning of the next notebook, Proust did not follow up on the phrase that signaled the reprise of the present pages (see above). The merging of the characters took place in Notebook 12: "The next day the first person that my grandmother saw in the hotel lobby was the Marchioness of Villeparisis, that old lady with whom she had been at Sacré-Coeur

and who, followed by her chambermaids carrying her coats, preceded by her
footman who went up next to the driver on the coach emblazoned with her coat of
arms into which she climbed, seemed within the hotel to move around inside her
own little world, descending the staircase, without having to submit to direct contact with the hotel, in a sort of extraterritoriality like that of ambassadors in foreign countries in the embassy is [sic] an enclave of their homeland. She wanted to
say hello to my grandmother. But already my grandmother had turned away"
(f. 50; Other Manuscripts, no. XIII). Next, Proust thought about making the portrait
of the old lady the counterpart to that of Swann, who would inherit the traits attributed here to the uncle: "Perhaps put here the dowager, my grandmother, the
Monsieur and his mistress" (Notebook 69, f. 7): see previous note. In 1912, when
he revised the first seaside visit, he asked for several blank pages to be set aside
in the typed version of Notebook 70 (f. 53), for the scene before Mme de Villeparisis and the grandmother spot each other for the first time at the hotel (f. 62), in
anticipation of reworking the portrait of (among others) the old lady. Consequently, he wrote it on loose sheets—the format of which perhaps rekindled his
memory of the present pages (NAF 16735, ff. 212–215; Other Manuscripts, no.
XVII; *JF*, II, pp. 38–40). Finally, Proust preserved the anonymity of the 1908 character since, until the twist of the encounter with the grandmother, nobody recognized her as the "Marchioness of Villeparisis." Certain character traits of the "old
lady" would be passed on to the hero of *Search:* see below ff. 56, 58.

4. *her black-and-white mourning dress.* White, purple, and gray were permitted along with black during "half-mourning," once the period of "full mourning"
was over. From Notebook 32, the focus would be on the hat worn by Mme de Villeparisis, a "small hat with mauve button loops such as I had hardly ever seen
anyone wear other than our concierge's wife and a completely black coat as worn
by certain visitors to the kitchen" (f. 36v). During the 1912 revision of the typed
version (see previous note), she went "more or less unnoticed or [was] considered
a figure of fun with her black wool dress and her unfashionable hat" (NAF 16735,
f. 214; Other Manuscripts, no. XVII).

5. *signally failed.* Staying in Cabourg from July 17, 1908, Proust noted: "chic
people enveloped in their milieu, nobles refusing to tolerate being unknown to
others at the hotel" (Carnet 1, f. 6v; *Cn*, p. 41).

f. 55

1. *a chauffeur.* Most of the elements of this account (ff. 55–58) would be retained in the version inserted into the typed draft of 1912 (NAF 16735): the old

lady's coterie of servants (f. 212) and the habit of taking her personal belongings to the hotel (ff. 214–215), the privilege of a sort of "extraterritoriality" she
enjoys (ff. 214–215), but also her secret shyness and her pride (f. 214), the mock-
eries directed at her behind her back (ff. 212–214), and the way she accepts a
life bereft of the charms of meeting new people (f. 213). See Other Manuscripts,
no. XVII, and *JF*, II, pp. 38–40.

f. 56

1. *like some not-very-chic client, perhaps.* The fear of being despised by the
hotel manager would be attributed to the hero from Notebook 12 onward: "[. . .] I
was obliged to remain in the entrance hall while [my grandmother] talked with
the hotel manager, trying to burrow deep within myself—as certain animals
retreat inside their shells—to protect myself from the injuries that this meeting
inflicted on my self-esteem, and from the melancholy of seeing people who were
already 'regulars' walking around as if they owned the place" (f. 43). Cf. *JF*, II,
pp. 23–24.

2. *greeted her so coldly.* In the revision of these pages, there was no longer any
mention of this cold greeting, nor the "precious old ornaments" and "personal
curtains [. . .] the screens and photographs and trinkets she'd brought with her,"
erecting "between herself and the outside world to which she would have had to
adapt, the dividing wall of her habits" so that "it was her home in which she
stayed that traveled, rather than she herself" (NAF 16735, ff. 212, 214; Other
Manuscripts, no. XVII). But the hero would not be spared this tedious contact:
the inhospitable characteristics of the bedroom in his uncle's country house
would be transported to the seaside in Notebook 12 (f. 49; Other Manuscripts,
no. XIII). See above, f. 13.

3. *holding a rose above the door.* This refers to a pictorial motif on the over-
door, but the reading of the passage is unclear.

f. 58

1. *and her over-delicate sensitivity.* A passage from Notebook 4, which rewrote
another episode from the "seventy-five folios," that of the remote house (f. 41v),
generalized this behavior (which we might easily imagine was based on the behavior of Marcel Proust when arriving at the Grand Hotel in Cabourg): "if one
wishes to know the land, in that great anxiety that we have to be what is not us,
to marry the land, to taste the secret life of those who inhabit it, wouldn't it be by

becoming an inhabitant, by being the castellan of that castle lost in the woods, by becoming a citizen of this hamlet, by paying taxes to the collector of Garmantes? But no! It's impossible, we never inhabit a new home. Like the snail we carry our home around with us, our atmosphere, our past, our habits" (Notebook 4, f. 39; Other Manuscripts, no. XII).

2. *with his mistress and two friends.* This is the first sketch of what would become the "little society" of four friends (*JF*, II, pp. 40–42), apparently inspired, at least in part, by some of Proust's acquaintances in Cabourg in July 1908 (see f. 59). Intended to illustrate another type of social indifference, more sincere than the old lady's though no less inadvisable, this piece would also be reworked, albeit quite late in the day—in 1912, on the loose sheets that would be added to the typed version of "Place-Names: The Place" (NAF 16735, ff. 212 and 216; cf. f. 54). Proust then split it, inserting the portrait of the dowager in the middle, an organization he would quickly abandon, returning to the order of the present pages in the definitive text. The main elements recur: the artistic tastes and personal elegance of the rich man's mistress (f. 212), the activities always carried out "together" (f. 216), the very late dinner eaten after everyone else has left the dining room or taken elsewhere (ff. 212, 216), the indifference to everything around them: "countryside," "sea," "people" (f. 216). See Other Manuscripts, no. XVII.

f. 59

1. *They came down to eat dinner only very late.* Dinner became lunch during the rewrite (NAF 16735, f. 212) to avoid the two types of dinner described in the present version: those that take place in the hotel dining room and those that are eaten in restaurants.

2. *a soft and perfumed veil but one that separated him from it nonetheless.* This image was part of a note in Carnet 1, which provides the key to its inspiration: "[. . .] Sohège and his mistress perfumed veil between him and the world" (Carnet 1, f. 8; *Cn*, p. 44). The note was written after Proust's arrival in Cabourg, on July 18, 1908. Paul Sohège, whose third wife Mme Singer died in 1904, was in litigation with her daughter, Winnaretta Singer, Princess de Polignac, over the 450 million francs inheritance; the 1909 edition of *Tout-Paris* (the Parisian version of *Who's Who*) indicated that he was still the owner of the Château de Blosseville in Villerville (Calvados). Proust liked this phrase and used it again when he rewrote the passage on loose sheets in 1912, but the "rich, elegant man" of the present pages, perhaps too easily identifiable, became a "rich young man": "while the friends of the rich young man envied him having such a well-dressed mistress,

the mistress's scarves stretched out before the little society like a perfumed, supple veil that separated it from the world" (NAF 16735, f. 216; Other Manuscripts, no. XVII; *JF*, II, p. 42).

f. 60

1. *not that way.* The portrait of the uncle begins here (ff. 60–65), completing the previous series by offering a counterpoint: on vacation, the uncle, unlike the old lady or the "rich, elegant man," his mistress and their friends, does not seek to protect himself from contact with the unknown life that surrounds him, but quite the contrary, even if the narrator's admiration for this attitude would later become more nuanced. But it is never mentioned that the uncle is in the hotel, and his portrait seems to become an end in itself. Proust took the essential elements from this portrait and used it to depict Swann, first in Notebook 4 (1909), after his portrait in Combray, then in Notebook 69 (1910), at the start of the first polished version of "Swann in Love," where it would remain (see *CS*, I, pp. 188–191; Other Manuscripts, nos. XII and XV). See the Commentary and the notes for the following pages.

2. *to his mistress to come.* See the notes from Carnet 1, made in Cabourg after July 18, 1908: "Mistress summoned," "Better to love what is local [. . .] Sad life of courtesans brought from home*" (ff. 6 and 6v; cf. *Cn*, p. 41).

3. *something that did not belong to it.* This idea was first taken up as a general truth in Notebook 2 of *Contre Sainte-Beuve*, in a defense of the "particular" and "individual" nature of beauty (f. 27v). "Marcel Proust," whose article had just appeared in *Le Figaro*, remembers his desire for a girl selling coffee with milk during a morning train journey: "And now, after two years, I sense that I will return there, that I will try [. . .] to kiss the redheaded girl who hands me café au lait. Another man brings his mistress and when the train starts up again he uses her to stifle the desire he feels for the local girls he met. But this is an abdication, a renunciation of the chance to know what the region has to offer us, to explore the limits of reality" (Notebook 2, f. 27; *CSB*, p. 103). In 1910, this observation was applied to Swann, toward the conclusion of the moral portrait of him drawn up at the beginning of "Swann in Love": "When traveling he did everything he could to make the acquaintance of the local women he liked and to send for his mistress only as a last resort, regarding such an act as a sort of abdication, a confession of his powerlessness to penetrate the new reality that was offered to him" (Notebook 69, f. 6; Other Manuscripts, no. XV). We find the "renunciation" of the present version in the definitive text: "If on his travels he met a family whom

it would have been more correct for him to make no attempt to cultivate, but among whom he glimpsed a woman possessed of a special charm that was new to him, to remain on his "high horse" and to stave off the desire she had kindled in him, to substitute a different pleasure for the pleasure which he might have tasted in her company by writing to invite one of his former mistresses to come and join him, would have seemed to him as cowardly an abdication in the face of life, as stupid a renunciation of a new happiness as if, instead of visiting the country where he was, he had shut himself up in his own rooms and looked at views of Paris" (*CS*, I, p. 189). See also f. 65.

4. *enclosed in his old relationships.* See Carnet 1, f. 8: "My uncle constantly making new relationships" (*Cn*, p. 44). "The question of knowing whether or not one should make new relationships while traveling [. . .]" (f. 53) is the one at the heart of the present chapter.

5. *in his "situation."* The unusual conception that the uncle has of his "situation" is a leitmotif of these pages: the word, which was first introduced when discussing the old lady ("the work we are obliged to do to adapt to new places, to new people, to perpetually rebuild on unknown sand the house of cards of one's 'situation,'" f. 58), is repeated here eight times, and nine times in the rewrite in Notebook 69 (ff. 1–7; Other Manuscripts, no. XV). It is notable that the uncle's desires lure him into every kind of milieu: "elegant women" (f. 60), the daughter of a judge or a farmer (ff. 61, 62), servants (f. 65); for Swann, on the contrary, it is the discrepancy between his brilliant situation and his conquests that is immediately emphasized in Notebook 69: "This wasn't the first time that Swann, for romantic reasons, lowered himself from his grand social situation and migrated to inferior circles" (f. 1; Other Manuscripts, no. XV). In Notebook 4, Proust ended his account before detailing the "favors that [Swann] asked of his famous 'situation'" (f. 62). In Notebook 26, the term "situation" served as the join to a possible addition to the present passage: "His worldly ~~situation~~ <relations> was [*sic*] for him merely a key that opened up romantic possibilities before being put back in his pocket," "His worldly situation was for him only a powerful tool that helped him open a locked door and was of no further use once he had entered the room. Often he liked to bring the woman he loved into his world [. . .]" (ff. 25v, 26v; *Cahier 26*, 2010, f. 25v).

f. 61

1. *that was everything.* Cf. Notebook 69, f. 2: "And soon [Swann] sensed that, as an acquired situation, his situation in St. Germain where there wasn't a

woman he didn't know or who had something new to teach him, his situation was no longer of any interest for him. It represented only a sort of potential value, like a bill of exchange, enabling him to create a new situation in Quimper-Corentin, or in some Quimper-Corentin in Paris, if he liked the judge's daughter" (Other Manuscripts, no. XV).

2. *a good impression.* Cf. Notebook 69, f. 2, on the subject of Swann: "His situation was something that could be taken down and transported; better still, it was like those huts of which the pieces, once they have been taken apart, can be transformed into tools that enable you to build a suitable home wherever you go" (Other Manuscripts, no. XV). Proust would in the end adopt the image of "those collapsible tents which explorers carry about with them" (Notebook 15, page conserved in the *Reliquat* NAF 16703, f. 94; *CS*, I, p. 190).

3. *to dazzle the one they loved.* The vanity of the uncle as described here, which "in itself [. . .] meant nothing" and was "used only in the service of love," is very different from the more common vanity attributed to the uncle in the first chapter, in which he gloried in everything (his gardener, his aristocratic connections, his family). In all likelihood the character here is starting to be split in two. His personality is again opposed to the grandmother's (cf. above ff. 1–3, 4, 5–6, 7, 15–16), and this does not change when he becomes Swann: "I cannot of course compare him to people like my parents who showed so little interest in anyone they didn't know that they could barely tell them apart and would not have been capable of recognizing them, but even supposing that my grandmother's soul was one day implanted in the body of a young man in search of good fortune, that soul was too free of all vanity to understand Swann might want the woman from Quimper that he met to *know* that he was friends with the Duchess of S. etc." (Notebook 69, ff. 6–7; Other Manuscripts, no. XV).

f. 62

1. *of total contact with life.* In Notebook 69, this regrettable arrogance toward women, now attributed to Swann (f. 7), was given an important explanation—the character's Jewishness: see on this subject the Commentary. It is notable that the context of the source passage should then be invoked by an editorial note on the facing page, the only one in all Proust's manuscripts, to our knowledge, that harks back to the "seventy-five folios": "Perhaps put here the dowager, my grandmother, the Monsieur and his mistress. Anyway show that all this is useless for Swann and that it's just so he isn't despised" (Notebook 69, f. 7; Other Manuscripts, no. XV). In 1910, then, Proust had planned to introduce to the beginning of

"Swann in Love"—no doubt in parallel and counterpoint to the portrait of Swann—different types of social indifference: the affected indifference of the dowager, and the sincere indifference of the grandmother and the four friends. There would remain a faint trace of this in *CS*, I, p. 189: see f. 54. Finally, the developed version of "the dowager [. . .], the Monsieur and his mistress" would in 1912 be added to the manuscript of "Place-Names: The Place": see ff. 54, 55, and 58.

2. *to a farmer.* Cf. Notebook 69, f. 2: "How many times did he sell the precious jewel that was a duchess's accumulated desire to be agreeable to him for way below its value to procure the dish that he fancied at that time, asking that duchess, with an indiscreet telegram sent on an absurd pretext, for a letter that would introduce him into the home of one of her farmers whose daughter had caught his eye" (Notebook 69, f. 2; Other Manuscripts, no. XV). Cf. *CS*, I, p. 190.

3. *by sphygmographic lines, always identical.* The sphygmograph, a kind of sphygmomanometer, an instrument for checking the pulse, recorded the beats of arteries (Littré). See Proust's translation of Ruskin's *Sesame and Lilies*, p. 93 note 1: "[. . .] is not the work of art, for the hidden rhythm of our soul—all the more vital since we do not perceive it ourselves—similar to those sphygmographic lines that trace the beating of our blood?"

f. 63

1. *the woman he liked best at that moment.* Proust had imagined this scenario as early as the first months of 1908, at the beginning of Carnet 1: "Character writing from time to time to ask if he can be introduced etc." (f. 3; *Cn*, p. 34). In Notebook 4, it was the only part retained from this portrait of the uncle, where it was—and this is the earliest example of such a transfer—attributed to Swann. Introduced by a simple join, it completed his extended portrait in "Combray": "I have perhaps already talked too much of M. Swann and yet I have given only one aspect of his person, undoubtedly the least interesting. Other traits of his nature, which I perhaps reconstructed later based more on my family's accounts of him than on my own observations, are so sympathetic to me, so close in a way to certain traits in my own nature that I would like to devote a few words to them. I had noticed at the house that we often received letters from M. Swann [. . .]" (Notebook 4, f. 60). The account carries on over two folios (ff. 60–62; Other Manuscripts, no. XII). In this notebook, the letters arrive even after Swann's "bad marriage," but—with a concern for verisimilitude—Proust modified this scenario with an addition: "I had heard my grandfather say 'it's like Swann's letters, it won't wash.' This

is to what [he was] alluding. Back when Swann wasn't married, [the family] would never go very long without receiving a [letter from] him" (Notebook 4, f. 61v). In Notebook 69, the distance was accentuated: "My cousin told me that at home, before the time when Swann had his liaison, we often used to receive his letters, and that as soon as he recognized the handwriting on the envelope, my ~~grandfather~~ <great-uncle> would say [. . .]" (f. 3). Proust finally returned to the grandfather, but kept the temporal distance: "I was often told later that when my grandfather, who wasn't yet my grandfather because it was around the time of my birth that Swann began the liaison that would lead to his marriage and would for a long time put an end to these practices, picking up his mail and recognizing Swann's handwriting on an envelope, would cry out [. . .]" (Notebook 15, page kept in the *Reliquat* NAF 16703, f. 95; cf. *CS,* I, p. 191). In "Swann in Love," the stratagem that Swann uses here—"getting back in touch with friends he hadn't seen in a long time"—occurs at the expense of friends of the narrator's family (ibid., pp. 191–192).

2. *the way my parents would always flatly reject his requests.* As soon as the character in question switches from the uncle to Swann, the narrator is no longer a direct spectator of events: the "parents" are replaced by the grandfather or the great-uncle and a cousin, and the scene is moved back into the past: see previous note.

3. *Florian.* This name, which does not seem to recur anywhere in the manuscripts or in Proust's work generally, suggests his intention to distinguish this character from his uncle Louis Weil. Otherwise these pages remain strongly marked by autobiographical features, as shown by the presence of a brother and by the possible resemblance between some of the grandmother's traits and those of Proust's own grandmother Adèle.

4. *On your guard.* This expression, uttered repeatedly by the father, could be seen as a sort of innocent family catchphrase. But the rest of the genesis would show more clearly its association with anti-Semitism. From Notebook 4 onward, it was the grandfather (briefly replaced by the great-uncle in Notebook 8) who said it. It belongs to a series of quotations from operas with Jewish subjects that he hums whenever he suspects his grandsons' friends of being "Israelites": "My grandfather claimed that each time we brought a new friend home from school to introduce him, he was always an Israelite. [. . .] he would launch into the chorus 'Archers on your guard, Be vigilant and silent' and after one or two adroitly asked questions he would shout '<Archers> On your guard, on your guard'" (ff. 46–47; Other Manuscripts, no. XII; cf. *CS,* I, p. 90). And even

though the manuscript of Notebook 4 is damaged for the passage corresponding to the present page (f. 61), everything suggests that this exclamation was repeated, as it was in Notebook 69: "[. . .] as soon as he recognized the handwriting on the envelope, my ~~grandfather~~ <great-uncle> would say: 'Uh-oh, it's Swann who's going to ask us for something. On your guard!'" (f. 3; Other Manuscripts, no. XV; cf. *CS*, I, p. 191, where it is once again the grandfather who says these words). The source of this quote has not been identified.

5. *short blonde hair.* See the reworkings in Notebook 4, ff. 61–62 (Other Manuscripts, no. XII), then in Notebook 69, ff. 3–4 (Other Manuscripts, no. XV). Cf. *CS*, I, p. 191.

f. 64

1. *the hour of waiting.* The last two phrases were condensed in Notebook 69, f. 5 (Other Manuscripts, no. XV); in the definitive text, the remark introduces the example of letters received: "It was not only the brilliant phalanx of virtuous dowagers, generals and academicians with whom he was most intimately associated that Swann so cynically compelled to serve him as panders. All his friends were accustomed to receive, from time to time, letters [. . .]" (*CS*, I, p. 190).

2. *for reasons that we will see.* The character of the uncle would be abandoned, or rather his transformation into Swann would lead to the disappearance of this character trait, which would consequently remain mysterious. But we might think of this note in Carnet 1 at the beginning of 1908: "Not seeking to possess due to inability to be liked and to inspire happiness" (f. 2; *Cn*, p. 32). This anticipation by the narrator does, however, at least suggest that this was a long-term plan for a novel.

f. 65

1. *the milkmaid with white sleeves.* We find here again the idea expressed at the start of the portrait of the uncle: while traveling, the act of summoning his mistress from Paris would be a "renunciation," an "expedient to the penetration of reality," in the words of a crossed-out version (f. 60). When it came to Swann, this would be one of the "traits of his nature" that the narrator finds "so sympathetic to me, so close in a way to certain traits in my own nature," then "truly remarkable" (Notebook 4, f. 60 and Notebook 69, f. 6; Other Manuscripts, nos. XII and XV). They were also united by the same desire, noted here, to be led to "a real knowledge of particular things, of individuals": "I admit that in this desire to go bravely to the limits of what reality offers us, I feel he is so close to me

that I will never weary of talking about him" (Notebook 4, f. 62). In Notebook 69, this was expressed as "a sort of sincerity in desire that drove him to consider women as distinctive individuals and prevented him from cheating with another the pleasure that another had inspired in him" (the first, crossed-out version), that "made him wish to get to know a particular being, to know this or that woman whom he happened to meet" (f. 6). Proust returned to this in 1912 in "Place-Names: The Place," at the end of the series of portraits of the dowager and the society of four friends, while Swann was not even mentioned, as if the present pages had been resurrected, down to the repetition of the phrase about "taking out" one's desire on someone: "Unfortunately for my tranquility I was nothing like those people, and I worried about many of them; I wouldn't have wanted to be despised by them; back then, I had not yet had the comfort of discovering the character traits of Swann who, if he'd summoned his mistress from Paris to take out on her the desire inspired in him by an unknown woman, would have thought he didn't believe in that desire, a particular reality for which one could not substitute an[other]" (NAF 16735, f. 217; Other Manuscripts, no. XVII). This echo did not make it into the definitive text.

2. *the* trottin. According to Littré, an old-fashioned term for a "young boy or young girl who does the shopping." According to TLFi, an "apprentice, young female fashion worker whose job was to go shopping and to deliver hats and dresses to people's homes." The term is used once in *Search:* see *JF*, II, p. 217. In 1907 and 1910, Proust writes to Reynaldo Hahn mentioning (though getting the title wrong) "Amour de trottin," a song by Félix Mayol recorded in 1903 ("On rue de la Paix the other day / I followed a *trottin* / Blond like an angel," and "Every night the little *trottin* / Comes to see me / After leaving a client / The kid's sweet, ill-bred, perverted / An urchin of the streets!"; see *Corr.*, VII, p. 281, and X, p. 177).

3. *it was.* The portrait of the uncle ends abruptly, and the rest of the bifolio was left blank. A fragment found in the Fallois archives treats the theme of an erotic pursuit doomed to failure at greater length and in the same comic tone, but in the first person: it is difficult to say whether this was written before or after the present passage. See Other Manuscripts, no. VI.

[Young Girls]

We have placed this collection of pages after the portrait of seaside vacationers, following the order of the definitive text. But it might just as easily have been written before. Proust gives two successive versions here (ff. 67–74), the first ending abruptly in the middle of the first bifolio. While the grandmother accompanies her grandchildren to the hotel in [A Visit to the Seaside], "Maman" is present here with her sons: a way of signaling that these are two separate vacations, perhaps separated by a few years. The summary of the novel placed in the original edition of *Swann's Way*, in 1913, distinguishes a first stay in Balbec ("Place-Names: The Place—First sketch of the Baron de Charlus and Robert de Saint-Loup") then placed in *The Guermantes Way*, from a second ("In the Shadow of Young Girls in Flower"), then placed at the beginning of *Time Regained* (both times, the hero is alone there with his grandmother). It was the invention of Albertine that would lead to the merger of the first two vacations and the birth of another version of the second one.

f. 67

1. *whom I would never see again.* This is the oldest known version of the appearance of the "little band" (*JF*, II, p. 146). See also the rewrite of folio 69. The term *"fillettes,"* although apparently ill-suited to the account that follows, was maintained through all the versions until the published text. The *fillettes* on this page, two of them to start with, then four or five, then "five or six" (f. 69), are perhaps connected to the "four faces" or "four young girls' faces" (f. 11), the "quintuple" love (f. 14) noted in Carnet 1 in 1908, after Proust had set off for Cabourg (ff. 11, 14; *Cn*, pp. 50, 55). Their number would continue to vary: "I saw four unknown *fillettes*" (Notebook 12, f. 111; Other Manuscripts, no. XIII); "I saw a spot growing bigger, a singular gang of five or six *fillettes*" (Notebook 64, f. 146v); "I saw [. . .] five or six *fillettes* advancing" (Notebook 34, f. 24; *JF, Sketch XLV.3*, II, p. 938). Note that in this passage they are "on the beach" (cf. f. 69): in the next version, although only the location of the hero is specified, they seem to be walking "along the esplanade in front of the casino" (Notebook 12, f. 111; Other Manuscripts, no. XIII), then "on the terrace" (Notebook 64, f. 146v), then advancing "from the far end of the seawall" (Notebook 34, f. 24; cf. *JF*, II, p. 146). An image of them on the beach remains in a draft, but only as a memory of their childhood, years earlier (Notebook 25, f. 41v; *JF, Sketch XLV.1*, II, p. 932); in Notebook 34, Proust tried, unsuccessfully, to combine the two locations (ff. 24–23v). The "seabirds" of the present version became "seagulls" in Notebook 12 (f. 111; Other Manuscripts, no. XIII), then a "flock of seagulls" in Notebooks 64 (f. 146v) and 34 (f. 24) and the definitive text, where it was translated as a "flight of gulls" (*JF*, II, p. 146).

2. *seemed not to exist.* The image of the "chattering conventicle" features again in the Gallimard proofs as a "compact, chirping conventicle, bizarre and

oddly shaped" (Rés. M Y^2 824, f. 293), then becomes "a compact, chirping mass, like a bizarre conventicle of birds" (see *JF*, II, p. 150). Their indifference, as if they belong to another species, is unaltered: in Notebook 12 they walked "without seeing the humans," "as if Querqueville had been made for them alone" (ff. 111, 112; Other Manuscripts, no. XIII). In Notebook 64, they retained "their customs and roles as seagulls, paying no attention to the bathers" (f. 146v).

3. *a beautiful* break. A *break* was an open-top horse-drawn carriage with four wheels. In *Sodom and Gomorrah*, the mechanic wants the Verdurins to replace "their break by a motor-car" (*SG*, III, p. 417).

4. *grooms*. The groom's job was to care for and train the horses. The Duke of Guermantes, in the courtyard of his hotel, "made one of his grooms lead past him at a trot some horse he had just bought" (*CG*, II, p. 332).

5. *long red hair*. In Notebook 26, where the "*fillettes*" of the present pages, seen again during a later visit, had become "young girls," we would find described again the "pink and golden cheeks, the almost red hair, the sparkling green eyes of Mlle" (f. 34), and before that a "red mane" (f. 31; cf. f. 55). A "Mlle Swann" was named among the little gang in Notebook 26 (f. 36), and Proust soon gave Gilberte that complexion, but after she had been deleted from Querqueville/Balbec: "Gilberte looked like the image of her mother if her mother's hair and skin had been soaked in a resplendent red dye, which one soon identified as her father's coloring" (Notebook 27, f. 92v). In the next version of the first meeting with a girl from the little gang, it was a brunette "with a slightly Spanish look" who captivated the hero, foreshadowing two other brunettes, Maria and then Albertine (Notebook 12, f. 116; *JF*, Sketch XLV, II, p. 937). But red hair would remain the benchmark of desire: "this dark one was not the one that pleased me most, simply because she was dark and because (since the day on which, from the little path by Tansonville, I had seen Gilberte) a young girl with reddish hair and a golden skin had remained for me the inaccessible ideal" (*JF*, II, p. 153). In Notebook 2 of *Contre Sainte-Beuve*, the narrator remembered his desire for "the redheaded girl who hands [him] café au lait" (f. 27; *CSB*, p. 103).

6. *a part of her person*. It would seem that the image of the "chattering conventicle" had inspired the shape of this hat, which, in turn, suggested the metaphor of the young girl-seagull that appeared in the next version (see above). In Proust's pastiche of Flaubert published on March 14, 1908, in *Le Figaro*, there was a lady whose hat had a parrot on top of it: "Two young people expressed surprise at this,

wanting to know if it had been placed there as a souvenir or perhaps out of a taste for the eccentric" (*PM*, p. 13).

7. *or like someone of another race.* Even in the definitive text, the young girls are described as if "they had decided that the surrounding crowd was composed of creatures of another race" (*JF*, II, p. 149). See also f. 70, where they "seem like a race apart from the young girls of my own world," and Notebook 12, in which the hero gathered from the attitude of the Spanish brunette that he "in no way belongs to the same race as her friends" (f. 122). But the idea that other people belong to "another race" is a reflection, first and foremost, of the "*fillettes*" belonging to another species. This idea recurred in Notebook 12: "Then as if we could enter the soul and language of one of those beautiful beasts we had seen at the zoo, so that in a sort of translation we would suddenly understand what it meant when they shot a look at us [. . .]" (f. 122v). The hero wondered about "that inhuman world" from which the eyes of the "dark one with the fat cheeks" looked out: "[. . .] had she seen me at the moment in which the dark ray emanating from her eyes had fallen on me? In the heart of what universe did she distinguish me?" (*JF*, II, pp. 151–152).

f. 68

1. *for most.* This false start is preceded by another one, crossed-out: "~~My uncle~~/~~In this hotel~~ In Maman this indifference to what surrounded her was sincere. She was unaware of what surrounded her. In others it had various causes. There was an old lady there." So Proust evidently considered rewriting the portraits of the uncle and the old lady, with "Maman" this time in the role previously played by the grandmother, unless those portraits had not yet been written.

f. 69

1. *One day on the beach.* In the more developed rewrite that begins here, the opening was initially different, highlighting the girls' social origin: "The local noble families came to C. every year to spend a few weeks and I would see on the beach sometimes two, sometimes five or six girls, two of them almost young women already, who did not mingle with the others and stared at them rather rudely. All of them, daughters of nobles or local rich people, wore clothes that struck me as the very height of elegance [. . .]."

2. *on which they rode off.* This detail was absent from the previous version: these girls are horse riders. See f. 70.

f. 70

1. *nobles or rich people who mixed with the nobility.* The *break*, the horses, the grooms: all of this already suggested wealth. Later, the girls' social rank would seem less prestigious, their fathers being revealed as "industrialists," whether "wealthy" or "recently ennobled," or "small provincial noblemen" (f. 71; see also f. 73). But nowhere in this original version can we find the idea that they might be working-class. This hypothesis was introduced in Notebook 64; in Notebook 25, which followed it, their poor education and their insolence immediately excluded the possibility that they might belong to the aristocracy: "I knew they were not young girls from the aristocracy, who are never so ill-mannered or insolent [. . .]. I was unsure if they belonged to the rich bourgeoisie who try appear elegant or to a lower class of people who go to inferior race tracks [. . .]. Seeing the outfit worn by the one with the dark eyes, I even descended toward an almost professional milieu of the daughters or sisters of bicycle-race coaches [. . .]. My first supposition was the right one. These were mostly the daughters of foreign exchange brokers who had left behind the world of foreign exchange brokers etc." A little farther on, Proust added: "I learned from the judge who was acquainted with one of their fathers that they were the daughters of rich industrialists, brokers etc." (Notebook 25, f. 38v; *JF, Sketch XLV.1*, II, p. 934; cf. Notebook 64, ff. 141v, 126v, 123v).

2. *in C.* It is tempting to read this as "Cabourg."

3. *a disdainful pride.* These characteristics, already suggested or noted in the first version (f. 67), were accentuated in Notebook 12: "faces by chance all delicious and all different but to which so much insolence, self-confidence, disdain, insensitivity, and arrogance provided that absence of nervousness, distraction, and human respect that is so favorable to beauty" (f. 111; Other Manuscripts, no. XIII).

4. *the young girls of my world.* The term "race," for Proust, is deliberately used to designate a human group with common characteristics that could register their belonging to a single class, whether social (the aristocracy, the "people of ancient race," Notebook 5, f. 67) or sexual ("The Queer Race," Notebook 6, f. 37). See also ff. 67 and 86.

5. *tennis shirts.* Horse riding, golf, and tennis were the reserve of the elite, leaving no doubt about the girls' social origins. In the next version, they play the same sports, with the possible exception of golf: "In their clothing and their entire person they were absolutely different. Jodhpurs, short skirts, riding boots,

waists made supple by all that exercise [. . .]" (Notebook 12, f. 111; Other Manuscripts, no. XIII). But from Notebook 64 onward, the picture became less clear:
"Two of them pushing bicycles, another in a long skirt and long veil who had
presumably just got off a horse, another carrying golf rackets [*sic*] [. . .]" (f. 146v).
The free-and-easy look of one of the girls pushing a bicycle leads the hero to think
of "*fillettes* from the world of cycling coaches, those very young mistresses that
some of the riders have" (f. 142v). On their social origin, see above. In the group
from Notebook 34, the figure of the girl "in a riding skirt, wearing a long veil"
who "had probably just got off a horse" is crossed-out (f. 24).

6. *people whom we did not know.* In her indifference toward strangers, Maman
is behaving here exactly like the grandmother in the previous version (see also
f. 68). Cf. Notebook 4, ff. 63–64: "The thought that one might take an interest in
someone one didn't know was something [my grandmother] could not understand and that she considered the very depths of vulgarity" (Other Manuscripts,
no. XII); rewritten in Notebook 12, f. 58: "The idea that one might be interested
in people one didn't know, and care about the opinion they might have of us,
would have appeared infinitely vulgar to her but above all inexplicable" (Other
Manuscripts, no. XIII).

f. 71

1. *chic but* mauvais genre. When uttered by Maman, "*mauvais genre*" might
simply signify a lack of distinction. We know that, in his correspondence with
Lucien Daudet, Proust frequently used the abbreviation "m.g." to indicate homosexuality (see Benoît Puttemans, "Quand Lucien Daudet joue au rat et à la
souris," *Bulletin d'informations proustiennes*, no. 47 [2017]: 33–34). We do not
really know what Albertine means when she uses this expression (*JF*, II, pp. 228,
238, 242), but it quickly becomes associated with Gomorrah in the novel (*SG*, III,
pp. 197, 247; *P*, III, p. 592).

2. *had invited us.* In the version of Notebook 12, the hero wishes that, in order
to be "placed" at the hotel in the eyes of "two pretty young girls" then of the
aristocratic Mlle de Quimperlé, they could be induced to learn that his grandmother knew the Marchioness of Villeparisis (f. 51 sq.; Other Manuscripts, no.
XIII). Does this "Duke of Clermont" have any connection with the Clermont-
Tonnerres mentioned in [Noble Names] (f. 78; see also f. 76)?

3. *or recently ennobled industrialists.* See above f. 70. In the definitive text,
the *fillettes* are part of the bourgeoisie: "I had, with regard to their social posi-

tion, made a mistake, but not the mistake that I usually made at Balbec. I was always ready to take for princes the sons of shopkeepers when they appeared on horseback. This time I had placed in an interloping class the daughters of a set of respectable people, extremely rich, belonging to the world of industry and business" (*JF*, II, p. 200).

4. *the warmest friendship*. The hero does not hesitate to use his connections, a fact that implicitly brings him closer to his uncle (ff. 62–64). In the definitive text, as soon as the hero discovers by chance that Elstir knows the young girls from the little gang, the artist "was no longer sufficient in himself": "he was now only the necessary intermediary between these girls and me" (*JF*, II, p. 203). In Notebook 12, the role of "Monsieur T." was played by an anonymous artist, and it was in Notebook 64 that he took on several elements of the present pages: see Other Manuscripts, no. XIV; ff. 72 and 74.

5. *my older brother*. As in [A Visit to the Seaside] (f. 53), the protagonist has a brother, but the fact that the brother is his elder here distances us from Proust's biography, which had been followed in "Robert and the goat," where Marcel was the senior of the two brothers (f. 21). Perhaps this is a wink to Lucien Daudet (who did have an older brother, Léon), who in 1908—at the time when Proust was writing these pages—dedicated a short story to his friend in which the hero is nicknamed the "Prince of Ties": see the Commentary. "[. . .] Lucien Daudet does have some rather garish ties," Proust acknowledged in a letter to his mother (November 4, 1896, see *Bulletin d'informations proustiennes*, no. 49 [2019]: 183).

6. *a sign of opulence*. This comic passage was reduced to a brief editorial note in Notebook 12—"Attempts to get to know them" (f. 117)—and it was only later, in Notebook 64, that it was reworked. There, we would find again the gifts intended as bribes, the outlandish outfit, and even the "parasol" with the "jade handle," which had by then become an "*en-tout-cas*," in other words a parasol that could also be used as an umbrella. See Notebook 64, f. 127v and ff. 123v–120v; Other Manuscripts, no. XIV.

7. *in a fever*. This is the first depiction of the hero's impatience while Elstir calmly paints instead of going out with him to meet the young girls (*JF*, II, pp. 202–203, 209–210). But in that passage Albertine had already appeared at the window of the studio, whereas here the appearance of the young girls does not occur until afterward (f. 72: "and just then through his window I spotted the six young girls [. . .]"). See Notebook 64, f. 122v; Other Manuscripts, XIV.

f. 72

1. *and kissed him.* The same plotline would be found in Notebook 64 and in the definitive text: coming back after the disappointing outing with the artist, there is an unexpected encounter (ff. 121v–120v; Other Manuscripts, no. XIV; cf. *JF*, II, pp. 209–210). But the hero's attitude then is the opposite of the exuberant one he adopts here: he feigns indifference so convincingly that he causes the introduction not to happen (Notebook 64, f. 120v, cf. f. 126v; Other Manuscripts, no. XIV).

f. 73

1. *artificial mountains.* Artificial mountains were all the rage in the late nineteenth century, being used in the construction of pleasure gardens, zoos, and amusement parks. Naturally this brings to mind the Parc des Buttes Chaumont.

2. *knickerbockers.* Knickerbockers were baggy shorts worn for sporting activities that fitted tightly below the knee. To the manager of the Grand Hotel in Balbec, wearing knickerbockers is a sign of social distinction, similar to "not taking one's hat off when one came into the hall" (*JF*, II, pp. 23–24).

3. *T. cried.* The artist, who would take over Monsieur T.'s role, would also consider the girls "ill-bred" (Notebook 64, f. 119v). See also above f. 70, where Monsieur T. "would constantly object to their poor education."

f. 74

1. *not consecrated me in their eyes.* In the definitive text, all that would remain from this long, optimistic review of the failed meeting were a few, more nuanced lines: "I caught sight of myself in a glass. To add to the disaster of my not having been introduced to the girls, I noticed that my necktie was all crooked, my hat left long wisps of hair shewing, which did not become me; but it was a piece of luck, all the same, that they should have seen me, even thus attired, in Elstir's company and so could not forget me; also that I should have put on, that morning, at my grandmother's suggestion, my smart waistcoat, when I might so easily have been wearing one that was simply hideous, and be carrying my best stick. For while an event for which we are longing never happens quite in the way we have been expecting, failing the advantages on which we supposed that we might count, others present themselves for which we never hoped, and make up for our disappointment; and we have been so dreading the worst that in the end we are

inclined to feel that, taking one thing with another, chance has, on the whole, been rather kind to us" (*JF*, II, pp. 214–215; cf. pp. 219–220).

2. *a tram passing.* In the version from Notebook 64, before the failed meeting (see f. 72), we find almost exactly the same backdrop: "At last he had to leave. Regretfully I led him back, still holding the now ridiculous *en-tout-cas.* We took one of those avenues lined with trees and here and there with such singular houses. For, despite the presence of a tram line, a gymnasium, a dentist's office, the houses looked like they belonged to the countryside [. . .]" (f. 121v; Other Manuscripts, no. XIV).

3. *the famous gang.* The first known use of this term by Proust. He employs it again a few lines farther down.

4. *He introduced me to his daughter.* From Notebook 12 onward—and perhaps in some intermediary manuscripts that have not reached us—the formal presentation to the desired young girl no longer took place in the middle of the street, but during a tea party at the artist's house (*JF, Sketch LXIII*, II, pp. 989–992).

5. *didn't have time to respond.* This scene was further developed in Notebook 12, after the introduction at the artist's house: on their way back from the beach, the hero and his grandmother (whereas here he is alone, "with Mama[n]" having been crossed-out) have to stand aside for a "roar[ing]" car, belonging to Mme de Chemisey. The "beautiful Spanish girl" was there (but without "the entire gang"): "the car slowed at the bend, and as she was passing me she raised her gloved hand and waved it in a sign of friendship: 'How've you been since the other day at XXX's house, see you soon'" (ff. 122–124; Other Manuscripts, no. XIII). Proust planned to rewrite this scene in Notebook 64: he set aside a blank page to indicate where to place the account of the tea party at the artist's house, then made a brief allusion to the girl's "hello" from the car (f. 118v; Leriche 1987a, p. 43). But the scene would disappear, according to an editorial note in Notebook 30 that planned to transfer to the Duchess of Guermantes at the Opera the "blue and flowered rainfall" of the girl's smile: "After smile should probably put my impressions from the smile of the young girl in Mme de Chemisey's car since that scene will be deleted" (f. 33; see *CG*, II, p. 358).

[Noble Names]

This "chapter" (ff. 75–82) could correspond to the first of the eight projects that Proust says he is "currently working on" in the letter [May 5 or 6, 1908] to his friend Louis d'Albufera: "a study on the nobility" (*Corr.*, VIII, p. 112). On

April 24, the fourth volume of *Récits d'une tante: Mémoires de la comtesse de Boigne* (Plon) was published, an event Proust had undoubtedly been awaiting, since he had reviewed the first volume in *Le Figaro* the previous year ("Reading Days," March 20, 1907). Two pages from the present "chapter" were directly inspired by that recent publication (see below, ff. 80, 81; Quémar, spring 1976, p. 16 and note 72). Moreover, it was in "Reading Days" that Proust first began to show an interest in the poetry of names, while insisting on the inevitable disappointment caused by the knowledge of people and countries (*EA*, pp. 530–531; below, f. 77). We have kept the title Fallois wrote on an insert in these pages, which he published at the end of chapter XIV of his *Contre Sainte-Beuve* ("Names of People," *CSB*, pp. 273–283), although he did leave out the last page (f. 82). This exception can be explained by the fact that he preferred the rewritten version of that page found in a draft notebook: see f. 82.

f. 75

1. *the impression of the residence and the desire for travel.* The association of the noble family name with the place-name, suggested here from the first mention of the "Château de Villebon" (f. 27), is pursued in the closeness between "the Villebon road" and the "Duchess of Villebon" (f. 41). It was in Notebook 4 that this began to be personified: "Then we joined the main road, which we took to return to Combray and where sometimes we would see a carriage pass and catch a glimpse of a young woman with golden hair. 'It's the Countess of Garmantes,' a farmer told us; what he meant by this was not that this lady was called the Countess of Garmantes, but that she was the countess who lived in the Château de Garmantes" (Notebook 4, ff. 34–35; *CS, Sketch LIII*, p. 809). In the long piece on the Guermantes in Notebook 5, Proust reworks the present idea and the poetic description of the journey that follows, including the association between the noble place-name and the "name read in a train timetable," which is crossed out here: "So many noble names, for that matter, have the charm of also being the name of a château or a railway station where, reading a timetable, we have often dreamed of getting off the train one early evening in late summer, when in the North the arbors, soon lonely and deep, with the train station lost in between them, are already reddened by dampness and coldness as they would be elsewhere at the start of winter" (f. 65; *CG, Sketch II*, II, p. 1029). Proust would show that this association of name and place, which seems consubstantial, can be the fruit of history.

2. *on a cheerful winter evening.* In the crossed-out lines that follow, Proust anticipated the disappointment connected with the transformation of "names,"

full of poetry, into "words": "Since childhood, we have been forever banishing poetry far from us by decanting intuitions of feeling into intelligence, by breaking up names to find the words they contain." Proust drew a tick next to this passage on the manuscript and later returned to "the inevitable disappointment arising from the encounter with things whose names we know" (f. 78), while vigorously championing the poeticization of the real through imagination and dreams (ff. 78–79). We know that in July 1913 he would consider these titles for his novel: "the Age of Names for the first [volume]. For the second: the Age of Words. For the third: the Age of Things" (*Corr.*, XII, p. 232).

3. *heraldic stained-glass windows.* The coloring of syllables in names is not exclusive to noble names (see "Place-Names: The Name," *CS*, I, pp. 381–382), but it is particularly emphasized for the Guermantes, "poetic and golden like their name" (Notebook 5, f. 64). In the present pages, the image develops and culminates with the moment when, the noble name no longer being merely a colored name ("the colored space of its syllables," f. 75) but becoming a name that is "colored and yet transparent" (f. 79), Proust brings in the metaphor of the stained-glass window ("in the rosy glow of its heraldic stained-glass windows"); then, in the transparency of a certain name, the "stained-glass window" gives way to the "display window" to which the noble mansion is then likened, in an image destined to a greater genetic posterity (f. 82). The opening of *The Guermantes Way* returns to the subject of the diversity and vicissitudes of the hues taken by names (*CG*, II, pp. 310–312), until they have "lost all color like a prismatic spinning-top which turns so fast that it appears gray" (ibid., p. 312).

4. *is in reality from Provence.* On this page and the next, Proust gives three examples of "transplanted" noble families: all had been settled in Normandy for a long time (two centuries, three centuries, and two centuries, respectively), all have a southern name (from Provence, Italy, and Provence, respectively). The only differences are the locations of their Norman château or mansion: near Bayeux, then Saint-Pierre-sur-Dives, and lastly in Falaise. Their characteristics are a mix of borrowings from fact and flights of fancy. See below and f. 76.

5. *less exotic and more French than their foliage and their flowers.* The comparison with acclimatization is taken up later for apple trees and then hydrangeas: see f. 76. This theme is found in "Combray," through the chinaberry trees and the buttercups, "transplanted from Asia perhaps centuries ago but naturalized now and always in the village" (*CS*, I, pp. 134, 166). Here botany serves as an allegory for social assimilation, by rewriting Maurice Barrès's theory of rootedness.

6. *the façade of red schist and grayish stone.* Given that the "grayish stone" here corrects a facade of "glass" (*"pierre"* and *"verre"* being closer in look and sound than "stone" and "glass"), one thinks of the Château de Balleroy, which Proust mentioned in an unpublished draft of his article "Impressions of the Road from an Automobile" (*Le Figaro*, November 19, 1907): "Having left St. Lô and needing to arrive in Lisieux before nightfall, with a long way still to go and little time remaining, we went fast. Soon at the end of the avenue that ran the whole length of a village we had not yet reached and went on far beyond it, I saw looming, always at the vanishing point whatever the tilt of the road, sometimes moving to our right and sometimes to our left but always rising above its ~~hillsi~~ <plateau>, surrounded by valleys, a ~~high~~ <noble> abode of pink schist and glass, <with its high windows> [. . .], Mansard's [*sic*] masterpiece, the Château de Balleroy. Soon we were on the road to Caen [. . .]" (Fallois archives; on the subject of Balleroy, we can find this in another draft from the same batch: "the sparkling abode of red schist and glass, with high windows"). While the location of Balleroy is incompatible with that of Saint-Pierre-sur-Dives, being more than seventy kilometers to the west, it does correspond to that of the "château near Bayeux" mentioned a few lines before. Proust, then, is here rewriting and redistributing certain abandoned elements from "Impressions of the Road from an Automobile": see also f. 76. He had visited the Château de Balleroy in August 1907, during one of his many excursions in Normandy with Agostinelli; the fairly detailed account of his visit that he sent to Georges de Lauris attests to the later transposition of this château into the Château de Guermantes (*Corr.,* VII, p. 264; *CG,* II, p. 315 note 1). On Balleroy, see also NAF 16729, f. 156: "the Château de Balleroy / [. . .] how I would have liked to arrive outside that château one early evening in autumn [. . .]."

7. *Falaise.* "Marcel Proust came twice to Falaise to spend a few hours," according to the edition of *Lettres à Madame C[atusse],* at the "old and charming abode" of Charles de Bionneau, Marquis of Eyragues, and his wife, née Henriette de Montesquiou-Fezensac ([J. B. Janin, 1946], p. 17 note 2). These visits to the "agreeable Eyragues" took place in the summer of 1907 during those automobile outings with Agostinelli; "I would like to return to Falaise," wrote Proust the following year to Lucien Daudet, when his health had deteriorated and he had "given up the long walks of last year" (*Corr.,* VII, p. 277, and VIII, p. 197). The Bionneau d'Eyragues family was indeed of Provençal origin (see f. 76), in the Bouches-du-Rhône département.

f. 76

1. *as in a novel by Barbey d'Aurevilly.* A note in Carnet 1 from 1909 associates the Eyragues of Falaise with the Barbey novel *Le Chevalier des Touches:* "It would be interesting to redo the Touffedelys salon with Eyragues [. . .]" (f. 43; *Cn*, p. 104; *Cn 1908*, note 440). Also mentioned here are some other places typical of the geography of Barbey's Normandy: Coutances, present in *Le Chevalier des Touches* and in *L'Ensorcelée*, and of course Valognes, described in *Les Diaboliques.*

2. *of two hermit crabs.* A draft of this image is found in the Fallois archives along with other antecedent texts of the "seventy-five folios" (see the Chronology): "~~The church~~/ Between the <~~compact~~> roofs of the houses there could be seen <rising, in a different material, openwork, pinkish like a seashell> the steeple of the church ~~openwork, slender, openwork,~~ pink ~~pinkish, like a seashe~~." Here, Proust inverts the elements that compose the vision: it is no longer a steeple between rooftops, but a rooftop between two steeples, "openwork seashells" with "pinkish turrets." But he returned to the initial order in the next version, in Notebook 3, for the morning impressions sparked by desires for travel "in some small town in Normandy <Caudebec or Bayeux>," to see "the church, ~~crumbly~~ <pink> and perforated <like a seashell> between the <steep> roofs of houses, ~~like an~~ <enormous> ~~seashell among pebbles~~" (ff. 24–25; cf. *P, Sketch I*, III, p. 1095). The comparison is developed at length in Notebook 7 when describing the steeple in Combray, with the memory of Falaise being reinstated, only to be immediately deleted: "There are <~~in Falaise~~ in a town in Normandy> two charming white 18th-century hotels that are in many respects dear and venerable to me, and between which the spire of St. Gervais soars up, as if part of the two facades, though in a material so different, so precious, so annulated, so chiseled, so pink and polished, that when one looks at it from the same beautiful garden [that] slopes down from the two hotels, and from where <since the church cannot be seen> it appears to soar upward from their roof, one immediately senses that it is not part of them and that it is as different as the pink and crenelated turret of a seashell is different from two pebbles between which it lies on a beach" (Notebook 7, ff. 23–24; cf. *CS, Sketch XXVI*, I, pp. 735–736 and p. 735 var. *b*). See the definitive text, *CS*, I, p. 65.

3. *from Provence.* Proust is thinking here of the Eyragues family. See f. 75.

4. *those beautiful pink hydrangeas.* Originally from the Far East, the hydrangea was brought to Europe at the end of the eighteenth century. In the list of "Pages

Written," Proust had noted: "The Castellanes, Norman hydrangeas [. . .]" (Carnet 1, f. 7v; *Cn*, p. 43). He returned to this theme on folio 11: "I have [. . .] in the Norman hydrangea something that invites deeper exploration but that I don't know what to do with" (*Cn*, p. 50), and again in folio 14: "Back to Gérard. Party at Cha[a]llis = my Norman nobles' hydrangea" (*Cn*, p. 55). The Castellane family, like the Eyragues family mentioned on the present page, is southern French, originally from Haute-Provence.

   5. *to Saint-Vaast*. Proust here links two municipalities from Calvados, Honfleur and Pont-l'Évêque, to two municipalities from Cotentin, in the Manche: Valognes and Saint-Vaast-la-Hougue.

   6. *with the count*. This little scene is a reworking and condensation of the conclusion to "Impressions of the Road from an Automobile," the important 1907 article from which an abandoned fragment had been recycled on the previous page (f. 75): "[. . .] *the automobile* had stopped at the corner of a sunken path in front of a gate overgrown with roses and deflowered irises. We had arrived at my parents' abode. *The mechanic honks the horn* so that the gardener comes out to open the gate to us, *that horn* whose strident, monotonous *sound* offends our ears, but that, like all things, can become beautiful if it is steeped in a particular feeling. In my parents' hearts it resounded joyously like an unexpected announcement . . . [. . .] at the far end of the garden *the horn* that they can no longer mistake, its *sound* become joyous, almost human, keeps *calling* out like the obsessive idea of their coming happiness, urgent and *repeated* like their growing anxiety" (*PM*, pp. 68–69, italics are ours; cf. Yoshikawa 1973, p. 138). Proust may have taken inspiration for this arrival from his visit, in September 1907, to the Marquis of Clermont-Tonnerre and his wife Élisabeth de Gramont at their summer residence, the Chalet de Glisolles near Évreux, driven there in a car by the "ingenious Agostinelli" (ibid., p. 66). See Carnet 1, f. 5: "Agostinelli at Glisolles" (*Cn 1908*, note 39; *Corr.*, VII, p. 288). A marginal note in Notebook 39, opposite the description of the Guermantes hotel, reads "Glisolles/ Balleroy/Eyragues" (i.e., three names tacitly presented in these pages and connected to the fantasy of the "noble name" through the Norman excursions of 1907) (f. 75).

   7. *Ploërmel*. With this mention of a Breton town, alongside the crossed-out names of Quimperlé and Morbihan, the geographical circle, up to this point restricted to Normandy, begins to be extended; by the next page, Proust would be writing about "foreign nobility."

f. 77

1. *in Vézelay.* It is Guermantes that is foreshadowed here, as it appears in the narrator's conversation with Maman in Notebook 7: "When you arrive in the cloister that leads into the château, you walk upon the tombs of the abbots who ran this monastery from the 8th century and who, beneath our feet, are stretched out under long engraved stones where, cross in hand, a noble Latin inscription at their feet, they lie"; "Imagine that they rose up[,] the towers of Guermantes, inde-structibly erecting the 13th century, an era when, as far as their view carried them, they could not catch sight of, to greet with a smile, the towers of Chartres, the towers of Amiens, the towers of Paris, which did not yet exist" (ff. 11–12 and f. 13; cf. *CG, Sketch VI,* II, pp. 1046–1047). This comes close to *CG,* II, pp. 313–314 where "the proud race of Guermantes" precedes the construction of Notre-Dame de Paris and the cathedrals in Chartres and Beauvais. The Cousin is a tribu-tary of the Cure, which flows by the foot of the Vézelay hill. This "Cousin, deep and teeming with fish," could also prefigure "that land of bubbling streams" where the Duchess of Guermantes teaches the hero to "fish for trout" (ibid., p. 313).

2. *the same* Revue de Paris *and* Comoedia. The *Revue de Paris* was a literary and historical bimonthly, a rival of *La Revue des deux mondes,* publishing psycho-logical short stories and novels since 1894, and championing the aesthetic of Maupassant and Mérimée, then Paul Bourget, Marcel Prévost, and Henry Bor-deaux. *Comoedia,* a daily paper devoted to theatrical life, was launched on October 1, 1907: placed here next to the conservative *Revue de Paris,* it represents a concern to appear "modern." Proust then reworks an idea from "Reading Days" (*Le Figaro,* March 20, 1907): "Very often this medieval impression given by their names probably doesn't survive spending any time around the people who bear those names and who have not absorbed or understood their poetry." And he added: "But is it reasonable to expect people to show themselves worthy of their names when the most beautiful things in the world have so much difficulty living up to theirs, when there is not a country, not a city, not a river the sight of which can assuage the desire for dreaming inspired in us by its name?" (*EA,* p. 531).

3. *the foreign nobility.* We recognize here the next part of the list of "Pages Written": "The Castellanes, Norman hydrangeas, English [and] German châ-teau owners" (Carnet 1, f. 7v; *Cn,* pp. 43–44). But what Proust describes here is more Scotland than England: see f. 78.

4. *this or that mediatized German lord.* Fallois did not manage to decipher "*mé-diatisés*" (*CSB,* p. 277). The mediatized lords—German lords who no longer

depended directly upon the Emperor—are listed in the second part of the *Almanach de Gotha* ("Genealogy of Germany's Mediatized Lords"), after the part devoted to "Genealogy of Europe's Sovereign Houses" and before the one on "Europe's Other Non-Sovereign Princely Houses." Certain families, such as the Guermantes, are both dukes in France and mediatized princes in Germany (*SG*, III, p. 338, note 4 by A. Compagnon). As Charlus reminds us: "in Germany, mediatised princes like ourselves are *Durchlaucht*"; in other words, of the "rank of Highness" (ibid., p. 338).

5. *Aldegrever's old stained-glass window.* Heinrich Aldegrever, a German artist and engraver (born 1502, died between 1555 and 1561). But this passage too was inspired by an automobile excursion in Normandy. In the same letter of [October 8, 1907] to Mme Straus in which he mentions the visit to Glisolles (f. 76), Proust writes of having "gone very close to Évreux in Conches to see a church that still has all its 19th-century stained-glass windows[,] many of them by a student of Dürer's. It's like a pretty little Renaissance German bible with color illustrations. The stained-glass windows are captioned below in Gothic lettering. But stained glass of that era does not really interest me; it's too much like *paintings* on glass" (*Corr.*, VII, p. 287). As Ph. Kolb makes clear, the Baedeker Guide (*Le Nord de la France* . . . [Leipzig, 1884], p. 177) attributed the "magnificent stained-glass windows" in the choir of the Sainte-Foy church in Conches-en-Ouche to Heinrich Aldegrever (*Corr.*, VII, p. 290 note 7). Today it is believed that they are the work of Romain Buron de Gisors, who had some engravings by the German master in his studio collection (see Françoise Gatouillat, "Voyage des hommes, voyages des oeuvres: Le vitrail, un produit d'exportation," *Revue de l'art*, no. 120 [1998]: 35–48, here p. 38).

6. *and inhabits his name.* Martin Luther took refuge in Wartburg Castle, which overlooks the town of Eisenach, in Thuringia, a long way from the Black Forest. Wagner set the singing contest there in *Tannhäuser*, which Proust would remember in Notebook 13 (see next note), and which would pop into Charlus's mind during the soiree at the home of the Princess of Guermantes: "[. . .] M. de Charlus the German prince must have been imagining the party that takes place in *Tannhäuser*, with himself in the role of Margrave, standing at the entrance to Wartburg and condescendingly greeting all his guests [. . .]" (*SG*, III, p. 49).

7. *no more princes.* This whole passage on the fantasy attached to the German noble name, including its ultimate disappointment, was reworked at length in a passage from Notebook 13 that was never published: "It was one of those mediatized princes, Lords of Franconia and Swabia, whose double-barreled names, borrowed from the gnome-filled valley where they drew their origin and from the

town in the enchanted forest over which they reigned[,] are the most moving pic-
tures we possess of German landscapes during the Middle Ages, the feudal and
legendary Germany whose endless obscurity would bloom in the 19th century in
a literature <a philosophy> and a music of light. Names that retain in the taste of
their first syllable the frankness, in the stammering repetition of the second syllable the affected naivety, the color of sugared almonds of the people from the
Rhine or the Black Forest. And just when one believes that this dark 1st name
<which is only half or one-third of the entire double-barreled name> [. . .] is over,
the serious people utter a final syllable [. . .] which shows that this 1st name is
already in itself a double-barreled name, like almost all names in that majestic,
abundant language, that final syllable often being some blue enameled *heim*
through whose somber and mystical translucency one can see, only as one sees
through the stained-glass window of a Rhineland church, the shredded greenish
or black branches of the whispering forest that are the 1st two syllables. [. . .] His
address, if one had to write to him[,] was this or that river haunted by goblins and
nymphs, the castle for which one knew he was leaving [. . .], a castle where
Wagner set an act from one of his operas, the others famous through Luther or
King Louis the German, [. . .] and for whom lands of fairies or gnomes that no
longer seem more than a name provide him with those revenues that [. . .] are
transformed into Panhard automobiles and a box at the Opera" (ff. 16–19). This
piece was reworked in a more concise form to introduce Prince von Faffenheim-
Munsterburg-Weinigen in *The Guermantes Way* (*CG*, II, pp. 553–554; cf. ibid.,
Sketch XXXII, pp. 1245–1248).

f. 78

1. *from Clermont-Tonnerre.* See the note in Notebook 14, f. 69v: "Very useful
inserts for later/Don't forget Mme de Clermont Tonnerre Mme de La Tour
d'Auvergne whom I know now." On Proust's visit to the Clermont-Tonnerres, near
Évreux, see above f. 76. "Princes des Dunes" would be one of M. de Charlus's
titles: see *SG*, III, p. 333, and earlier, Notebook 7, f. 33v, and Notebook 74, f. 16.
Fallois interpreted this as: "P . . . des ducs de C. T." (*CSB*, p. 277).

2. *that Turner painted so many times.* See note 4 below.

3. *the happy hour of a late afternoon.* We find almost the same image in the
piece on the "ways": "the white clouds, like natural sundials, showed by the
angle at which they received the light that the sun was very low and would soon
set" (f. 39). The present passage, more polished and added between the lines, was
probably written later.

4. *we know from Turner.* The memory of Turner comes here via Ruskin. In *Lectures on Landscape,* two plates created after Turner's *Liber Studiorum* correspond to Proust's description: "Near Blair Athol" shows a fisherman in a kilt, his feet in a steep-sided river, one arm raised in the act of casting out, and the next, "Dunblane Abbey," shows a Scottish abbey in ruins (*The Works of John Ruskin,* Library Edition [London: George Allen, 1906], vol. XXII, plates V and VI). The following year, in Notebook 5 (f. 49) then Notebook 10 (f. 46), Proust would make reference to other plates from *LiberStudiorum* reproduced in the same volume (plates XIII, "Aesacus and Hesperie," and XIV–XV, "Procris and Cephalus").

5. *Stevenson.* Proust may have in mind here Robert Louis Stevenson's *Kidnapped, or the Lad with the Silver Button,* 1886, of which he wrote in July 1907: "I believe that *Kidnapped* is considered one of Stevenson's more boring works. Personally I was charmed by it, all those Scottish landscapes" (*Corr.,* VII, p. 225).

5. *would come to sing.* Like the "you" employed earlier (f. 75: "You might tell me . . ."), this dinner in an imaginary town suggests that Proust is seeking the complicity of a society readership, that of *Le Figaro* perhaps: "Marcel Proust," still little-known as an author, attempts to amuse by imagining himself invited with his paronym "Marcel Prévost," the successful novelist (elected to the Académie Française the following year, in 1909). For a long time Proust was, to his dismay, confused with Prévost (1862–1941), whose novels he "loathed" (*Corr.,* VII, pp. 31, 59; X, p. 139; XI, p. 252). On April 28, 1908, in other words more or less the very time when he was writing these pages, he missed a soiree at the home of Madeleine Lemaire where Hahn sang and that was attended by the Australian soprano Nellie Melba (*Corr.,* VIII, p. 104 note 1; Quaranta 2011, p. 173).

7. *I will not cross the strait.* The author gave up on his Scottish dreams. Is this an allusion to the trip to England suggested to Proust by the Bibesco brothers in the fall of 1907? (*Corr.,* VII, p. 296 and note 2.) Proust did once cross the English Channel, with his friend Horace Finaly, but we are not even sure he set foot in England: "And one day, do you remember, the two of us took the boat to Dover and without even getting off we took the next boat back, returning home only a little seasick and with barely any memories" (1921; *Bulletin d'informations proustiennes,* no. 51 [2021]: 211).

8. *with known things.* See f. 75.

f. 79

1. *a stained-glass Tree of Jesse.* The Tree of Jesse is an important medieval iconographic motif, which, based on a verse from Isaiah (11:1–2), represents the genealogy of Jesus Christ from Jesse, David's father, via the kings of Judah. Émile Mâle mentions the stained-glass windows devoted to the Tree of Jesse in Saint-Denis, Chartres, and the Sainte-Chapelle in his *Art religieux du XIIIeme siècle en France* ([Paris: Ernest Leroux, 1898], pp. 218–219), a work with which Proust was familiar. He would reuse the image in *The Guermantes Way*, but this time recalling its religious meaning: "[. . .] those names which, at regular intervals, each of a different hue, detached themselves from the genealogical tree of Guermantes, and disturbed with no foreign or opaque matter the translucent, alternating, multicolored buds that, like the ancestors of Jesus in the old Jesse windows, blossomed on either side of the tree of glass" (*CG*, II, p. 832; cf. Notebook 42, f. 7; *CG, Sketch XXXII*, II, p. 1268).

2. *a Choiseul.* These names of great French families would recur in the finished novel. Alongside the Harcourts, crossed out here, Charlus counts the Choiseuls among the "leading families," although "far below the Guermantes" (*SG*, III, p. 475, notes 7 and 8). He claims that his title of baron "is earlier than the Montmorency title" (*JF*, II, p. 114; cf. Notebook 47, f. 21v: "I do not dispute that the Montmorencys found glory afterward, but who knew their name in the year 1000?" *SG, Sketch XI*, III, p. 1025). We also see the hero delight in visiting the poetic abode of Mme de Montmorency-Luxembourg, to the great annoyance of her niece, Oriane (*SG*, III, pp. 146–148).

3. *Van Huysum.* Jan Van Huysum (1682–1749), Dutch painter of flowers, some of whose works Proust could have seen at the Louvre. See *CG*, II, p. 511 and note 2.

f. 80

1. *Prince of Württemberg.* This is Philipp of Württemberg (1838–1917), son of Princess Marie of Orléans, Duchess of Württemberg, and of Duke Alexander of Württemberg. We find here the remainder of the list from "Pages Written": "[. . .] English [and] German château owners; Louis Philippe's granddaughter" (Carnet 1, f. 7v; *Cn*, p. 44). Marie of Orléans was the daughter, not the granddaughter, of Louis Philippe, as Proust would write elsewhere in this volume. See the next note.

2. *born in the Kingdom of the Two Sicilies.* For this ekphrasis of an imaginary stained-glass window, Proust draws on the fourth volume of *Récits d'une tante: Mémoires de la comtesse de Boigne,* which had appeared at the end of April 1908 (see f. 75), in particular the chapter "Mort de la princesse Marie d'Orléans, duchesse de Wurtemberg" (*IV. 1831–1866* [Plon, 1908], pp. 233–272). Marie of Orléans (1813–1839), the daughter of Louis Philippe and Maria Amalia of Naples and Sicily, had seen her betrothal to Prince Leopold of the Two Sicilies fail despite the dispatch to Naples of an "extraordinary ambassador," Admiral de Rigny (pp. 249–250); she sank into a "deep melancholy," which manifested itself during the wedding of her brother, the Duke of Orléans, in May 1837: "Her display of discontent extended to her choice of clothing. While we were all bedecked in embroideries, lace, and feathers, she alone was wearing an outfit of startling sobriety, which clashed strangely with those around her." She stood apart from the others, "not speaking to anyone and generally making no attempt to conceal her despondency" (pp. 252, 188–189). She was married a few months later to Duke Alexander of Württemberg, the first cousin of King William I of Württemberg and a "wonderfully handsome" young man (pp. 253–254); when she had to leave her family, "the spectators were irritated by the indifference she appeared to display to their tearful embraces [. . .]. The Swiss guards saw her pass, smiling at her husband [. . .] and this did not make a favorable impression, particularly among the servants, who bore daily witness to the love her family bore her" (p. 256). Back in France, pregnant, she gave birth to a son; although she "absolutely wanted to spend the winter in her Schloss Fantaisie, which she had not yet seen" (p. 263), she had tuberculosis so she agreed to go to Italy instead; as her health worsened, the family sent her brother the Duke of Nemours "to prepare a steamboat in Toulon to transport the Queen" to her side (p. 266), but by then it was too late. Proust reworked this page in *The Guermantes Way,* in which the stained-glass window becomes a shrine by Carpaccio or Memling: see *CG,* II, pp. 825–826, and notes 3, 5, and 6. On the Schloss Fantaisie, see the next note.

3. *that Schloss Fantaisie.* See the list of "Pages Written": "[. . .] Louis Philippe's granddaughter, Fantaisie" (Carnet 1, f. 7v; cf. *Cn,* p. 44). Mme de Boigne states that Marie of Orléans "expressed her joy that [her fiancé] possessed only one country house in Saxony [*sic*], bearing the singular name of 'Fantaisie'" (*Récits d'une tante: Mémoires de la comtesse de Boigne,* t. IV, p. 257). But the Duchess of Württemberg never set foot in the Schloss Fantaisie, the summer residence of the Margraves of Bayreuth.

4. *Ludwig II of Bavaria.* Ludwig II of Bavaria was the patron of the *Festspielhaus* in Bayreuth, but there is no evidence that he visited the Schloss Fantaisie,

only a few kilometers away. Was this a misunderstanding on Proust's part? Robert de Montesquiou, among many poems dedicated to Ludwig II, did write one about "that Phantaisie/Whose name is fanciful; enviable castle" (*Les Chauves-Souris* [G. Richard, 1907], p. 296; see also p. 297, "Schloss"). The "definitive edition" of *Les Chauves-Souris* had appeared in late May 1907, and Montesquiou had been assured that Proust would read it (*Corr.*, VII, pp. 173–177). Depicting Ludwig II as a "transcendent and matchless" type of "Great human Bat," "with [his] share of shame and pain" (p. VII), Montesquiou mentioned his many eccentricities and made a barely veiled reference to his homosexuality ("You who no feminine union has joined/[. . .] Tumultuous Bacchus [. . .]/Beside/Some Orestes," pp. 278–279, passim).

5. *these words of the Queen of France: "a castle near Bareut."* Proust perhaps borrows this expression from an extract of the "unpublished correspondence" of M. de Saint-Aulaire, French ambassador in Vienna, with Mme de Boigne, quoted as a note in the book: "[. . .] a beautiful castle near Bareuth [Bayreuth] that would make a suitable summer residence for our princess" (*Récits d'une tante: Mémoires de la comtesse de Boigne*, p. 255, note).

6. *Schloss Fantaisie, "a castle near Bareut."* A line omitted by Fallois (*CSB*, p. 281). This is the second time in a few lines that homosexuality has been mentioned, with this allusion to Prince Edmond de Polignac (1834–1901), which would be elucidated in the corresponding passage from *The Guermantes Way:* Prince X. rented Fantaisie "only during the Wagner festivals, to the Prince de Polignac, another delightful 'fantasist'" (*CG*, II, p. 826)—more likely he rented the castle to his extremely wealthy wife Winnaretta Singer, whose musical salon Proust often attended (see Leblanc 2017, p. 117). But Edmond de Polignac died in Paris.

7. *son of Louise de France.* This should read "Marie de France." Is it the proximity of Louis II that led to this mistake, repeated on the following page?

8. *for fear her tears would betray her.* Paraphrase of *Récits d'une tante: Mémoires de la comtesse de Boigne:* "[. . .] finding herself alone with her brother, she told him: 'Nemours, you know me well enough to be sure that I can bear the truth, but that I want it; tell me, am I very ill?' 'Very ill, no; but since last night, the doctors have been worried.' 'Thank you, my brother, I understand you.' Seeing Duke Alexander returning after he had moved away for a moment, she put her finger to her mouth and shushed him, and did not let her emotion show again. Except it was noticed that she became more affectionate toward her brother and

her husband; but after that she no longer asked to see her young child" (t. IV, p. 268).

9. *royal prince.* See above note 1.

f. 81

1. *which she thought would be so at home in her Schloss Fantaisie.* Mme de Boigne judges severely what she calls Marie of Orléans's "artistic mind" (*Récits d'une tante: Mémoires de la comtesse de Boigne*, t. IV, pp. 235, 257), but she does concede Marie's "remarkable" talent for sculpture (p. 247). See *Marie d'Orléans, 1813–1839: Princesse et artiste romantique*, ed. Anne Dion-Tenenbaum ed. (Paris: Musée du Louvre et Musée Condé, 2008).

2. *"my poor Mother."* See the list of "Pages Written": "Louis Philippe's granddaughter, Fantaisie, the maternal face in her debauched grandson" (Carnet 1, f. 7v; cf. *Cn*, p. 44). While Marie of Orléans, Duchess of Württemberg, was not the "granddaughter" of Louis Philippe, her son Duke Philipp of Württemberg could, according to Proust, be the "debauched grandson" of the last king of France. But this is really just a pretext for a private question: see the Commentary.

3. *to rescue the Princess.* Proust might have in mind here the departure from Cherbourg of Charles X and the royal family for their exile in England on August 16, 1830, under the command of Jules Dumont d'Urville, who did indeed later become famous for his expedition to the Antarctic; the Duchess of Berry, the daughter-in-law of Charles X who had just abdicated in favor of her son the Duke of Bordeaux, also undertook that journey. She is mentioned in volume IV of *Récits d'une tante: Mémoires de la comtesse de Boigne.* See the next note.

4. *the name of his father who rescued the Duchess of Berri on a boat.* Proust invents a fictional genealogy here: neither of Dumont d'Urville's sons survived him, and his name did not even appear in volume IV of *Récits d'une tante: Mémoires de la comtesse de Boigne* despite the fact that it begins with a long chapter on the Duchess of Berry ("Expédition de Madame la duchesse de Berry," about her extraordinary failed attempt to foment a legitimist uprising after the establishment of the July Monarchy). There is, however, an anecdote about the duchess at the time of her departure for exile in 1830, and the expression "set sail": "Wandering under the bridge, she had overheard the pilot suggesting that they enter the harbor at St. Helens, since the wind for Spithead was unfavorable, and she already saw herself *setting sail* for the rocky island where another fallen

great had recently ended his brilliant career" (*Récits d'une tante: Mémoires de la comtesse de Boigne*, t. IV, p. 7, italics are ours). The image of the Duchess of Berry "leaning" on the commander is invented, but it does reflect her light-heartedness, an aspect of her character related in detail by Mme de Boigne. Another reading is possible: according to Francine Goujon, Proust could be alluding to the expedition of the *Carlo Alberto*, the ship on which the Duchess of Berry, exiled in Massa, Italy, embarked in 1832 in a vain attempt to raise a rebellion in the south and west of France. The "owner of the ship" mentioned here would in that case be the commander of the *Carlo Alberto*, Count André-Adolphe Sala (1802–1867); his son, the "gray-haired man" and anti-Semite, would in that case be Maurice Michel Antoine Sala (1851–1905), father of Antoine Sala (1876–1946), an acquaintance of Proust and Antoine Bibesco who had inspired in them the term "salaism" to denote homosexuality (see *Corr.*, II, pp. 464, 469; III, pp. 42–43 and 74–75). But it seems unlikely that Proust would have given him the admiring portrait that follows.

5. *the son of the man I saw in the hotel dining room.* These characteristics would be used again for Saint-Loup, whom the hero also meets at the seaside. Saint-Loup "had in fact no respect, no interest save for and in the things of the spirit, and especially those modern manifestations of literature and art [. . .]; he was imbued, moreover, with what [Mme de Villeparisis] called '*Socialistic* spoutings', was filled with the most profound contempt for his caste and spent long hours in the study of *Nietzsche* and Proudhon. He was one of those intellectuals, quick to admire what is good, who shut themselves up in a book, and are interested only in pure thought" (*JF*, II, p. 92; italics are ours). Was Proust trying, through that mention of the "hotel dining room," to connect these pages in advance to those at the seaside (which he had probably not yet written, the present pages dating from late April or May 1908 and the chapter on the visit to the seaside to that summer in Cabourg)?

6. *before she leaves for sea.* First Proust attempts to attach this vision to Vittore Carpaccio's series of paintings *The Legend of Saint Ursula*, which he had been able to admire at the Accademia in Venice. He alludes here to the sixth painting, *The Dream of Saint Ursula*, in which an angel appears in a dream to Ursula, predicting her martyrdom: but here, all that seems to matter is the simplicity of the bedroom's decor compared to the hotel dining room, "so simple in its English decorations." (It is worth noting that Ursula, betrothed to the son of the king of England, was Princess of Brittany.) None of the paintings in the series, however, show the queen receiving "ambassadors who beg her to flee"; those that are represented in the first three paintings are, respectively, asking for Ursula's hand in

marriage, saying their farewells, and informing the suitor of the results of their embassy; only one of them, *The Ambassadors Depar*, takes place indoors, and it includes no feminine figure. A connection with the ambassador sent to Naples to try to ensure the marriage of Marie of Orléans (see f. 80) would also seem unlikely, because here they are trying to escape to sea. So it is probable that Proust is here no longer thinking about Carpaccio or the Orléans, but the "expedition of the Duchess of Berry" narrated by Mme de Boigne, one episode of which has already been mentioned: several ambassadors were sent to her in a vain attempt to beg her to escape to sea before being forced into exile, which is exactly what happened after her arrest in 1832 (see M. Berryer's diplomatic mission in *Récits d'une tante: Mémoires de la comtesse de Boigne*, t. IV, pp. 56–59). Note that in the version in *The Guermantes Way*, all allusions to the Duchess of Berry have been removed and the reference to Carpaccio is made at the beginning of the passage (*CG*, II, pp. 825–826).

f. 82

1. *than stained through glass.* This page was not published by Fallois: he preferred the later version from Notebook 5, ff. 64–65, which he placed at the beginning of the passage (*CSB*, p. 273). But as the present phrase suggests, Proust follows the opposite order here. The "noble names" first conjure the image of the multicolored stained-glass window, a multifaceted mirror of genealogy and history; next comes the transparent glass of the display window, associated with the subdued hues of porcelain, and with present society. The Belleuse family, whose name is not mentioned elsewhere by Proust, prefigure the Guermantes.

2. *. . . glass.* From Notebook 5 onward, the Guermantes would be regularly compared to Saxon figurines, and their home to a house of glass or a display window: "In Querqueville one day when we were talking about Mlle de Saint-Étienne, Montargis told me: oh she's a real Guermantes she's like her sisters she's like my Aunt Septimie, they're 'Saxons,' figurines from Saxony. [. . .] From that day I could no longer think about Mlle de Saint-Étienne's sisters or Aunt Septimie as anything other than Saxon figurines on show in a display window with other precious things. And every time we talked about a Guermantes property in Paris or Poitiers, I saw it as a pure and fragile glass rectangle inserted between houses, like a Gothic spire between rooftops, and behind the pane of which the ladies of Guermantes, who were not allowed to sneak in anyone from the outside world, gleamed in the gentlest colors, little Saxon figurines" (Notebook 5, ff. 58–59; cf. *CSB*, p. 269; *CG*, *Sketch II*, II, p. 1026); "the very place where [Mme de Guermantes] lived had to be as different from the rest of the world, as impenetrable

and impossible for human feet to tread upon as the glass shelf in a display window" (Notebook 5, f. 59; *CG, Sketch II,* II, p. 1027). Before the hero knows them, the Guermantes are as "poetic and golden as their legendary name, as impalpable as the projections of a magic lantern, as inaccessible as their château, as brightly colored as a transparent house enclosed in a glass cabinet, like Saxon statuettes" (Notebook 5, ff. 64–65; cf. *CG, Sketch II,* II, p. 1029). The image was kept for the definitive text: "In the entertainments which she gave, since I could not imagine the guests as possessing bodies, moustaches, boots, as making any utterance that was commonplace, or even original in a human and rational way, this vortex of names, introducing less material substance than would a phantom banquet or a spectral ball, round that statuette in Dresden china which was Mme de Guermantes, gave her mansion of glass the transparency of a showcase" (*CG,* II, p. 315).

3. *The universal church.* This phrase is possibly a memory from the introduction to *Art religieux du XIIIeme siècle en France,* in which Émile Mâle mentions the "universal Church of which the apostles are the symbol" (p. 14; my thanks to Sophie Duval for this reference). In Notebook 66, Proust darkens the transparency and reorientates the vision of the Guermantes reception room, turning the church into an oriental temple: "This plushly furnished room was very somber and nothing like the clear, bright glass palace I had imagined. [. . .] Sometimes during a soiree of the kind I had already attended [. . .], there had been for some reason one of those men who is a name and whose body, like the bodies of certain Oriental prophets, seems to reflect a national forest and an entire past. But here there were only such men, crowding around like the pillars of this mysterious temple. So that Mme de Guermantes's reception room was like a temple full of mystery and beauty crowded with a forest of precious pillars in cedar or sandalwood, each bearing wonderful inscriptions" (Notebook 66, f. 16v; *CG, Sketch IX,* II, p. 1062). In Notebook 39, the image of the oriental temple was abandoned, while the "prophets" were compared to "those whose gilded (?) wooden statues are lined up along the nave of the Sainte-Chapelle" (Notebook 39, ff. 26–27; *CG, Sketch IX,* II, p. 1066). In the end, Proust returned to his initial clarity and to the image of the church, with the temple no longer signifying only the building: "Then in the depths of this name the castle mirrored in its lake had faded, and what now became apparent to me, surrounding Mme de Guermantes as her dwelling, had been her house in Paris, the Hôtel de Guermantes, limpid like its name, for no material and opaque element intervened to interrupt and occlude its transparency. As the word church signifies not only the temple but also the assembly of the faithful, this Hôtel de Guermantes comprised all those who shared the life of the duchess, but these intimates on whom I had never set eyes were for me only famous and poetic names [. . .]" (*CG,* II, p. 315).

[Venice]

Before composing these pages in 1908, Proust had already written about Venice, though mainly in his role as a Ruskin scholar, in the prefaces and the notes of his translations of *The Bible of Amiens* (1904) and *Sesame and Lilies* (1906), and in his review of Mathilde Crémieux's translation of *The Stones of Venice* (1906; *EA,* pp. 520–523). This, however, is his first purely "narrative" collection of writings on La Serenissima. Two more or less independent pieces are juxtaposed: the first is about the Venice of the Grand Canal and Gothic palaces; the second seeks to understand the originality of the "street of water" and the aesthetic shock caused by St. Mark's Basilica.

f. 83

1. *While I was reading these pages.* The beginning of the piece is missing: the first words, inserted in an addition, are intended as a join. A tiny handwritten fragment in which two letters in Proust's hand can be made out remains stuck to the edge of the page, the remnant of a lost folio.

2. *these pages on Venice.* The "pages" in question probably belong to a book by Ruskin, mentioned here several times (ff. 83, 85, 85v). Nevertheless, Proust was familiar, not only with the writings of Taine, Gautier, and the Goncourt brothers on La Serenissima, but also "the dying Venice of Barrès, the posthumous carnival Venice of Régnier, the Venice of insatiable desire described by Mme de Noailles, the Venices of Léon Daudet and Jacques Vontade [. . .]" (*EA,* p. 521).

3. *drafts of cool sea air.* These impressions can be linked to a note from Carnet 1 written just after Proust's arrival in Cabourg on July 18, 1908: "Cabourg walking on carpets while getting dressed sunlight outside Venice/Cabourg descending the big stairs, quick movement of sun and wind on big marble spaces big hangings Venice" (f. 6; *Cn,* p. 40). Proust drew a sort of curly bracket to link the two final mentions of "Venice" with what came before. This memory of Venetian impressions inspired by analogous impressions of Cabourg might well have been what triggered the writing of the present pages.

4. *on a soft pillow.* In the long piece on Venice developed after this as part of *Contre Sainte-Beuve,* from back to front in Notebook 3, the comparison with the soft pillow would disappear, as it didn't work with the idea of resilience that Proust introduced: "a sapphire water [. . .] of a color so resilient that to relax your eyes you can rest your gaze upon it, [. . .] feeling your muscles go soft against the color's

surface" (f. 42v). Later in the same passage, that softness takes on the color of the water itself ("The street in broad sunlight was that spread of sapphire whose color was at once so soft and so resilient that my gaze could be cradled there while pressing its weight down upon it [. . .] without the azure weakening or giving way [. . .]," f. 38, cf. f. 36v). This combination was continued in Notebook 48, where "the soft color" of the water "was also, like a good bed, so resilient" (f. 55); this version was crossed out and replaced with a "turquoise color, at once so soft and so resilient" (f. 54v). But in the last revision of the Venetian episode, the softness disappeared again: "[. . .] this street was all of a sapphire water, refreshed by mild breezes, and of a color so resilient that to relax my tired eyes I could rest my gaze upon it without fear that it would yield" (Notebook XIV, f. 80; cf. *AD*, IV, p. 203).

5. *hidden by running water.* This image is developed later: see f. 85.

6. *the books.* These books are, presumably, Ruskin's works on Venice (*The Stones of Venice, St. Mark's Rest*) in the "Traveler's Edition." See f. 85, "the books by Ruskin," and f. 85v, "my Ruskins in my hand." Twice in his translation of *The Bible of Amiens*, Proust mentions having read these books with a feeling of elation in St. Mark's Basilica itself, surrounded by his friends: "This page [of *St. Mark's Rest*] has for me not only the charm of having been read in the baptistery of St. Mark's during those blessed days when, with a few other disciples 'in mind and in truth' of the master, we traveled through Venice on gondolas, listening to his sermon by the water [. . .]" (*BA*, p. 245; *PM*, p. 133; see also, for a "page from *Stones of Venice*," *BA*, pp. 83–84).

7. *in the scent of hawthorns.* This is the oldest trace of the desire to establish a parallel between Venice and what was not yet called Combray. We recognize the scenery of the walks along the "ways": fish and tadpoles (ff. 28, 34), buttercups (ff. 28, 36), little bridge (ff. 28, 31, 44), hawthorns (ff. 29–30, 31, 36, 40). From the piece about Venice in Notebook 3—and despite a brief mention, in Notebook 48, of those "deep shadows" in the "little canals" that could be seen "mottling the waters of the Vivonne" (Notebook 48, f. 61v)—it was the marketplace of a still anonymous "village" (f. 38v, passim), one sunny Sunday, that would be connected with the impressions of Venice (f. 43 sq.; *AD*, *Sketch XV*, IV, p. 689 sq.). We have the beginning of this here, with the pâtissier, the street crossed, the suggestion of a sunny day. Since the manuscript was damaged, we have had to replace a few words.

8. *Palazzo Foscari.* The Foscari Palace is located on the first bend of the Grand Canal as you leave the Piazzetta, on the left bank, at the corner of Rio Nuovo, just after the Palazzo Giustiniani, the other corner being occupied by the Palazzo Balbi.

It is the current headquarters of the University of Venice, known as Ca'Foscari. Ruskin wrote of the Palazzo Foscari that it is the "noblest example in Venice of the fifteenth century Gothic, founded on the Ducal Palace" (*The Stones of Venice*, in *Works*, vol. XI, p. 378). A passage from Notebook 2 of *Contre Sainte-Beuve*, the beginning of which is missing, mentions that palace "which spends all day gazing at its reflection in the Grand Canal and into all those eyes that stare at it enraptured" (f. 22v). But his desire to leave for Venice is stymied by a memory: "But in that moment the thought of the Foscari Palace brings me back to my grandmother, who died last year and who used to have a photograph of the palace on her table. And immediately the other being that I am, and whose life alternates so precisely with the one who wishes to leave, spreads over me and drives him out. Now all I think about is the horror of being separated from Maman" (ibid.).

9. *those who have inflamed your dreams.* The plural (from "will point at them") indicates that Proust had other palaces in mind, even if the only one he names is the Foscari. This entire passage would be developed at length in late 1910 in Notebook 48, and three other palaces would be mentioned by name: Dario, Mocenigo, and Contarini Fasan. See *AD, Sketch XV,* IV, pp. 696–697, the next note here, and f. 83v.

10. *the heroes of Ruskin novels.* More than thirty palaces are "characters" in the "Venetian Index" of *The Stones of Venice,* including the Foscari Palace. In the rewrite in Notebook 48, "the gondolier named them, each as individual as people, whom I recognized having seen their portraits" (f. 55). Proust plays simultaneously on the memory that the palaces seem to have of their first occupants, and on the personification of their architecture ("Arab costume," "beautiful lace tie," "the lobes of its 'oculi' in colored stone," f. 55v; cf. *AD, Sketch XV.4,* IV, p. 697). This passage would not be kept.

f. 83v

1. *"the glorious private architecture of Venice."* In the preface to his translation of *The Bible of Amiens* (1904), Proust stated: "I left for Venice so that I could, before dying, approach, touch, see embodied in palaces that were failing but still upright and pink, Ruskin's ideas on domestic architecture in the Middle Ages." Two years later, while reviewing Mathilde Crémieux's translation of *The Stones of Venice,* he defined the city as a "[s]ort of complete and intact museum of domestic architecture during the Middle Ages and the Renaissance" (*EA*, p. 521). This phrase made it to the final text of *Swann's Way,* among the young hero's incantations: "Venice was the 'school of Giorgione, home of Titian, the most complete museum of domestic archi-

tecture in the Middle Ages'" (*CS*, I, p. 384; cf. *AD*, IV, p. 204). It is true that Ruskin affirmed the importance of private architecture in Venice, inseparable in his eyes from its religious architecture: "Wherever Christian church architecture has been good and lovely, it has been merely the perfect development of the common dwelling-house architecture of the period" (*The Stones of Venice*, vol. II, IV, § 53, in *Works*, vol. X, p. 120). The Contarini Fasan Palace, which Proust mentions in the rewrite of the present passage (Notebook 48, see previous note), would be the best example of this: "The richest work of the fifteenth century domestic Gothic in Venice" (*The Stones of Venice*, in *Works*, vol. XI, p. 368).

2. *Palazzo Foscari.* In the version from *Contre Sainte-Beuve*, as they are arriving by train and Maman reads out loud a description from Ruskin, Venice "naturally lacked in my eyes, when the gondola stopped in front of it, the same beauty it had had a moment earlier in my imagination, because we cannot at once see things with the mind and with the senses" (Notebook 3, f. 34v; *AD*, *Sketch XV.2*, IV, pp. 693–694). In the rewrite of the present passage, the disappointment felt at the sight of the Foscari Palace is compared to that of an encounter with a person: "And a little farther on he pointed with his oar: 'Foscari!' 'Ah!' and I felt my gaze fastened upon that face of stone with the same fixity it would fasten itself to the face of a famous and admirable man pointed out to us in a crowd: 'Ah, so that's him,' at the moment when we are trying to find in his face all those things we have so often thought. In that way my eyes devoured the Foscari Palace [. . .]" (Notebook 48, f. 57, crossed-out version; next version in f. 55v: "Then he said to me: 'Foscari'—'Ah!' and as it slowly moved past and away from the gondola my gaze reached out the same way it does when trying to adapt to the idea of a celebrity pointed out to us in a crowd the ideas we had formed about him long before," *AD*, *Sketch XV.4*, IV, p. 697). This idea was reworked in Notebook 43 upon meeting the Princess of Guermantes: "Thus the disappointed visitor in Venice says to himself but this is Venice, it really is the city that inspired Barrès, Ruskin, Chateaubriand (?) to write all those pages that I read" (f. 21v). From the revision of the section on Venice in Notebooks XIV and XV during the war, however, these passages disappeared, and Venice was described as being more fulfilling than disappointing: the dysphoric episode was delayed until the moment of departure.

3. *on the day, come at last, of the resurrection.* Proust abruptly ends his account here, in the middle of the page, leaving the rest of the bifiolio completely blank, without giving any further indication of what he means by this "resurrection." In 1904, when he feared the disaffection of France's churches that might be caused by the Law of Separation, he wrote about "the whole and complete resurrection that is a High Mass in a cathedral," with the choice of term clearly deliberate,

even if it also referred, in all probability, to Michelet's definition of history as the "resurrection of life in its entirety" (on this subject, see Compagnon 2009, p. 41). While Proust, in his use of the adjective "glorious," emphasizes the Christian undertone, the context is very different, and the term is obviously not meant in its religious sense: it prefigures the aesthetic of "time regained" that, from the "preface" to *Contre Sainte-Beuve*—rewritten, let us remember, on folios identical to those of the "seventy-five folios"—Proust sketched out with recourse to the expression "poetic resurrection" (Other Manuscripts, no. VII; *CSB* Clarac, p. 213). In this way he introduced the episode of the toast: "every hour of our life, as soon as it is dead, is incarnated and hidden inside some material object. [. . .] The object where it was hidden [. . .] we might very well never encounter. And so it is that there are hours of our lives that will never be resurrected. Sometimes the object is so small, so lost in the world, there is so little chance that it will be found on our path. There was a house in the country where I spent several ~~years~~ <summers> of my life. Sometimes I would think about those ~~years~~ <summers>, but what I thought about wasn't *them*. There was a good chance that they would remain forever dead to me. Their resurrection was due, as are all resurrections, to simple chance" (Other Manuscripts, no. VII; *CSB* Clarac, p. 211, cf. pp. 214–215). We also find "resurrection" and "resurrect(ed)" in the following versions of the episode of the toast, in Notebook 8, where Proust associates them with the pagan image of Erebus and the dead (ff. 47, 48 and ff. 67, 68v; cf. *CS, Sketch XIV*, I, pp. 695, 697; *Corr.*, III, p. 196). But from the version after that, he avoided these terms: "All our effort to [. . .] evoke[,] in order to [. . .] bring back to life" the "souls of those we have lost" are vain, until, passing close to them "in our sight, they shudder, call out to us, break their tomb" (Notebook 25, ff. 4–5), the image of the tomb itself disappearing afterward: "they shudder, call out to us, and as soon as we have recognized them the spell is broken. Released by us they have vanquished death and return to live with us" (NAF 16703, f. 8). In the end, the term "resurrection" applied to the aesthetic of time regained would be found only in the final chapter, in the meditation on the epiphanies of involuntary memory ("these resurrections," "these resurrections of the past," "these resurrections of the memory," *TR*, IV, pp. 453, 456; see also pp. 457, 466, 497).

f. 85

1. *the books by Ruskin.* See f. 83.

2. *they went to wait for us.* This phrase presupposes that the author is accompanied. But in contrast to later versions of the Venetian episode from Notebook 3 onward, Maman is never mentioned.

3. *all the social personality that the word street implies.* In *The Stones of Venice*, Ruskin writes of "untrodden streets" (*Works*, vol. X, p. 6) and, in a passage from *Modern Painters* translated by Mathilde Crémieux in the same volume, of "those tremulous streets, that filled, or fell, beneath the moon" (*Works*, vol. VII, p. 375): both phrases would be put to good use in "Place-Names: The Name," with "tremulous streets" becoming "lapping streets" (Notebook 65, f. 2; *CS*, I, p. 385; see also p. 386 note 1). But of the original long meditation on the Venetian "street of water" that begins here, only one fleeting phrase would remain in Notebook 48: the "paradox accepted as the [most] natural thing in the world of all the complications and all the refinements of the life of a city founded in the middle of the sea" (Notebook 48, f. 54v; *AD, Sketch XV.4*, IV, p. 696). From Notebook 3 onward, this "social personality" whose native aspects Proust enumerates here would be reduced to tourist activities ("I wanted to take the train to St. Mark's and tomorrow, leaving home, to travel in a gondola along that great and wonderful street that flows every day past the boats full of enchanted visitors [. . .]," f. 41v), then to the worldly activities of the "most elegant women, almost all of them foreigners," with Venice resembling "any broad, fashionable Parisian avenue" (Notebook XIV, f. 95; *AD*, IV, pp. 208–209).

4. *by the rising water.* In Notebook 3, Proust would return to this impression with a simpler phrase ("the front doorsteps, still damp from the water that covered or abandoned them as the tide rose and ebbed," ff. 37v–36v). The source for this phrase, though half-forgotten, is a line from Ruskin (see *BA*, p. 106 and note 1: "slow currents of ebbing and returning tide"). Cf. Notebook XIV, f. 95; *AD*, IV, p. 208.

f. 86

1. *a foolish Oriental pasha.* In the Ottoman Empire, a pasha was the governor of a province, appointed by the sultan, or an honorific title given to a high official; the epithet "foolish" reinforces the pejorative connotation that the term has acquired. Given that our visitor is standing outside the cathedral, the Christ he refers to must be the one in the modern mosaic above the central portico, *The Last Judgment*, created in 1836 based on a mediocre sketch by the artist Lattanzio Querena; Ruskin dismisses it contemptuously ("flaunting glare of Venetian art in its ruin," *St. Mark's Rest*, VIII, § 104, in *Works*, vol. XXIV, p. 290; we can make out the original mosaic in Gentile Bellini's painting *Procession in St. Mark's Square*, which Proust saw at the Accademia and mentions in *Swann's Way: CS*, I, p. 164). But in truth, this bland representation of Christ does not in any way justify Proust's feverish description, unless he was trying to emphasize—

in a deliberately provocative way—the Byzantine influence on the architecture of St. Mark's. Obviously, however, its construction preceded the fall of Constantinople and the Ottoman Empire.

2. *the waves of marble that encroach.* This image is a reworked translation of a fragment from *The Stones of Venice,* at the end of Ruskin's description of the facade of St. Mark's Basilica: "[. . .] until at last, as if in ecstasy, the *crests* of the arches break into *a marble foam,* and toss themselves far into the blue sky in flashes and wreaths of *sculptured spray* [. . .]" (*The Stones of Venice,* p. 83, italics are ours). Proust appears to have cribbed from the original English book rather than Mathilde Crémieux's translation. On the transposition of this passage from *The Stones of Venice,* see also below.

3. *festival.* The adjectival use of this word is a hapax. The best gloss of this is given by Proust himself in a previous description of St. Mark's: "this low monument, with its long facade, its flowered flagpoles, its festive decor, its appearance like something from a World's Fair" (*SL,* note p. 55; *PM,* note p. 193). See the next note.

4. *stretched out.* Although this passage is essentially a rewrite of Ruskin's arrival outside St. Mark's in *The Stones of Venice,* this phrase crucially distinguishes Proust's version from its model. While Ruskin contrasted the Gothic church and the Venetian basilica, also noting its "long low" shape, he did so indisputably in favor of the latter, in accordance with a paradox highlighted by Robert de La Sizeranne in his preface to Mme Crémieux's translation: "Ruskin, this lover of pure Gothic, this admirer of old French cathedrals, devotes his most brilliant study of architecture to a Byzantine monument!" (*Les Pierres de Venise,* translated by Mathilde Crémieux, preface by Robert de La Sizeranne [Paris: H. Laurens Éditeur, 1906], p. xiii). Ruskin's description ends with these words: "[. . .] beyond those troops of ordered arches there rises a vision out of the earth, and all the great square seems to have opened from it in a kind of awe, that we may see it far away;—a multitude of pillars and white domes, clustered into a long low pyramid of colored light; a treasure-heap, it seems, partly of gold, and partly of opal and mother-of-pearl, hollowed beneath into five great vaulted porches [. . .]. Between that grim cathedral of England and this, what an interval!" (*The Stones of Venice,* pp. 82, 84). As far back as 1905's "On Reading," Proust was already insisting, as he does here, on the monument's "festival, low, stretched out" appearance, but he also described the brightly colored impression that so enchanted Ruskin: "Anyone who has seen photographs of St. Mark's in Venice can believe (and I am talking here only about the monument's exterior) that he has

some idea of this church with its cupolas, but in fact it is only by closely approaching, so closely you can touch it with your hand, the multicolored curtain of those laughing pillars, it is only by seeing the strange and serious power coiled around the leaves where birds perch on those capitals that can only be distinguished close up, it is only by standing in the square itself that you have a real impression of this low monument, with its long facade, its flowered flagpoles, its festive decor, its appearance like something from a World's Fair, that you feel erupting in these important but incidental features that no photograph can convey, its true and complex individuality" (*SL*, note p. 55; *PM*, note p. 193). Everything in the present version that places the Byzantine aesthetic in violent, provocative opposition to that of the Gothic was watered down in 1910, in the only known version that echoes this one, in Notebook 48. Repeating the image of the "multicolored curtain" from 1905, Proust returns to Ruskin's enchantment and removes anything recalling the image of the unpleasantly "stretched out" monument, the phrase he had used in 1909 in another context (Notebook 7, f. 10; cf. *CG, Sketch VI*, II, p. 1046); and while he again invokes the vision of Christ as a "pasha," he tempers his rhetoric: "The 1st time we arrived outside St. Mark's, pulling back that invisible curtain which seems to unveil when we see [them] for the 1st time the works of art we have heard so much about, and, perhaps because our idea, immediately lodging itself inside them [. . .], gives them a sort of intense interior soul, expression, attitude, it was like an apparition. The far end of the square was dominated by this stretched-out, multicolored tableau vivant with its beautiful oriental pillars, holding up in a sort of apotheosis, ~~long and not raised very high~~, an ambivalent and somewhat Turkish Christ, while the rest of the square was given over to other epochs [. . .]" (Notebook 48, f. 62; Yoshida 1987, p. 169, read "a somewhat drab Christ*" (*turc* and *terne* are visually similar in Proust's handwriting); cf. *AD, Sketch XV.4*, IV, p. 698. But this blander albeit still "Oriental" version, vaguely Flaubertian ("it was like an apparition"), was never reworked, and in the final text there is only the briefest mention of the arrival outside St. Mark's and even that is in a completely different context (*JF*, I, p. 521), while there is also the comic image of a "large photograph" in which "I might myself be the tiny figure [. . .] in a bowler hat, in front of the portico" (*CS*, I, p. 386).

5. *at the very back we see Our Lord.* The apse "at the very back" of St. Mark's is decorated with a mosaic representing a *Christ Blessing*, reworked in the sixteenth century but whose Byzantine character remains unscathed. Ruskin does not seem to have commented upon it.

6. *some fat, suspect Syriot.* A Syriot is an inhabitant of the Greek island of Syros. Almost certainly, Proust had in mind the Ottoman province of Syria and

created a demonym on the model of "Cypriot." In the version from Notebook 48, these new derogatory epithets were combined with the "foolish Oriental pasha" (see above) to become "an ambivalent and somewhat Turkish Christ," a less inflammatory phrase that was never used again (f. 62; cf. *AD, Sketch XV.4*, IV, p. 698; see above). The aesthetic approach seems narrowly nationalistic and bigoted, apparently in complete opposition to that championed by Ruskin: "the Venetians deserve especial note as the only European people who appear to have sympathized to the full with the great instinct of the Eastern races"; Ruskin hoped to "enable the traveler to judge with more candor and justice of the architecture of St. Mark's than usually it would have been possible for him to do while under the influence of the prejudice necessitated by familiarity with the very different schools of Northern art" (*The Stones of Venice*, in *Works*, vol. X, pp. 98, 113). Since Proust did not belong to that group of people who saw St. Mark's as "a barbaric monstrosity" (ibid., p. 117), the passage could be read in a different way: in reality, he could be speaking in favor of the capacity to recognize under the confusing variety of aesthetic forms produced by "beings of another race" the identity of tendencies toward virtue. If the epithet "Oriental" were taken to mean "Jewish," and "effeminate" were taken to mean homosexual, this Christ flagellated by insults could even be a secret self-portrait (see the Commentary). A series of similar adjectives would be attached to M. de Charlus, "this painted, *paunchy* personage, sealed up like some box of *exotic* and *suspect* provenance [. . .]" (*SG*, III, p. 429, italics are ours). Swann, in an abandoned passage from Notebook 4, would remind the anti-Semitic grandfather that those virtues of which he believed the Jews "devoid" ("generosity, charity, solidarity, forgiveness of insults, probity, delicacy") were "in fact Jewish virtues" (f. 47; *CS, Sketch VIII*, I, p. 667).

7. *certain.* The manuscript does not end with a period.

Chronology

The lost "seventy-five folios" had been called the "1908 novel."[1] But is it possible now to calculate the precise chronology of the writing of its various "chapters"? Since Proust never dated his manuscripts and his correspondence was, in this case, usually vague, we must cross-reference the few clues at our disposal: possible allusions in the manuscript, referring to events attested elsewhere; the material characteristics of the folios, of a type that Proust could have used for other projects with better-known dates; and the corresponding notes from Carnet 1. Lastly, the start of *Contre Sainte-Beuve* almost certainly marked the end of Proust's work on the "seventy-five folios" and the moment when they were set aside, although that certainly doesn't mean that Proust did not refer back to them later. Far from it.

Had Proust already acquired the impressive double pages that compose our manuscript by the summer of 1907? It was on folios of this type that he took notes on Sainte-Beuve from an article by Paul Bourget published in *Le Figaro* on July 7. However, he might also have set this article aside and used it some time later.[2]

Two "chapters," [An Evening in the Countryside] and [Noble Names], include allusions to the trips that Proust took in Normandy in the summer and fall of 1907 with his driver Alfred Agostinelli;[3] the article that celebrated those trips, "Impressions of the Road from an Automobile," published

---

1. Bardèche 1971, t. I, p. 211 sq.; Quémar 1976, p. 26 note 73; Leriche 2012, p. 72 note 2.

2. NAF 16636, ff. 13, 14, 16–17. *CSB* Clarac, p. 218. It was the obituary of the Viscount of Spoelberch de Lovenjoul. See Pugh 1987, p. 37; Leriche 2012, p. 71 note 1, and p. 70 for codicological information.

3. See the Commentary.

in *Le Figaro* on November 19, 1907, as well as one of its drafts, also left traces:[4] this provides a *terminus a quo* for these sections of fall 1907.

According to Philip Kolb, the episode "Robert and the goat, Maman leaves on a trip" (which was what Proust called it)[5] at the end of [An Evening in the Countryside] could have been written in January 1908. Proust wrote a letter that month to Auguste Marguillier, the editorial secretary of the *Gazette des beaux-arts,* asking him to procure "English engravings" showing a child and his pet animal.[6] Kolb believed that Proust was looking for inspiration for the description of a child whose face, while it "had the magnificence of [. . .] English children close to the animal," expressed, "under all that luxury, which only heightened the contrast, the fiercest despair" (f. 22).

On [February 2, 1908], Proust told his friend Geneviève Straus that he wanted to "start work on a fairly long project,"[7] but was this the "seventy-five folios"? In the same letter he thanked her for her New Year gift of "little almanacs," four elegant, oblong pocket notebooks, the largest of which—known today as Carnet 1—he quickly began using to note down dreams, impressions, thoughts from reading, snatches of plotlines. But nothing before a few months corresponds to the contents of the "seventy-five folios." A brief notation, however, does presage the portrait of the uncle in [A Visit to the Seaside]: "Character writing from time to time to ask if he can be introduced etc." (f. 3).

In February and March 1908, Proust devoted part of his time to writing the series of seven brilliant *Pastiches* of the "Lemoine Affair" that appeared in *Le Figaro*'s literary supplement:[8] it was on a double page of the same

4. Ibid.

5. Carnet 1, f. 7v; *Cn,* p. 43. See below.

6. See Kolb 1956, and 1971, pp. 793–794. Letter to Auguste Marguillier, [just before January 8, 1908], *Corr.,* VIII, p. 25: "[. . .] would it be possible for you to send me provisionally a few of your English engravings, particularly those where an animal is shown next to a person or persons? I don't know if they would be what I'm looking for, but perhaps I would take one or two of them if the format isn't too small."

7. Letter of [February 2, 1908], *Corr.,* VIII, p. 39.

8. The authors pastiched were Balzac, Faguet, Michelet, Goncourt (February 22, 1908); Flaubert and Sainte-Beuve (March 14, 1908); Renan (March 21, 1908). After the appearance of the seventh, Proust wrote somewhat insincerely to his friend Robert

type as the "seventy-five folios" that he revised the Flaubert pastiche (published on March 14).[9]

On [April 21], using almost the same words he'd written to Mme Straus in February, Proust solemnly (but vaguely) announced to his friend Louis d'Albufera: "I bid you farewell, I am going to begin a very important work."[10]

On April 24, Plon published the fourth volume of *Récits d'une tante: Mémoires de la comtesse de Boigne*, about which Proust had written an article for *Le Figaro* the previous year:[11] he took several anecdotes from it, which appear at the end of [Noble Names] (ff. 80–81).[12]

On [May 5 or 6, 1908], Proust wrote again to Louis d'Albufera, this time to enumerate a long list of projects: "[. . .] I am currently working on: a study on the nobility / a Parisian novel / an essay on Sainte-Beuve and Flaubert / an essay on Women / an essay on Pederasty / (not easy to publish) / a study on stained-glass windows / a study on gravestones / a study on the novel."[13] While disparate, this list prefigures the array of themes in the future *Search*, even the *Contre Sainte-Beuve* project (since the "essay on Sainte-Beuve and Flaubert" seems to have emerged from the pastiches of those two authors in *Le Figaro*, in which Sainte-Beuve was supposedly criticizing Flaubert's "novel" on the Lemoine Affair). And yet this list is no help at all to us, with only the first item, "a study on the nobility," echoing a passage in the "seventy-five folios." It is possible that Proust started working on that study following the publication of *Récits d'une tante* and was planning to expand it as a work in its own right. Although there are reading notes at the beginning of Carnet 1 on Balzac, in preparation for the possible "Parisian

---

Dreyfus: "now it's over I'm not doing anymore. What a stupid exercise" (*Corr.*, VII, p. 67). And yet almost immediately afterward he thought of having them printed together as a booklet (ibid., pp. 91, 107). The pastiche of Régnier would be published on March 6, 1909.

9. See *Pastiches*, p. 93; NAF 16632, ff. 30–31, 32–34. Folios 32, 33, and 34 are folios of the same dimension, but single.

10. *Corr.*, VIII, p. 99.

11. "Reading Days," *Le Figaro*, March 20, 1907 (*EA*, pp. 527–533).

12. Quémar, spring 1976, p. 16 and p. 26, note 72. Folio 82, which Fallois did not include in *CSB*, begins a new development on the same theme as "noble names."

13. To Louis d'Albufera, [May 5 or 6, 1908], *Corr.*, VIII, pp. 112–113.

novel," this project (like the others) would never be started: at least, no draft has yet been found of it. It is striking that in his verbose confidences (or pseudo-confidences) to Louis d'Albufera, Proust does not mention the autobiographical project of "Robert and the goat."

The most important document we possess in our attempt to date the "seventy-five folios" is Carnet 1, the gift from Mme Straus in early January 1908 that Proust began using in February.[14] On folio 7v, we read the following list, clearly written in a single sitting as the handwriting becomes increasingly rushed:

Pages written
Robert and the goat, Maman leaves on a trip.
The Villebon way and the Meséglise way
Vice ~~interpre~~ seal and opening of the face. Disappointment as a possession, kissing the face ~~under~~.[15]
My grandmother in the garden, M. de Bretteville's dinner, I go upstairs, Maman's face then and since in my dreams, I can't fall asleep, concessions etc.
The Castellanes, Norman hydrangeas, English [and] German château owners; Louis Philippe's granddaughter, ~~1~~/Fantaisie, the maternal face in her debauched grandson.[T]
What I learned from the Villebon way and the Meséglise way.[16]

The lower part of the page is not filled: it remains available for any possible additions. Unlike the eight projects listed in the letter to Louis d'Albufera in early May, the title "Pages Written" supposes a single, unifying project that Proust did not mention, perhaps the "fairly long project," the "very important work" announced earlier to his friends.

14. According to Philip Kolb's chronology, *Cn 1908*, p. 38.
15. This might alternatively be "without"; the original is difficult to read and could be either "*sous*" or "*sans.*"
T. Or "little son." The French "*petit fils*" is ambiguous.
16. Carnet 1, f. 7v. Proust really did write "Meséglise" and not "Méséglise" (*CSB*, p. 14; *Cn*, pp. 43–44; *Cn 1908*, p. 56).

According to Fallois, the contents of the "seventy-five folios" are "clearly designated by [this] note."[17] However, while there is undeniably a similarity between this list and the "seventy-five folios," Fallois's affirmation needs to be qualified:

– The list in Carnet 1 makes no allusion to three of the six episodes in the "seventy-five folios": the visit to the seaside, the encounter with the young girls, and the chapter on Venice. So presumably Proust had not yet written them;

– On the other hand, the list does mention a few episodes that are not part of the "seventy-five folios" as it has reached us: "Vice seal and opening of the face. Disappointment as a possession, kissing the face";

– Lastly, the list begins with "Robert and the goat, Maman leaves on a trip" and separates the walks of the "ways" from what "lessons" they taught: consequently, if the "chapters" containing these pages had already been written (or, more precisely, if they were already in the state of those chapters in the "seventy-five folios"), this would mean that Proust was here choosing to divide up the contents, separating and reorganizing them in accordance with a sort of plan. But it hardly seems plausible that he would change his mind now about the place he had found for the lessons of the "ways" only at the third attempt in the "seventy-five folios." It also seems unlikely that he would wish to begin his novel with "Robert and the goat," which was deliberately positioned after the bedtime drama, as its more parodic, lighter-hearted counterpart.

So, with the probable exception of [Noble Names]—perhaps finished, as we have seen, in early May 1908 (and which corresponds to the summary in the carnet)[18]—and part of the walking of the "ways" (since Proust mentions here the "Méséglise way," which must already have replaced the "Bonneval way"),[19] the pieces listed in folio 7v of Carnet 1 do not designate the "seventy-five folios." These are earlier incarnations, when the evening

17. *CSB*, p. 14.
18. See Yoshikawa 1973, p. 138 note 2; Quémar 1976, p. 16.
19. See ff. 27–32.

kiss and "Robert and the goat," when the "ways" and their lessons, had not yet been joined in the manner that they are in the "seventy-five folios,"[20] but were written separately.

These preparatory manuscripts have not reached us. However, we do now possess certain manuscripts that are connected, in one way or another, with the genesis of the "seventy-five folios." For example, a piece found in the Fallois archives, written on large double folios of graph paper in a less impressive format, undoubtedly corresponds to one of their antecedent texts, even if it is not the version designated in Carnet 1. It consists of a portrait of the grandmother in the garden and a version of the evening kiss, evidently a very early fragment.[21] It is important to note that it was on absolutely identical folios that Proust wrote the drafts (also found in the Fallois archives) of the article "Impressions of the Road from an Automobile," which appeared in *Le Figaro* on November 19, 1907. This could suggest that Proust returned to writing his "personal" novel in the fall of 1907.

As for the "page written" listed in Carnet 1 but nowhere to be found in the "seventy-five folios"—"Vice seal and opening of the face. Disappointment as a possession, kissing the face"—we do have a credible candidate for it: a manuscript found in a batch with the previous manuscript in the Fallois archives, and written on the same graph paper. Its text is included in this volume.[22]

Although they are not mentioned in the list of "Pages Written," three other manuscripts with identical material characteristics that were found in the same batch are probably also associated with the genesis of the "seventy-five folios."[23] One of them prepares, very briefly, an image later

---

20. This would explain why the first appearance of the theme of the lesson of the "ways" is featured in the "seventy-five folios" in abridged form, as a marginal addition placed there by an editorial note (f. 32): Proust is looking for a place to add a passage already written elsewhere (the following attempts are in f. 35, then ff. 40–41).

21. Other Manuscripts, no. III.

22. Other Manuscripts, no. V.

23. The five manuscripts written on the same paper had been put by Fallois in a folder entitled: "handwritten graph-paper folios Swann." It is possible that their grouping in this way goes back to Proust himself.

found in [Noble Names];[24] the second has a clear thematic link with the end of [A Visit to the Seaside];[25] the last, as we have seen, concerns reminiscences.[26]

If we could date the moment when Proust drew up his list of "Pages Written" in Carnet 1, that would give us a *terminus a quo* for most of the "seventy-five folios" (the ones not mentioned, namely [A Visit to the Seaside], [Young Girls], [Venice]) and a *terminus ad quem* for those listed there in a preliminary state (namely [An Evening in the Countryside], [The Villebon Way and the Meséglise Way]), assuming that [Noble Names] was already, in all probability, well-advanced as early as May 1908.

Since the notes mentioning Cabourg began in the Carnet on folio 5v[27] (i.e., two pages prior to the list of "Pages Written" [f. 7v]), one automatically assumes that Proust wrote the list *after* his arrival at the Grand Hotel on July 18, 1908.[28] However, the list has been inserted, on the verso page reserved for it, between what are clearly continuous notes.[29] It could therefore have been written independently, more or less at any time between the end of April—after, having read the new *Récits d'une tante*, Proust wrote his pages on "Louis Philippe's granddaughter, Fantaisie"—and the first days of his stay in Cabourg, beginning July 18, 1908.

24. This is the seashell-steeple rising between the roofs: "~~The church~~/Between the <~~compact~~> roofs of the houses there could be seen <rising, in a different material, openwork, pinkish like a seashell> the steeple of the church ~~openwork, slender, openwork, pink pinkish, like a seashe~~" (complete transcription). This motif is integrated in a new form in [Noble Names]: see f. 76 and note 2. These lines in which it is sketched are written on the back of a bifolio whose recto is filled with the revision of two pages of some kind of essay, unconnected with the themes of the 'seventy-five folios', in which Prosut distinguishes three periods (natural, artistic, historical) in the poetic quest.

25. Other Manuscripts, no. VI.

26. Other Manuscripts, no. IV; Commentary.

27. "Maman rediscovered during journey, arrival in Cabourg [. . .]," "Avenues of Cabourg [. . .]" (f. 5v); Cabourg is also mentioned three times on folio 6. The concentration, in these pages and those that follow, of notes referring to Proust's relationships suggests that they are contemporary to that trip.

28. See the letter sent from Cabourg to Henry Bernstein, [just after July 18, 1908], *Corr.*, VIII, p. 184: "I've been in Cabourg since Saturday"; cf. p. 183.

29. Moreover, the last notes of the previous recto (f. 7) spill over onto the facing verso (f. 6v), which would not have been the case if the next verso (f. 7v) had been available. On this subject, see Pugh 1987, p. 109 note 32. In his carnets, unlike in his notebooks, Proust did not write from recto to recto, but continuously.

This would fix the revision of [An Evening in the Countryside], as well as the writing of the second and third versions of [The Villebon Way and the Méséglise Way] on the large double pages that constitute the "seventy-five folios" no earlier than the end of April or the start of May 1908. Two notes from Carnet 1 suggest that the version of [An Evening in the Countryside] that we possess was written after Proust's arrival in Cabourg in July. One mentions a hostile bedroom: "Smell of a room, the body isn't used to it, and suffers, the soul notices." (f. 8v). This could be the origin of the "smell of vetiver" in the "seventy-five folios," transferred to the family house in the countryside[30] (before returning, later in the writing process, to the hotel bedroom at the seaside). The other note suggests that Proust dreamed of his mother on the train to Cabourg: *"Maman rediscovered during journey,*[31] arrival in Cabourg, same room as in Evian, the square mirror!" (f. 5v). It is the fourth dream of a dead relative to be mentioned by Proust since the start of that carnet,[32] and the only one that wasn't turned into a little story. But it could be the same dream that is featured in the "seventy-five folios" (f. 18), because that dream is associated with the three previous dreams in the next part of the genesis.[33] In the note of "Pages Written," which *already* mentions dreams of Maman ("M. de Bretteville's dinner, I go upstairs, Maman's face then *and since in my dreams,* I can't fall asleep, concessions etc."),[34] either these are different dreams from the one featured in the "seventy-five folios" (perhaps the other dreams from Carnet 1), in which case the list of "Pages Written" must have been written by Proust before his arrival in Cabourg, or the dream he had "during the journey" must already have been written, only in a version that was not yet the one in the "seventy-five folios."

As far as [A Visit to the Seaside] is concerned, it was certainly written in Cabourg. The piece is clearly prefigured in Carnet 1 by a series of notes written after his arrival (i.e., after folio 5v), all within a few pages: notes

---

30. See f. 13.

31. Italics are ours. See Yoshida 1992, p. 45.

32. See ff. 2, 3v, and 4 (*Cn*, pp. 31–32, 36).

33. In Notebook 65 (ff. 39–44), then the four dreams are divided between Notebooks 50 and 48 (*SG, Sketch XIII*, III, pp. 1032–1034, 1045–1046, 1048).

34. Carnet 1, f. 7v. Italics are ours.

mentioning the dowager's pride[35] ("chic people enveloped in their milieu, nobles refusing to tolerate being unknown to others at the hotel," f. 6v), heralding the little society of four friends[36] ("Sohège and his mistress perfumed veil held between himself and the world," f. 8), preparing the portrait of the womanizing uncle[37] ("Mistress sent for," f. 6, "Better to love someone local," f. 6v, "My uncle constantly remaking his relationships," f. 8). Likewise, the Venetian inspiration is clearly announced by the note: "Cabourg walking on carpets while getting dressed sunlight outside Venice/Cabourg descending the big stairs, quick movement of sun and wind on big marble spaces big hangings Venice" (f. 6). As for the separate piece on the [Young Girls], on the other hand, nothing comes near it in Carnet 1: the "young girl" ruined and kept (ff. 3, 3v) being reserved for the "2nd part of novel"; the "four faces" or "heads of young girls" (f. 11), the "quintuple" love (f. 14), notations obviously written after leaving Cabourg, are all too vague; the "pink-stained" silhouette of the actress Lucy Gérard (f. 6v) would be used in the novel, but not until the next year, in Notebook 4, and for Mlle Swann.[38]

Back from Cabourg on September 26 or 27, Proust stayed in the Hôtel des Réservoirs in Versailles before returning to boulevard Haussmann in the first days of November.[39] In a letter of [October 23] to his friend Mme de Pierrebourg, who had just published a novel, he wrote:

> [. . .] But above all where you live [. . .] is in your love for Odette [*character in Mme de Pierrebourg's novel*]. And that feeling, or at the very least, Odette's love for her mother, some already quite old pages that I've written about mine will perhaps <if I publish them one day> show you that I am not completely unworthy of understanding it and that, if I have rendered it less skillfully, and very differently, at least I was made to admire in another writer the most moving expression of that

35. See this volume, f. 54.
36. See this volume, f. 59.
37. See this volume, ff. 60–62.
38. Notebook 4, f. 32; *CS, Sketch LIII*, I, p. 808.
39. *Corr.*, VIII, pp. xxi, 15–16.

love. The "goodnight" scene near the bed . . . you will see: completely
different and certainly inferior. You are a novelist! If I could create
beings and situations like you, how happy I would be![40]

Proust surely had in mind here the episode he had just written in the
"seventy-five folios,"[41] and this supposedly disillusioned letter did not signify the abandonment of the project of publishing the "goodnight kiss," but
quite the opposite. Rather it was a pre-emptive attempt to protect himself
from possible accusations of imitation: his own pages on the subject were
"already quite old" (meaning: he wrote them first) and the feeling of the
scene is "rendered [. . .] very differently."

Exactly when did Proust set aside the project corresponding to the
"seventy-five folios" to devote himself to an essay on Sainte-Beuve's method?
The systematic reading notes on criticism in Carnet 1 do not begin until
the end of November.[42] A series of reminiscences and obscure impressions
is noted on three large bifolios identical to those that make up the "seventy-
five folios" and serves to introduce the critique of Sainte-Beuve.[43] It seems
to precede the letter to George de Lauris, which dates from the [end of
November or the first half of December 1908], whose contents Proust
repeats to Mme de Noailles:

> I want to write something about Sainte-Beuve. I have sort of con-
> structed two articles in my mind (review articles). One of them is a
> classically formed article, like Taine's essay but less good. The other
> would begin with the description of a morning, Maman would come
> close to my bed and I would tell her about an article I want to write

40. Letter to Mme de Pierrebourg, alias Claude Ferval, about her novel *Ciel rouge*,
Lettres, pp. 457–458.

41. Philip Kolb saw in this an allusion to the scene from *Jean Santeuil*, while Françoise Leriche wondered if it wasn't the "mysterious work" that Proust had told Lucien
Daudet in 1906 that he wanted to write "all about" his mother (*Corr.*, VIII, p. 252 note
10; *Lettres*, p. 459 note 8).

42. Pugh 1987, p. 37.

43. NAF 16636, ff. 1–6; Other Manuscripts, no. VII.

on Sainte-Beuve. And then I would develop it. Which do you think best?[44]

The project, then, had already begun, in several forms. We might think that by this point, at the latest, Proust must have set aside his seventy-five (or seventy-six)[45] folios. But he would quickly return to them, in Notebook 3,[46] the first notebook of the narrative *Contre Sainte-Beuve*.

44. Letter to George de Lauris, *Lettres*, pp. 465–466. See also the letter to Anna de Noailles, ibid., p. 466. Kolb dated those letters to [circa mid-December 1908], *Corr.*, VIII, pp. 320–321.
45. See the Note on the Manuscript.
46. See Other Manuscripts, no. VIII.

Bibliography and Abbreviations

*Editions of Works and Manuscripts
by Marcel Proust and Abbreviations*

Agenda: L'Agenda 1906. Critical edition by Nathalie Mauriac Dyer, Françoise Leriche, Pyra Wise, and Guillaume Fau. Éditions de la Bibliothèque nationale de France and OpenEdition Books, 2015. Available online: https://books .openedition.org/editionsbnf/1457.

BA: John Ruskin, *La Bible d'Amiens*. Translation, notes, and preface by Marcel Proust. Paris: Mercure de France, 1904.

Bodmer: Du côté de chez Swann. Combray. First corrected proofs, 1913, facsimile. Introduction and transcription by Charles Méla. Paris: Gallimard; Cologny (Geneva): Fondation Martin Bodmer, 2013.

Cahier 26: Cahier 26. Edited by Françoise Leriche, Akio Wada, Hidehiko Yuzawa, and Nathalie Mauriac Dyer. Vols. I and II. Turnhout: Brepols and Bibliothèque nationale de France, coll. "Marcel Proust. Cahiers 1 à 75 de la Bibliothèque nationale de France," 2010.

Cahier 53: Cahier 53. Edited by Nathalie Mauriac Dyer, Pyra Wise, and Kazuyoshi Yoshikawa. Vols. I and II. Turnhout: Brepols and Bibliothèque nationale de France, coll. "Marcel Proust. Cahiers 1 à 75 de la Bibliothèque nationale de France," 2012.

Cahier 71: Cahier 71. Edited by Francine Goujon, Shuji Kurokawa, Nathalie Mauriac Dyer, and Pierre-Edmond Robert. Vols. I and II. Turnhout: Brepols and Bibliothèque nationale de France, coll. "Marcel Proust. Cahiers 1 à 75 de la Bibliothèque nationale de France," 2009.

Cn: Carnets. Edited by Florence Callu and Antoine Compagnon. Paris: Gallimard, 2002.

Cn 1908: Le Carnet de 1908 [Carnet 1]. Edited and introduced by Philip Kolb. *Cahiers Marcel Proust 8.* Paris: Gallimard, 1976.

Corr., I–XXI: Correspondance de Marcel Proust. Edition by Philip Kolb. 21 vols. Paris: Plon, 1970–1993.

CSB: Contre Sainte-Beuve, followed by *Nouveaux mélanges.* Preface by Bernard de Fallois. Paris: Gallimard, 1954.

CSB Clarac: *Contre Sainte-Beuve.* In *Contre Sainte-Beuve,* preceded by *Pastiches et mélanges* and followed by *Essais et articles,* edition by Pierre Clarac and Yves Sandre. Paris: Gallimard, "Bibliothèque de la Pléiade," 1971.

EA: Essais et articles, edition cited.

JS: Jean Santeuil, preceded by *Les Plaisirs et les jours.* Edition by Pierre Clarac and Yves Sandre. Paris: Gallimard, "Bibliothèque de la Pléiade," 1971.

Lettres: Lettres (1879–1922). Revised selection and annotation by Françoise Leriche, with the support of Caroline Szylowicz, based on *Correspondance de Marcel Proust,* edited by Philip Kolb. Unpublished letters, selection, and annotation by Françoise Leriche. Preface and afterword by Katherine Kolb. Paris: Plon, 2004.

Pastiches: L'Affaire Lemoine: Pastiches. Critical edition by Jean Milly. Geneva: Slatkine Reprints, 1994.

PJ: Les Plaisirs et les jours, edition cited.

PM: Pastiches et mélanges, edition cited.

RTP, I–IV: *À la recherche du temps perdu.* Edition published under the direction of Jean-Yves Tadié, with the collaboration of Florence Callu, Francine Goujon, Eugène Nicole, Pierre-Louis Rey, Brian Rogers, and Jo Yoshida (t. I), Dharntipaya Kaotipaya, Thierry Laget, P.-L. Rey, and B. Rogers (t. II), Antoine Compagnon and Pierre-Edmond Robert (t. III), Yves Baudelle, Anne Chevalier, E. Nicole, P.-L. Rey, P.-E. Robert, Jacques Robichez, and B. Rogers (t. IV). Paris: Gallimard, "Bibliothèque de la Pléiade," 1987–1989.

    CS: Du côté de chez Swann (Swann's Way).

    JF: À l'ombre des jeunes filles en fleurs (In the Shadow of Young Girls in Flower).

    CG: Le Côté de Guermantes (The Guermantes Way).

    SG: Sodome et Gomorrhe (Sodom and Gomorrah).

    P: La Prisonnière (The Captive).

    AD: Albertine disparue (The Fugitive).

    TR: Le Temps retrouvé (Time Regained).

SL: [John Ruskin], *Sésame et les lys.* Translation, notes, and preface by Marcel Proust. Paris: Mercure de France, 1906.

Other Editions of Texts and Manuscripts by Marcel Proust Consulted for the Present Edition

Albertine disparue. Edition of the last version revised by the author, by Nathalie Mauriac and Étienne Wolff. Paris: Grasset, 1987.

"Bricquebec": Prototype d'"À l'ombre des jeunes filles en fleurs." Edited and introduced by Richard Bales. Oxford: Clarendon Press, 1989.

Le Mystérieux Correspondant et autres nouvelles inédites. Texts transcribed, annotated, and introduced by Luc Fraisse. Paris: Éditions de Fallois, 2019.

Textes retrouvés. Collected and introduced by Philip Kolb, with a bibliography of publications by Proust (1892–1971). Revised and expanded edition. *Cahiers Marcel Proust 3.* Paris: Gallimard, 1971.

Manuscripts

Fallois Archives.

Proust Collection at the Bibliothèque nationale de France. This fully digitalized collection is accessible on Gallica (gallica.bnf.fr) and via the ITEM-CNRS homepage: item.ens.fr/fonds-proust-numerique.

Correspondence (Other than Corr. and Lettres)

Index général de la correspondance de Marcel Proust. Edited under the direction of Kazuyoshi Yoshikawa. Kyoto: Presses de l'Université de Kyoto, 1998.

Kahan, Sylvia, and Nathalie Mauriac Dyer. "Quatre lettres inédites de Proust au prince de Polignac." *Bulletin Marcel Proust* 43 (2003): 9–22.

Books and Articles Consulted

Biography, Realia

Bloch-Dano, Évelyne. *Madame Proust.* Paris: Grasset, 2004.

Cattaui, Georges. *Proust: Documents iconographiques.* Geneva: Pierre Cailler, 1956.

Duchêne, Roger. *L'Impossible Marcel Proust.* Paris: Robert Laffont, 1994.

———. "Un inédit proustien: Le testament de 'l'oncle Adolphe.'" *Revue d'histoire littéraire de la France* 104 (2004/3): 673–685.

Fallois, Bernard de. "'L'Histoire d'un roman est un roman.'" Interview with Nathalie Mauriac Dyer. *Genesis* 36 (2013): 105–112 (available online).

Fournier, Albert. "Du côté de chez Proust." *Europe,* "Centenaire de Marcel Proust," August–September 1970, 246–263.

Francis, Claude, and Fernande Gontier. *Marcel Proust et les siens,* followed by *Souvenirs de Suzy Mante-Proust.* Paris: Plon, 1981.

Henriet, Jean-Paul. *Proust et Cabourg.* Paris: Gallimard, 2020.

Larcher, Philibert-Louis. "Le Pré-Catelan d'Illiers, parc de Swann." *Bulletin de la Société des Amis de Marcel Proust* 10 (1960): 242–248.

Mayer, Denise. "Le Jardin de Marcel Proust." In *Cahiers Marcel Proust 12, Études proustiennes V*, pp. 9–51. Paris: Gallimard, 1984.

Naturel, Mireille. "Du lieu de pèlerinage au réseau européen: Le cas de la maison de tante Léonie." *Revue d'histoire littéraire de la France* 109 (2009/4): 831–840.

Panzac, Daniel. *Le Docteur Adrien Proust, père méconnu, précurseur oublié.* Paris: L'Harmattan, 2003.

Tadié, Jean-Yves. *Marcel Proust: Biographie.* Paris: Gallimard, 1996.

Wise, Pyra. "La Marraine et le parrain de Marcel Proust: Quelques découvertes." *Bulletin d'informations proustiennes* 47 (2017): 75–87.

Critical Works on Proust (Selection)

Boucquey, Éliane. *Un chasseur dans l'image: Proust et le temps caché.* Paris: Armand Colin, 1992.

———. "La Mémoire involontaire du lecteur de la *Recherche*." *Bulletin d'informations proustiennes* 30 (1999): 93–101.

Compagnon, Antoine. *Proust entre deux siècles.* Paris: Éditions du Seuil, 1989.

———. "Ce qu'on ne peut plus dire de Proust." *Littérature* 88, no. 4 (1992): 54–61.

———. "Proust, mémoire de la littérature." In *Proust, la mémoire et la littérature*, pp. 9–45. Paris: Odile Jacob, 2009.

———. "Proust, 1913." Lecture at the Collège de France, 2013. Online.

———. "Proust essayiste." Lecture at the Collège de France, 2019. Online.

———. "'Le Long de la rue du Repos': Brouillon d'une lettre à Daniel Halévy (1908)." *Bulletin d'informations proustiennes* 50 (2020): 13–32.

———. "Proust sioniste." Series, Collège de France website, 2020.

———. "Lucien Daudet, 'rat musqué.'" In *Le Cercle de Marcel Proust III*, under the direction of Jean-Yves Tadié, pp. 53–74. Paris: Honoré Champion, 2021.

Duval, Sophie. "Du Moyen Âge de 1913 à celui de 1919: Combray, Chartres, Reims et l'art gothique dans *À la recherche du temps perdu*." *Littera: Revue de langue et littérature françaises*, Société japonaise de langue et littérature françaises, 4 (2019): 49–67 (available online).

Goujon, Francine. *Allusions littéraires et écriture cryptée dans l'œuvre de Proust.* Paris: Honoré Champion, 2020.

Kristeva, Julia. *Le Temps sensible: Proust et l'expérience littéraire.* Paris: Gallimard, 1994.

Leblanc, Cécile. *Proust écrivain de la musique: L'allégresse du compositeur.* Turnhout: Brepols, 2017.

Lejeune, Philippe. "Les Carafes de la Vivonne." *Poétique* 31 (September 1977): 285–305.

Leriche, Françoise. "La Citation au fondement du *Côté de Guermantes?* Hypothèses pour un séminaire." *Bulletin d'informations proustiennes* 22 (1991): 31–36.

Leriche, Françoise, and Nathalie Mauriac Dyer. "Les Proust aux 'lieux': Du *Traité d'hygiène* à *Sodome et Gomorrhe*." *Bulletin d'informations proustiennes* 31 (2000): 65–96.

Mauriac Dyer, Nathalie. "*À la recherche du temps perdu*, une autofiction?" In *Genèse et autofiction*, edited by Jean-Louis Jeannelle and Catherine Viollet, pp. 69–87. Louvain-la-Neuve: Academia-Bruylant, 2006.

———. "Un degré d'allusion racinienne de plus: Pour une relecture de l'adieu aux aubépines dans *Du côté de chez Swann*." *The Romanic Review* 105, no. 3–4 (2014): 147–160 (available online).

Murakami, Yuji. "L'Affaire Dreyfus dans l'œuvre de Proust." Doctoral thesis, Université Paris-Sorbonne, 2012.

Critical Works on the Genesis of "In Search of Lost Time"

Bardèche, Maurice. *Marcel Proust romancier.* 2 vols. Paris: Les Sept Couleurs, 1971.

Bonnet, Henri. *Marcel Proust de 1907 à 1914.* Paris: Nizet, 1971.

Brun, Bernard. "'Une des lois vraiment immuables de ma vie spirituelle': Quelques éléments de la 'démonstration' proustienne dans des brouillons de *Swann*." *Bulletin d'informations proustiennes* 10 (Fall 1979): 23–38.

———. "L'Édition d'un brouillon et son interprétation: Le problème du *Contre Sainte-Beuve*." In *Essais de critique génétique*, pp. 151–192. Paris: Flammarion, coll. "Textes et manuscrits," 1979.

———. "Le Dormeur éveillé, genèse d'un roman de la mémoire." In *Cahiers Marcel Proust 11, Études proustiennes IV*, pp. 241–316. Paris: Gallimard, 1982.

———. "Brouillons des aubépines." In *Cahiers Marcel Proust 12, Études proustiennes V*, pp. 215–304. Paris: Gallimard, 1984.

———. "Étude génétique de l'' ouverture' de *La Prisonnière*." In *Cahiers Marcel Proust 14, Études proustiennes VI*, pp. 211–287. Paris: Gallimard, 1987.

———. "Brouillons et brouillages: Proust et l'antisémitisme." *Littérature* 70 (1988): 110–128.

Eissen, Ariane. "Inventaire du Cahier 65." *Bulletin d'informations proustiennes* 18 (1987): 31–36.

Fau, Guillaume. "Le Fonds Proust au département des Manuscrits de la Bibliothèque nationale de France: Notes pour un cinquantenaire." *Genesis* 36 (2013): 135–140 (available online).

Goujon, Francine. "Édition critique de textes de Marcel Proust (Cahiers 59, 60, 61, 62, 75)." 2 vols. Doctoral thesis, Université Paris-Sorbonne, 1997.

———. "'Je' narratif, 'je' critique et écriture intertextuelle dans le *Contre Sainte-Beuve.*" *Bulletin d'informations proustiennes* 34 (2004): 95–110.

Keller, Luzius. *La Fabrique de Combray.* Carouge, Geneva: Éditions Zoé, 2006.

Kolb, Philip. "Le "Mystère" des gravures anglaises recherchées par Proust." *Mercure de France* t. 327 (August 1, 1956): 750–755.

———. "La Genèse de la *Recherche:* Une heureuse bévue." *Revue d'histoire littéraire de la France* 71 (1971 / 5–6): 791–803.

Leriche, Françoise. "Vinteuil, ou le révélateur des transformations esthétiques dans la genèse de la *Recherche.*" *Bulletin d'informations proustiennes* 16 (1985): 25–39.

———. "Inventaire du Cahier 64." *Bulletin d'informations proustiennes* 18 (1987a): 37–59.

———. "Note sur le cahier "Querqueville," les thèses d'Akio Wada et de Takaharu Ishiki, et sur l'activité de Proust en 1909." *Bulletin d'informations proustiennes* 18 (1987b): 11–21.

———. "*Louisa* / Sonia, Wanda, Anna, Madeleine, Carmen, Odette, Suzanne, les avatars d'un personnage du *Contre Sainte-Beuve* au 'manuscrit Cortot': Transformations génétiques et stratégie mondaine." *Bulletin d'informations proustiennes* 19 (1988): 59–83.

———. "Hésitations énonciatives et génériques dans la genèse du roman proustien." *Bulletin d'informations proustiennes* 42 (2012): 69–84.

———. "De la 'naissance' de la *Recherche* à 'l'œuvre des manuscrits': Étapes dans la réflexion sur les processus génétiques proustiens." *Marcel Proust aujourd'hui* 10 (2013): 9–31.

Marchal, Bertrand. "À la recherche du jardinier perdu." In *Cahier Marcel Proust,* under the direction of Jean-Yves Tadié, pp. 13–17. Paris: L'Herne, 2021.

Milly, Jean. "Étude génétique de la rêverie des chambres dans l'"ouverture' de la *Recherche.*" *Bulletin d'informations proustiennes* 10 (Fall 1979): 19–22 and 11 (Spring 1980): 9–31.

Pugh, Anthony R. *The Birth of "À la recherche du temps perdu."* Lexington, KY: French Forum, 1987.

———. *The Growth of "À la recherche du temps perdu": A Chronological Examination of Proust's Manuscripts from 1909 to 1914.* 2 vols. Toronto: University of Toronto Press, 2004.

Quaranta, Jean-Marc. *Le Génie de Proust: Genèse de l'esthétique de la "Recherche."* Paris: Honoré Champion, 2011.

Quémar, Claudine. "Sur deux versions anciennes des 'côtés' de Combray." In *Cahiers Marcel Proust 7, Études proustiennes II,* pp. 159–282. Paris: Gallimard, 1975.

————. "Autour de trois 'avant-textes' de l'ouverture' de la *Recherche:* Nouvelles approches des problèmes du *Contre Sainte-Beuve.*" *Bulletin d'informations proustiennes* 3 (Spring 1976): 7–39.

Ritte, Jürgen. "Anatomie d'un fait divers: Un brouillon inédit des 'Sentiments filiaux d'un parricide' de Marcel Proust." In *Cartographie d'une amitié: Pour Stéphane Michaud,* edited by Philippe Daros, pp. 151–164. Paris: Presses Sorbonne nouvelle, 2017.

Saraydar, Alma. "Un premier état d'Un amour de Swann.'" *Bulletin d'informations proustiennes* 14 (1983): 21–28.

Sebban, Nicole. "La Publication des manuscrits inédits: Liste des inédits proustiens publiés (1922–1991)." *Bulletin d'informations proustiennes* 22 (1991): 111–142.

Vigneron, Robert. "Genèse de *Swann.*" *Revue d'histoire de la philosophie* (January 1937): 67–115.

Wada, Akio. "Chronologie de l'écriture proustienne (1909–1911)." *Bulletin d'informations proustiennes* 29 (1998): 41–65.

————. *Index général des cahiers de brouillon de Marcel Proust.* Osaka: Graduate School of Letters, Osaka University, 2009 (available online at the ITEM website).

————. *La Création romanesque de Proust: La genèse de "Combray."* Paris: Honoré Champion, 2012.

Yoshida, Jo. "Proust contre Ruskin: La genèse de deux voyages dans la *Recherche* d'après des brouillons inédits." 2 vols. Doctoral thesis, Université Paris-IV, 1978.

————. "L'Après-midi à Venise: Autour de plusieurs textes inédits sur la basilique Saint-Marc." *Cahiers Marcel Proust 14, Études proustiennes VI,* pp. 167–189. Paris: Gallimard, 1987.

————. "La Grand-mère retrouvée: Le procédé du montage des 'Intermittences du cœur.'" *Bulletin d'informations proustiennes* 23 (1992): 43–64.

Yoshikawa, Kazuyoshi. "Marcel Proust en 1908—Comment a-t-il commencé à écrire *À la recherche du temps perdu?*" *Études de langue et littérature françaises,* Société japonaise de langue et littérature françaises 22 (1973): 135–152.

Table of Concordance

À la recherche du temps perdu	The Seventy-Five Folios	In Search of Lost Time
CS, I, pp. 7–8	ff. 12–13	
CS, I, pp. 10–12	ff. 1–3	
CS, I, p. 13	ff. 7–10	
CS, I, p. 23	ff. 7–9	
CS, I, p. 24	f. 10	
CS, I, pp. 27–30	ff. 7, 10–12	
CS, I, pp. 31–35	ff. 12, 14, 16–19	
CS, I, pp. 37–38	ff. 19–20	
CS, I, pp. 131–134	ff. 31–32, 33–34	
CS, I, pp. 137–138	ff. 29–30	
CS, I, p. 143	ff. 20–23	
CS, I, pp. 143–145	ff. 41v, 27, 40, 41, 35 passage crossed out), 29	
CS, I, p. 148	f. 31	
CS, I, pp. 163–166	ff. 32, 35, 34	
CS, I, pp. 168–169	ff. 41v, 27, 40, 51	
CS, I, p. 177	f. 30	
CS, I, pp. 188–191	ff. 60–65	
JF, II, pp. 26–28	ff. 12–13	
JF, II, p. 35	f. 53	
JF, II, pp. 38–46	ff. 54–60, 70–71, 53	
JF, II, pp. 76–78	ff. 36–37, 39	
JF, II, p. 146	ff. 67, 69	
JF, II, p. 150	f. 67	
CG I, II, p. 315	f. 82	
CG II, II, pp. 825–826	ff. 80, 81	
CG II, II, pp. 831–832	ff. 79–80	
AD, IV, pp. 266–269 (Notebook XV, ff. 69–72)	ff. 41, 27, 33	

Acknowledgments

To my dear friend Jean-Jacques Neuer, my immense gratitude.

This edition could never have been published without providential support. My gratitude, first and foremost, to Jean Milly, Gilles Mauriac, and Michel Dyer. I am grateful to all my family and friends, and in particular to the Marcel Proust estate.

I also thank the Bibliothèque nationale de France and, at the Department of Manuscripts, Isabelle le Masne de Chermont and Guillaume Fau.

It would be presumptuous to claim that I alone prepared the texts of the unpublished Marcel Proust manuscripts presented here: I am hugely grateful to Bertrand Marchal, who transcribed the folios in parallel with me before we compared our work. I, and all of the book's readers, owe him a great debt.

This edition was also helped enormously by Francine Goujon and Sophie Duval, whose attentive and rigorous rereading was essential.

It goes without saying that any mistakes remaining are my responsibility.

My thanks, too, to Éditions Gallimard and Jean-Yves Tadié, who wrote the preface: I was greatly touched by his first reading.

The groundwork for this edition was laid over many years by the work of numerous researchers into the life, work, and manuscripts of Marcel Proust. I dedicate it to them, with gratitude, particularly those who were not able to read the "seventy-five folios": Claudine Quémar, Henri Bonnet, Philip Kolb, Anthony Pugh, Jo Yoshida, Richard Bales, Bernard Brun.

Finally, all my thanks to the English translator of this edition, Sam Taylor.

"In the infinite stillness of love lies shattered the sword of human will."